Spark

The Shining Falcon

"A gloriously rich tapestry of pageant,
adventure, and magic, with wonderfully
intriguing and believable characters"
Esther M. Friesner,
author of *Sphinxes Wild*

❖

"A world based on Slavic history and mythology,
a world both exotic and disturbingly familiar . . .
darkly brilliant and shimmering with magic"
Morgan Llywelyn,
author of *The Lion of Ireland*

❖

"I gulped the entire book in one day,
as if it were a box of chocolates."
Nancy Springer,
author of *The White Hart*

Worlds of Fantasy from Avon Books

THE CRYSTAL WARRIORS
by William R. Forstchen & Greg Morrison

THE DRAGON WAITING
by John M. Ford

THE GRYPHON KING
by Tom Deitz

A NAME TO CONJURE WITH
by Donald Aamodt

THE WHITE RAVEN
by Diana L. Paxson

THE XANTH SERIES
by Piers Anthony
VALE OF THE VOLE
HEAVEN CENT
MAN FROM MUNDANIA

THE WINTER OF THE WORLD TRILOGY
by Michael Scott Rohan
THE ANVIL OF ICE
THE FORGE IN THE FOREST

and coming soon in the trilogy

THE HAMMER OF THE SUN

Avon Books are available at special quantity discounts for bulk purchases for sales promotions, premiums, fund raising or educational use. Special books, or book excerpts, can also be created to fit specific needs.

For details write or telephone the office of the Director of Special Markets, Avon Books, Dept. FP, 105 Madison Avenue, New York, New York 10016, 212-481-5653.

THE Shining Falcon

JOSEPHA SHERMAN

AVON BOOKS ◆ NEW YORK

THE SHINING FALCON is an original publication of Avon Books. This work has never before appeared in book form. This work is a novel. Any similarity to actual persons or events is purely coincidental.

AVON BOOKS
A division of
The Hearst Corporation
105 Madison Avenue
New York, New York 10016

Copyright © 1989 by Josepha Sherman
Cover illustration by Kinuko Craft
Published by arrangement with the author
Library of Congress Catalog Card Number: 89-91271
ISBN: 0-380-75436-3

All rights reserved, which includes the right to reproduce this book or portions thereof in any form whatsoever except as provided by the U.S. Copyright Law. For information address Avon Books.

First Avon Books Printing: November 1989

AVON TRADEMARK REG. U.S. PAT. OFF. AND IN OTHER COUNTRIES, MARCA REGISTRADA, HECHO EN U.S.A.

Printed in the U.S.A.

R-A   10 9 8 7 6 5 4 3 2 1

Dedicated
to the memory of
Jacob and Raissa Altschuler

1

FALCON AND CROW

HIGH OVER KIRTESK, the prince's city, a falcon sported in the clear sky—a falcon like no other, glinting bright in the sun, silver in the morning light.

Below, leaning gingerly out of a window in the white and gold royal palace, old *boyar* Semyon, chief of the princely council, eldest of that noble lot, craned his head back to watch, and gave a wry, amused little smile.

"How like his father he is! Escaping from the court like this, if only for a time—our Prince Finist may be a wise young man, wise in statecraft, wise in magic, but sometimes the wind does call to him!"

Across the smooth, paved square, another watched that flight. Ljuba, lovely Ljuba, hair a knee-length fall of burnished gold, eyes deep and lustrous blue, royal Ljuba, cousin to the prince, stood at a sheltered window in her own small palace, staring after that falcon with eyes which blazed with undisguised passion.

God, to fly like that!

Oh, Ljuba could master the shifting to a second, avian shape—of course she could. Magic ran through all the royal line; it always had. And each member of that line had, as part of his or her birthright, an avian shape almost as easy to the wearing as the natural human form. But for Ljuba what should be a simple thing, a gentle shifting of shape, was far from easy. For her, the change ate at her strength, pointing out her shame, the fact that the magic she'd inherited was weak, weak.

1

True, she'd had the will to study on her own, seeking through arcane scrolls the knowledge that should have been innately hers, the touch of Power in her blood giving her at least a slight edge over any totally nonmagical would-be sorcerer trying to learn spells by rote. True, her understanding of secret, magical herbs was second to none; there was a certain satisfaction in seeing her potions work, watching torn flesh heal or fever flee.

But that was such a small thing. To wield something of Finist's effortless magic, to feel the Power running through one's veins, strong and sweet . . . The true-shape forced on her by her own weak magic was no graceful falcon, but a crow, nothing but a common, ugly crow. She seldom flew, at least not when anyone could see.

Flight's the least of it!

Watching Finist's shining, easy, self-confident skill, Ljuba felt a sharp, irrational stab of hatred for her dead mother, hatred at her for having been only petty nobility, for having left her daughter barely enough Power to prove royal blood, for having left her so far from the direct line of succession that even Finist's sudden death wouldn't improve her rank.

No, should Finist die, unwed and childless as he was, his uncle would take the throne: "Vasili." Ljuba spat the name. *Gentle Vasili—priestly Vasili, there in his quiet mountain monastery.*

He'd sworn an oath once, had Vasili, years back, presumably lest he be used by plotters against his brother, Finist's father. He'd sworn never again to enter Kirtesk.

But let our Finist die, and we'll see how quickly dear Vasili bows to fate and overcomes his scruples. He's still young enough to wed, to sire heirs. Heirs! And where does that leave me?

Ljuba glared up at her cousin with a new fierceness, heart pounding. Finist didn't even suspect! He thought she *chose* to isolate herself from court with her herbs. He knew she'd have no reason at all to attack him.

So my dear cousin leaves me alone with my studies— Oh, fool!

She'd stumbled on it almost by accident, after all the years of trial and failure, she'd discovered the one potion that just might bring her power . . . But something within her hesitated. Something within her wanted to turn away, arguing that she wasn't ready, it wasn't time, afraid to act, afraid—

No. She had to face the truth. On her own, she would never be able to win the throne, or wield true Power, or do anything at all of any worth. The only way Ljuba was ever going to have any chance to rule Kirtesk was by ruling Finist himself!

Wildly she flung up a hand. The air about it shimmered faintly—heat-haze shimmer, magic haze—as the long, graceful fingers began to weave intricate patterns. The faintest of crooning syllables left Ljuba's lips, the sound caressing, compelling . . .

"Come to me, Finist, come to me . . ."

Again the charm was repeated, again . . .

But the falcon, wheeling easily in the free sky, showed not the slightest sign of heeding.

FINIST, the wind whistling through his feathers, wasn't being quite as frivolous as either his counselor or his cousin might think. No, he was making use of an advantage no magicless prince could claim: he was analyzing his city's strengths and weaknesses from the air, his falcon's vision rendering even the smallest detail crisply clear.

And what he saw was pleasing. No piles of disease-breeding refuse in *his* city! Kirtesk might not be as grand or as large as some other royal cities he might name—such as Radost and Stargorod, far to the west—but it was clean and neat and nicely ordered there in the early morning sunlight, all the streets paved with proper planking. Aside from that paving, there was little use of wood; save for the occasional one-story, gaily painted house with its intricately carved shuttered and doorposts, most of Kirtesk's buildings were made of stone, two or sometimes, daringly, even three stories high, their steeply sloping, many-gabled roofs shingled with slate that glowed a clean blue-grey in the sunlight.

The Pact still stands.

He meant that pact his magical ancestors, long generations back, had sworn with Those of the forest at Kirtesk's founding. There was a good deal of the Old Magic still alive in that vast, surrounding forest, the raw Power of elemental nature that was so much stronger than anything mere humans could control, and it was wisest to keep on its good side. The Pact had stated simply: so long as the humans of the city never harmed the forest, the forest would never encroach on the city. Kirtesk's planking came only from dead or diseased trees.

Finist nodded to himself. The Pact was a fine and just thing. And stone houses were far less likely to catch fire.

The prince caught a smooth current of air under his wings, enjoying the silken play of it about his body, and made one more wide sweep over Kirtesk, studying the stone wall surrounding it—another source of pride, pact notwithstanding, since even Stargorod had to make do with a mere wooden palisade—then headed back towards the royal palace where it burned dazzlingly bright against the cloudless sky.

Motion far below caught the falcon's eye, and Finist glanced down to see a group of folk headed that way, moving shyly, dressed mostly in homespun: farmers come, as was their right this third day of the month, to present petitions. He watched them point up towards his gleaming self, nudging each other, making self-conscious little bows, and Finist sighed. So much for free time.

He flung himself into one last, wild loop in the air for the sheer joy of flight, then came swooping down through an open palace window, folding his wings at the last possible moment to make it safely through the narrow opening, then throwing them wide again to kill his speed, coming to a smooth landing on the marble floor. The change began as he willed it, the swift, dizzying not-quite-pain, not-quite-pleasure as bones and sinews stretched and lengthened, as the sense of smell returned in a dazzling rush of sandalwood, leather, silk, as colors brightened and vision dulled to the merely human once more.

Patient servants stood waiting as the falcon-shape rapidly blurred, grew, then resolved itself into the form of a tall young man, somewhat breathless, hair silvery and tousled, eyes bright amber. Quickly and efficiently, used to their shape-shifting master, they dressed him in regal robes stiff with gold thread, combing the wild, bright hair into docility, placing a thin golden circlet on Finist's head while he caught his breath and adjusted to being human again.

"So," he said at last, grinning. "Thank you, all of you. And now, to business."

With that, the Prince of Kirtesk, all wildness hidden, swept regally down to the great audience hall.

LJUBA had watched helplessly as the falcon disappeared blithely into the royal palace. Now, with an angry, weary little hiss of a sigh, she let her hand fall.

That spell would have caught an ordinary man. It had, several times before this; Ljuba was not one to risk an untested spell. *But I should have known. What's enough to snare an ordinary man is never strong enough to snare a magician!*

She massaged tired fingers, trying to ignore the whiny little inner voice that whispered, *It's fortunate you failed, now you don't have to try again, now you'll be safe . . .*

After all, though Finist was a gentle enough man, if he should learn that she meant to master him, he, the prince . . . There were certain rumors in the royal family of past members who'd erred in some unpardonable ways, and who, instead of facing the axe, had endured instead a binding into the avian form—a permanent binding. In such a case, the human thoughts would slowly fade, the memory of being human fading with them. Soon *self* would be lost, and only bird remain.

Ljuba bit her lip, clenching her fists to stop their trembling. The thought of such a fate, of such a total, total loss! It had been enough to waken the child-Ljuba screaming many a night. And now, grown though she was, the fear remained, softening her, blocking her from doing what she must—

No! Ljuba smacked a hand down angrily on the windowsill. *I will* not *be afraid!*

And, after a time, she almost managed to believe it.

All right, then. Maybe she couldn't control Finist by mind alone. Maybe she didn't have the strength for great magic. But Ljuba had no intention of giving up her chance at the throne.

I would be so good for this land!

Better than Finist, surely. Finist spent so much time on commoners, insisting that a realm could only run smoothly if peasants and merchants and crafters were content. He wasted his magic on such creatures, and refused to see the wider picture! She had told him again and again that if only he channeled his magic, he could become a truly mighty prince. Kirtesk could go from being a simple little city-state, wealthy only in trade and happy peasants, to a realm of true power, one to be feared by other lands. But each time he'd merely laughed and told her he had no intention of becoming a tyrant. A tyrant! Was it tyranny to want the best for your land?

For a moment, Ljuba toyed with the image of herself on the throne of Kirtesk, ambassadors from many lands bowing to her in fear and awe . . .

Nonsense. Daydreams were all well and good, but they accomplished nothing. There was still that potion, though, the potion to sap the will . . .

Eh, but to be convincing, any changes in Finist were going to have to be slow, subtle. She would have to be close to him for a long time—as his mistress, perhaps . . . or his wife.

Ljuba had never had any difficulties in seducing men. Finist, magician or no, would be no exception, particularly after he'd had a taste of her potion to encourage him! Yes, fine, that was the first step. And since they were only distant cousins, there would be no legal bar to their marriage. His *boyars* were always after him to wed. A few well-placed suggestions to them—oh, she probably wouldn't need any magical force behind the words at all, not if she used proper tact. And with a prince already besotted with her . . . All she had to do was act, feign love for as long as it took, till she quickened with Finist's child.

Ljuba stared thoughtfully out the window, a cool, predatory glint in her eyes. That much of the plan would work, she was sure. But then would come the dangerous part . . . After they'd been peacefully wed for a respectable time, she would have to increase the dosage of her potions, but with delicate care. If Finist came to suspect, she was doomed! But if only she were wary enough, Finist wouldn't have a chance of suspecting. He'd begin to fade, slowly, with never a sign of traditional poisons or bespelling. Everyone knew that the royal magic had been known to turn on its wielders: Finist's own grandfather, Prince Vseslav, had actually died of a miscast spell. And even should someone, by wild mischance, guess at the truth, it wouldn't matter. With Finist helpless, mindless, and his wife bearing his only heir . . .

The boyars will accept me on the throne. They won't have a choice!

A discreet cough made Ljuba whirl. "Anya. What is it?"

The maidservant's curtsey was a quick, respectful, nervous thing. "Mistress, the—the *boyar* Erema would speak with you. If it pleases you."

"It doesn't!" Ljuba snapped. Akh, would she never be rid of the man? She could sense him standing just outside the room, feel the turbulence of his longings—curse him! He'd been her lover once, the bland, dull courtier; he'd been one of her first magical experiments. No longer! But the released power of her spell aimed at Finist had had to go somewhere, and with Erema Mikhailovich still aching for her, he'd drawn it to him like a lodestone. "Bah, tell him to— No, wait."

Ljuba straightened slowly, thinking, *What if . . . ?* Erema was her tool now, and it was surely never wise to cast away a tool.

"Very well. Bid him enter."

"Shall I . . . stay, mistress?"

"No, fool!" Ljuba caught and held the servant's gaze, controlling Anya's more submissive personality with her will. "And no one shall know of this visit. Is that understood?"

Anya's face was dull. "No one shall know, mistress."

As the servant cast open the door, the *boyar* rushed in on a storm of passion, a young man, dark-haired, supple. *Virile of body,* thought Ljuba dryly, *soft of mind.* He fell to one knee before her, kissing the hem of her embroidered caftan like the romantic fool he was. For a time Ljuba looked down on him, unmoved, smiling thinly, then reached down to catch his face between her hands and raise his head so he must look at her.

"Erema. What would you do for me?"

His eyes were glazed with magic and desire. "Anything!"

"Would you do my bidding, hmm? Would you obey me, no matter what?"

"Oh, my dear one, yes! Yes!" His voice was thick with passion. "I—I would take arms against the prince himself if you would only take me back again! The embrace of your sweet arms—"

"Akh, yes," interrupted Ljuba absently. "We shall see."

But she was thinking fiercely, *And now the first step is taken at last. Oh, Finist, here is the beginning of your fall!*

11

SUSPICION

It was dark in the palace corridors, dim and quiet and cool, cool enough for Danilo, *boyar*, counselor to Svyatoslav, Prince of Stargorod, to be glad of the warmth of his fur-trimmed caftan. A fine-figured man, Danilo, though no longer young: distinguished, greying of hair and beard, proud of bearing. And right now, quite lost in thought, barely aware of the servants following at a respectful distance, barely seeing the familiar, gloriously bright murals covering every bit of wall, gold leaf glowing even in the muted light.

The marriage should do well. It should do well, indeed. Mikhail's son—eh, marriage will steady him. And my dear Vasilissa . . . Lissa loves young Afron already, or so Maria tells me.

Akh, Maria. Danilo had but the two children, the two daughters, Vasilissa, the elder, the betrothed, and Maria: sensible, clever Maria. If Lissa had inherited most of their poor dead mother's beauty, Maria had her wit and warmth.

Now I must see to her betrothal as well, Danilo told himself firmly. *I should have done it years ago. But . . . I hate the thought of losing her.*

Perhaps he'd come to depend on Maria too much. After all, in those dark years after his wife's death, when he'd determined never to wed again, he hadn't been able to turn to Vasilissa—no, the delicate thing, he couldn't burden her. It had been Maria, for all that she was the younger

9

child, who'd pretty much run the household, and run it well.

But he was being selfish, thinking like that. Custom insisted a young woman be wed, and wed Maria would be. Though the girl did keep swearing in that calm way of hers that she would marry only for love.

"For love!" muttered Danilo. Well now, he was long past such youthful foolishness. Love notwithstanding, he intended to find her a husband who was a fine, noble man. "Someone who's worthy of—"

He broke off with a start at the sight of the figure that had suddenly appeared out of the shadows. "Forgive me, Danilo Yaroslavovich," said a man's voice. "I didn't mean to alarm you."

Danilo peered into the dimness, trying to place that teasingly familiar voice, making out the shape of a fine-boned, pale face, a neat, dark beard—

"Alexei! How did you get in here?"

The young *boyar* grinned sharply. "I told the guards I had an appointment with you. They, ah, believed me."

Danilo snorted. "They believed your gold, you mean." If old Svyatoslav, suspicious enough at the best of times, knew that his guards could be so easily bribed, he'd have their heads! "Alexei," Danilo began again, then stopped, belatedly aware that his servants, uneasy, had surged forward. Impatiently he waved them back, very much aware that for safety's sake he should say nothing to Alexei, he should simply have the man thrown out.

But Alexei was giving him a hesitant, charming, innocent smile, a very familiar smile, and memory prodded Danilo. Even though he knew the man was about as innocent as a fox with a mouthful of chicken, he found himself remembering a younger Alexei, alone and friendless, the not-quite-respectable *boyar*'s son, half peasant, who'd looked at him with just those hopeful, fearful eyes, the youngster he'd impulsively made his aide . . . It hadn't been that bad a choice; Alexei had proven clever enough, and most of the time his charm had seemed quite genuine. But, Danilo realized with flawless hindsight, there had always been that other Alexei, the inner, secret Alexei he'd never been able to reach, a slyness, a bewildering hardness beneath the innocence.

Maybe not so bewildering. Serge, Alexei's father, had always been a hard man himself, a cold man obsessed with status, never forgiving himself for his weakness with that pretty peasant girl, never forgiving his son for being less than pure of blood.

Maybe, Danilo thought with a touch of guilt, *if I'd spent more time with the boy . . .*

Dammit! Even now, Alexei still had the sly knack of making everyone else take the blame for his behavior.

No longer. Danilo had done what he could. He'd tried to show the boy there was such a thing as trust, and honor, and stability, and if he'd failed—

No, dammit, *he* hadn't failed! This wasn't a matter of some minor error in Danilo's account books or a midnight romp with a merchant's daughter. Alexei wasn't a child anymore.

"I doubt this is a chance meeting," Danilo said dryly. "You'd speak with me. Of what?"

"You know of what." The younger man fell in beside him, voice soft and earnest. "Were you to speak with our prince about me—"

"No."

"Please, hear me out. I've changed, truly I have. I—"

"No!"

"Danilo! We—we were friends once."

"Until you betrayed my trust!" Danilo glanced back at the curious servants, then caught the younger man by the arm and virtually dragged him into the privacy of an alcove. "Alexei, I *did* speak to him once in your behalf! Have you forgotten? I vouched for you. And Prince Svyatoslav believed me. He gave you a position in his retinue, an honorable post. And how did you repay him? How did you repay *me?* You tried to steal from the royal coffers!"

"Oh, I only—"

"Don't lie to me! Do you know how close I came to being banished for your crime? You know, you surely must know, how quick to mistrust our prince can be— Yes, and even then, I was fool enough to pity you! Even then I was fool enough to risk my post and maybe even my life to argue in your behalf. And if I hadn't done so, you'd still be languishing in the royal prison. So don't come whimpering to me, man. I've done with you!"

The handsome head drooped. "It's true." Alexei's voice was resonant with sorrow. "I was wrong. I admit it." He glanced up beseechingly. "And I thank you for your help, you surely know that."

"Alexei . . ."

"I have no genuine excuses. But I—I was younger then, and frightened, and foolish. I had debts—"

"Debts! You practically ran through your father's entire estate!"

Alexei's eyes glittered. "I was a fool. I won't make such a mistake again. Please, just tell the prince—"

"Again, *no!*"

"You're holding my birth against me, aren't you? That's it, isn't it?"

"For God's sake, man, don't whine. And stop trying to blame your mother's blood for your faults. There are men of full peasant stock I'd trust sooner than I'd trust you!"

"But can't you simply—"

"*No!* Alexei, you lie as easily as you breathe; it took me too long to realize it. There hasn't been any miraculous reformation. Oh no, you're the same sly, slippery Alexei you've always been. I've already endangered myself—yes, and my family, too—for you, and I'm not about to be such a fool again! The prince has been gracious enough to allow you back into the city. Be content with that."

"You can't mean it. Surely—"

"Can't I?"

"Danilo! You're my only hope!"

"Then you'll be hopeless! Good day to you."

There was stunned silence. And then, "You'll regret this." For an instant the studied innocence was quite gone from Alexei's voice, and Danilo whirled to stare at him.

"What's this? A threat?"

"Oh no, of course not."

Alexei bowed, straightening slowly, watching the *boyar* leave, then clenched his fists to stop their trembling. How could Danilo do this to him? Danilo, with his so superior airs, looking down on the poor little half-peasant, always lecturing him, always trying to get him to "do the right thing," which meant think like Danilo, act like Danilo—

Damn Danilo! One word from the *boyar,* and Alexei would have been returned to rank, to wealth . . .

To safety. Alexei shuddered. He had been so sure the man would forgive him just this one more time. How could Danilo turn against him? Saying his own life had been in danger—what nonsense. The man was a court favorite. Surely he'd have been able to wriggle out of peril, come what may.

Talking about his position and his safety—What about my safety? Doesn't he care what happens to me?

That made Alexei abruptly remember the creditors who were all but breathing down his neck, of his gambling debts and—worse—those to whom the debts were owed, and he began to tremble in earnest.

All right. So Danilo would play his sanctimonious little games, would he? Two could play at games. Maybe Danilo wouldn't sponsor him at court. But the man would still help him, like it or not. After all, Danilo was vulnerable. He had his daughters, his dear Vasilissa and Maria . . .

And for all the cold fear sickening him, Alexei managed a thin smile. "A threat, Danilo?" he said aloud, so softly it was a whisper. "No threat. A promise."

IT was market day in Stargorod, the great open square at the city's heart crowded with booths set up on cobblestones worn smooth over the generations. The air was heavy with musk and lavender, cumin and cooking oil, and fairly rang with laughter, song, the squealing of frightened pigs and the singsong chants of the merchants. Colors flashed, red, blue, gold, as pennants, cloaks, and wide-sleeved caftans caught the shifting breeze. Those city folk not actively engaged in buying or selling furs or gems or cabbages and carrots were busy watching the dancing bear or the jugglers or the minstrel with his sweet-stringed *gusla.* For this one day, *boyars* and commons swirled together in a wild, happy wave.

Only Maria Danilovna stood motionless, Maria of the long brown braids and worried brown eyes, barely aware of the servant—loyal, stocky Sasha—standing protectively by her side. The young woman bit her lip, trying to keep her face impassive all the while her heart was pounding wildly as other servants hunted all that large, crowded square for her sister.

Where can she be?

They'd come to the great market together, Maria and Vasilissa, with the retinue of servants no noblewoman went without. Vasilissa, as ever, had been lecturing her younger sister on the decorum proper to a *boyar*'s daughter. No, Maria mustn't stop to listen to a mere peasant storyteller, love the old tales though she might, and no, Maria mustn't think of buying some mere peasant-woven ribbons, pretty though they might be. And, as ever, Maria had been letting the lecturing drift by her, interjecting a docile "Yes, Lissa," or "Of course, Lissa." She'd learned from sad experience that it was the easiest way to keep the peace.

But then the running monologue had stopped, a fact that had taken Maria, her thoughts far away, a moment to realize. When she'd looked up in surprise, she'd found to her shock that Vasilissa was gone. Somehow, despite all that entourage of servants, she'd managed to slip away, to simply—disappear.

Maria fought down images of her beautiful, elegant, naive sister in the hands of ruffians, slavers. Surely Lissa had more sense than to get snared by such as those! And yet, behind the lecturing and the facade of stern propriety was a certain . . . fragility of mind, a fragility their father simply refused to see, sheltering the young woman as he would some rare, delicate flower. Lissa saw things sometimes, ghosts or spirits or visions from the past: things that just weren't there. The aftermath of one of these sightings or wide-awake dreams or whatever they were (Maria flinched away from that all-too-easy word, "madness") tended to leave her almost morbidly depressed. But she was, Maria knew, capable of the most incredibly swift shifts of mood, of action taken without a thought to the consequences.

"It'll be all right," Sasha soothed roughly. "You'll see, young mistress, it'll be all right."

Maybe it would, at that. Maybe Lissa had wanted some

time alone . . . No, with her betrothed, of course! There was no denying that Vasilissa had fallen madly in love with her handsome husband-to-be, while he . . . At least he was in love with the idea of being in love, thought Maria, wishing her father had picked a man of strong enough character to give Lissa the strength she lacked. But Afron was every bit as flighty as Vasilissa, and if the two of them had decided it would be daring and romantic to snatch some unchaperoned kisses, they would have conveniently forgotten the tongues eager to gossip.

"Akh, Lissa, I'm not against the idea of love, I'm not. But I only wish you wouldn't—*Lissa!*"

That last was a shout, because she'd caught a sudden glimpse of her sister. And that had almost certainly been Afron with her, the two of them running guiltily down that alley.

But—had there been a third person with them, beckoning them on?

"*Boyarevna* Vasilissa!" cried Sasha. "*Boyarevna,* wait!"

Of course she didn't wait. Maria gave a sharp little sigh. Much as she'd like to simply let the two have their fun, her father would be the first to suffer if the ridiculous laws of propriety weren't observed. "We can't wait for the others. Sasha, hurry!"

The alley, little more than a space between houses, twisted its convoluted way between windowless, wooden back walls, splitting off again and again into a maze of paths. It was so abruptly quiet back here after the noise of the market that Maria's ears rang.

"I don't see her," she said over her shoulder to Sasha. "There are so many ways—"

A sharp whistle of air cut into her words, a *crack* of a blow. Maria whirled just in time to see the man crumpling to the ground.

"Sasha!"

Horrified, she dropped to his side. Was he . . . Thank the Lord, he was still breathing. There was an angry red mark on his forehead, a round pebble on the ground—a sling, someone had struck him down with a sling!

But who—why—

And then they strolled into view: four rough men, roughly clad, one of them still swinging his sling casually in one hand, and all of them with hard, predatory smiles.

And here I am, thought Maria desperately, *a young woman alone, dressed in what's obviously an expensive caftan—oh, wonderful!*

Trying to buy time, she snapped, "What do you want?"

They chuckled. "What do you think?"

While they were wasting those few seconds in swagger, Maria had the chance to palm Sasha's knife and quietly slip it into her wide sleeve. Now what? No point in wasting breath in screaming—not with only blank walls to hear her, and everybody probably at the market anyway, the market with all its noise. And she was no warrior-woman out of the ballads, to defeat all these scum. That left only . . .

Maria burst up and away without warning, hearing startled curses behind her as she ran with all her might. If only she could find her way back through this maze to the market's safety!

Of course the men weren't going to let her go so easily. Maria heard footsteps pounding loudly in her ears. But when a rough hand snatched at her sleeve, she slashed out wildly with the knife. There was a yelp of pain and her sleeve was abruptly released, and Maria ran on, grinning in a way that rather shocked herself. Now, if only she could somehow manage to lose the rest of the men—

No, oh no! There were more of them, coming at her from a new direction! *This can't be a casual attack!* she thought in terror. *It can't be. This has to have been planned!*

No time to worry about it. She was being herded, no doubt about it, herded into this one passageway—that ended in a blank wall. Trapped, Maria whirled to face her hunters, knife in hand, fierce with rage and fear.

But she was no trained fighter, and there were just too many of them. They were being overtly careful not to hurt her, and that care added to her terror. She lunged, but then the knife was being jerked out of her grasp, and strong arms were pinning her against the wall for all her frantic scratching and biting and kicking.

Even in the heat of that desperate struggle, some cool, sane part of her mind was noting, *They're wearing boots. Under those rags are fine leather boots!*

What good did that do her? In a moment they'd have her down, and then—

And then, amazingly, the rough arms were falling away from her. Amazingly, her attackers were running in all directions, pursued by someone's servants—Alexei! Here he was in all his dark-bearded handsomeness, asking her earnestly:

"Are you all right? My dear, are you all right?"

Only sheer pride kept her from bursting into tears. Lost in helpless shudderings, Maria could only nod.

"My home is nearby," Alexei was continuing in a solicitous tone. "You remember, I have a house in the city. Come, you'll be safe there."

She was too shaken not to go with him. He must have spoken to her, but Maria didn't hear a word. Indeed, she didn't really begin to come back to herself till she was in the *boyar's* small hall, seated across a table from him, holding a cup of wine that she needed both hands to steady lest she spill it all over herself. God, that had been a narrow escape!

No; if she kept thinking about it, she'd collapse. And still that cool, sane little voice in her mind was insisting, *Something's not right.*

Maria let her gaze wander about the small room, noting signs of barely concealed poverty in threadbare rugs, worn furnishings. The walls had once been painted in bright, old-fashioned style, stiff, archaic figures against a sky-blue background, but now the paint was sadly faded, so stained and peeling that it was difficult to tell if the images were holy men or heroes. One figure, so worn that only its eyes remained, seemed to stare at her, pleading or pitying, till Maria, fighting down a shudder, looked down at her winecup instead, noting for the first time that it was of cheap, common pewter, not silver. It was true then: Alexei was at the point of bancruptcy, too proud to soil his hands with work, too drawn by the love of gambling to save himself.

But why was he studying her like this? Why did his eyes

glitter with passion? All at once Maria began to wonder very much about that so obviously planned attack, and the fine leather boots on men in rags, and the perfectly timed rescue.

"Alexei," she began slowly, "I'm very grateful for your help. But how is it you chanced to be there just at that very moment?"

He gave her a charming smile. "Why, good fortune, Maria Danilovna. Good fortune. You see, the city guards can't be everywhere, and so I have my own men patrol the area about my house. It happened that I was with them this day."

"I see." But her hands were beginning to tremble anew, and Maria clenched them fiercely about the winecup. *"Boyar* Alexei, I may be wrong about this. And if I am, I sincerely crave your pardon. But—what had you to do with Vasilissa?"

His expression of surprise was just a bit too perfect. "I? Why, nothing, *boyarevna!* She's betrothed, isn't she? What should I have to do with a betrothed woman?"

"Then you'll deny I saw Lissa and her betrothed—and you—running towards this house?"

"Why, my dear, what a thing to say!"

"Alexei, stop it. I'm not the little girl who was bedazzled by your charm. Did I or did I not see you guiding them here?"

His elegant glance seemed to caress her, gently admiring. "No longer a little girl at all," he murmured, voice smooth as dark velvet. A small shiver of response ran up Maria's spine, and angry at herself, she snapped:

"Answer me!"

"Temper doesn't become you." He paused, then added thoughtfully, just before she could explode, "Of course, it is possible that I might have yielded to romance and let a certain young couple have a bit of privacy on my small lands."

Maria stiffened. Very carefully she put down the half-filled cup of wine lest she hurl it into his smiling face. "And you made certain I'd see them, didn't you?"

"Did I?"

Curse it, she wasn't going to let that smooth voice beguile her! "You timed the whole thing very nicely, Vasilissa and my attackers, and the so-called rescue—it must have taken every one of your servants."

"Oh, it did," he admitted, smile fading just a bit. "But how did you suspect?"

"My God, Alexei, if you're going to set a trap for someone, think of the details! Ruffians don't wear expensive boots."

"Ah. Of course."

The smile had gone completely; Alexei never had liked being corrected, Maria remembered. She hurried on, "The whole thing was a trap for me? But—but why? What could you possibly hope to gain?"

"You," he said simply.

"What!"

"You, my dear." The velvet was back in his voice. Before she could move, his hands had snared hers, so quickly she barely had a chance to release the winecup, holding her with a grip so firm it was almost painful. His eyes burned into hers, sending renewed shivers racing through her.

"Alexei, let me go."

"Not yet. Not till you hear me out. Don't you see, Maria? Did you never guess? Do you not remember that kiss?"

Maria felt herself blush. They'd both been barely more than children, he enough her senior to have little to do with her. Till that day he'd cornered her in an empty hallway and seen her for the first time as girl rather than child. "I slapped your face."

"But you didn't tell your father."

Tell him what? That Alexei had let her go the moment after his lips had brushed hers, suddenly remembering who and what she was? That for all her shock and anger she hadn't exactly disliked the experience? "It was nothing."

"But you do remember."

She tried to pull her hands free, but he only tightened his grip. Some women might have enjoyed the feeling of being held helpless like this, Maria supposed in growing unease, but the man's air of casual superiority infuriated her. "Are you actually trying to *seduce* me, Alexei?"

"And would that be such a terrible thing?"

"It would be an astonishing foolish thing!"

"Akh, Maria, did you never guess? Did you never before notice how I watched you all the years you were growing up, you and your sister—oh, hers is the quick, elegant beauty, but you, with your radiant charm . . . Many a time I ached, burned, to take you in my arms, Maria, but your father would never let me—"

"Stop it." No other man had ever spoken to her like this; they'd all been too dazzled by Vasilissa. She might have believed him. She wanted to believe him. But in his contempt for her sense, her willpower, he'd gone too far. This was just too polished a speech to be genuine. Maria thought of all the poor, simple, silly young women who must have been snared by it, and torn by regret and pain and a rage that nearly left her breathless, she gasped out, "Alexei, let me go."

"No, my dear, not till—"

"Stop it!" With a surge of panicky strength, she twisted her hands free. "What do you *really* want?"

Alexei paused, studying her, still smiling faintly. "Akh, fierce young woman. Clever woman! I spoke the truth. I want you."

"Liar!"

The smallest hint of anger flickered into life in his eyes. He continued, with only the slightest roughening of the urbane voice, "Why, my dear, such a bitter word doesn't belong on such lovely lips."

"Liar, I say!"

She started to scramble to her feet, but he caught one wide sleeve of her caftan and pulled her sharply down again. "I told you that temper doesn't become you, Maria." The velvet had been replaced by steel. "But I will kiss it away and—"

"You never learn, do you? *I don't want you.*"

"You will."

He leaned slowly towards her, eyes hot. And Maria slapped him. It wasn't as hard a blow as she'd have liked, what with the table so awkwardly between them, but she made a point. Alexei released her with a hiss, face gone cold and deadly.

"That was a foolish thing, Maria. So now, my dear, you want the truth? I do want you. Oh no, not from any overblown sense of the romantic. But, as I said, you're a clever woman. Figure it out."

"I won't play games with you."

He sighed. "So be it. You know I'm still in disgrace with our most unforgiving prince. Without a court position, my fortune is fading rapidly. I barely have enough gold left to maintain this house in proper style."

The chill, calculating passion in his eyes frightened her. As coldly as she could manage, Maria spat, "What's this? Am I supposed to pity you?"

"My dear, I hardly care. Your father might have helped to restore my place in Svyatoslav's good graces. But he refused me. This time he isn't going to be so hasty."

"You can't actually be planning to hold me for ransom!"

"Oh, no. My intentions are quite honorable." He added with deliberate malice—revenge on her for her blow—"I would have preferred your pretty, pliable sister, but she is already as good as wed. That left only you."

Maria stared at him in disbelief. "You can't be meaning to *marry* me!"

"Can't I?"

"But there are dozens of unmarried women. Go to them!"

Alexei shook his head gently. "No. Your father alone has both the wealth sufficient to replenish mine and the social rank high enough to bolster my . . . sadly sagging reputation. And there's a certain lovely justice in my becoming his son-in-law, don't you agree?" His smile hardened. "Think, girl. We're alone. There's no one to help you. One way or another, Maria, I do mean to have you. One way or another, there will be a wedding."

She refused to let him see her fear. Unable to meet his gaze, she moved quickly to the room's one window, staring blankly out, mind racing with panic—

Until she noticed the garden below. Soft earth . . . and it wasn't so far to the ground, not so far at all, and the wall beyond it looked quite scalable . . . She remembered her younger days, scandalizing the household with her tree climbing . . .

But then Alexei was at her side, putting his hands possessively on her shoulders, and Maria pulled away, returning to the table.

"There will be no wedding," she said firmly.

"Come, let's be civilized." Alexei moved smoothly to her side. "You'll have to marry someone. And who's to say the man your father picks won't be old, or ugly, or cruel? I'm still young, and I know you don't find me uncomely, and as your husband, I'll treat you kindly enough. And when I'm your father's son-in-law," continued Alexei blithely, "why, he'll treat me kindly as well, and we'll all live happily forevermore, just like folk in a minstrel's tale."

"No! Alexei, this is ridiculous. Let me go. Let me go, and I won't say anything about—"

"Oh no, my dear."

With that, he lunged at her. Maria didn't wait to learn what he intended. With one quick twist of the wrist, she neatly flipped the contents of her winecup full in his face. Alexei gasped, clawing the stinging wine out of his eyes, but Maria was up and away, out the window before she had a chance to think twice about it, hanging by her hands for an instant, then letting go, falling, landing in a breathless but undamaged heap. Back in the house, Alexei was swearing in a choked voice, but he hadn't called to his guards, not yet—

"Maria!"

It was a horrified gasp. Maria scrambled to her feet to find Vasilissa staring at her, a rather rumpled and red-faced Vasilissa, and with her an equally disconcerted Afron, tall and golden and weak of chin. Maria caught her breath enough to say sharply, "We're leaving. Now."

"But where—how—Maria! Wait!" Lissa grabbed her by the arm, whispering frantically, "You can't tell Father where we were!"

Maria glared, jerking her arm free, ready to spit out some furious reply. But the childlike panic she saw in those big eyes made her bite back what she was going to say and mutter instead, "I wasn't planning to."

"But what on earth are you doing here?" Vasilissa, shaky with relief, was struggling to slide back into proper aristocracy. "Alone, with a man—"

"I wasn't the only one! And this is hardly the time or place for a—a chat!" Maria whirled to the two men at the gates. "Guards! Open those gates! Stand aside!"

It was her father's tone of voice. And it worked. Startled, the guards obeyed. But then they were looking uneasily past her, and Maria spun about to see Alexei, winestains darkening the front of his clothing, anger darkening his pale face. "Good day, my lord," said Maria hastily, and virtually dragged her sister out to safety, praying Alexei wouldn't try to stop them.

But Alexei made not the slightest move to stop them. As Maria and Vasilissa and the sheepish Afron hurried off, Alexei merely stood, as though turned to stone.

"My lord?" It was one of the guards. "My lord, should we go after them?"

"No, you fool! Leave me."

"But—"

"Leave me!"

The guard bowed, cringing from that cold, cold face, never guessing at the terror lurking behind the frozen facade or twisting at Alexei's bowels.

His creditors; his debts. The debts that now he could never hope to pay . . . Assuming those creditors let him live long enough to worry about it . . .

Oh, God!

How could things have gone so wrong? It had seemed such a simple, foolproof plan: frighten the girl, play the gallant rescuer, have her fall about his neck in gratitude . . . But she'd thrown him off balance right at the start by being so damnably clever about those leather boots— Why hadn't he remembered to warn his men not to wear them?

Yes, but even so, Maria had been weakening beneath his charm; he'd felt it. He should have been able to win her over quickly enough, with pleasure in the winning for both of them; clever creature though she was, she was still only a young woman, innocent in the ways of men. But— dammit, how *could* things have gone so wrong?

I had her! I had her, and a way out of this mess, and I let her escape!

So what if the foolish thing had thought she wasn't willing? It would have been so simple, so easy—some quick, rough bed-sport (who knew? she might even have enjoyed it!), a few tears, and the girl would have agreed to wed him. She would have had to wed him, or have the whole city know she'd been ruined.

But he'd underestimated her and her nerve, there it was. He'd let her escape. Now she would go straight to Danilo. And that, realized Alexei in new horror, would be the end of everything.

Danilo again! Alexei bared his teeth in a hating grin, remembering all the years he'd needed to be humble to the man, all the years he'd forced himself to bow beneath that condescending kindness.

Danilo, always in his way. Proud Danilo, honorable Danilo— *Damn* the man!

Alexei drew in his breath with a sharp hiss. All right, then. No more playing about. It would have been simpler, safer, to have married Maria, but there was still a way out. In his strongbox were certain letters, forged with care by a scribe who knew how to let himself be bought, and how to stay bought. They had cost Alexei a good deal of gold, those letters. But what price glory? Or his life?

It was a risky plan. It might not work, and failure might well mean his death.

And if he played the noble fool, and did nothing? Why, it was just a matter of which death he preferred: the mercifully swift axe of the headsman—or the clubs and daggers of his creditors: a dark alley, and pain, and himself left broken, to bleed out his life in the filth . . .

No, he mustn't think of that. He must think only of seeing himself elevated, and Danilo humbled! And old Svyatoslav was such a suspicious sort . . . Oh, it might work after all. It *would* work! And when it did, all hail Alexei—and farewell Danilo.

III

THE WOLF

Now, WHAT GOOD IS IT, thought Finist, *to have oh-so-wondrous magical gifts if you can't use them to reshape this unwieldly monster of a throne?*

It was a splendid thing up here on its high dais, too rich in history for him to dare any tampering. Cut from the trunk of some enormous dead tree about the time of the Pact, the throne had originally been left as plain wood, polished and covered with intricate carvings symbolizing forest, field and magic. But over the generations, changing tastes had seen it plated with gold, then enamelled, then encrusted with so many gems that it fairly blazed with light.

Unfortunately, the original carvers had had a ridiculous idea of royal grandeur, and the throne was far too wide; it was impossible for Finist to reach both armrests at the same time. The thing was also too deep for him to rest his back against its back without his feet dangling foolishly off the floor. And, thought the prince, it was damnably hard on the royal backside, even with a bulwark of cushions. The only way to get comfortable was to sprawl sideways. And that, Finist conceded with an inner grin, would hardly look regal.

At least his discomfort was merely physical. Finist glanced out at his *boyars,* those supposed "equals among nobles" who, he knew, actually had a stern pecking order in which status depended on their service to him and their ancestors' service to his ancestors. He bit back an impa-

tient little sigh at the sight of them in their overstuffed
sobriety sitting in neat rows on the benches lining the audience hall. Custom decreed they attend any meeting other
than that of the Inner Council, so here they were, all of
them looking bored to the point of yawning, yet none having the nerve or spontaneity to simply beg his pardon and
leave. Their dullness was incongruous in that great,
grandly ornamented hall: thick stone pillars supported the
sweep of its vaulted roof; and ceiling and pillars and walls
were rich with color, blazing with paintings of Kirtesk
history done in reds, yellows, blues, glinting with gold,
reflected dazzlingly by the polished marble floor.

But even more incongruous in their plain, honest greys
and browns were the reasons he sat here—the stream of
petitioners, farmers, artisans, common folk, come to him
with problems of farms or taxes or inheritances. Suddenly
Finist tensed, feeling a faint psychic stirring, a feather's
touch brushing his consciousness: Ljuba. His cousin must
be watching the proceedings, as she often did, through a
magic-treated mirror. It was her right, after all, as a member of the royal family. And even this sometime interest
in the outside world, Finist supposed, must be healthier
for a young woman than that self-imposed semiexile of
hers spent in what was generally unproductive arcane
study.

Not that she would be finding much of interest in peasant affairs. *Elegant enough for you?* Finist asked her silently, sarcastically, though of course, she couldn't hear
him.

Forget Ljuba. Now, to business.

In the slow hours that followed, Finist counselled where
he could, occasionally calling on this or that *boyar* for
advice, making those decisions he thought just, using his
magic to determine honesty or falsehood—not that there
were many who'd dare lie to a magician—and wondered,
deep within him, if the line of supplicants would never
end. Thank Heaven, this day came only once a month!

He could, of course, have simply declared the audience
at an end at his whim. But his father had never done such
a thing, not when there might be someone genuinely in

need of his help, and neither, Finist conceded reluctantly, would he.

At last the final group of petitioners approached the throne. Finist leaned forward, studying them. No farmers, these straight-backed, leather-clad men. Woodsmen, he guessed, fearless souls from one of the small villages that dared nestle within the boundaries of the vast forest which covered much of the land, the forest that was still full of the Old Magic. Finist raised an eyebrow. It must be some great problem indeed to bring such proud, self-sufficient folk all the way to his court.

But right now they didn't look particularly proud, shifting nervously from foot to foot, eyes never quite meeting his gaze.

"Well?" prodded Finist at last. "What would you? Come, speak."

That merited him a quick, wary glance from the lean, middle-aged man who seemed the group's leader. And Finist drew a startled gasp at the sorrow he glimpsed in those weary eyes.

"Come," the prince repeated, more gently. "Speak."

The weatherbeaten face reddened. "It's just . . ." He glanced pointedly at the bored *boyars*. "Eh, what it is, is that we need your magic, my prince. But we . . . uh . . ."

"You'd just as soon not have everyone here knowing your troubles," Finist concluded. Intrigued, the prince studied the man for a silent moment, wondering . . . Royalty always has its enemies; he wasn't so naive as to believe he mightn't have some secret foes. Yet he sensed no treachery in the man, only that awkward, painful sorrow. Eyes half-closed, arm outstretched, Finist quested with his mind for the aura of hidden weaponry on the group, hunting for the cold, cruel tang which meant iron—that metal most deadly to magic and magicians—for any other concealed weapons . . . Nothing.

"So be it." Finist got to his feet in a swirl of robes, moving smoothly down the dais' narrow stairway, ignoring the stirrings of surprise from his *boyars*. "The rest of you, wait here. You"—pointing at the sad-eyed man— "come with me."

* * *

THE Ruby Chamber was a much smaller audience chamber, less formal despite the elegance of silken rugs imported from the East and the glowing red walls delicately ornamented in patterns of gold. It was one of Finist's favorite meeting rooms, since it was one of the few to boast the luxury of a wide window, reminding him comfortably of the sky's freedom just outside. It also had, much to his relief, no cumbersome throne, only a relatively simple chair of polished wood thickly padded with red brocade and raised on only a few token steps. Here he sat, watching the woodsman's silent unease.

"Now," Finist said firmly when it seemed the silence would go on forever. "Your story. First, you are . . ."

"Feodor, my Prince, son of Igor."

"So. Talk to me, Feodor Igorovich."

"I—it's about a wolf," the man began.

"A wolf. You'd hardly be wasting my time about some animal you could hunt yourself, now, would you? What's the matter, then? Is this wolf rabid?"

"No, no, nothing like that." Feodor's voice shook. "The—the wolf is—one of us. Stefan. Stefan has—has become a wolf." At Finist's startled, skeptical stare, he added fiercely, "It's true! I— Stefan's my son! I know him! You have to help him, my Prince, you must!"

"Slowly, slowly!" Finist wasn't quite so willing to believe, not so quickly. "How could such a transformation have come about? Was your son playing with dangerous secrets?"

"My God, no! Stefan would never— He's a *good* boy, my Prince, he'd never think of dabbling in—in— He wouldn't!"

"Softly, now. Tell me exactly what happened."

Feodor sighed. "All I know for certain is that one night Stefan disappeared. We hunted for him all the next day, but couldn't find a trace of him. The next night . . ." The man swallowed convulsively. "The next night the wolf appeared: Stefan. Every night since then, he's prowled the village. He—hasn't hurt anyone yet, or even taken any livestock; he only roams around the village palisade. But—but surely it's only a matter of time before he—before he—" Feodor choked, and couldn't go on.

"Before he forgets he's human," Finist said softly.

It was possible, it was very possible.

He shook his head impatiently. "Akh, Feodor, there doesn't have to be anything magical about this! Tell me, does Stefan have himself a girl?"

The peasant hesitated. "Marfa, Boris' daughter. They'd had a fight, Stefan and Marfa; that's why he ran off. But—"

"There you are! Stefan might even have run here, to Kirtesk. I'll have my guards—"

"No!" Feodor, in his distress, didn't even notice he'd interrupted his prince. "The wolf! What about the wolf?"

"It's probably only a youngling cast out from its pack."

"*No!* I know my son! I saw the wolf! Those aren't the eyes of a beast, they're the eyes of my son! Please, you're the only one who can help him. I—I'll do whatever you command. Only please, help my son!"

Uneasy, Finist stepped down from his chair, moving to stare thoughtfully out the window. Could it be? There was magic enough in the forest, Heaven knew, strange beings and Power older than anything he wielded.

No, this was ridiculous! It was probably just as he'd said, a lovers' quarrel—

But what if it wasn't? What if, somehow, a young man had been bound into beast form, trapped till he came to forget his very humanity? No magician could be free of that nightmare . . .

"Yes," Finist said. "If it lies within my power, I will help."

Of course, Finist had no need to waste time in riding all that way back with Feodor and the others. He had a much swifter means of travel, and so that night a silvery falcon sped towards the forest and the village within it.

Village? thought Finist. It was little more than a few huts sheltered within a palisade of wooden stakes, there in the middle of a clearing. Still, the prince conceded, these folk were his subjects, as surely as any of the nobility.

He stood alone in the growing darkness outside the palisade, sniffing woodsmoke from the village, hearing the rustlings of the forest, waiting, shivering a bit in the chill from the cooling earth, rather wishing he'd brought more with him than the one lightweight, silken caftan. But then, there was a limit to the bulk his talons could carry easily. He'd refused to allow the villagers to wait out here with him, fearing that if the wolf really was Stefan, the shock of capture might well drive an already shaken human mind past recovery. *But I wish I'd at least had the sense to borrow a warm cloak.*

The wolf appeared suddenly, materializing out of the forest and padding silently towards the village palisade, for the moment unaware of him. An adolescent wolf, this, still too long of limb, lanky, but surely no more than a lonely, curious, perfectly ordinary wolf.

Or was it? Finist stirred slightly, and the animal started, staring at him. For an instant, the prince saw something glint strangely in those greenish eyes; for an instant he wondered uneasily if this mightn't be a rabid beast after all, and him standing there without a weapon to hand, his magic not being of the dramatic, fireball-hurling sort.

He'd risk it. *But if the wolf charges me,* Finist thought with a flash of wry humor, *he's going to see the fastest avian transformation in royal history!*

Warily, the prince let down his mental guards, sending out a careful, wordless query . . . brushing the other mind, the lupine mind . . . No; he'd felt the animal thoughts of wolves before, the basic instincts for food and pack, but there were no such thoughts here, only a half-formed vagueness, and behind it the hint of some lost, frightened consciousness . . .

Finist hastily drew his senses back into himself lest he too get snared by vagueness. "So-o . . ." he breathed. "Feodor was right. You *are* Stefan, aren't you? I wonder who transformed you, and how."

The wolf froze at the first sound of his voice, ears up, and stared at him intently.

"No," the prince continued softly, "the problem is that your untrained mind doesn't know how to deal with the change. Humanity is sliding away from you. And how am I to draw you back?"

The wolf couldn't hold his gaze any longer. With a worried little whine it began pacing back and forth, giving him quick, nervous glances.

"If I'm to do you any good, I must lay hands on you," Finist told it, taking a slow, cautious step forward. "But will you let me approach you, Stefan?"

He continued his patient, wary dance, now a step forward, now a step back, being always careful never to come between the uneasy creature and the safety of the forest, keeping up a steady, soothing croon as though this really was no more than some frightened beast. Finist knew he didn't dare move any faster: push the confused creature that was wolf-Stefan too hard, and he'd be sure to either run off or attack in sheer panic.

"So, and so . . . Another few steps and I'll be at your side, and maybe you'll actually allow me to touch you, and I'll be able to—"

"Stefan!"

A small, feminine form came hurtling out of the forest towards the wolf. This had to be Marfa, hiding in wait for her transformed lover, meaning only good—but Stefan didn't know her, not as he was. All he knew was that this screaming human was cutting off his escape.

"No!" Finist shouted. "Get away!"

Too late—the wolf was springing.

So Finist sprang first, catching the thin grey form in mid-leap, hurling them both to the ground, the wolf snarling like a true wild thing, Finist trying frantically to pin the lithe body writhing and snapping in his grip, trying to hold those powerful jaws together. God, the strength of the thing!

And then, in the middle of the struggle, Finist, hot animal breath in his face, glanced wildly up to catch the merest glimpse of a fine-boned, so familiar face, long hair shining like burnished gold even in the dim light: Ljuba. Ljuba, here? Impossible; she hated the forest, fearing its wild magic—besides, if she were here, she'd be helping him, wouldn't she? Aie, watching his council meetings was one thing, she had a perfect right to do that, royal lady that she was, but spying on him was something else entirely! Angry, Finist glanced up again and saw nothing but forest, and nearly got himself raked by the frantic wolf's claws for that moment of inattention. Panting, he fought till he'd managed to lock his legs about the straining beast. Slowly, painfully, he forced the lupine head about, forced the wild eyes to meet his gaze.

"Stefan. You are Stefan. I call you, I—"

He broke off with a gasp as fangs snapped and nearly closed on his arm. Finist caught the wolf in a fiercer grip, feeling Power blaze up within him, a fire in the blood, and began again, calling Stefan, coaxing, summoning, dragging the lost essence that was Stefan back and back and back . . .

And suddenly the lithe grey form went limp and submissive in his arms, gazing pleadingly up at him with human eyes.

"Stefan," murmured Finist, releasing his grip gladly, the fire fading within him. "Now—let's see how to—break the charm . . . Get you back into your rightful shape."

But there was a flicker of movement: Marfa, come to take the wolf's head in her arms, sobbing over him with adolescent fervor—or guilt? Finist studied her a moment, eyes widening in sudden comprehension.

"Marfa," he said sternly, and she turned to him, plainly terrified of his magic, his royalty, but determined to be brave: a small, pretty, defiant thing. The desperation in that slight frame touched Finist, and he sighed. "Why, Marfa? Why do this thing?"

"I—I didn't—"

"Don't lie. Not to me. Why did you do it? Do you hate Stefan so very much?"

"I don't hate him!" It was an anguished wail. "I never—Oh, Stefan! Stefan, forgive me! I—I was so angry, I didn't think; we'd sworn to be true to each other, and then Anna told me, that night the two of you had—had— How could you?"

Wolf-Stefan gave a little whine, seeming to shrink into himself, abashed, eyes fixed on her face, pleading, *Forgive, please, forgive!*

Marfa hesitated. Then, with a little sob, she let her hand fall to his head, stroking the rough grey fur.

"I never expected it to work. Not really." Her murmur was meant more for Stefan than Finist. "It was only an old story, you know the one, about how to make the wolf-charm. Nobody *really* believes it." She stopped short, biting her lip. "But I thought, what if? It probably wouldn't work, but if it did, it—it wouldn't last, it would just change you long enough to—to teach you a lesson. Stefan, I didn't know! I didn't know you—you'd have to stay a wolf forever!"

Finist sat back with a sigh, rubbing tired muscles. "He doesn't."

Human and lupine heads shot up to stare at him, eyes fierce with hope. "How . . . ?" Marfa began.

"You still have this, ah, wolf-charm, I take it?"

She nodded, hand going to her bodice. "I've been carrying it with me to keep it safe. I was afraid if I didn't, something might happen to it and hurt Stefan. I mean, hurt him worse than—than—"

"Never mind that. First, girl, go back into the village and get Stefan something to wear. Go on! With any luck at all, he'll be himself again soon enough. And I doubt he'll want to be caught walking around stark naked."

"Oh!"

Reddening, she went. Finist glanced down at Stefan, who was staring after her with longing eyes. *Well, now, he really does love her!* thought Finist, surprised at how pleased the thought made him.

And Marfa came scurrying out again, a bundle of clothing clutched in her arms.

After that, it was a simple matter of lighting a small fire with a flash of will and having Marfa cast her homemade charm—an ugly little thing of scraps of fur and knotted twine—into the heart of it. These odd little backwoods spells did tend to work, there being enough Power in the forest to fuel them, but they also tended to be ridiculously easy to break.

The charm burned to ash quickly enough. And with its destruction, wolf melted smoothly back into man—into boy, rather: a lanky, yellow-haired, green-eyed youngster who hastily scrambled into his clothes while Marfa modestly hid her eyes. Then, their prince quite forgotten, the two young lovers rushed into each other's arms, stammering apologies and declarations of undying love. Finist got slowly to his feet, watching with wry humor and, much to his amazement, a touch of rueful envy. What must it be like to be the recipient of such blazing love? What must it be like to *feel* such love? Princes seldom found out . . .

Eh, no self-pity. In a short while the two youngsters would be remembering his presence. And the villagers, who must surely be spying through the cracks in the palisade, would get over their awe and come rushing out. Finist decided he just wasn't up to their idea of celebration, which would, he knew, include a good deal of heavy drinking.

Magicians, for obvious reasons, didn't dare risk the loss of control found in drink.

But he wasn't quite finished here. Finist paused, considering. Marfa had plainly gone through enough mental anguish to make any punishment from him mere anticlimax. But still:

"Marfa." He tried again. "Marfa!"

This time the girl heard him, pulling hastily free of Stefan's embrace and whirling about to face the prince, face reddening anew. "Oh. My—my Prince?"

"Marfa, do you realize how narrow an escape this was? Had I not arrived when I did, it might have been too late for Stefan. There might not have been a chance to save his human mind. Do you understand what that means?"

To judge from her stricken face, she did. Finist continued relentlessly, "He would have been animal, Marfa, no more than a beast for the rest of his days. Now, my dear, you're not going to experiment with any more of the old tales, are you?"

"N-no, my Prince." It was a very meek reply.

"And neither you nor any others of the village are going to ever try to play with Powers they really don't understand, are they?"

Both youngsters winced at the coldness in his voice.

"No, my Prince."

"Good!"

With that, Finist raised his arms to begin the shift to falcon-form, hearing Marfa and Stefan hastily stammering their belated thanks to him as they realized he meant to leave.

But just as he'd gathered his will together, Finist felt the faintest psychic echoes, barely enough to catch his attention, but quite recognizable. Ljuba! Then he *had* glimpsed her here, spying on him! Anger rippling through him, the prince soared up and out, maneuvering on bright wings through the maze of night-blackened trees, warily, determinedly, following his cousin's trail.

That she fully meant for him to follow her, he hadn't the slightest doubt.

LJUBA stood in shadow, shivering in the night, wishing she had something more than the long veiling of her loose hair to shield her. Damn! She should have thought to carry some sort of clothing with her, as Finist did. But she didn't believe her crow's claws up to the task, and besides, she'd had a lovely, seductive picture of herself in the moonlight, a golden lure to snare her cousin. He'd be tired, and triumphant, and angry at her, a mix of emotions to guarantee his resistance to her would be at its lowest . . . If she'd been foolish enough to try to snare him right away with one of her potions, he would certainly have detected it. But trap him once with the lure of her body alone, and the next time they met, he'd hardly have potions on his mind.

Yes, but how attractive could gooseflesh be? Or— dammit—insect bites? And the forest . . . just didn't want her here.

It never did.

Whenever she was forced to enter it to gather herbs vital to her potions, she could sense the hostility of the Old Magic, that raw Power that *was* the forest, frighteningly unpredictable, terrifyingly uncontrollable, to her and the ordered, civilized, scroll-reading magic she represented. Now Ljuba felt its presence all around her, like some great, dangerous beast that knew she feared it. Surrounded by gnarled, ancient trees, vague black shapes heavy with slow age, she had to make a conscious effort not to sag beneath the weight of a night that had grown far darker than a clear, moonlit night had any right to be.

The things I do for Power, she tried to jest, struggling to hold fast to her rapidly diminishing confidence.

It didn't help to recall that Finist seemed to get along

perfectly well with the Old Magic. To him, this forest was a friendly place, more full of mischief than malice, and he'd go wandering in it whenever time permitted. Keeping the Pact, he called it. Assuming, Ljuba thought, that the Pact their ancestors were said to have made was anything but myth.

No denying, though, that Finist did have a way with the devils living here that was so comfortable it verged on the pagan. He insisted that they weren't devils at all, merely forest entities of various magical sorts. Ljuba knew better. Her spells didn't work in this barbaric place, their small Power crushed by the force of Old Magic; her mirrors could sooner show her what was happening in faraway Stargorod than here! If ever she came to power, Ljuba told herself bitterly, she'd see all these hostile, pagan trees cut down.

The forest knew it. Overwhelmed by its menace, she'd made a damnably stupid mistake and shouted out that threat the last time she'd come here to gather her herbs . . .

A bush rustled. Ljuba started, biting back a gasp—

Oh, fool! It was Finist, only Finist, following the trail she'd left him. A glint of silvery feathers, a swirling shape, and he stood before her, eyes angry. Ljuba forced a smile.

"Cousin. I did hope you'd find me."

He wasn't wasting any time on formality. "Just what game do you think you're playing? What are you doing here?"

"Why, waiting for you!"

"Spying on me, you mean. Why?"

Ljuba hesitated. "I was puzzled," she said after a moment, and just then genuine bewilderment was in her voice. "Finist, why do you bother?"

"Eh?"

"These are only woodsfolk, peasants, nothing! Why do you bother with them?"

He raised a brow. "These are my people, cousin. They trust me. How can I betray that trust?"

"Oh, nonsense! That can't be the whole story!"

A hint of anger flickered in his eyes. "Have you never thought I might have pitied them?"

"Finist, please. I'm not one of your simple peasants."

"You want a materialistic answer, do you? All right, here: the peasants produce the land's food, its resources. Take care of them, they take care of you, and the land flourishes. Plain enough?"

She still didn't see it. After all, if peasants refused to produce, they were traitors and should be punished. But there was still that anger hot in his eyes, and Ljuba, who knew when to yield a point, only sighed in wonderfully feigned innocence. "Do you know, no one ever bothered explaining things like that to me?" She gave a fetching little shiver. "The night's so chill. And—dark. I don't see how you can enjoy this forest, even by day! It's so . . . unfriendly."

"Not to me. Cousin, enough. Why were you spying on me? And why, in Heaven's name, didn't you help me with that wolf?" He paused, eyeing her speculatively. "Hoping to see me die, cousin?"

"Good God, no!" That was heartfelt enough. "Don't be so suspicious. I could see you weren't in any real danger. Besides . . ." Ljuba smiled faintly. "I could hardly have displayed myself to the whole village like this, could I?"

She took a smooth step out of shadow, and was gratified to hear Finist's involuntary gasp at his first clear sight of her, those amber eyes widening, drinking in the vision of golden woman veiled in golden hair . . .

Then his eyes shifted resolutely to her face. "A bit chilly for this, isn't it?" Finist asked dryly.

"Maybe we aren't all so clever in carrying clothes in flight!" she snapped before she could stop herself.

After all, it was difficult to be seductive when she was still shivering, and itching, and scratched in a dozen tender places. And when Ljuba tried to take a second step forward, she trod right on a rock that seemed knife-edged, and fell forward with a little shriek.

Finist caught her. Ljuba stole a quick, wary look up at him and saw nothing in his eyes but concern . . . Maybe this was going to work after all! That cursed rock had hurt her enough to bring tears to her eyes, and now Ljuba let herself go and sobbed.

What man could have resisted? She felt Finist's arms close about her, and buried her face against his chest, very well aware that only one thin layer of silk separated them.

"Here." Finist's voice was husky. "Let me see if you've cut your foot."

"No, no, I only bruised it." Ljuba looked up at him, eyes still bright with tears. "Finist, oh, Finist, I never dreamed, I never dared hope . . ."

"I . . . This isn't . . . We shouldn't . . ." He made one valiant, gallant attempt to free himself, but Ljuba's arms were about his neck, her lips were meeting his. He turned away, but only to bury his face in the warm mass of her hair, and Ljuba smiled, feeling his control slipping, feeling the disciplined, magical mind drowning beneath the flood of the body's demands. Right now he was helpless, helpless, and with a small, fierce cry, he surrendered and bore her to the ground. Ljuba stared up at the hostile forest with wild, triumphant eyes, thinking defiantly, *You see? He's mine!*

And then she forgot all about clear thought for a time.

IV

ACCUSED

FOOLISHNESS, FOOLISHNESS, this tradition that insisted he leave his safe palace and come down here to the market-place with its peasants and riffraff and Heaven knew what else, just to officiate over the closing of market day. But one must, after all, keep in touch with one's people—unpleasant and potentially dangerous though that might be.

Prince Svyatoslav of Stargorod, tall, aging and thin, gathered his voluminous golden robes about himself lest they sweep up the market dust, and proceeded on his regal way, only the darting of his gaze revealing his unease. Oh, they all seemed sincere enough in their welcome, these cheering crowds, but who knew what they were really thinking? A prince must learn from childhood to trust no one—he'd learned that harsh lesson early. He flinched from memories of blood, of terror, of the palace revolt that had left his mother and uncle dead before his eyes. God, and then, when he'd newly come to the throne, little more than a boy, when he'd been fool enough to begin to dare trust again, his cousin, his friend, the one man he'd thought safe, had betrayed him: Prince Rostislav had tried to depose him! Well, Rostislav had gotten himself exiled—lucky to keep his head—and Svyatoslav would never again make the mistake of giving his trust to anyone.

Least of all in this marketplace!

At least he could keep his royal bodyguard all about him, his loyal, spearbearing *achrana*.

But what was this? Those guards in the lead had stopped in a tangle of confusion, and Svyatoslav perforce had to stop short too, thinking wildly, *Assassins!*

It wasn't assassins. It was one man, only one, lying prostrate in the street before him, arms outstretched on the ground in total submission, total supplication, face hidden. Svyatoslav hesitated, uncertain. He hadn't reached this mature age by taking chances. But he could hardly act as though the man wasn't there, and simply step over him. And to have the *achrana* cut a safe path through the crowd to avoid the man would hardly suit the royal dignity.

"Who are you?" the prince snapped, angry at having his routine disturbed. "What do you want?"

The prostrate figure slowly raised his head, moving with great caution since he was ringed by spears. "Sire. Grant me a boon, I pray you. Grant me speech with you."

An indignant Svyatoslav had recognized the man. "Alexei Sergeovich, I have nothing to say to you! You have nothing to ask of me!"

"Sire, no. You misunderstand. I—I don't speak for myself. I have news of something you must know. For the safety of the Realm. For your own safety."

Svyatoslav straightened as sharply as though he'd been slapped. "What news? Get up, man! Tell me! What are you talking about?"

Alexei got carefully to his feet, eyeing the spearbearing guards warily, then turned his attention fully to the impatient prince. "About . . . Well, I'm afraid we're talking about treason, Sire," he said softly.

BOYAR Danilo thought nothing of it when the guards fell in behind him. Some military ritual or other—the palace was full of guards constantly shifting from post to post. Nothing to concern him, surely.

But then they moved forward to surround him, and he found himself facing soldiers who were trying with embarrassed shifts of eye not to meet his glance, but whose weapons were very close to hand. "What nonsense is this?" Danilo asked sharply. "Stand aside. Eh, stand aside!"

They did, but only to permit a stout, somber, richly robed man to approach.

"Gleb Igorevich!" Danilo hailed the prince's under-steward. "Gleb, what's the meaning of this?"

The under-steward wouldn't look directly at him, either. Instead, in a rushed mumble he read from a scroll:

"Danilo Yaroslavovich, *boyar* and member of the Inner Council of Svyatoslav, Prince by the Grace of God over Stargorod and—"

"Yes, yes, get to it, man! Tell me what all this is about!"

Gleb shot him a quick, uneasy glance. "It would seem, *boyar*," he began apologetically, "that our prince has accused you of high treason."

The blood surged so painfully in Danilo's head that he staggered, his only thought a wild *God, God, all the times I spoke so lightly of the prince's suspicious nature, all the times I boasted so smugly and never, never thought suspicion could ever fall on me— I've done nothing wrong, nothing!*

Gleb was watching him with more than a little sympathy, and Danilo knew he should say something, but all he could manage was a weak echo: "Treason . . ."

"Yes, my lord. You are herewith ordered to appear before the prince and his royal court to plead your case, and I'm commanded to see that you get there."

"But—this is ridiculous! This is the most impossible, unbelievable— You know me, Gleb! You know I'd never—"

"*Boyar*, I'm sorry. Truly, I am. But . . ." Gleb's very stance said plainly, I don't dare say more, I don't want to risk my own neck. "I have my orders."

Danilo fought to control himself. "Am I not to be allowed to know the specifics of this—this monstrous charge? Am I not to be allowed at least a chance to prepare my defense?"

Gleb sighed, studying the scroll. "No . . . it would seem not." He gave the *boyar* a wry smile. "It appears to me that you must have made yourself some very nasty enemy. I . . . can only wish you luck." His face went flatly formal. "And now, *Boyar*, will you come with me?"

* * *

OF course, Danilo had participated in many a royal court of law before this. *But never like this!* his mind screamed. *Never as victim!* And victim he too plainly was meant to be, ringed with guards like some common criminal, none of the assembled *boyars*—his friends, his colleagues— daring so much as to look at him: cold-eyed Yelenko, Chief Steward and Royal Judge, waiting patiently to read the charges, and Prince Svyatoslav up on his throne watching the proceedings with all the softness and charity of a marble statue.

"*Boyar* Danilo Yaroslavovich," began Yelenko without preamble, "you come before the Throne accused of that most grievous of crimes, high treason against your sovereign lord—"

"How accused?" snapped Danilo. "Who dares accuse me?"

Yelenko looked reproachfully down his long nose at this interruption. But at a quick gesture from the prince, he intoned, "Let the accuser stand forth."

"Alexei!" shouted Danilo. "My God, I should have known!"

Yelenko frowned. "The *boyar* will kindly refrain from comment."

"Refrain! How can I refrain? If that—that scoundrel dares accuse me of any crime at all, he perjures himself in the eyes of Heaven and—"

"*Boyar* Danilo." Yelenko's voice was chill. "Any further outburst and"—he glanced at his prince for confirmation—"and I fear, *boyar* or no, you must be gagged."

Choking on his rage, Danilo subsided, glaring at Alexei, who was very much the picture of innocence, quietly clad, eyes modestly downcast. He hadn't shown by so much as the flicker of an eyelash that he'd heard the *boyar*.

"Alexei Sergeovich," continued Yelenko, "tell us now what words passed between yourself and Danilo Yaroslavovich."

"I admit that I met with him with intentions of trying to better my position," Alexei began humbly. "But before I could speak more than a few words to the *boyar*, he dragged me into a private alcove."

"Is this true?" Yelenko asked Danilo severely.

"Yes, but—"

"Continue, Alexei Sergeovich."

"I—I hardly dare. It seems that the *boyar* . . . had been in communication with—with the exiled prince, our liege's banished cousin."

"Now, that's an outright lie!" shouted Danilo. "My Prince, I swear by all that's holy, I've never had any dealings with Prince Rostislav!"

"*Boyar*," said Yelenko coldly, "this is your last warning. Be silent." He turned to Alexei. "Continue."

"Ah . . . the *boyar* told me Prince Rostislav was planning to return, planning to overthrow our rightful ruler. And he promised me advancement if I sided with him."

"And did you agree?"

"I did not. We parted with angry words on both sides."

"I see." Yelenko glanced up again at his prince for instructions. Svyatoslav gave a sharp little hand signal, and Yelenko nodded obediently. "Bring forth the witnesses."

As Danilo watched in disbelief, he saw some of his own servants brought forward, those who'd been with him in the palace that day. They bowed timidly to the prince, then stood looking uneasily about, giving Danilo quick, nervous glances.

"Are you prepared to swear by Holy Word that what you say is truth?" asked Yelenko.

"Uh, yes, my lord."

"Fine. Your master is Danilo Yaroslavovich?"

"Uh . . . yes, my lord."

"Don't be afraid. You are not on trial. Merely answer my questions. You saw him meet with the *boyar* Alexei?"

"Well, yes, my lord," began Misha. "But—but he didn't exactly meet with the *boyar*, the *boyar* met with him, if you get my meaning—"

"Just answer the question. Did you see him meet with the *boyar* Alexei?"

Misha subsided. "Yes, my lord."

"Did you hear words exchanged?"

"Yes, my lord."

"But your master realized you were listening? What did he do then?"

"He—took the *boyar* by the arm and pulled him into an alcove."

"Ah. And did this sudden urge for privacy seem odd to you?"

They stared at him blankly. Yelenko sighed. "Did your master often have secret meetings?"

"Oh, no, my lord!"

"But he did, indeed, hold a secret discussion with the boyar Alexei?"

"Well . . ."

"Answer my question! Did your master hold a secret discussion with Alexei Sergeovich?"

The servants stirred uneasily. "Yes, my lord," they muttered at last.

"But—but this is nothing!" cut in Danilo. "Please, my Prince, let me finish. Alexei and I did talk, but it was only about his position at court. Prince Rostislav's name was never mentioned, I swear it! I've served you loyally and faithfully these many years; there's no proof—"

"No proof?" Svyatoslav spoke for the first time, eyes like stone. "Bring forth the evidence. Let the traitor read his guilt in his own words!"

Danilo stared in growing horror at letter after letter, all in his handwriting, all addressed to the exiled prince, all offering terms of comfort, of aid. All saying, in no uncertain terms, words of treason.

"But I never wrote these—" The letters fell from nerveless hands. "I never . . . My God, I'll swear to that on whatever holy objects you name! I never wrote these letters! I am innocent!"

"Liar!" Svyatoslav's voice shook with passion. "I thought you, of all my *boyars*, would never betray me— Traitor!"

Danilo, drowning in shock, cried, "At least grant me the right of trial by ordeal!"

"No! You shall die, and your treason with you!" Overwhelmed by the force of his outrage, the prince fiercely waved Yelenko aside. "Hear my decree: Danilo Yaroslavovich, you are declared traitor to the crown. Your lands

and estate are hereby forfeit, and shall descend to my loyal servant, Alexei Sergeovich, who has shown himself by his actions this day worthy of pardon for any previous misdeeds. And you, Danilo Yaroslavovich, shall have two days' grace in which to repent, and then, as befits your rank and crime, you shall die by the axe!''

"My children!" cried Danilo in anguish. "What of my daughters?"

The pain blazing in that cry cut through the fog of Svyatoslav's rage. He hesitated, said gruffly, "I will not make war upon young women. They shall, by my royal mercy, become my wards," then shouted, "Enough! Guards! Take this traitor away!"

MARIA slumped in her chair, too drained by the day's events to even weep. First had come the news of her father's arrest, then she and Vasilissa had been virtually dragged here to the palace, to this suite that, for all its comfort, was still all too plainly a prison.

And we've only two days before father . . . dies. What are we going to do?

Vasilissa would be of little help. As though there hadn't been enough shocks, Afron and his father had come to visit shortly after their arrival. The red-faced, embarrassed young man had torn free of Lissa's frantic embrace and, with quick, nervous glances at his cold-eyed father for approval, had told her bluntly that he didn't love her, that he'd never loved her. The truth of the whole thing was, of course, that his father had broken the betrothal out of fear of being linked with a man the prince had named traitor. But for Lissa it had simply been one shock too many. Now she huddled in bed, seeing nothing, saying nothing.

Did they have to be so cruel? Maria asked herself. *They know Father's no traitor! Those letters were forgeries, they had to be forgeries!*

If only she could find a way to see the prince, to plead her father's case with him. But Svyatoslav considered women, particularly young women, little more than fools, hardly worthy of notice. And he'd flatly refused to grant Maria any sort of interview before the week's end, four days away. By that point, of course, it would be far too late.

"Damn him!" Her audacity rather shocked Maria, but she said it again, as savagely as she could. "Damn him! He's a—a weak, cowardly fool— He's no longer my prince! I—I renounce him!"

Well and good, but cursing the man wasn't going to help her father. Maria glanced desperately at Vasilissa, suddenly aching for comfort, but her sister, escaping in the only way she could find, was lost in slumber.

That's no escape at all. Maria sighed wearily. *There must be a way out of this . . . Bribe a guard? With what?* The guards hadn't even allowed enough time to gather up their mother's jewels. Everything of value was still back at the estate, with the servants . . . *The servants!*

Maria sat bolt upright. No one noted an underling's comings and goings, not in a busy palace. And her father had told her often enough that even with such an edgy prince as master, the royal guards had become shamefully lax and lazy in these times of peace . . . Yes, and Svyatoslav held such a low opinion of her sex that he'd never expect anything more from her than helpless tears. Why, he'd stationed only the one bored guard at the door!

"Yes!" gasped Maria after some nervous consideration. Putting on her haughtiest manner, she called sternly, "Guard!" and smiled to herself as the door opened and a weatherworn male face peered in.

"Lady?"

"Guard, my sister and I came here so—so abruptly that we had no chance to bring with us any of the necessities of life."

"All will be provided, lady."

"All will *not* be provided! We left behind our jewel case, the gems left to us by our mother."

"I'm sorry, lady." His face was unmoved. "But I don't see what can be done about it. You must stay here."

"Yes, yes, I know that. I only meant . . ." Maria let her voice trail off pathetically, thinking wryly to herself that Lissa really was better at this sort of thing. She let tears well in her eyes—which wasn't difficult just then—and pleaded softly, "Can't you help us? There—there's a servant at home, Sasha. He knows where everything is. Can't you get word to him? If he brings us the—the small red lacquer case, yes, and—and the blue and yellow clothes chest . . . that's all we need . . . Can't you have him bring that to us? It—it's not so much, not really . . .''

The tears weren't feigned at all by this point. Maria, past the point of speech, let herself go and simply sobbed. The guard stirred, uneasy and embarrassed.

"Uh . . . lady. Lady, please. Don't . . . uh . . . don't cry. We'll get a message to this Sasha, you'll see."

Maria managed a watery smile. "Th—thank you."

But as soon as the guard was gone and the door closed, she nearly choked herself, mixing tears and helpless gusts of giggles till she thought she'd be sick. Oh God, oh God, he'd believed her! Now if only Sasha understood what she wanted. If only he'd remained loyal!

HE had.

"I . . . wasn't really sure this was what you wanted, mistress. I mean, a chest of the kitchen staff's clothes—''

"Hush, hush, this is exactly what I wanted! And the lacquer box of herbs, too? Good." Maria froze. "Were the boxes searched?''

Sasha grinned. "Oh, they opened them, all right. Figured they would. So I put one of your pretty caftans on top of the kitchen stuff, and your mother's gems on top of the herbs. They palmed a couple of trinkets, payment and all like that, but they never questioned me.''

"Sasha, you're a wonder!''

As he reddened, pleased, Maria hastily dropped some of the herbs into a bottle of mead the prince had oh-so-graciously granted the sisters. Sasha's grin widened.

"That's the herbs you use to make sick folks sleep! Want me to be the good host to the guard outside, eh?''

"You really *are* a wonder! Yes, go ahead!'' Maria was busily shaking her sister. "Lissa, love, wake up! Come, wake up! Get into these clothes. Yes, I know they're ugly—never mind that! Hurry! We're going to get Father out of prison!''

THEY made an awkward trio, Sasha hotly embarrassed at having his arms about two young noblewomen, Lissa wild-

eyed and shrinking from his touch, Maria terrified that her
sister would faint or scream or somehow manage to give
them away. But nothing terrible happened, no one stopped
them or even looked closely at them, these three who were
plainly kitchen servants of the lowest order staggering
drunkenly along the prison corridors, making the guards
who saw them laugh; the good Lord knew there was little
enough to laugh at down here.

Of course *boyar* Danilo wasn't being held in some plain,
verminous cell. He was being allowed a certain amount of
comfort, a room to himself as it were, and light, and clean
bedding. There were only two guards at his door. Why
waste more? He wasn't going anywhere!

"Wanna see him!" whined Maria. "Wanna see the
mighty lord!"

The guards grinned at each other. "Give us a kiss, then,
love," said one.

Lissa cringed. Before she could say something that
would give them away, Maria hastily waggled a hand in
denial. "No, no, got something better 'n that, see?"

She held up the bottle of mead.

"Swiped from the royal cellars, eh?" said a guard. "We
could have you reported for that, you know."

"And waste the mead?" The other guard laughed. "Not
a chance! Go ahead, wench. Look at the fine *boyar* all you
want."

Maria stood on tiptoe, peering through the narrow window at her father, aching to see how sad and hopeless he
sat, longing to call to him, all the time waiting, heart
pounding, for the sounds that would say the drugged mead
had had its effect . . . What if they didn't drink enough?
What if they realized something was odd about the taste
of it and refused to drink it at all? She doubted she and
Lissa and Sasha could silence two trained guards, not
without noise. And to actually kill someone . . .

But just then she heard a soft thud, a sigh, a snore.
Maria breathed a quick prayer of thanks, then dropped to
the side of one of the slumbering guards, carefully with-
drawing the precious keys. Her hands were shaking so
much she had to fumble with the lock, and there seemed

an impossible number of keys to be tried . . . What if other guards came checking? What if— There!

Her father looked up with a start as the door creaked open. As he recognized Maria, his eyes widened in astonishment. But Danilo was too well schooled in the various shocks of diplomacy to do anything but silently rush out of the cell, enfolding his daughters in a quick, fierce hug. Sasha, meanwhile, had been slipping out of the kitchen disguise he'd been wearing over his own clothes. Maria asked him in a hurried whisper, "You'll be all right?"

"Of course, mistress. I'm supposed to be in the palace, remember. No one's going to be suspicious if they see me leaving, not so long as I'm leaving by myself."

Danilo had been coolly donning the discarded rags. "Yes, but I doubt you've got permission to be down in the prison area. If anyone sees you leaving here, they're going to be sure you were aiding, and abetting the . . . traitor. Be careful!"

"Yes, my lord. But you . . . ?"

Danilo glanced at his daughter and gave a quick grin. "They saw three kitchen scullions enter, they're going to see three scullions leave. No one's going to care about us, not if we go out through the kitchen."

"Sasha," added Maria, "God be with you."

"And with you, mistresses, master."

"Indeed," muttered Danilo. "Come, hurry!"

THEY made it into the vast royal kitchen with so little trouble that, perversely, Maria felt almost disappointed, as though all the tension had been for nothing. *Don't be a fool,* she told herself sharply. *You aren't safe yet.* Surrounded by the bustle and noise and varied cooking smells, she bit her lip, wondering now just how long those sleeping guards were going to remain asleep. How long before someone came to check up on them? How long before an alarm was sounded?

It was too much for Vasilissa. Trembling, she sank to a bench, moaning, "I can't go on! I can't!"

"Oh, Lissa!" Maria fought down a sudden hot urge to slap her sister. *That* wouldn't help anything. Instead, she bent to catch Lissa by the shoulders, whispering desperately, "Lissa, please! We don't have time for this now!"

To her horror, she realized they'd attracted the attention of one of the kitchen sluts. "She sick?"

Maria forced a grin. "Just . . . you know . . . woman troubles."

With a shrug, the slut turned away, and Maria bent to her sister again. "Do you want Father to die? Well? Do you?"

"Of—of course not." Tears welled up in the beautiful, vague eyes, and Maria ignored her surge of pity and pulled her sniffing sister to her feet.

"Then come on!" she hissed.

Danilo, meanwhile, had casually strolled to a pile of refuse-filled sacks. With a slight gesture to his daughters, he flung one of the sacks over his shoulder with the self-confident air of someone doing a familiar job. No one objected. *Of course,* thought Maria, and she hurried to follow her father's lead. "Come on, Lissa!"

Quickly Maria picked up a sack, staggering a bit under the unexpected, smelly weight, and stared at her sister till Vasilissa had done the same.

"Just follow me," murmured Danilo. "We should be able to make it to the refuse heap, and from there, out of the palace."

Single-file, they left the kitchen, Maria tense with the expectation that someone was going to notice. But no one said a word.

We're going to make it, we're actually going to make it . . .

A hideous screaming of trumpets blared through the palace—

The alarm had been sounded.

V

GHOSTS

"WE'LL NEVER ESCAPE!" Vasilissa's weak gasp of terror was almost drowned beneath the trumpets' blare, the blasts of *Alarm! Alarm!* "We're trapped!"

"Not yet, we're not." Danilo had thrown aside his sack and was searching on hands and knees amid a pile of debris. "Somewhere about here . . . Yes, here it is! Now, if only I can still get it open . . ."

As his daughters watched fearfully for guards, he pulled aside a narrow, rusty grating.

"I *thought* I remembered this!" Danilo gave a quick grin. "Come, daughters, follow me!"

He was leaping down into darkness even as he spoke. "Come on, I'll catch you. It isn't deep."

Vasilissa was too stunned by fear to resist, sliding obediently down after her father. Maria found herself hesitating, held by the fear of the unknown. "Hurry!" her father hissed, and she told herself, *If Lissa can do this, so can you,* and blindly jumped.

Danilo was right, it wasn't a long drop. As he reached up to carefully replace the debris-covered grate, Maria looked warily around. This was some sort of tunnel, narrow, sloping down and away from the kitchen—must be an old drain.

"Let's see now," muttered Danilo. "It's been years, but . . . This way."

They edged their cautious way forward into smelly, stale darkness, over a stone floor covered thickly by rotted

51

kitchen scraps. Or at least Maria hoped they were only innocent kitchen scraps . . . She had flint and steel in her pouch, but this was hardly the place to strike a light, not when someone might see the flare.

"I was right," her father whispered triumphantly. "It's still here!"

He pulled his daughters aside, up into a new tunnel, a wider passage, almost airy by comparison with the first, dimly lit every now and again by slits that let in the sunlight.

"Where are we?" breathed Vasilissa.

"Somewhere under the main courtyard. Just a little further, and we'll be able to stop, and safely build a fire, too . . . Here we are."

It was a plain stone chamber, almost dry, almost clean, smelling of earth and age. Maria looked about as best she could in the semidarkness, bewildered.

"What *is* this place?"

"Part of the original palace." Danilo's voice was casual.

"But that was supposed to have collapsed centuries ago!"

"Most of it did. This room and some of the hallways survived. It seems that the new palace was built right over the ruins of the old." A hint of amusement quivered in his voice. "I found this place when I was a boy, exploring behind your grandfather's back. Never dared tell anyone I'd been here, though. At any rate, I doubt anyone's going to come looking for us down here."

Vasilissa had been standing in silence all this while, arms hugged about herself. Suddenly she murmured, "There are old ghosts in this place."

Maria felt a little prickle run down her spine at that hopeless whisper. "Oh, nonsense, Lissa. There's no such thing."

"I feel them, all around . . . There! Did you see?"

"Dear, it's only a shadow."

Lissa was staring blankly ahead. "They're smaller than us . . . bronze swords . . . their hair is dark . . . their eyes are dark . . . so dark . . ."

Maria and her father exchanged startled glances. Lissa

could almost be describing folk of the old stock, those who'd lived here long before the Norrund invasion four hundred years past had brought greater height and fair coloring into the region.

She could also, thought Maria, wincing, simply be . . . seeing things again.

"Come now, Lissa. It's been a long and trying day and—"

"I do see them. I—"

"Stop that!" Maria caught herself, began again, a little more gently, "I'll tell you what, Lissa. If any ghost comes bothering you, you let me know, and I'll . . . Oh, I'll make up some sort of spell to chase it away from—"

"Maria!" Danilo snapped. "Don't jest about evil!"

Startled, she stammered, "I—I only meant—"

"Magic *is* evil! It goes against the laws of God! And you are not to joke about it!"

There was a moment's stunned silence. Then Maria heard her father sigh. "Akh, I'm sorry, child. It's just . . . Only a short time ago I was in that prison cell, sure I was doomed. I haven't quite caught my breath yet. But there are times when you seem a bit too fond of the old tales. And you know how I feel about such dark things."

It was hardly the time or place to argue. Maria said in a sort of resigned, reluctant humility, "Yes, Father."

"But we can't stay here!" Vasilissa cut in fearfully.

"I'm afraid we must," Danilo said gently. "But only for a short time, Lissa. Not forever."

Maria blinked. "Of course not!" she said in sudden comprehension. "Father, there's a way out of here into the town, isn't there?"

"Indeed."

"But we can't leave right away, not with everyone sure to be looking for us. No, all we have to do is wait until next market day!"

She saw her father's teeth flash in a quick grin. Market day was the only time when the guards had to keep the city gates open. And they couldn't possibly keep track of everyone's comings and goings.

"That—that's a week away!" gasped Vasilissa. "We'll never last it out!"

"We will."

"No! What will we do for food? For—for light?"

Maria thought for a moment. "What if I stole back up into the kitchen? They didn't notice us before; they'll certainly not pay any attention to one more scullion! And then every night I'll be able to slip down here with food and—"

"No," Danilo interrupted. "It's too dangerous."

"There doesn't seem to be much of a choice. I'm the only one who can go. You couldn't go back up into the palace yourself, Father! Someone would be sure to recognize you." She glanced quickly at her wild-eyed sister. "And Lissa can't go, either. We—we certainly can't leave her alone down here. Father, it *has* to be me!" She took his silence for consent and hurried on, "It'll be all right, you'll see," and prayed she was right.

CLAD in stolen peasant garb, aching from days of unaccustomed labor, Maria moved slowly with the marketday throng filing out of the city. Somewhere up ahead were her father and sister. They'd decided it would be safer to split up, but now Maria wasn't so sure. Overwhelmed by loneliness in the middle of that crowd, she clenched her hands to stop their shaking, and fought back the urge to simply bawl like a babe. The guards were still looking for them. And what if some ambitious soldier recognized the missing *boyar* in that filthy, limping beggar? What if Lissa's nerves gave way completely?

Akh, Lissa . . .

That dark world of tunnels had terrified the young woman, keeping her from sleep. And when sleep came, it brought such foul dreams that her father and sister had been hard put to muffle her screams. God, and she'd grown so silent lately, so . . . empty.

The great gates were right ahead. Maria edged sideways a little, trying to look as though she were part of a large, rowdy family group. But now the guards were stopping them, checking their faces with bored inattention. Maria held her breath. They shouldn't be able to recognize her, but if they did . . . The menfolk of the group were complaining loudly, the womenfolk— Ah, but one of them was a beauty, a true beauty, and the guards were all paying rough, gallant attention to her, and no one was aware in all the confusion of the one dirty little peasant girl slipping carefully past them . . .

And she was out! Out of Stargorod, and on the road that wandered through the fields till it vanished into the vast forest. No place to stop, not here, not out in the open . . . But she couldn't see her father or sister ahead of her. Could they have already reached the forest's shelter? Or had they been caught? No; she'd have heard the outcry if that had happened. She must just keep trudging along, never looking back, never daring to hurry lest she draw attention to herself . . .

Head down, Maria didn't realize how far she had walked, until suddenly the sunlight was cut off, and she glanced wildly up to see forest all around. She was safe!

But a strong hand closed about her arm, and pulled her from the road into darkness.

VI

EXILE

EVEN AS MARIA opened her mouth to scream, she recognized the man who'd caught her arm, and gasped instead, "Sasha!"

The servant hastily released her. "Didn't mean to frighten you, young mistress. But I figured the sooner we get you out of sight, the better. Your father and sister are waiting, lady. Follow me."

He led the way down a narrow, twisting forest path that Maria guessed must surely be a deer trail. It seemed to go on forever, but at last came out in a small glade. And there, indeed, were her father and sister, seated on a weatherbeaten wagon, to which was harnessed a stolid workhorse Maria recognized as belonging to the estate. Her father, holding the reins as though he'd done this sort of thing all his life, gestured to her. "Hurry, child. Get in."

As she scrambled up to sit beside Lissa, she glanced back at Sasha, who was watching as though he might not approve. "But this is marvelous, Sasha! How did you manage it?"

He grinned. "Well, getting the rig and old Brownie off the estate wasn't hard. Not with all the fuss that's going on there now. No one's going to miss either of them. Not that *boyar* who thinks he can just come in and take over, that's for sure! He wouldn't know how to run an estate if— Eh, don't mean to go running off like this."

"But, Sasha," Maria cut in, "what about you? The

guards we drugged wouldn't have admitted they'd been drinking mead on duty, but surely they would have remembered you . . . We've endangered all the servants, haven't we?''

The man laughed. ''Not a bit, young mistress. Oh, naturally, I was questioned; we all were. But no one from the palace could identify me. Folks at court don't really notice servants' faces. And of course, all of us on the estate have been covering for each other. Guards or no guards, work had to go on, right? Misha and Ivan brought the wagon out into the fields. They brought back a cart—and the guards, being cityfolk, never noticed the difference. Didn't even notice when Serge took old Brownie here for a ride—making sure the blacksmith did a good job on his shoes, we told them—and came back leading a black pony instead. Well, this sort of thing went on till the guards gave up on keeping track of us. I snuck out while Anna and Katia were having a nice, loud, distracting fight. And no one even tried to follow me.''

Maria giggled in spite of herself. ''But if Svyatoslav finds out . . .''

''How can he? The prince has no idea how many or how few of us there are. He can't put us *all* in prison, not when he's given a *working* estate to his pet *boyar.*'' Sasha grinned triumphantly. ''I didn't know when you'd get out of the city. The gossip told me that you hadn't been caught. So I hid the rig and waited. Old Brownie here's a sensible nag, not the sort to carry on or try to go wandering off.''

''Sasha,'' Danilo said softly, ''we can't repay you for this.''

''You already did.'' The man's eyes were suddenly solemn. ''Took me in that day, years back, remember? When no one else wanted a boy who'd been called a thief? Only thing left to me would have been outlawry. Or maybe starvation.''

''You weren't a thief.''

''That I wasn't.'' Sasha stirred suddenly, staring earnestly up at Danilo. ''But now, you're sure you know how to get there?''

''Your directions were very clear.''

''Well. They're all dead and gone on that farm, remember. No one's going to come claiming it. And no one's going to know to look for you there, either. The tools and seed and all should keep you going till it's safe to come home." Sasha hesitated, uneasy. "I hate to be just leaving you like this."

"Nonsense, man. You have your wife and family to concern you. God be with you, Sasha."

"And with you, master, mistresses. And with you."

THE trail they were following was just barely wide enough for the wagon, and for a time Danilo was too busy keeping them from getting stuck to be very talkative. But at last the trail joined up with a road that, muddy and full of ruts though it was, was a marvel of smoothness and width by comparison. Maria cleared her throat.

"Ah, Father?"

"Mm?"

"Where are we going?"

"Sasha, bless his kind and clever soul, told me all about a place where we should be safe. It's an old farm; the owners died some twenty years back, leaving no heirs. No one else ever moved in. Till now." He shot his daughter a wry glance. "How do you fancy yourself as a farmer's daughter?"

Better than as an orphan! But she kept that thought to herself. "I know we've got seed, and the tools to plant it. But what are we gong to do about anything else?"

"There's supposed to be a small village about a day's journey from the farm, a 'mind your own business' sort of place, where we'll be able to get whatever we need without anyone asking awkward questions." He shook the reins at Brownie, who'd taken advantage of the conversation to snatch a mouthful of leaves. "We'll manage. After all, this is just a temporary setback. Svyatoslav may be stubborn, but he'll come to his senses soon enough. And then we'll be able to come home."

Did he really believe that? Maria glanced at her father, but his impassive face gave no clue to his thoughts, no clue at all.

* * *

IT had been a long and torturous journey, even with stops every now and then to rest the horse and their own aching bones. It had been a frightening journey, too, what with never knowing whether someone from Stargorod might have picked up their trail, and never knowing whether they might simply lose themselves forever in this apparently endless forest. Vasilissa was no help, convinced that dark woodland magic was all about them. And who knew but that this time she might be right?

But at last Danilo said with some relief, "Ah. This has to be the riven birch Sasha mentioned. The trail we want should be just beyond it . . . Yes." He glanced wryly at Maria and said, too softly for Lissa to overhear, "Know why the forest hasn't engulfed it? Sasha told me the farmers who cleared it had sworn pacts with the forest. And so the forest Folk, instead of turning the trail into part of their everchanging mazes, let it remain. Even, as the poets say, unto this day." He eyed the overgrown way dubiously. "More or less, at any rate. I think we can still get the wagon through here. Hold fast, daughters! A short way, and we'll be arriving at our new home."

THE three of them got slowly and stiffly down from the wagon, staring. For a long time there was silence.

"You mean that's it?" asked Maria faintly.

What more could have been expected after twenty years of neglect? It might have been a neat little farm at one time, but the forest had gone a good way towards reclaiming it. What had been a wooden palisade was now only so much sagging, splintered kindling. Within it, a tangled wilderness might once have been a garden. What outbuildings there'd been had pretty much caved in. The farmhouse itself, being of good, sturdy logs, seemed to have suffered the least, though there were shingles gone from the roof and vines twining up the walls. An empty doorway gaped forbiddingly.

Silence fell once more. Maria, heartsick, glanced back at her father and sister. And what she saw there made her spirits sink even lower. Vasilissa's face was ashen, as might have been expected, her stance that of the proud but doomed, also as might have been expected. But Danilo—

Danilo, who'd come through so much, who'd seemed so invincible, so unquenchable, had plainly come at last to the end of his strength. In his despairing eyes was the sudden acceptance that this exile was real, that there wasn't going to be any word from Stargorod, any miraculous last-minute escape. Maria felt sudden hot tears welling in her eyes . . . No, the last thing she dared do now was collapse. *Someone* had to stay strong.

Since no one else seemed about to do anything, Maria moved forward to study the debris.

It really didn't look so bad up close. Of course, the garden would have to be virtually torn up by the roots and replanted. She hoped the season was right for such things, and the soil . . . The outbuildings were as ramshackle as they'd looked from a distance, but there seemed to be enough good planks left to make a solid shed or two. They were going to need a shed, and some new fencing, if they were going to keep animals . . . They would need chickens, she supposed, and maybe a goat or two . . .

Greatly daring, she stepped through the gaping farmhouse doorway, then stopped, trying not to breathe too deeply. Some wild things had plainly been using the house as their den. They were gone, but their stench and mess remained. Spiderwebs muffled every corner. But the stove, of the massive, nearly room-filling sort favored by peasants, was still in place, not a crack in its tiles, and it looked quite useable. Walking warily, Maria inspected the rest of the house: three small rooms, one with the framework of a bed still intact. They'd all need a proper cleaning and airing, but after that, they might be almost comfortable . . .

Yes. All in all, things might be salvageable.

Maria returned to the doorway, hesitating a moment at the sight of her despairing father and sister, trying desperately to hold fast to self-confidence and organize her thoughts.

"All right, now," she said, as firmly as she could. "Things aren't so bad, really. Father, do you suppose you could unhitch poor Brownie and see if you can find him some shelter? And Lissa, won't you come and see if you can get this stove working?"

Watching life slowly returning to her father and sister with action, she stood for a moment with hands on hips, ablaze with sudden fierce determination.

"I wonder," said Maria Danilovna, *boyar*'s daughter, "what I can use for a broom."

VII

ENSNARED

FINIST FLEW AIMLESSLY through the night, circling over his sleeping city of Kirtesk, nearly invisible in the darkness, unable to sleep. His mind was too full of thoughts of Ljuba.

Why had she done it? Why, after all these years, suddenly set out to seduce him? Oh, he'd always been aware of her beauty, he would have to have been a clod of earth not to have been aware, but till now it hadn't mattered. Till now his dislike of her had been strong enough to master any sense of true desire. He'd always been careful, so careful—

Enough. What had happened that night in the forest was over. And surely Ljuba saw as clearly as he that they'd been lucky to get out of it with nothing worse than a frenzied coupling that had little joy to it. He'd treat the whole thing as an accident, he'd find some cool, formal way to let his cousin know it would never happen again.

But if only it had been someone other than Ljuba . . . someone special . . . The plaintive thought rather embarrassed him. Yet he found himself remembering Marfa and Stefan, the youngsters so madly in love, and surprised himself with a pang of envy. Ah, God, what must it be like, feeling such tenderness for someone, being the object of such tenderness? Love—

Wasn't for royalty. So he'd been taught.

And it certainly wasn't possible with Ljuba. It was all too easy to remember her as she'd been, the child-Ljuba

62

spelling a puppy into immobility, heedless of the little animal's terror: it was only a puppy, after all. And later, the adolescent Ljuba, already beautiful enough to catch men's breath in their throats, working practice magics on her servants, small, harmless spells to be sure, but worked quite against their wills: they were only servants, after all. Well, he had put a stop to that sort of thing as soon as he'd learned about it. But even now Ljuba hadn't changed, not really. For all her loveliness, there was still a certain emptiness at the heart of her. And, he supposed, no wonder—

Dammit, now he was going to start pitying her! That was easy enough to do; he'd realized even as a boy that her father ignored his daughter's existence, her mother all but hated her, though of course, he hadn't realized the reason, not then.

Devil take it! These mental meanderings had brought him right to her window! There Ljuba sat, alone in her bedchamber, brushing and brushing the long fall of golden hair, and Finist paused in spite of himself, perched on the windowsill, caught by the charming picture she made, there in the dim light of the single candle.

He paused too long. Ljuba sensed his presence and looked up. "Why, cousin! Please, enter."

What else could he do? There wasn't any way to speak to her while in falcon-form, and he certainly couldn't just fly rudely away. *What's this?* Finist chided himself at his sudden unease. *A prince who's dealt with boyars and ambassadors is afraid to simply talk with one virtually magicless woman?*

Ljuba was politely holding out a cloak. *A bit late for modesty between us,* thought Finist, but he accepted it, transforming and wrapping himself in its shelter. Maybe this wasn't the best of times to speak with Ljuba about that night, but there might not be a better time. At least right now they had privacy.

"Ljuba . . ."

"Wait, let me give us more light." She moved smoothly from candle to candle, till the room was aglow in soft, flickering gold. "That's better. Finist, I know why you've come."

"I don't think you do."

"Oh, yes." She gave him a slow, sweet smile, eyes veiled behind long lashes. "After that cold, damp night, I knew you would be wondering, as I was, if our pleasure wouldn't have been more . . . pleasant here."

Before Finist could find a way to tactfully deny her, a hot little voice in his mind whispered, *Why not?*

Nonsense. He had more restraint than that.

You don't have to look for love, you don't even have to like the woman, just take what's being offered—

No! Dammit, he wasn't some mindless, rutting stag!

After all, the voice insisted, *it's not as though you were close kin. And you both do know the charm to prevent conception. Why not? You weren't her first lover, no more than she was yours; she's no helpless little princess who must be kept as a chaste prize for some other prince. Why not?*

He'd almost think Ljuba had managed to feed him one of her sorcerous potions—but that was impossible; she hadn't so much as touched him. No, this ridiculous wave of passion could only be his own fault, and he had better say what he'd come to say and leave and hope the cold night air would restore him to himself.

"Ljuba. That night was a mistake. You know it, and I know it."

There was more he should be saying. But . . . God, it had grown so stifling in here. He couldn't think . . .

"We mustn't—I won't—"

Damn. That wasn't making any sense at all. How could Ljuba bear the scent of all these candles? Burning wax and fragrance, heavy as perfumed fog . . . so heavy he felt he could surely brush it aside if he could only manage to raise a hand . . . Struggling for breath, trying in vain to blink his blurring vision clear, he saw his cousin through the fog, still as a statue in some pagan place, a goddess cold and perfect and merciless, and a new wave of passion staggered him—

No, and no! He would not let his body rule him! Desperate and angry, Finist turned to leave . . . tried to turn . . . but something was going very wrong. He could still think, but he couldn't seem to move. Struggle though he would, he just couldn't get his legs to obey him. Somehow he found himself still facing Ljuba, and all at once admitted fiercely, *Yes, here in this room, here in this bed! I'll burn this passion from me and be done with it!*

The cold statue melted into warm, willing life as he pulled her into his arms.

THE forest was dank and close about him, no longer friendly, but hostile, hating, so dark he stumbled blindly through a never-ending maze of trees. There must be a way out, if only the forest would let him go. But now vines were reaching out for him, weaving their silken way about him, tightening no matter how he struggled, gently, firmly tightening as he realized in helpless horror that they were draining the strength from him, the magic, the very soul—

"No!" Finist sat bolt upright, eyes wild. What—

A dream. Only a dream. He was still sheltered and warm in Ljuba's bed, she was still peacefully asleep beside him. And she was lovely, no denying it, relaxed and defenseless in sleep, the yellow candlelight soft on curve of cheek, of shoulder, of breast. Even now he felt a returning stir of desire . . .

"No," Finist repeated, softly, fiercely. Even in the throes of his lust, he'd tried to be gentle, he'd tried to please them both, he'd tried for at least a semblance of love. But as before, there'd been no joy in their coupling, not even relief, nothing but anger and a vague sense of revulsion, almost as though there were something unnatural about this most natural of acts.

She can't *be bespelling me, I'd know it! I wasn't fool enough to eat or drink anything from her hand, she wasn't wearing any ointments or sorcerous perfumes . . . Yet . . . I—I just can't seem to think . . .*

The candles weren't helping. Their light was beginning to hurt his eyes, while the smell of the scented wax lay so heavy in the air that he found it difficult to breathe. And his head was pounding. Feeling like a man wading through syrup, Finist reached out a heavy arm to pinch out a flame. There. That seemed to relieve the pressure, however slightly. He wasn't sure his legs would hold him, but if he stretched out a bit more, he could reach a second candle and extinguish it, a third . . . Yes, the air did seem to be clearing faintly, at least to the point where he didn't have to struggle for each breath. Now his muddled mind seemed to be clearing, too . . .

Clearing, indeed.

"My God." Finist sat bolt upright. "What a fool I am!"

As Ljuba stirred, blinking in confusion, Finist struggled to his feet. Head still reeling, he fought his way to the window, casting open the shutters to take deep lungfuls of cold, clean night air, feeling the haze leave his brain. Quickly, holding his breath, he reached for the remaining candles, hurling them out, watching in grim satisfaction as they fell, trailing small tails of fire, till they hit the cobblestones far below.

"Finist . . . ?" Ljuba's voice was pathetically weak, and her eyes, when he whirled to face her, were wide and fearful.

"Oh yes, cousin," hissed Finist, "fear me!"

"I—I don't understand."

"Don't you? How clever you were! Your potions were worked into the candlewax itself, weren't they? So simple a trap! If I hadn't been so—so damnably besotted, I'd have realized it from the first."

"I didn't mean—"

"Don't lie to me! Why did you do it, Ljuba? Answer me!"

Her head dropped. "I . . . wanted you. But you . . . just never looked at me, not as a man sees a woman." She glanced up, face pale. "What are you going to do to me?"

What *could* he do? Ljuba lied as easily as she drew breath. But what if this once she was telling the truth? He could hardly banish her for that! Seduction of a man old enough to know what he was doing was hardly a treasonable offense! And if he made matters public at all—oh, wouldn't *that* do wonders for his royal image? Devil take it, Ljuba knew he wouldn't—couldn't—publicly chastise her, not his cousin, not under these circumstances!

It took every bit of regal self-control to keep his voice level. "This time, you are forgiven. But I promise you this, cousin: try any magics against me again, any magics at all, and I'll find a way to see you declared a traitor to the crown.''

"But, Finist, you don't understand—"

"I understand enough!"

If he stayed there a moment longer, Finist knew he'd do something he would regret. With a swirling of shape, he was falcon, and soaring up out of that stifling room. Behind him, he could hear Ljuba calling frantically, "Finist! I did it because—Finist, wait!"

Then, as he fled away into the night, came one last, despairing wail: "I did it because *I love you!*"

VIII

THE LOVERS

PRINCE FINIST OF KIRTESK flew from his cousin's palace, his anger slowly cooling in the night chill. After all, hate the thought though he might, he had to admit that she could never have seduced him, even with those ridiculous candles, if he hadn't consented, somewhere deep within himself.

Akh, Ljuba, what am I to do with you?

How lovely if he could merely do as other princes did: marry off an unwanted or dangerous female relation to some foreign potentate, or force her into a convent! But Ljuba had never shown the slightest interest in marrying anyone. And as for a convent— The falcon gave a sharp squawk of laughter at the idea. Even were he sufficiently cold-hearted to attempt it, a magician could hardly be wed or incarcerated against her will!

What does she really want of me?

That despairing *"I love you!"* still echoed in his mind. For a moment he wondered uneasily, could it be . . . ? But he couldn't believe that, not from Ljuba, not from his cousin who'd made it very clear over the years that she'd never loved anyone or anything in her life. If she were some magicless commoner, he could have the truth from her in a moment, read easily from eyes or face. But Ljuba, of course, knew enough to know how to shield her thoughts.

She certainly wasn't just seeking bed-sport. What else could someone who was related to the royal line want, except: *power?* His wings missed a beat as the realization struck him. *And here I thought all this time that she was quite satisfied with whatever she could gain from her studies.* Intellectual *power.* Ljuba had to know she hadn't a hope of inheriting the throne; Finist would never have dared allow her so much freedom otherwise. *But could it be she's decided that isn't enough? Maybe she's decided that the path to true power can only lie in becoming the royal mistress. Or—good God, my wife!*

Stunned by that, he came to a rough landing on his windowsill, scrambling into the room, transforming from falcon to man.

"My wife? Oh no, Ljuba. That, you'll never be!"

FOR a long time, Ljuba had huddled motionless in her bed, too dazed, too fearful, to move. But at last she uncurled, stretching stiff muscles, the memory of her desperate cry returning to her: *I love you!*

Whatever possessed me to say such a ridiculous thing? For no reason she could name, Ljuba felt a little shiver run through her. *It isn't true . . . And yet . . . Bah, of course it isn't true! No wonder he didn't believe me!*

Ljuba got to her feet, moving slowly to the window, half expecting to see the glint of silvery feathers against the night. But of course, by now the sky was quite empty, and she pulled the shutters closed, leaning wearily against them, her body remembering his strength, his unexpected gentleness . . .

Stop that! He was a man, just another man.

The man she must control. She never, never should have tried those candles. It was too strong, too blatant. He couldn't *not* have suspected.

Maybe all wasn't lost. There was still the potion. And all she had to do was find a way to introduce it into his bloodstream—

Oh, easily said! She couldn't get near his food or drink, and now she wouldn't even be able to get near *him.*

Damn him! He'll never trust me again!

Why should that thought hurt so much . . . ?

Stop it!

Angry at herself, Ljuba slammed a fist against the shutters. Then, grimly, she began to consider what options were left to her: grimly, she began to plan.

And after a time, Ljuba began to smile.

FIRE beat in his brain, fire raced along every nerve, every sinew. Didn't she know? Didn't she care? His lady, his sweet, sweet lady . . . Young *boyar* Erema shivered with delicious memory, thinking of her by candlelight, sleek and soft and golden. He remembered her in his embrace . . .

"Ljuba . . ."

They'd been apart for so long, so painfully long. And then she had called him to her side, and he so radiant with joy his head had fairly swum. She'd poured wine for him with her own dear hands. And then, while he drank, she had told him the cruelest of words: that it was done between them—finished. She'd left him for another. Her cousin. Her royal cousin.

Erema groaned, remembering how shamelessly he had begged her, hating himself for this humiliation, yet powerless to stop in the heat of his passion.

Keep away! he had warned himself afterward. *Keep your pride.*

But he couldn't eat, or sleep, or think of anything but Ljuba. And now at last he had surrendered. He'd abandoned pride and come to her once more, praying for just a crumb of mercy.

"Ljuba . . ." Erema moaned again, staring pleadingly up at her from where he'd dropped to his knees. "Don't leave me. I—I will die—Don't leave me . . ."

Ah, the fire in his brain! He couldn't think, couldn't move, only hear her speak, each word a separate flame. "Oh, my dear Erema, I don't want to leave. But I must."

"No!"

"Don't you see? I have no choice. My cousin's magic is far too strong for me. If he summons me, if he makes me his slave, how can I resist?"

The fire, the fire burning at his brain . . . Somehow Erema managed to gasp, "I will save you!"

"Do you mean that?" Her voice was fierce in its intensity. "Erema, you swore once you would do anything I bade. Is that still the truth?"

Frantic with the fire's heat, Erema grabbed the goblet she handed him, gulping down the contents without even tasting them. But the fire burned on, unchecked.

"Yes!" he gasped. "Anything!"

A knife was in his hand, though he couldn't recall how it had gotten there. As he stared down at its keen, strangely darkened blade, he heard Ljuba's voice, sharp as the knife: "Remember!"

Remember what? Had she been talking to him? He wasn't sure . . .

"Erema! Do what I've told you. Scratch Finist's arm with this blade, and his hold over me will be broken. Remember, it must seem an accident! And do no more than scratch him."

She might have said more, but now Erema found he couldn't seem to hear her. The fire was all around, the fire . . . He nodded obediently, but all he could see was the knife in his hand. And all he could remember was the name of Finist.

Finist, his rival. His foe.

IX

THE ACCIDENT

HE MUST KEEP the knife hidden. That much he knew. No one must see it, not till he was near the prince. And then, and then . . . Erema laughed softly to himself, pleased with his cunning. Why, already he'd made his way through the palace unchallenged, already he'd learned that Finist stood alone and unguarded up on a rampart!

Just for a moment, the fire in his mind seemed to fade; for a moment Erema swayed, hand to head, confused. What was he doing here? Seeking to harm the prince? No, that couldn't be! He'd always been jealous of Finist, of his easy grace, his powers. But to turn traitor— Frightened and angry, Erema pulled out the knife with trembling hands. But the sight of that dark blade made his head swim. He felt so weak . . .

Ljuba. He must remember Ljuba. As long as he could hold her image in his mind, a talisman, a shield against the fire, he was safe. But Ljuba was in peril. That was it, of course; how could he have forgotten? Ljuba was in peril. And he must protect her!

The fire seized him once more. And Erema, thinking only of Ljuba, reached the stair to the rampart, and began to climb.

SHE mustn't let Erema get too far ahead. Her instructions had been so very simple: show Finist the knife, tell him you thought it might be enchanted, then "accidentally" graze his arm with the blade. Simplicity. But there was always the chance that that young idiot of a *boyar* might make some fatal mistake, let Finish read the truth from him, let Finist get a good look at that treated blade before it could be subtly wiped clean . . .

Damn! There seemed to be an impossible tangle of courtiers through which she must weave her way, each and every one of them seemingly determined to delay her, with their "Why, good day, lady!" and their "Good health to you," all the polite, inane, time-consuming courtesies to which she must nod and smile, all the while burning with impatience—Oh, damn them! Were they so unused to the sight of her here in the royal palace that they must stare and block her way? Ahead of her, Erema had already started his climb. She dare not let him get too far ahead!

There was no help for it. Heedless of the surprised murmurings all around her, Ljuba caught up the full skirt of her caftan, and ran.

FINIST leaned moodily on the rampart's low balustrade, looking out over his city, his thoughts all on the past.

In the old days of the royal house, he knew, cousin had married cousin freely, attempting to enhance and strengthen the family magic. And for a time, it would seem, such a practice had worked. Then such experiments had stopped, perhaps a hundred years or so ago, with nothing at all in the records to indicate why. But Finist suspected the answer. Writings dated to just before that period had mentioned that in some members of the royal line, the innate magic had begun to take some dark and devious turns.

Too much close breeding weakens animal stock. Why should it not do the same to human stock as well?

Ah, and Ljuba . . . There was a secret he'd never shared with anyone: the chance that the woman might be closer kin than she believed. Finist could only dimly recall the night when he'd still been very much a child, and sleepless, and using his budding talents to wander the palace unnoticed. He'd chanced to overhear Ljuba's mother speaking angrily to someone. What she'd said hadn't made all that much sense to him then; he'd been too young. But if he was remembering correctly, the gist of it had been that Ljuba's father wasn't her *real* father, that her real father might have been someone closer to the direct royal line . . .

His father? Surely not. Still . . . *Akh, this is ridiculous! I can't even be certain of what I heard that night!*

But this was a foolish train of thought. When he married, as he must, sooner or later, he hoped for at least a touch of the joy that burned between those two young lovers, Marfa and Stefan . . .

Finist shook his head impatiently. Here he was, continuing to meander foolishly in his thoughts, not even realizing one of the guards was speaking to him.

"Ah, my Prince? My Prince, I hate to be disturbing you, but you didn't say you didn't want to be disturbed, and here's *boyar* Erema to see you, and him saying that it's important . . ."

Finist held up a hand to silence the man's ramblings, and glanced past him to where Erema waited anxiously. Now, what? Finist gestured to the young *boyar* to approach. "What is it, Erema? You look unwell."

"Uh . . . I . . ." Erema stopped short, blinking in bewilderment. Finist studied him with a touch of bewilderment on his part as well. Had the man been drinking? There was nothing to be read from him but waves of wild confusion, of a certain strange psychic fire— And the man was bearing iron, cold iron! But Erema was continuing, more strongly, almost like a man reciting something well learned by rote, "I've found something I think you might wish to examine, my Prince."

EREMA dimly heard himself saying the words Ljuba had taught him. But they meant nothing, there was only Ljuba, the dear one, Ljuba who was in peril from this man, and though his hand began, almost of its own accord, to draw out the dagger as though to merely show his prince a curiosity, he knew he must act, act now to free his love, his Ljuba, from this foul sorcerer!

FINIST tensed as Erema began to draw a dagger out of the wide sleeve of the *boyar*'s elegant caftan. But the man was moving so slowly, so carefully, that surely he couldn't mean any threat. And Erema was saying, innocently enough, "I think this knife I've found may have some manner of enchantment on it. Perhaps you would deign to examine it, my Prince?"

Now! thought Erema. *Now, when he least suspects!* The fire blazed up within him, searing, blinding, destroying all doubts, and wild with hatred, he raised the knife to strike—

FINIST felt the savage change in the man's aura, he saw Erema's grip on the knife go from innocent to deadly, and before he could think twice about it, he was springing back— But he'd made a mistake, he'd let Erema corner him against a wall, and Erema, eyes wild and insane, was lunging at him—

HE's gone mad! thought Ljuba. The quick realization that her potions had probably driven Erema over the edge crossed her mind, but there wasn't time to worry about it, not with Finist's life at stake! This fool of a guard was never going to let her pass in time, and Ljuba screamed in fury, a scream that swiftly became the harsh cry of a crow—

EVEN as the knife came plunging down at Finist, a great, dark crow hurtled, shrieking, at Erema. A powerful feathered body struck his head with a sickening thud, sending the stunned *boyar* half over the edge of the low balustrade, the knife flying from his hand. Finist reached out a quick arm to snatch Erema back from the edge, but he was the barest of instants too late: his fingers closed only on empty air as, with a wild cry, Erema fell out and down, plunging helplessly from the rampart.

For a moment, Finist could only stand frozen in sheer, dazed horror, then he was falcon, plummeting down to where Erema lay in a crumpled heap. The crow flapped her way down to land beside him, returning to human form long enough to gasp:

"I—I didn't mean— He was going to kill you—"

She broke off abruptly, staring at Finist. In man-shape once more, he stared back at her over the *boyar*'s lifeless

form, seeing no shock, no horror, nothing but a wild relief
that he, himself, had survived—*for her sake*, realized Finist with a touch of despair, *not for mine, not for our people, only for her own sake*—akh, Ljuba!

But by now, courtiers and guards were racing out to see
what had happened, and before Finish could say anything
aloud, Ljuba, aware suddenly of her nakedness, swiftly
returned to crow form and flew quickly away. Finist bent
over Erema's body, trying to keep himself from shaking
with reaction as he sought desperately to find any lingering
sign of life at all.

"I, uh, I'm afraid he's dead, my Prince." It was a sub-
dued Semyon, the old counselor, solicitously wrapping a
hastily borrowed cloak about Finist. "We'll never know
why he tried to do what he—"

"No!" The sharpness was more in response to Erema's
violent death and Ljuba's callowness than anything logical. Trembling, Finist said harshly, "He's not gone, not
yet, not so far away that I can't recall him!"

"My Prince!"

"Dammit, Semyon, the man tried to assassinate me! I
want to know why, I want to know who was behind—
Move aside, *boyar*, and let me work!"

He'd never tried anything like this. Deep within himself,
Finist knew this was perilous ground, very close to verg-
ing on the forbidden, the Dark Arts, but caught in a net
of his own passion, he refused to give way. He knew the
proper spell, in theory at least, and so, shrouded in his
cloak, crouching over the body like a true necromancer,
Finist called up the fire of Power within him and began to
force out the strange, painfully twisting syllables. They
burned at his mind till he could have screamed, sending
the blood surging through him so fiercely he thought he
must faint, or die. But he couldn't stop, not now. He could
feel the spell beginning to work. He could feel Erema,
Erema's spirit, being drawn back to him, though it fought
him . . . but now Erema was slipping away again, and
Finist couldn't stop him. The pain, akh, the pain! This
was wrong, he knew it was wrong, his innate magic was
all of Light, of Nature, and this dark spell was tearing at
him, tearing at his very essence—

And suddenly Erema was gone, and the unspent force of the spell was recoiling savagely on Finist. With a groan, the prince came back to himself, fallen helplessly into Semyon's arms, his heart pounding so fiercely that he knew he'd escaped killing himself by only the barest of margins. Drained, Finist lay in his counselor's fatherly support, and knew nothing more for a long while . . .

ALONE in her chambers, Ljuba huddled in silent shock, trying to control her breathing, trying to curb her racing thoughts. That had been such a frighteningly narrow escape! Erema had nearly ended everything then and there, Finist's life, all her hopes— His death was for the best, though she'd be a long time in forgetting the sight of his face as he fell . . . But at least this way there'd be no awkward questions. And she still had the potion, though it certainly wouldn't be wise to try to use it again right away. Not with Erema's death so fresh in Finist's mind. No, thought Ljuba with a shudder, far better to do nothing at all suspicious for a time, apparently as innocent of plots as some little nun, so that Finist would have no reason to suspect—

The knife! She'd forgotten about the knife! If it still somehow bore traces of her potion on the blade, if Finist chanced to find it or some well-meaning idiot brought it to him—Oh God, he'd know it had come from her hand; how could he not? She'd be giving him the perfect chance to be rid of her. All he had to do was accuse her of Erema's murder, and . . .

"No," Ljuba vowed softly, "that won't happen."

Wearily she got to her feet, stretching muscles already stiff from the unaccustomed flight and attack. Wearily she dressed herself. Then, not daring to consider that she might fail, Ljuba went in search of that dangerous knife.

It couldn't have fallen that far from the palace wall . . . Somewhere about here . . .

"Ah!"

Ljuba hastily stifled her sigh of relief, looking warily about. A guard walked by, giving her a rather uncertain glance, but bowing politely enough. Two courtiers followed, so deep in conversation they didn't even notice her. *Go on!* she urged them silently. *Go away!*

There, now, she was alone for the moment. Ljuba bent as though merely adjusting the lace of one elegant leather shoe, and quietly slipped the knife into her sleeve.

"Lady?" asked a sudden voice, and she whirled, heart racing, to see the guard, returned. "Is something wrong?"

"Nothing," Ljuba assured him, feeling the knife nestled safely in her sleeve. "Nothing at all." And, nearly giddy with relief, she gave the man a dazzling smile.

X

PEASANTS

FINDING A BROOM, thought Maria wearily, was proving to
be the least of their problems, a simple matter of tying a
bundle of long twigs to a stout stick with a scrap of the
rope blessed Sasha had thought to include in their sup-
plies. While their father struggled, swearing under his
breath when he thought his daughters couldn't hear him,
to provide Brownie with at least a makeshift stable out of
one of the half-ruined sheds, she and Vasilissa set about
sweeping out the farmhouse as best they could, holding
their breath against the various smells, till at last Lissa
burst into tears because her delicate hands were beginning
to blister.

Maria was in no mood to be sympathetic. "And you
think mine aren't? Stop whining!" She brushed her di-
sheveled hair back impatiently. "If you don't want to
sweep anymore, why don't you go get us some water instead?"

Vasilissa, still sniffling a bit, obediently disappeared,
only to come hurrying back inside. "The rain barrel's
nearly empty, and there's something green and disgusting
growing in it."

"Ugh. We'll have to see about scrubbing that out. But
for now . . . we passed a stream on our way in here. If
you take one of the buckets—"

Lissa stared at her in horror. "Go into the forest, you
mean? Maria, no. I can't."

"Whyever not?"

"Don't you know? Maria, *They* are out there! They won't pass that palisade, but They are out there, just beyond it . . . Don't you *feel* Them?"

"Oh, Lissa, *now* what?"

"Demons, Maria, forest demons . . ."

"There aren't any demons!"

But the young woman's eyes were so wide with unreasoning fright that there was no arguing with her. Maria gave a wordless cry of frustration, snatched up a bucket herself, and started forth, trying to make some useful plans as she went.

Demons in the forest, indeed. It was too lovely out here, quiet and green, the stream sparkling in sunlight shifting through thick leaves, to believe in them. Far easier to accept the existence of beings out of the old tales, the sly, mischievous nature sprites which, if they were sometimes perilous for humans to meet, at least had no concept of true evil. Maria sat on the streambank and looked about with undisguised pleasure, revelling in the moment of solitude, breathing in the clean, spicy air, feeling a sudden sense of peace such as she'd not had a chance to enjoy in . . . she couldn't even remember how long. Granted, this was wilderness, and there might be dangerous creatures about, bears, she supposed, or wolves, but right now she was finding it very difficult to worry about them.

Eh, but pleasant though this was, she couldn't afford to loiter, and Maria reluctantly scrambled to her feet. Tonight they would have to sleep under the wagon for shelter, and eat whatever dried provisions Sasha had included. At least they would have clean water to drink, even though the filled bucket was proving far heavier than she'd expected and—curse it all, she'd hit the lip of it against her knee and gotten herself drenched! But by tomorrow, Maria told herself with a sort of clenched-teeth cheerfulness, the farmhouse would be clean enough and aired out enough. They'd have a roof over their heads once more.

SHE had forgotten—they all had—that the roof leaked. They remembered it the next night, when the rains came.

"I should be able to replace the missing shingles myself," muttered Danilo from their dubious shelter back under the wagon. "They're only slabs of wood, after all. Damn! I'll have to waste a day cutting new ones from the planking of the sheds instead of going into the village to get us a plow of some sort. The roof has to be fixed before we can— But we have to get started on the soil right away if the seeds are to be planted in time for any sort of harvest and— Akh, I forgot, we've also got to do something about getting some chickens—making a coop for them—getting food for them—for us . . ."

He broke off in dismay, staring helplessly at his daughters. And Maria, just as overwhelmed as he at the ordeal before them, could find nothing hopeful to say, nothing at all. Instead, she and Vasilissa silently moved into Danilo's arms, and the three of them huddled together in desperate, loving courage.

"I can't do any more," Vasilissa whimpered. "Maria, I can't."

Maria didn't even bother looking up from her weeding: cabbages, turnips, carrots, whatever grew quickly and could be stored for a long time; the village women, if not exactly friendly towards strangers, had, at least, been willing to teach her the basics of gardening. "You can."

"I can't! I'm just too tired."

"I'm tired, too." It was an automatic response, without any real fire behind it; long days of endless labor, of helping Danilo clear and plow resistant soil—praying all the while that it was rich enough to support crops—of sowing seed and chasing away a never-ending troop of thieving birds and beasts, of cooking and mending and rebuilding, had dulled any anger she might have felt. Groaning, Maria sat back on her haunches, trying to ease complaining back muscles. *A fine boyarevna I look now. Broken nails, sunburned face . . .*

Still, they'd come a long way from that first, terrifying day in only . . . just how long was it? Maria blinked to realize she'd quite lost track of time. Were they a month into their exile already? Two months? There had been, thank Heaven, not the slightest sign of pursuit from Stargorod, and that other way of life and its dangers already seemed vague and unreal. There were more immediate perils now. Maria glanced about. It had been full summer when they'd arrived. The weather was still warm, but now that she studied it, the forest all about them did seem to be already slipping past that last, lush peak of growth.

And what happens when the weather turns chill?

Fighting down the increasingly familiar ache of fear, Maria forced herself to concentrate only on what they had managed to accomplish so far. They'd made good use of the wood salvaged from the ruined outbuildings. The roof was at last reasonably rain-proof, though replacing the shingles had proven to be even more tedious, lengthy, and perilous than Danilo had predicted, particularly since he'd had to spend so much time perched atop the house. There was a reasonably secure stall for Brownie, a pen for the one aging pig Danilo had been able to buy in the village, and a ramshackle enclosure for chickens. Maria smiled faintly, thinking that for a time it had seemed they were feeding every fox in the forest on those stupid birds—

Damn! They were out again!

"Oh, Lissa, you forgot to latch the gate again."

"I hate those chickens! They're smelly and disgusting—"

"You like the eggs well enough." Maria was busy catching up the foolish creatures, which didn't put up more than a token struggle, and dumping them back over the fence; not bothering to use their stubby wings, they landed like so many plump, feathered rocks and promptly set about scratching peacefully in the dirt of their pen. "Lissa, if you don't want to tend the chickens, take care of the pig instead."

"Oh, but he's so big and ugly!"

"Then don't look at him! Curse it all, Lissa, I can't do everything around here!"

"Maria!" It was Danilo, returning from the hunt, spear over his shoulder, a brace of rabbits dangling down his back. "Don't talk to your sister like that!"

"But—"

He'd reached her side, whispering, "You know how delicate she is! She can't stand hardships."

Maria wanted to shout, *And I can?* But she was too painfully aware of how drawn her father's face had become, of the guilt and shame radiating from him—that he should have brought his daughters down into *this*—and Maria contented herself with saying, half choking on suppressed frustration, "The snares worked, I see."

THE year was turning, all too swiftly, towards winter. The forest fairly blazed with color, a wild tapestry of birch-leaf gold and oak-leaf copper picked out in threads of somber larch-green, all beneath a sky clear and sharp as blue enamel. The air was crisp enough to hurt the lungs and dazzle the mind.

If one had time to let the mind be dazzled.

Driven by terror, the exiles prepared for the coming ordeal of winter as best they could, wasting few moments on unnecessary speech, caulking the chinks between the logs of their house with mud and moss, setting racks of meat—deer and rabbit—to dry, piling up turnips, carrots, the grain they'd bought in the village, in every spare corner of the house and barn. There was no time to spend in soothing the fears of Vasilissa, who grew more house-bound and afraid with every shortening day. But though she still sensed demons everywhere beyond the charmed ring of their palisade, she could at least be useful, pickling cabbage or beets, though at times she sobbed with fright into the mixture over Things only she could see.

Maria went on wider and wider expeditions into the forest as the days grew short, hunting nuts, fruit, anything edible, anything that might last the length of the winter, hardly aware of the forest except as a source of potential food. Akh, and of firewood, wood to keep them warm and alive . . . Unable to coax Vasilissa out with her, she foraged alone for dead branches and twigs, dragging them back in an old shawl, while Danilo used their one precious axe to join with the villagers in cutting down dead trees; neither he nor Maria saw anything at all incongruous in the once proud *boyar* coming back triumphant because he'd managed to gather a whole wagonload of wood.

They'd been putting off the matter of the pig for as long as possible. "It's no good," said Danilo at last. "We can't carry him through the winter. And we need the meat."

"Can't we just call in the butcher?" Vasilissa asked

without thinking, then added softly, "Oh." Her eyes widened at the thought; her face paled. And suddenly, hands over mouth, she was running out to their rickety outhouse.

"So much for Lissa as pig-slayer," Maria said.

Later, she regretted that feeling of smug superiority. Neither Danilo nor she had the vaguest idea of how to kill a pig. After a long and horrifying struggle, Danilo finally managed to brain the madly squealing beast with a club, and cut its throat. Maria grimly held a basin to catch the blood, telling herself it was precious food, thinking of blood puddings, sausages. She steeled herself to watch the full basin.

And then she too was hurrying off to be sick.

STILL the winter came on, tearing the last leaves from the trees, leaving the trunks and branches dour and lonely in the long twilights and chill nights. Vasilissa cried out to find the water frozen in the washbasin one morning, and she and Maria went frantically over the garden one more time, trying to glean the last turnip from the freezing soil. At last Maria straightened, shivering through thick layers of clothing.

"That's it, Lissa. There's no more any of us can do now. Except wait."

"And pray," her sister added softly.

THE forest lay quietly under the snow, bearing about it an air of tranquility and deadliness, making Maria think of some alien creature well aware of the presence of three little humans, well able to destroy them, but simply not caring enough to make the effort. Stay out in cold sharp enough to shatter a knife, she told herself, and the creature would most certainly strike to kill.

There was nothing for the three of them to do now, save see to Brownie, secure and shaggy in his dense winter fur, and to those chickens weather-wise enough to stay huddled together, safe within their coop. The days grew short and crisp, with air that froze the lungs, long nights filled with distant wolf-song. And all at once there *was* time, too much time, long spans of huddling before the stove and staring blankly into the fire, or mending clothes that had

been mended twenty times over, or checking and recheck-
ing the stores that were already dwindling—they were getting heartily sick of turnips and smoked pork, and
beginning to dream about fresh fish, sweet cakes, precious
salt—and conversation.

For a while Maria tried to entertain the three of them
with storytelling and the music of her sweet-stringed *gusla*.
But words seemed out of place in the heavy winter silence,
and music thin and unbearably lonely.

They'd long ago lost track of the calendar, making one
half-hearted attempt to celebrate what they estimated must
be Yuletide, but slowly they lost interest in measuring the
count of days, resigned as any animals. As the painful
time dragged on, day into night, night into day, Vasilissa
shrank so much into herself that Maria had nightmares of
her never being able to reenter the living world. Didn't her
father see what was happening?

But Danilo, reacting in his own way to the boredom and
the fear, was lost in the memory of the injustice done him.
The firelight made his brooding face look alien, cruel.
Maria shuddered, and deliberately picked fights with Vasilissa, as much to stir her sister's blood as to help Maria
hold to her own sanity, and prayed for the winter to end.

But no one seemed to hear her.

XI

AWAKENINGS

SHE LAY FULL-LENGTH AND LANGUOROUS in the warm spring meadow, the new grass soft and cool against her bare skin, her long hair shining golden in the sunlight, so attractive a contrast against the bright young green that she kept turning her head lazily from side to side to admire it. Birdsong and insect chirpings were dreamy and soft in the quiet air, and the sweet scents of growth were all about her. Ljuba laughed softly for sheer pleasure, and a falcon's chuckle answered her.

Finist. Finist had come swooping silently down to a landing, altering shape smoothly till he was man again, sprawled lazily beside her, his long, supple body as golden in the sunlight as her own.

"Ljuba . . ." Her name was a caress on his lips. "The winter was long and lonely."

"You've forgiven me? Those candles—the enchantment—I did it only because I love you."

"Akh, my dear . . . What man could resist you? What man could fault you?"

"Finist . . ." She reached out an arm to encircle his neck, pulling him, unresisting, down across her, welcoming his strength. His lips brushed her cheek, nibbled teasingly at an earlobe. But then, bewilderingly, he was murmuring:

"But there is still the little matter of Erema, and the knife."

"I had nothing to do with any—"

"You killed him, didn't you? You destroyed him, mind and body."

"Finist, no!"

"You killed him to get at me. You killed him to steal my throne."

"No, oh, no!"

AND with that, gasping, Ljuba awoke in her bed, with chill winter sunlight stealing through the slats of shutters closed against the cold.

"God, what a ridiculous dream."

"Lady . . . ?" asked a sleepy voice, and Ljuba turned her head sharply to stare down at the form there beside her. Finist . . . ?

Good Lord, no. This man was dusty brown of hair, suntanned of skin . . . a guard, though for the life of her she couldn't remember his name. Young, handsome, and a fervent enough lover, if not subtle. She'd taken him into her bed to help combat the tedium of at least one of the long, seemingly endless winter nights . . .

And to combat a certain loneliness, too: Finist . . .

For a moment more, she felt the dream linger about her. Then, with a sudden cry of anger, Ljuba was on her feet, clutching a blanket about herself.

"Up!" she commanded. "Get up and get out!"

Then, as the bewildered guard stumbled to obey, Ljuba thought better of it, and called him back.

"Here. Drink."

"Wine? Ah, lady, your pardon, but I really don't—"

"Drink!"

Hastily, he obeyed. Ljuba watched his eyes go dreamy and vague from the effects of the drug in the wine, and purred, "You spent the night alone. Alone, do you understand?"

"Alone," he agreed dully.

"Now—get out of here."

Dourly, she watched him leave. Ever since the near-disaster of Erema's death, Ljuba had realized that her only safe course of action to allay Finist's suspicion would be to lead a quiet, apparently blameless life, at least for a time. Even if it meant her lovers must be drugged to ensure their silence. Even if at certain crucial moments she heard herself call out a royal name, longing for silvery hair against her own, amber eyes hot with passion . . .

Dammit, no, I am not *in love with the man!*

Then why were there tears in her eyes?

Akh, blame it on this interminable winter! Days of being pent-up indoors because of cold or storm were beginning to wear on her nerves.

Ljuba flung open the shutters with a crash, welcoming the blast of chill, restoring air. She'd decided that her time of quiet innocence should last until the spring; no one could be expected to live anything but a quiet life in winter, anyhow.

But, wondered Ljuba with a touch of wan humor, was *she* going to be able to last till then?

"ENOUGH!"

Finist hurled the parchment down with savage force, glaring at the counselors who stared at him in amazement.

"But . . . my Prince . . ." Semyon began tentatively.

"Enough, *boyar!*" Finist struggled for control. "We have spent the entire morning going over and over these ridiculously petty boundary quarrels as if we could actually do something about them. I told you this was useless, but no, you wouldn't believe me! *Boyars,* we *can't* settle anything now, not in the middle of winter with snow covering everything!"

"But surely we could . . ."

The last threads of temper snapped. "Surely you could get out of here, all of you!"

With nervous glances at each other, they gathered up their scrolls and maps and scuttled out of the chamber. Only Semyon dared to linger. "My Prince, I understand. We've all been short of temper lately. It's the season. The winter wears on all of us, particularly you younger folk—"

"Don't patronize me, man."

"But—"

"I gave you a command. Get out!"

Semyon's sigh expressed volumes. But, shaking his head, he obeyed. Alone, Finist turned to the window, unbolting the shutter and flinging it open, welcoming the wave of cold that swept into the hot chamber. Akh, he hated this room, the claustrophobic little Golden Chamber, all pretty yellow silk, with its low ceiling and one small window, but it was one of the few rooms in the palace warm enough to suit his shivering *boyars*. As though they weren't swathed in enough furs to warm a village!

Leaning on the windowsill, looking out over his silent, white-shrouded city, his breath frosting the air, Finist reluctantly had to admit that Semyon was right. It *was* the weather wearing at all of them; once the joyousness of Yule and Winter Solstice and New Year's celebrations were past—his people were nothing if not ecumenical in their holidays—there was nothing left but long nights, short days, and cold. No one travelled, save by sleigh or skis for brief jaunts; there wasn't any journey worth the risk of a frozen death. Even Finist was restricted. Winter flights, with no warm thermal currents to ease his wings, burned up almost more energy than they were worth. In the forest, he knew, the magical folk were almost all in their various forms of hibernation; even the *leshiye,* those tricky, shape-shifting forest lords, slept.

But we foolish humans stay awake. With far too much time in which to think.

And, as it had so many times already in the nearly six months since the incident, his mind wandered back to the still-unsolved puzzle of Erema's mad attack and Ljuba's so fortuitously timed rescue.

Finist gave a sigh of frustration. Once he'd recovered from the strain of his ill-starred attempt into necromancy—and what a damnably foolish thing *that* had been!—he'd gone in search of the *boyar's* knife. But there'd been no trace of it. And his appeals to courtiers and servants alike had met only with blank, innocent stares. Anyone in the palace could have picked up the blade, or simply thrown it away!

Nor had he any more success in tracking down any plot behind Erema's attack. There hadn't been, thank Heaven, any secret, slowly fermenting revolution brewing. No, it really was beginning to look more and more as though the

young *boyar* had been acting on his own insane behalf.
Unless Ljuba . . . Dammit, he knew—no matter how il-
logically—that Ljuba had something to do with it. Yet there
wasn't any proof, there never had been, not the slightest
shred, magical or mundane. And lately his lovely cousin
had been living as innocently and quietly as a little nun
(*hardly a nun,* thought Finist, *not Ljuba!),* being as remotely polite to him at the Yule celebrations as though
there'd never been that feverish night, those heavy-scented
candles . . .

She, it would seem, had taken his warning to heart.

And he? Try to ignore it as he would, he kept recalling
that frantic *I love you!* And for all and all, as the winter
dragged on, he was beginning to find his magician's will
sorely tested. What if he visited her just once more, without the candle-spell or any other enchantments this time,
just to see what would happen if . . .

The very thought of it stifled him. God, had he come
to this, lusting for a woman he neither liked nor trusted?
All at once the walls of the Golden Chamber were too
close about him. Finist thrust his head out of the window,
gulping in lungfuls of air so clean and cold it ached. It
wasn't enough. Recklessly he tore off his regal robes, letting them fall unheeded. Falcon once more, Finist took
flight, trying to outrace his thoughts.

Oh, God, would this winter never end?

DEEP in the forest, it grew colder still, and terrifyingly
bleak. In the farmhouse, the exiles lived in growing fear
of death by freezing or starvation. The latter seemed increasingly more likely. Their careful hoard of food had
run alarmingly low. But there was no larder to raid, nothing to do but cut their rations and move as little as possible
to conserve their strength. Faces grew gaunt and tempers
short, and Maria began to wonder if a quick death at the
hands of Svyatoslav's executioner might not have been
more merciful after all . . .

And then one morning she woke to an unfamiliar, reg-
ular sound. For a time she lay still, trying to puzzle it out,
then at last threw a blanket over the clothes in which she'd
been sleeping for warmth, and struggled to pull open the

complaining door. A blast of cold air staggered her—but it no longer had that bitter bite to it. The farm was bright with sunlight. And the sound she'd heard—

Was the steady drip of melting icicles.

"Spring," breathed Maria. "Oh, dear God . . . Father, Lissa, come, hurry! It's spring!"

XII

LESHIYE

You COULD ONLY LIVE with fear so long, thought Maria, whether it was fear of capture or of starvation, before it stopped being fear and changed to something else entirely. Hopelessness, perhaps. She glanced to her father, laboring behind Brownie with the plow, breaking up the newly thawed soil, his face as carefully empty of thought as any serf's. By now, they dared believe the winter had passed them by and left them alive. And it seemed pretty clear that even if Svyatoslav's men were still looking for them after so long, they weren't going to be found. But Danilo had never quite come back from the grim, hungry time, slipping little by little into his own dour world, a world as remote from reality as any of Vasilissa's wild fantasies of forest demons waiting to pounce. Maria sighed, looking down at her work-roughened hands without really seeing them. She'd hoped the dawning of spring would help Lissa. Instead, those demons were becoming more and more real to her; the young woman stumbled through the day as though shrouded in gloom, and there was seldom a night in which she didn't wake sobbing or screaming.

If only I could get through to her. Yes, and poor father, too.

But Maria sadly suspected that the only cure for them would be a return to their former life. And that seemed about as likely as an angel descending from Heaven.

Enough of this, Maria told herself. *At least we've got a house and a garden, and that's a good deal more than we might have had.*

She bit her lip. If only she didn't always have to be the brave one! If only, just for a short time, there were someone else, someone on whom *she* could lean! A muffled oath from her father made Maria look up. He was wrestling with Brownie, trying to mend a snapped rein. Before Maria could move to try to help him, Vasilissa, who'd been hanging wash on an improvised line, gave a wail of anguish. Maria whirled to her, thinking her sister must have hurt herself. But no, Lissa, helpless as ever, had only managed to drop the end of the line into the dirt.

"Oh, Lissa," Maria scolded, "I just washed those clothes!" She stopped with a sigh. "Lissa, girl, stop crying. It's only an accident. Lissa, stop it!"

"If—if only you'd help me . . ." her sister began plaintively.

"Never mind that!" Danilo cut in angrily. "Maria, come here and hold Brownie for me!"

Maria started forward, only to trip over the spilled basket of laundry. Vasilissa gave a new, despairing wail, Danilo uttered a short, sharp oath, and Maria, who'd found herself standing in one place, turning from father to sister to father again, gave a sudden wild cry of despair.

"Father, you know you can handle Brownie alone! Lissa, you just pick up that line and retie it yourself. I'm going to get us some water!"

She snatched up the buckets and fled.

MARIA let out a slow sigh of relief. Ah, the quiet, the wonderful forest quiet. Nothing around her but tree rustlings and the stirrings of small animals and birds. Surrounded by new leaves and ancient, slow vegetable life, she sat on the trunk of a fallen tree, and sagged, letting the vast, nonhuman, impersonal forest peace sweep through her, flooding her till she felt drained of all petty human cares. That there was danger in the forest, Maria admitted, even without those nebulous demons her sister conjured—danger from bandits or bears. But she wasn't going to worry about that. The forest seemed to be one great living being, and if it wasn't actually welcoming her, at least it wasn't trying to drive her away. It asked nothing of her, nothing at all, and Maria sat where she sat and revelled in its simple . . . neutrality.

But, decided the young woman reluctantly, she supposed she'd better be getting back. Her father would start to worry if she was away too long.

Slowly she got to her feet, bending to pick up the wooden yoke with the two water buckets, then straightening, lingering a moment to breathe in the sharp, spicy greenness of the air.

And then a loud, harsh *clang* cut into the quiet. Maria froze in alarm, then winced as she realized it had been the cruel sound of a trap snapping shut. She didn't begrudge hunters their need to earn a living, but she couldn't help hoping that whatever was snared had been killed outright, mercifully.

But what was that faint, terrified sound like sobbing?
That's the voice of a child!

The thought of the cruel strength of those iron jaws made Maria fling down the yoke and go racing toward the frightened sobbing.

"Where are you? Little one, I'm coming to help you. Where are you?"

The sobbing had stopped abruptly, as though some little wild thing, trapped, was trying desperately not to attract attention to itself.

"Oh, please, please, don't be afraid of me! I'm not going to hurt you! I only want to help you, child. Let me know where you are."

There, now, if she stood still, she could vaguely make out something, the faintest of muffled whimperings . . . Following that slight sound, Maria pushed through a tangle of bushes that somehow didn't seem to be hindering her—almost as though the forest knew she meant well. *No, that's ridiculous!*

But there before her was the savage shape of the hunter's trap, and firm in its shut jaws was a small, trembling bundle.

"Oh, poor little one! Let me see . . ."

The small form pulled sharply away from her, one pudgy-fingered hand over its face in fright, but not before

Maria, falling back on her haunches in disbelief, had gotten a good look at the childish body and face. Childish, yes—but certainly not a human child! Slowly the stubby hand fell. Wild, dark eyes peered up at her, echoing the forest's own wildness, peered up out of a snub-nosed, triangular, green-furred face, not quite fox, not quite boy.

"Oh," said Maria. "Well. I, uh, I don't know who you are, child"—*or what,* she added silently—"but I still do mean to help you."

The terrible iron jaws had miraculously not crushed the child between them. In fact, the child didn't seem to be more than bruised, protected from genuine harm by the way its baggy, furry caftan—*fur over fur?* thought Maria wildly—had chanced to bunch up to form a cushion.

"You were fortunate, ah . . . child. Wait, now. There's usually some sort of release lever to these things, a hunter showed me that once when he stopped at our house, and— ah! There we are!"

The child was up and away in a silent rush of motion. And Maria could have sworn she saw the bushes hastily part to let it pass.

"Oh, now, that's impossible!" she said aloud.

"Not so."

It was a woman's voice. Or . . . almost a woman's voice. Maria spun wildly, trying to locate the sound. And then she stopped, staring. This time the bushes *did* part, of their own accord, and a figure moved silently forward to stop just before the young woman. And if the child had been only remotely akin to humanity, this being was so alien— No, here in the forest, she, Maria, was the alien, and this one was part of the forest's own wild soul. Small and lithe, her green-furred form covered by the folds of a loose animal-skin caftan, the being shifted her weight from foot to foot with the unconscious grace of a wild thing, watching Maria from a narrow face as keen of feature as that of a fox. She had the sharp, not unpleasant smell of a wild thing to her, too. And she had horns, neat little goat horns.

Suddenly Maria remembered one of the old tales she loved so well. Fantastic as it might seem, the tale had just come to life before her eyes!

"Leshiye!" she gasped. "That's it! You're one of the *leshiye,* the lords of the forest!"

Mischief flickered in the dark eyes. "I am *lisunka,"* she corrected in a voice that sounded both human and animal. "My husband is the *leshy*-lord of this forest."

"I see." Maria, remembering just how alien these odd folk were said to be, how full of strange humors and rages, began to wonder uneasily if her deed of goodwill was going to wind up being the end of her. But when she curtseyed politely to the *lisunka,* the being only laughed, the rustling of leaves in wind.

"No, human-girl, no. We have nothing to do with the narrow human ways you call courtesy." She stirred herself, listening. "My husband comes. He is not so easy with human-folk as I. Stand, and watch, and say nothing."

Maria had no intention of disobeying. She saw nothing but a deeper shadow among the forest shadow, she heard nothing for a time but a bewildering series of sounds that were like no language she'd even imagined. But then the *leshy* said, quite clearly, "You have saved our child. Human-girl, the forest is in your debt."

That sounded so portentous that Maria could only stammer, "But I didn't—I mean, I'm glad I was able to help the little one, and I'm glad he—uh—she?—uh—wasn't hurt. But all I did was release a lever. Surely you could have—"

"We could not. The trap was of cruel, deadly iron. We could not touch it. And the child would have slowly died. The forest *is* in your debt, human-girl. We shall honor that debt someday, when most you need it."

Suddenly, bewilderingly, the *leshy* laughed—and that sound wasn't even remotely human. "But now, human-girl, go home. Go home before the night comes! Go home!"

There was a wild rush of wind, a shaking and lashing of the branches that made Maria shield her face with her arms—and the *leshy* was gone.

"Go home, eh?" Maria echoed. "Believe me, I intend to!"

But even through her fear and bewilderment, a sense of

sheer, joyous wonder warmed her all through the rest of that day, and through the long, wearisome days that followed.

The leshiye *are real. Magic is still alive in the world!*

XIII

STORMS

THE WIND WAS RISING outside the window of the Ruby Chamber, calling to him, fiercely alluring. And how Finist ached to answer! But within the audience chamber, his counselors droned on and on about taxes, treaties, the price of corn and wheat, all the minutiae of daily life . . . Despite his best intentions, the prince felt his attention beginning to wander. Once more he found himself musing over that one unsolved puzzle: Erema.

I still could swear *Ljuba had something to do with his attack!*

But there wasn't any proof. And Ljuba, over the winter, had been quietly building up support among the palace folk, being oh-so-gentle, so willing to help anyone who needed her potions or healing charms.

What a lovely act it is. He could almost believe she'd taken his warning seriously. But to believe that Ljuba had changed so drastically in so short a time? *I'm not that much of a fool!*

His counselors had paused, aware suddenly of his inattention, and Finist reluctantly signalled to them to continue. After all, he'd summoned them. And he must, in all courtesy, hear them out. Even now, after three full turns of the hourglass.

But how can they expect me to concentrate now, when the wind is calling?

His heart had begun to race in time to its wild song.

Finist glanced down at his hands clenched on the arms of his chair, and saw a shimmering of feathers—

"Prince Finist? Ah, Prince Finist, one thing more, if it please you. We know you're young, but . . ."

That brought him back to himself with a start. When they began with his youth, there was usually something to follow that he wasn't going to like. "But what? What now? We've already established that the land's peaceful and prosperous. What more can you possibly want to discuss?"

The *boyars* glanced uneasily at each other, and Finist stirred with impatience, listening to wind-song.

Then Semyon said warily, "The matter of a wife."

"That again!" He looked about at all the suddenly hopeful faces and sighed. "Eh, well, let's hear it. Whom would you propose this time?"

They hemmed and hawed for a time. "We . . . uh . . . agree with Your Highness that most of the candidates so far have not been, uh, quite suitable, for one reason or another. But that brings us back to our original suggestion. What better wife for you, Your Highness, than your cousin?"

"Ljuba!" It was an involuntary explosion of sound. Finist caught himself, and said, more guardedly, "You know how she feels about me. And how I feel about her."

The counselors looked at him blankly. "But . . . your pardon, my Prince," began one of them, "but what has that to do with anything? The Lady Ljuba's of the blood royal, after all, and young and healthy, and, ah, very beautiful."

They quite misunderstood his sudden silence. "And of course, she does have something of the Power," Semyon added enticingly.

It was too much for Finist. "Of course she does!" he spat. He was hardly about to tell them his vague suspicions as to Ljuba's true parentage, but even so . . . "Look you, all of you, I may be young, as you never fail to remind me, but I'm not a child! I know I must wed someday, I know a prince must have his princess, and a royal heir in the cradle. But that princess will never be Ljuba! Leave it at that!"

Akh, those tolerant, amused little smiles! They were all watching him, secure from the vantage point of their greater years, watching him as though he were a little boy rebelling against being sent to bed before—Oh, enough!

Finist shot to his feet, hearing the confusion behind him as he turned sharply to the window, leaning on the sill, drinking in the sound and feel of the wind all around him. A storm was surely on the way, but right then, half-smothered with thoughts of propriety and Ljuba, he didn't care. He'd done his duty, he'd listened politely to the *boyars'* reports, he'd been docile and correct and kept his true thoughts in check. No longer!

The prince laughed aloud in sudden keen joy, and sprang onto the sill, taking deep lungfuls of the clear, free air. As he tore off the encumbrance of his silken caftan, he could hear Semyon cry plaintively:

"But my Prince! Where are you going?"

"Wherever the wind takes me!"

And with that, he jumped. There was a moment of human helplessness, then he'd willed the change, and felt the sharp, familiar tug of air against wings as he braked his fall and began to spiral up in fierce freedom, sunlight bright on his feathers. The wind caught him and he laughed, a falcon's shrill cry, and soared out over his city. Some people in the streets far below heard him, and looked up, waving or bowing, and he dipped a wing in courteous reply.

Aie, but the wind up this high was cold and crisp, tugging at him, strong enough to sweep him right out over the city and the wall, out across the fields and beyond, growing stronger by the moment. *Wonderful,* he thought, *wonderful!*

But the storm's force was still growing. Deafened by the increasing roar all about him, vision blurring despite nictitating membranes, Finist gasped in shock as a new gust of wind slapped at him with painful force. Before he could recover, he was thrown aside by what felt like a solid wall of air. For a moment, tumbling, helpless against that merciless strength, he let the wind push him as it would, trying only to keep his wings unbroken, praying he wouldn't suddenly be slammed to the ground like some storm-lost sparrow. Abruptly dropped by the capricious winds into relative calm, Finist struggled, panting, to level out again.

God, how was he going to get out of this? He couldn't
fight a storm and live!

Fool! the prince shouted to himself. *You felt the wind's
warnings; you should have heeded them!*

Too late. Dazed, breathless, deafened, he was caught,
dragged along, powerless as any true bird, terrified and
exhilarated, a helpless part of that wilderness, sweeping
verst after *verst* westward with a dizzying blur of field and
forest, endless dark green forest, far below.

Avian lungs labored for breath. Akh, and his wings
ached as though they were being torn slowly from his
body. Ridiculous, to be trapped like this. He had friends
in the upper air, but he couldn't call on them, not in this
speechless falcon form, yet if he changed shape, he'd fall.

Eh, wait now, what if I did . . . ?

What other choice had he? And so, human, Finist fell,
arms and legs spread to keep himself level, down through
layers of wind, freezing without the warmth of feathers,
down and down till— Ah, the winds were weaker here!

With a final surge of effort, Finist became falcon once
more, crying out at the strain on his aching wings. But the
winds were weaker still—

And suddenly he was free of them, half diving, half falling, tumbling and spiralling to a carpet of trees below him.

It was as clumsy a landing as ever he'd made, leaves
blinding him, twigs lashing at his body, but at last his
desperately outstretched talons caught at a branch and held,
and he was in a tree, alive and unbroken.

For a long, shaken while he perched there, too exhausted to move, craving sleep as a starving man craves
food. But he couldn't stay up here, not safely. An over-
tired avian body tended to slip back into human form of
its own accord. He hadn't gone through that stormy ordeal
merely to die from a fall out of a tree. Finist groaned,
then fluttered painfully to the ground. He huddled under
the shelter of a bush, past the point of caring that some
woods creature just might like the taste of falcon. He didn't
smell like a proper falcon, anyhow . . . human scent under
the bird . . .

His last coherent thoughts faded away.

Completely drained, Finist slept.

XIV

THE ROBBERS

FINIST AWOKE shuddering with cold, aching in every joint and almost too stiff to uncurl.

Uncurl? His last memory was of being falcon . . . Then he really had shifted back to human-shape in his sleep.

Where was he? It was difficult to concentrate; that brief nap had helped, but not enough, and the chill was fogging his mind. All he knew for sure was that he'd been driven far to the west, and that he'd come down in the middle of a forest—hardly surprising, since most of the lands about his own were forest.

And as his mind cleared, Finist could sense the life of that forest all around him. He was foreign here, and all the forest-magic was awake and stirring in response to the unfamiliar presence of his Power as it never would have bothered to react to a magicless human. Finist quickly sent out a soothing *I come in peace, I mean you no harm,* and felt the sense of *other* fade away.

Before Finist could do anything more, he was shaken by a mighty sneeze that completely shattered his concentration. Akh, he couldn't worry about the forest now, not while he was shivering so fiercely. Worse, judging from the angle of fading light through the trees, and the rising chill from the earth, the hour must be somewhere in the late afternoon. He'd never survive the night, not like this!

Groaning, Finist staggered to his feet. At least most of the damage from his wild flight and fall was minor,

102

scratches and bruises, already healing. But if he didn't find clothing . . .

Hear me, he sent to the forest-presence, *I must make use of some of your Power, just a bit. Is it granted?*

The branches about him rustled after a moment, rustled when there was no wind, and the prince took that for consent. Well and good, but it wasn't going to help him if this spell didn't work . . .

Luck was with him. Finist found tufts of deer fur caught in underbrush almost right away, and managed to disentangle them despite trembling hands. Closing his eyes, sending his will out to touch the forest-magic, feeling Power swirl dizzyingly about him, he condensed a tiny bit of that fierce life-force, using the fur scraps as focus, into a sort of backwoods caftan and boots. The prince opened his eyes with a sigh, looking wryly down at his crude handiwork. At least it should prove warm enough. He slipped the makeshift caftan on, then sagged to the forest floor in renewed weariness.

His mind was working again—working a little too well, reminding him that he was in someone else's domain, reminding him of all the horror stories he'd ever heard of what might happen to royalty caught in foreign lands: torment, death, ransom enough to destroy his people . . . Finist glanced down at his ugly clothing and gave a dry little laugh.

At least I don't have to worry about being conspicuous!

Inconspicuous? With silver-bright hair and amber eyes? Finist groaned again, trying to concentrate only on the warmth of his caftan, trying to put off the moment of magic as long as possible. His falcon-shape might be as natural to him as his human form, but any other form certainly wasn't. There'd be a price to pay for even minor shape-altering—besides an increase in weariness—and after a moment his tired brain remembered it: he'd still be able to shift into falcon-form, yes, but every time he returned to human shape, it would be to the conjured form, not his own, until someone called him by his rightful name.

It seemed a small enough price to pay for safety.

So Finist called together as much will as he could find within himself, and set to work. It wasn't easy, and he wasn't helped by the forest's curiosity, all about him, peering around the edges of his concentration. But after a while, he'd managed to broaden and flatten high cheekbones, darken hair and eyes to a dull brown . . . Enough. He let himself fall back to the forest floor, staring blankly up at leaves.

Akh, but did his people think him dead? Finist knew he didn't have the strength to fly all that long way back, even assuming he could figure out where "back" might be. But as soon as he could find a quiet pool into which to gaze, he'd be able to contact someone. Semyon, probably, since the trustworthy old *boyar* had been taught by Finist's father to receive psychic royal messages—which simply meant that while Semyon didn't have any innate magic, he had enough inner sensitivity to let his mind, once properly trained, *feel* the particular psychic vibrations that meant royal scrying, and *hear* whatever his ruler sent to him.

Finist gave a long, weary sigh. Until he had the energy to locate that pool, Semyon and everyone else were just going to have to wait.

Suddenly the forest was stirring angrily all around him. Finist sat up abruptly, straining to hear what it heard, to sense what it sensed. There was a confused jumble of someone else's thoughts . . . Finist was no reader of minds, but surely he felt more than one someone, anxious, hostile—

Alarmed, the prince stole silently forward, and soon found himself overlooking a muddy, rutted road, and on that road, a shaggy brown horse pulling a small wagon and objecting with ears and switching tail to his driver's attempts to keep him at a trot. That driver was a bearded, middle-aged man in a work-worn blue caftan.

And surely his is the worry I sensed. But why should the presence of one innocent farmer so upset the forest?

After a moment, Finist realized the truth. There were still the other, hostile presences, and suddenly he knew they were:

"Robbers! Watch out!"

At his shout, the driver reined in his horse so sharply the animal almost reared. And the thief who'd launched himself at the wagon missed completely, sprawling across the horse's powerful haunches, scrambling frantically out from under massive hoofs. But now the other bandits were swarming out from hiding, grabbing at horse and driver, knives flashing. The driver held them off as best he could with his whip, but he was surrounded, as surely doomed as a stag cornered by wolves.

But these ragged wolves didn't expect an attack from a falcon. Filled with the sudden fierce energy of crisis, Finist—not about to watch a murder—shifted shape, launched himself wildly into the air, and dove at them, talons outstretched. The prince felt flesh tear and heard somebody shriek. He cried out in triumph, a falcon's scream, and turned to strike again. But one of the bandits flailed out blindly with his staff, and caught Finist a glancing blow that sent him tumbling back into the forest. He hit the ground with enough force to send him breathlessly back into human-shape, gasping for air.

Ai, the robbers had torn the whip from the driver's hand! Finist dove into his discarded caftan, and lunged at the robbers with a stout branch the forest-presence had graciously granted him. Magic or no, every prince was well trained in weaponry. Finist had even experimented with peasant weapons, and that branch was as good as any quarterstaff. It connected squarely with one man's head, and he crumpled. As Finist rapped another man sharply on the arm, the driver took advantage of the confusion to snatch a club from one of his attackers and copy the prince. And for a time there was chaos.

But chaos yielded quickly to order, because few thieves want to risk injury by standing and fighting. Soon those would-be robbers broke and ran, leaving behind only the man Finist had stunned.

There was silence. Finist and the driver grinned fiercely at each other, too winded to speak. Just as Finist decided he'd recovered enough to say *something*, the fallen robber stirred and groaned, and all humor fled the driver's face, leaving it bleak and cold. Grimly he leaped from the wagon and caught the robber by the throat.

"Who sent you?"

Finist had time to recognize a western dialect not dissimilar from his own tongue while their captive struggled to free himself.

"No one!" the thief gasped at last.

"Liar!"

"No, no, no one! Saw you, thought you'd be an easy mark— That's all, I swear it!"

"I think he's telling the truth," Finist said softly.

For a moment more the driver clutched his captive. Then he sighed and released his hold. "Yes. Of course he is. The woods are full of such trash."

The robber took advantage of the moment to scramble off. The driver held up a hand to Finist. "No, let him go. And we'd best not linger! Hurry, my friend."

But Finist's crisis-born energy had chosen that moment to desert him. Had he not grabbed frantically at the side of the wagon, the prince would have simply crumpled. The driver hastily threw a supporting arm around him.

"You're hurt!"

"No. Just . . . bruised a bit. And weary. I've had a . . . strenuous day."

He let the driver help him into the wagon, and they started off. The nervous horse was very willing to move on, even managing a lumbering sort of canter. Finist clung to the wagon's seat and winced every time they hit a hole, but despite the jolting—or perhaps because of it—he found himself thinking clearly once more.

Now, this was odd: a driver with a shabby caftan and a wagonload of vegetables worries not that he's been attacked by robbers, but that those robbers might have been sent by a much more dangerous foe . . . A driver, for that matter, who speaks to those robbers in a cultured, educated voice . . .

Finist found himself thinking about those vegetables. After all, he had expended an alarming amount of energy, and he'd best restore it as soon as possible.

"Ah, would you mind if I helped myself to a carrot or two?"

The driver gave him a startled look. "No, of course not."

But Finist paused, uneasy at the man's new uneasiness. "Is something wrong?"

"Oh, no." The man was a bit too quick with that. "I was only wondering what a man whose voice shows breeding is doing wandering all by himself in the middle of the forest."

Ah. "I could wonder the same thing about you," the prince murmured, and saw the driver tense.

"I live here," flatly. "And you? Where are you from? The west? No? Not from any of the cities? Stargorod, perhaps?"

This last was said with such cold emphasis that Finist looked at him in bewilderment, wondering for an uncomfortable moment if the man was quite sane. "No. My home's to the east. Why?"

For an instant their glances locked. Then the man turned away, as though relieved and embarrassed. "No reason, no reason. It's just that I . . . have a family. I worry about them lest— Never mind. Young man, I haven't properly thanked you for the rescue. You handled that branch like a trained warrior."

Caught in the middle of a carrot, Finist could only mutter something noncommittal, and the man chuckled.

"If you're that hungry, come home and dine with me on something more filling than roots!"

"Oh, gladly!"

But now the driver was shaking his head. "Odd . . . Did you see that falcon, attacking almost as though it knew what it was doing?"

Finist shifted his weight uneasily. "Nesting birds will attack humans."

"But the color of it!"

"There are albino animals. I suppose a falcon, too, could be—"

"No, no, it wasn't white, I saw it clearly! Its feathers were actually silver!"

Finist pretended to be deeply engrossed in his carrot, knowing all too well how intolerant and fearful of magic people tended to be outside of his own lands. They rode in silence, the driver stealing quick, curious glances at him.

"Lost your weapons, eh? And your possessions?"

"You . . . could put it that way," the prince answered carefully.

"This wasn't your first encounter with robbers, then."

"Let's just say I haven't been fortunate lately."

"Ah." The driver hesitated, then added, "I am Ivan Mikaelovich," which was so common a name as to be almost surely false. *Not,* Finist told himself, *that it's any of your concern.*

"And I am Fin—" He stopped in mid-syllable, belatedly remembering caution.

"Finn, is it?" The man waited, but when Finist gave him nothing more, he added tactfully to no one in particular, "There's many a son of noble blood not, ah, recognized by his father; many a son cast loose to find his own way."

If that was what he wanted to think Finist—the result of some lordling's illicit affair—it was as good a disguise as any. The prince smiled vaguely. "So they say."

"Off to see the world, are you?"

"In a manner of speaking."

"Might I ask where you were headed?"

That struck Finist as wryly funny. Remembering the words he'd so lightly tossed to Semyon, back in Kirtesk, the prince started wearily to laugh.

"Where was I headed? Why, wherever the wind took me!"

XV

GLIMPSES

AS THE CAPTAIN of the palace guard warily approached the throne, the throng of courtiers in the vast audience chamber fell silent, so silent that the click of the man's bootheels echoed loudly against the marble floor. Prince Svyatoslav of Stargorod saw the man wince at the sound and hesitate, and he frowned, tensing angrily.

Now, why does he wear such a hangdog expression? Unless he's failed me? Aloud, the prince said sharply, "Well, man? What news?"

"Akh . . . My Prince, we searched everywhere, but I— We . . ."

"Out with it! Did you find the man or not?"

The captain took a deep breath, then, like a man rushing to his doom, confessed, "No, my Prince. We did not. In fact, we found no trace at all of either the *boyar* or his daughters."

"But that's ridiculous! Danilo couldn't have vanished into thin air. He must have left *some* clue!"

"No, my Prince. It's a vast forest, and . . . well, since the *boyar* was no woodsman, I think we can safely assume he's dead by now."

"No, we can assume nothing! Have you questioned his servants?"

The captain sighed. "All of them. But without applying force—"

This time it was Svyatoslav's turn to sigh. "No." Much as he'd dearly love to torture the truth out of those sly peasants, he had his royal image to consider. The people already seemed to be uncomfortably on the side of the vanished Danilo; if he put an entire household to the torture, they just might revolt. An image of rebellion and bloodshed sped through Svyatoslav's mind, and he shuddered. But Danilo *was* a traitor, and he could hardly let a traitor go unpunished—what if the man had gone to join Rostislav?

The captain was staring at him. Svyatoslav recovered his composure with an effort. "I am not pleased," he said sternly. "Not pleased at all. Captain, I begin to wonder if you're not in sympathy with the traitor yourself."

"I!" The man's eyes were horrified. "Oh no, my Prince! I am loyal to you, only to you, you must believe that!"

"Are you? Then I shall give you one last chance. Go out there and find me the traitor Danilo, and bring him back to me—or you shall die in his place!"

GOD, he'd never thought things would work out this way! Alexei, gnawing at his lips, paced back and forth in the bedchamber that had once belonged to *boyar* Danilo. It had been difficult enough to do what must be done, to speak softly and innocently, to see a man condemned to death—a man he knew to be innocent. But now, to know Danilo was still alive, to know he might be anywhere at all . . . If he should return, if he should bring proof against Alexei . . . The young man shuddered. It wasn't fair, it just wasn't fair! Why did Danilo always torment him? Why couldn't the man have died?

But this sort of whining wasn't doing any good at all. "Sasha!" Alexei called sharply.

No response. The young *boyar* stifled an oath. Damn the man! Damn them all! It had been like this ever since he'd taken charge, slow service, ineptitude that could only be deliberate. If he hadn't thought to hire his own cook, he'd have been afraid of being poisoned every time he took a bite. And who knew but that someone might not get to the cook— No, he was getting as bad as old Svyatoslav!

If he could afford it, Alexei thought, he'd be rid of the lot of them, bring in his own staff.

But even Danilo's funds wouldn't go quite that far, not after Alexei had used them to repay . . . debts. At least he still had his own guards.

Oh, yes, if he could ever get anyone to call them! He shouted for Sasha again. But of course, there still wasn't a response.

"Damn you! If you weren't the overseer of this estate, I swear I'd have the life flogged from you," Alexei hissed, and went in search of the guards himself. The prince's men hadn't been able to find the *boyar* so far; now Alexei would mount his own search. He would end this ridiculous, uneasy way of life once and for all.

ALL winter there in Kirtesk she'd led that quiet, virtuous life *(Virtuous?* her mind taunted. *What about those lovers?),* all winter Ljuba had waited, watching Finist carefully, waiting for his suspicions to die from lack of evidence and sheer inertia. Now the spring had come, and with it, nothing but horror and denial.

Finist couldn't be dead! She'd have known it, she'd have *felt* it!

Ljuba wiped back limb strands of golden hair from her face and began anew, staring into her mirror, whispering the proper phrases till the surface clouded . . . clouded . . .

"Finist," she murmured. "I must see Finist. I will, I *shall* see Finist . . ."

And once again the mirror seemed to be clearing, just as it had all the hundred times so far. Again she saw only a tantalizing hint of—what? Trees? The forest?

"I *will* see Finist, damn you!" she muttered. *"I will see Finist!"*

And Ljuba threw into her magic all the strength left within her, focused . . . and yes, this time the scene was clearing. She could see a face—

But it wasn't Finist's face. A strange sharp face, like some unholy mix of fox and human, green-furred and feral, stared back at her, wild eyes fierce with mockery. *Leshy,* thought Ljuba, horrified. "You *will* show me Finist!" she told it savagely.

The *leshy* only laughed, as though it had heard her quite clearly.

But that's impossible! It can't *be seeing me. It* can't *be hearing me.*

"Can't I?" said a faint, mocking voice. "Forest-hater, tree-threatener, did you think I'd not recognize the *feel* of you?"

And then, eyes glinting with delight, the being made an obscene gesture at her. Furious, terrified, Ljuba hurled a candlestick at it. But of course, she only hit the mirror.

As the young woman sat, panting, drained, in the middle of glass shards, she heard someone gasp.

"My lady! Lady Ljuba! Are you hurt?"

It was Semyon, the old fool of a *boyar*. Ljuba got wearily to her feet, gingerly brushing off her clothing. "No, I'm quite well."

"Then, did you—"

God! The man had been asking her the same questions over and over: Did you see Finist? Do you know where he is? And Ljuba's frustration and fear erupted into wild anger. "No!" she shouted. "No, I did not see him! No, I do not know where he is! No, I—I don't even know if he's still alive!" She stopped short, horrified at what she'd just said. "He *is* alive," Ljuba said, very softly. "I'd know it were he slain. He is still alive, Semyon. And, come what may, I will find him."

XVI

SECRETS

THAT ROUGH WAGON RIDE seemed to last forever. Finist found himself aching to fall asleep right then and there, but every time his eyes would close, he'd be jolted rudely awake again.

Something besides mere physical discomfort was bothering him, too, and that was the fact that his host plainly regretted his charitable offer. At last Finist said sharply:

"Look you, remember I'm a stranger here. I know nothing of your ways. Or your politics."

That struck home. The man gave him a quick, keen look, and Finist added flatly, "I'm no thief, either, if you're thinking of your treasure."

The man snorted. "Treasure." Then, more softly, "I have a treasure, yes. A living one: my daughters."

"And I am no ruffian, either. All honor to my host's kin."

That seemed to set the other's mind at ease, at least for the moment. And soon after that—praise be to Heaven, thought Finist—they reached an end to that uncomfortable ride.

Finist paused in the middle of dismounting from the wagon, looking about. There was nothing unusual here, a small farm consisting of a shabby log house surrounded by the few outbuildings to be found on such a poor place, the lot surrounded by a crudely cut palisade of wooden stakes. But his host's daughters . . . If the driver's voice had hinted of noble breeding, his eldest daughter fairly radiated it, tall and slender and lovely as she was, elegant even in the simple blouse and overdress any peasant woman might wear, with a delicacy of bone that spoke of generations of aristocratic stock.

This, Finist learned, was Vasilissa. He bowed, and she smiled with studied politeness, eyeing his plainness with an equally polite dismay. But their eyes met for an instant; and in that instant, a bewildered Finist saw her dismay turn to fear. Hand to her mouth, the young woman shrank back, watching him with eyes gone wild and wide.

No one else seemed to find anything odd about her reaction. Confused, hazy-minded from fatigue, Finist almost took the younger woman with her for a servant. It wasn't so surprising. She looked too . . . capable for aristocracy, at ease in her peasant dress as though simple wool and fine silk were all the same to her. Not as tall as her sister, not as elegant, too tanned of skin for courtly beauty, too sunbleached of hair. But her smile seemed genuine, and her brown eyes friendly.

This, it seemed, was Maria.

But that was all Finist learned, for the last of his much-abused strength had faded. He was dimly aware of entering the farmhouse, finding it neat and scrupulously clean despite the shabbiness; he was dimly aware of sitting down abruptly. But after that, he remembered nothing but falling into a deep well of sleep . . .

HE awoke to a vision of warm brown eyes and a gentle smile—Maria, at his bedside.

Unfortunately, he also awoke to a feverish head and an aching throat. *Wonderful,* thought Finist wryly. *My body's taking revenge on me for abusing it.* Even magicians, it would seem, could become quite mundanely ill.

He started to croak out some embarrassed apology to his hostess, but she waved him to silence.

"Don't be silly. Everyone falls sick sometime." She draped a damp, cool cloth across his forehead—oh, wondrous coolness!—and continued softly, "Besides, I'm in your debt. You saved my father's life."

"I only did what—"

"Hush, now. Spare your throat. I know what you did. He told me. I repeat, I am in your debt."

THE next day found Finist on his feet again, albeit still miserable, queasy and dizzy, albeit over Maria's protests. But he couldn't go much longer without letting his people know what had happened to him. And he was only too well aware that on such an impoverished farm, with only the three family members and no servants, he would very quickly become a burden.

He made it all the way out of the house. But the next thing Finist knew, he was sitting down hard on a bench just outside the farmhouse's log walls, telling himself firmly that of course he'd meant to sit down.

And for a time, sit was all the prince did, drawing strength to him from sunlight and Warm Mother Earth. There before him, back to him, was the older daughter, Vasilissa, with a woven basket of laundry, hanging the wet clothes with all the frustrated and inefficient clumsiness of some queen forced to do peasant labor. She made such a bad job of it that at last Maria hurried to join her.

"Look, it's simple. I'll show you how—"

"I don't care!" sobbed Vasilissa. "This is servant's work!"

"Lissa, dear, face facts. It's our work now."

"No, I won't believe it! Maybe you enjoy being a—a peasant, but I don't! I won't! I won't forget how it was!"

Maria's voice trembled. "Don't you think I hate this, too? But the past can't be changed. Oh, my dear, can't you see that?"

She reached out a hand to her sister, but the sobbing Vasilissa slapped it away and turned to run into the house. She stopped short with a strangled gasp, and Finist, embarrassed, realized the sisters hadn't known he was there. He started to apologize, but Vasilissa gave him a horrified glance and raced inside. Maria continued to hang the wet things, trying to pretend nothing was wrong. Finist hesitated, wishing very much he was someplace else, but at the sound of the young woman's soft, hopeless sigh, he knew he had to say something.

"Lady?" he called softly.

"Maria," she corrected.

"Maria, then. Forgive me, I didn't mean to overhear, but . . . is there any way I might be of help?"

She turned to give him a weary smile. "Oh, it's nothing. All families have their little quarrels."

"Of course," said Finist noncommittally. "Why is your sister so fearful of me?"

"She—she's not. It's just . . . We see so few strangers . . . Please, don't worry about it. You need concern yourself only with getting well."

But Finist's heart ached with pity at the despair in those bright eyes, and he wondered, *What's the secret here? Who are these people?*

He didn't think he'd get an answer.

SOMEHOW, he never seemed to be alone that day. *Which means I'll probably have to wait till night to contact Semyon. If I last that long.*

Stubbornly, dizzily, he made it through the day, stubbornly sat down to dinner with the family—for all that his head ached and his stomach was rebelling at the very thought of food—in the small, neat main room. He politely ignored the fact that the table consisted only of bare, weatherworn planking. The chairs were ancient things precariously held together with bits of rope. There wasn't room for much else; the great stove took up most of the space. *Do they realize the stove's meant for sleeping atop at night? Apparently not. Only true peasants would know that.*

Maria, Finist saw, was cook as well as laundress; seeing how lightly balanced her sister's mind seemed to be, he was rather glad of that. Who knew what Vasilissa might choose to slip into his food?

But during the entire meal, the young woman showed no sign of strain: her manners were quite polite, her bearing refined. She said not a word. *I might be able to help her,* thought Finist. He had never tried to heal a sick mind, but when his strength fully returned, he might— *Ha, and have her father try to burn me as a sorcerer?*

Dinner finished, they sat for a time and made polite conversation. "Tell me, Finn," said the man who called himself Ivan, "what wonders have you seen in your travels?"

"Wonders." After a moment's thought, the prince smiled to himself and began to describe his own lands and their magical ruler. Seeing his host and the eldest daughter stirring uneasily, Finist sighed, his suspicions confirmed, and dropped the subject. "Aside from that, I've seen forest, and more forest."

"They say the forest is magical, too," murmured Maria, surprising the prince a bit. He grinned at her.

"Oh, it is!" Finist began some small, light tale about a woodsman outwitting a *leshy,* but before he'd gone more than a few words into it, Vasilissa said sharply, "No!"

Startled, he stopped, and she stared at him, wild-eyed. "How can you joke?" she gasped. "The forest is too big, too cold, too cruel— It wants to crush us, I feel it."

In the next moment, she was up and away to her room. There was a brief, awkward silence, then the prince said carefully, "I'm sorry. I didn't mean to give offense."

Ivan sighed. "Of course not. Talk of the old, pagan evils frightens my daughter."

"Oh, but the old ways aren't all evil!" Finist protested, only to be silenced by the man's glare.

"Sorcery *is* evil, Finn."

"Well, yes, it is, I can't argue about that. But all magic isn't evil!"

"Enough!"

"But—I only meant—"

"I know what you meant! You are a guest here, with guest rights. But such rights do not include immoral words!"

"They weren't—"

"Enough, I say!" The man stopped, restraining himself with obvious effort. "Finn, you are young. Young men think speaking of evil so lightly is daring, worldly. But evil is real, and ugly, and no jest!"

"Oh, agreed, but—"

"And the evil that is magic is no jest, either! I will not have such talk in my house!"

Finist sighed, not used to being scolded like some silly, foul-mouthed child. *But I still need the shelter of this man's roof, at least for now,* the prince reminded himself. And so he contented himself with merely bowing his head in compliance.

Ivan got coldly to his feet. "It grows late. Daughter, come." He caught her by the wrist as though she were some errant child. "Finn, I bid you good night."

Maria gave him one quick, apologetic look over her shoulder, then Finist was alone and uneasy in a suddenly hostile place.

XVII

TRUST

ALONE IN HIS ROOM —which was Maria's room, actually, he assumed, his arrival having exiled the poor thing to her sister—Finist did his best to put the family and their mysterious problems out of his mind. Now was his chance to contact Semyon, and with this small hand mirror as focus, he should be able to manage . . .

But he couldn't. Still dizzyingly and maddeningly weak, the prince found himself having to struggle to control his will, fighting to master himself with an effort he hadn't needed since he was a small boy. There, now, the mirror was beginning to properly fog over . . .

No, it wasn't. Head aching, Finist sank to the bed, stifling a groan. This house wasn't helping him, filled as it was with the fear and hatred of magic, and right now he just didn't have the energy to overcome it.

This is ridiculous! I can heal wounds, treat disease— but I can't seem to be able to do anything against this simple, mundane illness that—

The prince broke off with a sharp, impatient sigh. Forget illness! If he couldn't manage to contact Semyon from in here, then he'd simply have to go outside. The night was clear, not too chilly; he shouldn't take any harm from it. And with the forest all around him, with all its magic, he should at least manage to do something!

FINIST stopped short as he reached the farm's wooden palisade, suddenly aware of another presence just on the other side. He stood listening fiercely with a form of hearing that had little to do with the physical.

"My lord *leshy,*" the prince said after a moment. Though the being was little more than a vague shape there in the darkness, the *feel* of it was unmistakable.

"Magician-man," came the rustling-leaves reply. "This is not your realm. Why are you here?"

There was just the faintest touch of menace behind the words. Finist was on good enough terms with the *leshy*-lord of the forest surrounding his own lands, but he wasn't about to underestimate the wild magic of these strange beings. "I thought we'd settled that before," the prince said quietly. "I told the forest I'm here only by accident. As soon as I've the strength, I'll leave."

There was the sound of a faint sniffing. "Phaugh! You smell of human-sickness!"

"I don't doubt it." Finist leaned against the palisade, head swimming, in no mood or condition for delicate diplomacy. "It's something strictly of humanity, *leshy,* nothing to affect either you or your forest. But I must enter the forest. I must contact my people, and I can't work the proper spell in here."

The *leshy* gave a foxlike bark of a laugh. "Not surprising! Not surprising! They are of the dead places, these folk, the cold stone city places! They fear and hide, and deny anything they cannot touch, or hold, or measure!" There was a long silence, during which Finist knew the being was studying him. "So," it said at last. "Come out here, magician-man. There is a still pool you may use for your scrying."

Finist gave the ghost of a chuckle. "And of course, you wouldn't dream of leading me astray, eh? You wouldn't plan to bewilder and lose the poor human, would you?"

The *leshy* hissed indignantly. "I? Not I! Why would I do such a thing?"

"Because you are what you are, like all your kin, sly as foxes and tricky as the wind. But I warn you, I do know a few tricks of my own."

It cost him almost more strength than it was worth, but Finist managed to conjure a hint of flickering silver flame at his fingertips, and heard the *leshy* hiss again, this time in wonder.

"No tricks, magician-man, no tricks! The forest does not hate such as you, human though you be. Come, come!"

Finist dared follow that dimly seen, capering figure, wondering as he did if he was being a fool to trust a trickster. But the *leshy* led him truly, and the quiet pool was surely better than any hand mirror for his purposes. Ignoring the forest's curiosity, Finist set about once again focusing his will. It still wasn't as easy as it should have been, but the wild life-force all around him did help, and at last the prince saw his own image fading, to be replaced by greyness. Now, and now . . . He said the proper Words, concentrating as sharply as he must, feeling the Power growing and growing . . .

And suddenly it was done. Semyon's image was before him, there in the pool, the old *boyar* staring in amazement at the image *he* saw, a wan, brown-haired, brown-eyed stranger in an ugly fur caftan.

"It's me," Finist told him wryly.

"Prince Fin—"

"No, no, don't say it! I still need this shape."

"But—but, my Prince, where are you? Are you all right? Are you—"

"Alive and unhurt and quite safe."

"You don't look it."

"Akh, it's just a minor thing, really. I took a slight chill, a touch of fever, the sort of thing everyone gets—"

"Except you! My Prince, you're almost never ill! Are you sure—"

"Semyon, yes. Truly. I promise you, all's well. And it may take a bit, but I'll return as soon as I'm able." His strength was beginning to fade again. Before Semyon could take any fresh alarm, Finist added hastily, "Till then, good Semyon."

He broke the contact just before it would have slipped away from him, and huddled by the side of the pool for a time, shivering and overwarm in one. *"Damn* this sickness!"

But now the *leshy* was at his side, hunkering easily down

on its haunches, studying him, though all he could see clearly of it were the bright, glittering, green-glinting eyes. "I heard your words," the being told him. "They are not yours, then?"

"Eh?"

"Those ugly, armored humans who are searching the forest."

Finist stared blankly at the *leshy*. Not his men, that was impossible; even had they known where to look for him, they never could have come from Kirtesk so quickly. Then who . . . ? Ordinary hunters definitely didn't go travelling in armor! A sudden thought struck Finist. *I wonder,* he mused, *just how important* are *these mysterious hosts of mine?*

But maybe the whole thing was mere coincidence. And right now he wasn't up to solving puzzles.

"No," said the prince belatedly. "Those men are certainly not mine."

The *leshy* let out a whoop of joy. "Good! Good! Then I may play with them! I shall lead them up and down and about, and they shall find nothing, nothing, till they chance to find their way out of the forest and leave us in peace!"

And with that, the being was gone in a rustle of leaves and a stirring of the wind. Finist sat where he was for a moment, considering soldiers who were about to be lost in pathless woodland for a time, then shook his head. They should count themselves lucky to be getting out of a *leshy*'s domain with nothing worse than a fright! What excuse they might give to whomever had sent them . . . But it wasn't his affair. Finist sneezed, shivering, and got wearily to his feet. He found his way back to the farm with little trouble—the *leshy* seemed to have left a faint psychic trail for him—and made his way silently into the house, very glad the family had no noisy dog to sound an alarm. No one stirred as he stole back to his room, and collapsed.

And there Maria found him the next morning, sprawled helplessly across the bed, drained of strength, quite feverish, and completely disgusted with the whole concept of illness.

* * *

"AND I don't care what you say," Maria stood over Finist, glaring down at him. "Finn, you are staying in bed, and that's the end of it!"

"But—this is ridiculous! I'm quite well, and—" His tirade was interrupted by a sneeze.

"Good health," responded Maria automatically, then gave a sharp little laugh. "So! Quite well, are you?"

"I only—"

"Oh, Finn! You've already made yourself much worse by insisting on getting up the first time! Do you want to give yourself lung disease?"

"Of course not! I only . . ." Finist sighed. "I just hate feeling so weak."

"Who wouldn't?" The young woman's voice softened a bit. "All right. I know you're angry at your body for betraying you. But I *won't* have you doing harm to yourself just because you don't have the common sense to take care of yourself!"

Finist stared at her, astonished, all set to make some properly regal retort. But then he surprised himself by bursting into laughter. "So be it!" he conceded. "You win."

She nodded in satisfaction, and turned to go. "If you need anything, just call."

"Ah, wait just a moment. There *is* one thing. Maria, where am I? Or, rather, where exactly is this farm?"

Her glance was wary. "Some fifty *versts* or so southeast of Stargorod. Why?"

"Just trying to orient myself." Fifty *versts*, eh? A long distance afoot, a short one by wing. That wind really *had* carried him a long way from Kirtesk!

Finist came back to himself with a start. "Oh, but I'm being selfish. I didn't mean to keep you here. Please, go about your own business. I promise," he added with a little smile, "I'll be good."

Her answering grin was so unexpectedly sweet and bright with mischief that a startled Finist felt his heart sing in response. *Oh, don't be foolish,* he told himself, and determinedly shut his eyes, quieted his thoughts, and forced himself back into healing sleep.

* * *

AT first, Maria admitted to herself, she'd almost been ready to hate him, this stranger who'd rudely thrust himself into the established order of things. But how good it had been to see someone new!

Vasilissa didn't think so. *Poor Lissa, so sure that because Finn came out of the forest, he has to be something demonic.*

What he was, was plain, no denying it. But for all that plainness, there was a charm to the man. When he wasn't railing at her for keeping him in bed or making him drink his soup, that was. No—she had to admit it—he had a certain charm even then.

If only she knew who he really was. If only she knew—

Oh, this was stupid! Just because the man was polite, and pleasant, and the only one who actually seemed to listen to her, she was acting like some little ninny of a girl. He would be well in no time, and then he'd be on his way again, and that would be the end of that.

ENOUGH of this! Finist scolded himself. Maria was a sweet young woman and a kind nurse, and that was all.

True, they'd found they shared a love of music. True, they'd found they shared a love of the old tales, too. They'd even discovered in each other some of the same wry sense of humor. But Maria had never shown the slightest interest in him as anything other than an invalid. And he had no intention of making a fool of himself. Why, the woman wasn't even pretty!

Not conventionally pretty.

Not anything as blandly dull as pretty . . .

Nonsense!

Yet there was no denying her eyes were lovely, whether warm with concern or flickering with annoyance as they were right now for refusing to let her hand feed him any more soup. And her lips had such a charming curve to them. Indeed, the longer he gazed at them, the more he found himself wondering just what it would be like to taste their sweetness, to hold that warmly rounded body in his arms . . .

Hastily he turned away, embarrassed. This was his hostess, and he mustn't even think of abusing her hospitality. Scrambling for something safe to say, he came out with:

"Is that a *gusla* I see? Do you play?"

"A bit." Maria raised a wry eyebrow. "Trying to distract me from the soup?"

He shook his head, grinning, and saw her look away as though trying not to laugh. "Very well." Her voice was studiously level. "I'll try to pick out a tune or two, if you promise to finish the soup on your own."

"Agreed."

MARIA bent intently over the little *gusla,* pretending to be very concerned with the exact tuning of its strings. She didn't dare look up at Finn, not just yet. She wasn't quite sure what had happened, or why, but as she'd stood over him, some little devil deep within her had suddenly made her very much aware of him, not as a patient, but as a man, had made her aware of the clean male scent of him, of the lines of that lean, elegant body . . . *Boyar*'s daughter that she was, she'd never known more than the hastiest, most chaste of male kisses, but she wasn't naive, either. And in that confusing moment of awareness, she'd found herself wondering what it would be like to lie in a man's embrace, in *his* embrace.

Hot with embarrassment, she hadn't known what to do or say. And he must have been aware of it. Of course he'd been aware. Gentleman that he was, he'd given her the excuse of the *gusla* to give her time to get herself back under control. Gratefully she strummed the shining metal strings, trying to lose herself in the music—only to realize, horrified, that she was playing a love song.

"I think I hear my sister calling," Maria said hastily, scrambling to her feet. "I'd better go."

"No, wait!"

"I'm sorry, I'll be back later. But right now, I really must leave!"

Once she was out of the room, Maria stopped, shaking her head ruefully. That had been a truly ridiculous performance. She would go back in there, and this time she would remember that she was his nurse, nothing more than that.

* * *

SOON enough the day came when Finist could stand without falling over and walk about the farmyard without panting after every step. He stood soaking up the strength of the warm sunlight, and told himself he had imposed here long enough. Surely he was strong enough by now to leave, strong enough even to fly all that long way back to his own lands.

And yet, the prince realized with a shock, he really didn't want to think of leaving. Bewildered with himself, he found himself picturing a certain sweet, strong, sensible face, brown eyes warm and bright and clever— *Oh, come now!* he chided himself. *I thought you'd gotten over this! She tended you; it's natural to feel warmth towards your nurse. Think only of your people, your royal duties!*

But look—there was Maria, going down by herself to the stream, graceful even burdened as she was with the yoke and water buckets, and he couldn't keep his gaze from following her.

Filled water buckets were heavy; she should not have to be carrying them alone. Even Vasilissa—

But Vasilissa, predictably, was having another of her nervous fits, huddling in her room, sure that sorcery surrounded them all. Finist raised a thoughtful brow. At first he had considered her no more than a typical example of too much close aristocratic breeding, her sudden mood shifts—from deepest depression to frenzied bursts of activity—made all the worse by her father's pampering. But . . . could she, in her unstable mind, be sensitive to his true magical self? Yes, that was it. Such things had happened before. She was able to vaguely sense Power. Not that there was anything Finist could do about it. And her father and she were both so very sure magic was evil.

Indignant for Maria and for himself, Finist caught up with her as she struggled with the buckets and their yoke. "Here, let me help. That's too heavy for you."

She shot him a look of insulted pride. "No, it's all right. I can manage."

But he insisted, and she insisted, and of course, it ended with them spilling the water. Finist reached out hastily to steady the wildly swinging buckets, and somehow found himself holding Maria's hands instead, the two of them staring straight into each other's eyes. For a startled moment they stood like that, linked on more than the merely physical level.

And something deep within Finist said, quite calmly, *Of course. She is the one.*

But then that amazing moment had passed. Maria pulled her hands free, blushing a bit, steadying the buckets as best she could. Finist, shaken, could only watch her, speechless. And, forced to accept what he'd seen in her eyes, he could have cried aloud for frustration, because he'd seen the dawning of affection, even of something more—for Finn! All for Finn!

But how else could it be? He wasn't Finist to her. Thanks to his disguise-spell, she couldn't even know Finist existed.

Confused, overwhelmed, the prince couldn't think straight. What if he somehow got her to repeat "Finist" after him? That would break the spell and—

And probably frighten her. Her family hated and feared magic; he couldn't bear to see Maria shrinking back from him in terror—

Enough. Grimly, Finist forced his wild emotions back under control. "This time," he said shortly, "let me help. That's no work for a lady." The sight of her alarm at that dangerous word, "lady," brought his frustration blazing out of him as anger. "Yes, of course I know! How could I not know? Every word you speak betrays you, every word your father or sister—oh, yes, your sister. If ever a young woman was out of place away from servants and pampering, it's she! She has only the one servant here, and that's—"

"Stop that!" she snapped. "Do you think I enjoy this? Do you really think I like being a—a slave? *Someone* has to do the chores if we're to eat and drink and be sheltered, and who else do you see, eh?"

Abashed, he muttered, "I didn't mean—"

"And Lissa—Don't you think I've tried and tried and tried to get through to her? Dear God, how I've tried!" The buckets and yoke slipped, unheeded, to the ground. "Dear God," said Maria again, very softly. "Finn, you don't understand. You see, Vasilissa was never . . . strong, but she wasn't always like this. She was in love once; there was to have been a wedding. But then . . . things changed. Her betrothed believed what was said of us—even without proof, he believed. His family broke the betrothal, and with it, the last of my poor sister's strength. Now all she can see is doom, terror and doom, and I—I don't know what to do to—"

She stopped, biting down on her lip, and Finist, aching, almost took her in his arms. But . . . they would be Finn's arms. Instead, he echoed softly, "Things changed. Maria, what things? Is there really nothing I can do to help?"

She gave him the faintest wisp of a smile, raising a hand to nervously brush back her hair, stalling, plainly aching to confide, plainly fearing to trust. "If only there were."

"Maria." Finist hesitated, suddenly remembering the *leshy*'s talk of armored men in the forest. "Maria, I know your father has some powerful enemy. No, don't flinch. He made that fact very clear the day the thieves attacked him. But you can't believe I'm from that enemy. Oh, you can't!"

"I— No, I can't believe anyone's that good an actor."

"But you're afraid that I might betray you? I might go running off to said enemy with hopes of reward? No. I am neither as poverty-stricken as I might look nor a betrayer of hospitality."

Or of you, my heart, said a gentle voice in Finist's mind. But he resolutely shut it away.

Maria sighed. "My father," she began cautiously.

She was interrupted by a sharp voice shouting, "Maria!"

Her father came hurrying up with a hoe still in his hand. "Maria, what do you think you're doing?"

"I—"

"We need that water back at the house! Now, hurry!"

Maria bowed her head in resigned obedience. "Of course, Father."

The man waited till she was out of earshot, then turned fiercely to Finist. "And what do you think *you* were doing?"

"Why, helping your daughter with the water buckets!"

"By holding her hands and whispering to her?"

This was a situation the prince certainly had never had to face before. And for a moment he could only stammer, "What in the name of— Good God, man, I'd never harm Maria in any way, I—care for her—"

"Care for her! You! A landless, nameless—"

That was just too much for Finist's patience. "Enough!" he snapped regally. "My lands are far finer than these, my name as high as any! Now stop this nonsense and tell me what really troubles you. You're not really worried that I might be trying to dishonor your daughter. You trust Maria's common sense too much for that! You heard what I was asking her, didn't you?"

The older man's face grew very cold. "Young man, I have offered you my hospitality. Now I must demand that you leave."

Leave Maria? Leave her to poverty and near-slavery? An angry Finist caught her father's glance, his will, fiercely sending *honor* at him, and *trust*, and *honesty* . . . realizing suddenly that beneath that cold, wary wall, this man, no less than Maria, ached for the chance to confide. Of course he didn't trust Finist. How could he trust a stranger? But the prince's magical persuasions gently wore away at the wall till all at once the man shuddered and said, very softly:

"It would be good to speak openly again, so good . . ."

"Speak, then," Finist urged gently. "No harm will come of it."

"Ahh . . . You . . . Finn, you who are more than you seem, know that I too am more. I am—I was—Danilo Yaroslavovich, *boyar* at the royal court at Stargorod, advisor in the prince's Inner Council."

"So-o! Prince Svyatoslav is your enemy?"

"No, not really. It was Alexei, may Heaven curse him, young, sly, treacherous Alexei . . ."

And while Finist listened in disbelief, Danilo told of the incredibly fragile claims of treason, of the farce of a trial, of the sentence of death and the imprisonment.

"But you escaped."

"I escaped," the man echoed flatly. "My poor Lissa still has dreams of that, and wakens screaming. But," he finished bleakly, "here we are, safe at least for now."

Shaken, pitying, Finist released his psychic hold, saying softly, ''Forget this. Forget,'' and saw the man quietly return to his gardening.

Svyatoslav, mused Finist. He knew that oh-so-suspicious ruler, though they'd never actually met, not with so much forest and distance separating their two realms. But they'd corresponded, as politic princes do. Finist had always known the other prince was a wary sort. But tactful words on parchment hardly told the whole truth. Now, to realize just how unstable, mistrusting a man ruled Stargorod . . .

It was shocking, genuinely shocking, that a prince of the blood should prove so weak. Worse than weak—willing to believe an unproven tale—a lie—and condemn one of his Inner Circle to death, just like that!

Finist hadn't the slightest doubt that Danilo had been telling the truth; the man couldn't have lied to him, not while under that gentle psychic compunction.

To waste a good, honest, intelligent man—Svyatoslav, you fool!

And what of this *boyar* Alexei? Finist thought of Maria, worked like some hopeless serf; he thought of fragile-minded Vasilissa, tormented by fear; he thought of Danilo, living in shame and worry; and his fists clenched. Indeed, what of Alexei, living in his stolen glory, dooming his rival without a qualm, thinking himself safe—

Perhaps someone should open Alexei's eyes for him!

And would you feel this way if it wasn't for Maria? the prince asked himself frankly.

The answer was yes. For royal injustice is the bitterest, cruelest of all, since there's no one strong enough to correct it—save another prince.

It shouldn't take that long, now that I can travel by wing. I can meet with Svyatoslav and talk some sense into him, without being away from my own realm more than a few days longer . . .

He sought out Maria. ''I—'' No; he certainly couldn't tell her anything of the truth. ''Maria,'' the prince began again lamely, ''no matter what's already happened, no matter what else may come to pass, don't lose hope. Things will yet be well for you.''

Her smile was weary as age. "Finn, you're a kind man. I only wish I could believe you."

THAT night and the next, Finist secretly tested his magical strength till he was satisfied it had fully returned, till the renewed Power raced wildly through his veins.

He said no good-byes. On the third night, Finist stole silently away to avoid awkward questions. Alone and unobserved in the forest—unobserved by humanity at least—the prince shifted into falcon-form and launched himself into the air. Of course, flight would have been easier by day; flight was always easier when there were the sun-warmed currents of air to ride. But any flight was glory! Finist spiralled up and up on steady wings, crying out his joy, a falcon's sharp cries.

And then, catching the wind under his wings, he soared out into the night towards Stargorod, and justice to come.

XVIII

AT COURT

"I REPEAT," said Semyon wearily to the earnest faces staring at him, "Prince Finist told me, and I can only believe him, that he's well and unhurt, and will be returning to us in a few days."

There was a rumble of confused conversation from the other counselors: "But where—" "Why—" "Safe? Is he really—"

"Yes!" exploded Semyon. "The only thing wrong with him, as far as I could tell, was a touch of the sort of fever—"

"Fever!" That triggered a whole new eruption of alarm, and Semyon sighed and shouted, in his most officious voice:

"Order! *Boyars*, order! Prince Finist is not, definitely not, seriously ill! He assured me of that himself, and I, for one, have no reason to believe he was lying!"

"Yes, but are you sure he wasn't under duress?" came the anxious cry. "How do you know our prince isn't a prisoner somewhere, and—"

"He's not a prisoner!" shouted Semyon. "If he were, we'd have had some sort of ransom demand by now, wouldn't we? I saw him, I tell you, I saw him surrounded by free and open forest, and we all know our prince has nothing to fear from the forest. So enough of this hysteria. Let us take Prince Finist at his word, and get down to business so he'll have a neatly running land to which to return!"

* * *

". . . TO which to return!" The words echoed faintly in Ljuba's ears, as though they'd come from even further away than the royal palace, as she stared intently into her mirror, watching the *boyars* as fiercely as ever hawk watched prey.

Finist spoke to Semyon, not to me. He never even thought of me. The insulted little thought raced through her mind, but the young woman angrily shut it away. Of course he had sent his image to Semyon! Who else would he trust to take charge? Ljuba could only hope, with the *boyars,* that the prince really was alive and soon to return. *But what if I tried to take power now,* came the seductive little thought, *now, while he's away?* She gave a short, humorless laugh at that, only too well aware of her limitations. Oh, Ljuba supposed she might, with care and a judicious use of potions, control Semyon's will. But control the entire council? Impossible.

All she could do was watch, and wait, and—interfering forest demons or no—try to find Finist. She'd see for herself that all was well.

THE city of Stargorod was buzzing with excited curiosity. "Did you see them return?" "Did you see the terror in their eyes?" "They came out of the forest, didn't they? What did the forest do to them?"

Prince Svyatoslav was wondering the same thing. These were hardly the elegant, well-disciplined soldiers he'd sent to hunt for Danilo. And their captain! Svyatoslav had expected some fear to be in the man's eyes. After all, he'd blatantly failed to find the *boyar,* and he couldn't have forgotten his prince's threat of death. But the captain's eyes reflected more than a simple fear of execution.

"What is this?" asked the prince, straightening regally on his throne. "Why do you come before me in such a sorry state? And *where is Danilo?*"

"Dead, my Prince." The captain's voice was flat. "Almost certainly dead."

"How do you know?"

"My Prince, my investigations proved that he could only

have escaped into the forest. He wouldn't have had time to reach anywhere else.''

"Agreed!" said Svyatoslav impatiently.

"So we went after him. We went into the forest, into that—that forest . . .''

"Go on, man!''

"I never believed the old stories, I always thought them for children and fools. And I am no fool, my Prince, you know I am no fool. But when we entered that forest, it was as though we'd entered a sea, a pathless green sea.''

"Nonsense, there are roads!''

"You misunderstand, my Prince. There may be roads, but—we couldn't find them. Whenever we didn't actually watch it, the path beneath our feet would somehow . . . vanish. Whenever we'd managed to pick up another, it would simply . . . end, usually right in the middle of a swamp, or a thicket of thorns so fierce I swear only our swords let us cut our way free.''

Svyatoslav shook his head angrily. "Grown men, getting themselves lost and frightened!''

"No, it was more than that! I tell you, there were strange demons in that forest, green, capering things that mocked us, and vanished before we could attack them, things that jested at the very name of God! My Prince, the—the very trees were moving in that forest, blocking our way—oh, Heaven, if we hadn't turned to flee at last, I swear they would have crushed the life from us all!'' The captain shuddered, eyes wild with memory. "I'm sorry, my Prince. I have always been loyal to you. But now . . . Do what you will with me, but I am not going back into that forest. Condemn me to death if you must. A clean death at the hand of the executioner would be far, far better than dying in that sorcerous place.''

Svyatoslav stirred uneasily, wondering if this whole thing were some drunken fancy. But the man had never been given to drinking, and his fear did seem to be shared by his men. "What's that?'' the prince asked belatedly. "Oh, no, no, of course I'm not going to have you put to death. Go, man, get yourself something to eat and drink.''

But the prince hardly noted the relieved guard's grateful bow. *The forest has never been anything but a forest till now. Sorcery . . . Dear Heaven. Dear Heaven, what if Danilo really is alive in there? What if he's formed some sort of unholy alliance with the forest demons? And what if he's seeking . . . revenge?*

AND in Danilo's estate, Alexei waited and waited for the men he'd sent to find the *boyar* to return from the forest. But return they never did.

XIX

SPELLBOUND

FINIST CROUCHED in shadow in Stargorod, panting gape-beaked as a falcon pants, trying to catch his breath. The moon was nearly full this night, and it had glinted off his feathers most dramatically as he'd soared over the walls of the vast, sleeping city, nearly getting him speared by some overzealous guards before he'd finally managed to elude them and find a safe rooftop landing.

They really are *alert against magic, aren't they? I wonder what set them off like this.*

If it was Svyatoslav's own nervousness, he might do better not to approach the man right away. But he did have a second plan . . .

After a time, Finist recovered his breath, ruffling his feathers back into place.

Now, let me see about finding a certain treacherous young boyar.

He had a fairly good idea of the location of Danilo's estate, thanks to what the man had told him, and to the scattered bits of thoughts and words and dreams which chanced to drift by the prince when he opened his perceptions to them. He took flight in a long, silent glide, enjoying the feel of cool night winds sleek under his wings, and circled the city—wary of the guards—till he was sure of his location. Finist entered Danilo's home as falcon, and stood at last by the sleeping Alexei's bedside as man, looking thoughtfully down at the elegant, youthful face, frown-

136

ing a bit as he noted the weak mouth and the dark stains of strain under the *boyar*'s eyes.

So you haven't been exactly enjoying your new status, have you?

But this was no place to linger. Alexei's manservant was sleeping on a pallet at the *boyar*'s feet, and if that servant chanced to wake while Finist was defenseless in the middle of his magic, it would almost certainly be the end of everything.

Alexei isn't going to voluntarily confess his wrongs. Not without a bit of . . . prodding.

So Finist stood motionless at Alexei's side, gradually slowing his rate of breathing to match that of the young *boyar,* Finist's heartbeat to the *boyar*'s heartbeat . . . gradually shutting out everything about him till only Alexei remained, only Alexei . . . till the patterns of the man's thoughts lay clear before him. Alexei's surface thoughts only, of course; not even for Maria's sake was Finist going to overcome his training in magical decency and invade another's inner self. But surface thoughts were enough. And Finist saw just what he'd expected to see: a narrow, clever mind, full of pride, envy, ambition and weakness, and never a true understanding of morality. And so, gently, Finist sent a dream to him:

Danilo stood before him, boyar *Danilo, clad in spotless white. "You betrayed me!"* the dream-voice cried. *"You would have had me slain!"*

"Had to . . ." Alexei muttered in his sleep. "You stood in my way . . . Always in my way . . . Had to do something . . ."

"You would have had me slain!" the fierce voice repeated. *"You destroyed me, forced me and mine into exile, disgrace, and all for your own advancement!"*

"Had to . . ." Alexei insisted. "Had to remove you . . ."

"And are you proud of what you've done? Traitor, do you think yourself safe from me? Do you think yourself safe from justice?"

"Go away," moaned Alexei. "Go away . . ."

"Sleep no more, ambitious fool! Hear me: I shall haunt

you, night by night, I shall haunt you till you confess your crime. Traitor, sleep no more!''

Finist had pushed too hard. Alexei awoke with a wild cry, so suddenly he nearly caught the prince. But by the time the servant had managed to spring to his feet, Finist was gone, and all the two alarmed men saw were shadows; all they heard were the sounds of wings.

A good beginning, thought Finist, glancing back.

Of course, any *boyar* cold-blooded enough to let an innocent man die for his own gain wasn't going to be broken by one little foul dream. Nor had Finist expected it.

But there just might be a chance of wearing Alexei down.

There wasn't. On his second midnight visit, Finist found the *boyar's* room barred both by holy relics—which might have stopped some evil spirit, but not a mortal magician— and, more alarmingly, by armed guards.

Alexei, it seemed, was no fool.

And I don't have the time to wait him out. Bah, I should have known this wouldn't work. I'll have to try a different approach.

Oh, indeed. But the only other approach was one with which he wasn't too happy; he didn't care for the fact that Svyatoslav's fear of magic had spread all over Stargorod. Still, like it or not, he was going to have to pay that suspicious prince a visit after all.

With a sigh that sounded odd, coming from a falcon, Finist took flight once more, headed towards the many-domed royal palace, the gold paint ornamenting the roof glowing palely in the moonlight, a background against which the falcon's silvery feathers disappeared nicely.

The window of Svyatoslav's bedchamber was far too narrow for any human to enter, but a falcon could and did squirm through. Shifting silently to man, shivering in the sudden chill of being abruptly featherless, Finist glanced quickly around the dim, starkly furnished room, ready to take off again if someone spotted him. But there was no one here save Svyatoslav, not a sound save the man's soft breathing. Aside from the great, canopied bed, there was nothing in the room except the ubiquitous clothes chest, the type of thing everyone used, and a few elegant, thick-piled carpets, wonderfully warm to Finist's bare feet. No servants, of course. Anyone as suspicious as Svyatoslav was hardly about to risk having even the most loyal of servants sharing his room with him.

Naturally, there were armed guards just outside; Finist could sense their presences easily. But they were safely on the other side of that old-fashioned doorway, the sort so low they'd have to enter one at a time and bent nearly double. The prince grinned at that, and moved softly through the darkness to the head of the bed, gently pulling aside the curtain.

He was indeed no young man, this Svyatoslav, though not as old as Finist had pictured him. But the harsh lines of suspicion etched into the thin face gave the illusion of greater age, made him look drawn and cruel. For a moment Finist hesitated, uncertain.

But this was neither the time nor the place for delay. Quickly Finist moved to the clothes chest, rummaging about as silently as he could until he found a heavily embroidered cloak that fit him reasonably well. Wrapping its folds about himself for warmth and modesty, the prince drew back a nonthreatening distance from the royal bed and coughed gently till Svyatoslav began to stir.

"Prince Svyatoslav," Finist murmured, then repeated the name more emphatically, and the man sat bolt upright, staring. Before Svyatoslav could even begin his shout of alarm, Finist added hastily, "I'm quite unarmed," and let the cloak fall open to prove it.

Shock does odd things. The first thing Svyatoslav thought to say was an indignant "That's my cloak!"

"Ah, yes. Forgive me." Finist caught it about himself once more. "The room *is* rather chilly."

"But who—how—"

He shot a quick, desperate look towards the door, and Finist hurried to assure him, "No, no, your guards haven't betrayed you! I came in through the window."

"Do you think me a fool? No man could—"

"I could. As a falcon."

Dawning comprehension lit Svyatoslav's eyes. "Prince Finist!" he gasped, then gasped again, hastily signing himself, because, of course, the saying of Finist's name aloud finally broke the disguise-spell and rid him of being Finn. "The sorcerer!"

"No, not exactly. Magician, rather." The prince bowed as formally as he could under the circumstances, clutching the cloak about himself. "Yes, I am Finist, Prince of Kirtesk. But, my word and honor upon it, I'm not here to do you harm, magically or physically."

"Then why *are* you here? Why this unorthodox invasion?"

"I'm sorry. But I couldn't exactly have appeared in your audience chamber, now, could I?"

Svyatoslav had the good grace to look abashed. True enough, had Finist contrived to enter there as plain Finn, he would have been dragged off by guards before he'd had a chance to open his mouth. As Finist, he would have been risking his neck, magic or no, because alone, with no retainers, he would almost certainly have ended up either as Svyatoslav's "guest" till some royal ransom had been paid, or—more likely, judging Svyatoslav's fears—bound to a stake as a sorcerer.

"I concede the point," said Svyatoslav flatly. "But now, I repeat, why are you here?"

Finist drew a wary breath. "There's something I feel we really must discuss. It's about one Danilo Yaroslavovich."

Svyatoslav tensed at the sound of that dangerous name. But he gestured grimly for Finist to continue. And, doing credit to his royal training, he heard Finist out without once shouting for help or snatching for a weapon or holy item. But it was only too clear that he didn't believe a word Finist said.

There was a moment's chill silence when the prince had finished. And then Svyatoslav asked bluntly, "Why should you care? The man means nothing to you."

"But justice does. Prince Svyatoslav, *boyar* Danilo is still loyal to you. He always was loyal. I know it."

"Through your . . . magic?" It was delicately said.

"Ah, yes, but surely you can't let the man suffer when there's no proof he—"

"There was proof." Svyatoslav's voice was ice.

"The documents. But did he write them? Did he actually write them?"

"Of course he did!"

"I wonder . . ." Finist hesitated, trying his best to be tactful. "Prince Svyatoslav, I can understand your shock and anger at the thought of betrayal—"

"Of treason, dammit!"

"Of treason. But . . . in all the excitement, perhaps certain paths were left untrodden."

"Meaning?"

"Your royal scribes must be like mine in that they keep in their records all the court correspondence."

"Of course they do! What of it?"

"Why, surely there are other letters written by the *boyar*—"

"There are! But those treasonous documents *were* written by Danilo! I know his hand! And, yes, I did have them checked against other samples of the man's writing. There could be no mistake!"

Finist sighed. "Forgers?" he suggested gently, and saw by the man's uneasy squirm that Svyatoslav, in his rage, hadn't even considered such a possibility. "Forgers can be remarkably accurate, you know."

"Out with it, man! What are you saying?"

"Simply this: Prince Svyatoslav, I believe I can prove once and for all who actually wrote those damning documents."

"By magic."

"Yes. Harmless magic. I will swear to that on whatever holy items you require. That's right," Finist added wryly, "I really can touch such things; I don't vanish in a cloud of smoke at contact."

"Of course you don't!" said Svyatoslav so hastily Finist knew he'd been wondering just that. Reddening, the older man snapped, "Come, what are you proposing?"

"Prince Svyatoslav, what I mean to do is cast a compulsion-charm over the documents."

"And just what does that mean?"

"Simply that whoever actually penned them will—must—come to us. If that someone does turn out to be *boyar* Danilo— Well, my apologies to you for bothering you, and let justice be done. But if that someone is somebody else . . ." He let his voice trail off suggestively, and saw a flicker of interest in Svyatoslav's wary eyes. "But I can't act without your permission. Will you grant it?"

"You . . . will swear this is white magic only?"

"Magic is neither white nor black," said Finist softly. "It's a tool, a gift, no more, no less. I won't swear to a falsehood. But I *will* swear that I'm using that gift for honor, yes." When Svyatoslav still hesitated, the prince continued impatiently, "Look you, being who and what we are, we both *must* be interested in supporting the cause of justice. Will you grant me permission to act?"

"I . . ." For a moment Svyatoslav seemed to have forgotten all about Finist's presence, his eyes seeing only the past. "Danilo had ever been faithful to me," he said after a moment. "Or so I dared believe. To see him suddenly shown to be false . . . God! I wanted to kill him with my own hands!" The man stopped, controlling his passion with a visible effort. "But now . . . if there is any chance at all that I was wrong, that he might be proven innocent . . ." Passion surged up once more in Svyatoslav's eyes, but this time it was the passion of hope. "So be it!" Quickly he flung a night-robe about himself and sprang from his bed. "Prince Finist, do what you must!"

ONCE decided, Svyatoslav proved himself a man of no patience at all. Groggy courtiers were roused, yawning, from their beds, blinking in bewilderment at Finist. The royal scribes were found, the treasonous documents brought forth. Finist, hastily clothed in a caftan borrowed from the older prince, bright, tousled hair quickly combed into submission, glanced about at his curious, wondering, sleepy-eyed audience, and gave an inner sigh. He'd really rather not have to perform like some court entertainer. *But at least I've got Svyatoslav almost trusting me, for the moment. Let me not waste the chance.*

Carefully, he narrowed his perceptions to one of the documents he held in his hand, seeing that parchment, only that parchment . . . But this wasn't going to be so easy. So many people had handled it, leaving psychic traces of themselves behind to confuse things, like so many loose and trailing threads. There was the matter-of-fact grey that could only belong to one of the royal scribes, there was the wildly swirling rainbow bright with fear and rage that must surely have been left by Svyatoslav himself . . .

Yes, but there was another, very tenuous psychic thread, barely to be sensed, the same shade, almost exactly, as the ink upon the parchment. Finist smiled to himself and began, gently and very, very carefully, to reel in that fragile, floating thread . . . He'd hooked his fish, as it were, he could feel it, he could feel someone, somewhere, stirring all unaware of the spell, starting dreamily towards the royal palace . . . The thread was growing stronger as that someone approached, stronger . . .

And Finist was back in reality, taking deep, steadying lungfuls of air, wiping damp strands of hair from his face, hearing the murmurings of the courtiers all around him. Ah, and here was his catch, not *boyar* Danilo, certainly not, but a thin, sly little rat of a man, blinking in bewilderment as the last haze of the compulsion-spell faded from him. This was the forger; Finist hadn't the slightest doubt of it. This was the man who was about to prove Danilo Yaroslavovich innocent of treason beyond any question.

Yes, but if I stay here, Svyatoslav may just think I influenced the man's words in some arcane fashion!

Everyone's attention was on the forger; it was ridiculously easy for Finist to wrap himself in his magic and steal quietly away. He shifted quickly to falcon and perched, unseen and unnoted, in the rafters, watching the commotion below him.

Now the little forger was realizing where he was, and whom he faced. Confused, terrified, he stared at his prince like some mouse petrified before a snake.

"Have you ever seen these documents before?" Svyatoslav's voice was a purr.

"No, I—I haven't."

"Are you sure?"

"No! I—I mean, yes, I don't—I didn't have anything to do with them! They—they're treasonous!"

Svyatoslav tensed. "And how would you know their

contents without having read them? You wrote these documents, confess it!"

"No! I—"

"Confess it!"

The forger panicked completely. "Yes—no! I . . . yes. I . . . I wrote them." White-faced, he stood waiting for his doom to fall. But Svyatoslav wasn't finished with him.

"For whom? Come, speak! For whom did you write them?"

The miserable man hung his head. "I—I don't know. I mean, I—I never saw his face."

"Liar!" cried Svyatoslav fiercely. "Guards! Take this fool away and have him put to the question!"

That, of course, meant torture. Finist saw the forger pale, and heard him mutter to himself, "I don't owe him any loyalty." The little man straightened with a sort of desperate, almost hopeless courage. "My Prince, will you spare me if I confess?"

Svyatoslav paused only a moment, then he nodded. "I will. Speak, and you will not be harmed. Who hired you?"

The forger hesitated, licking his lips nervously. Then he burst out: "It was Alexei Sergeovich! *Boyar* Alexei ordered me to write those documents!"

SLEEPY, bewildered, frightened, the dazed young *boyar* had been virtually dragged before the royal presence. Finist looked at him thoughtfully, wondering, because Alexei already looked lost, drawn and wan, and this was even before he'd heard the charges brought against him. *So-o,* thought Finist, *I* wasn't *wasting my time in visiting you! You do, indeed, seem to have some manner of conscience, Alexei.*

"Alexei Sergeovich," Svyatoslav began, "you come before us accused of perjury and the attempt to see an innocent man slain for your profit. Do you confess your guilt?"

A man's own conscience could be a crueler tormentor than any executioner. Without the weight of his newly realized guilt, Alexei, Finist suspected, might have been smooth-tongued and cunning enough to clear himself. But now, off balance, still confused by his sudden awakening, the young *boyar* hadn't the slightest chance. Instead of framing some clever, ambiguous reply, Alexei stammered, "No, I—I didn't— Those letters—" He lunged blindly at the cringing forger. "You betrayed me! Damn you—"

"Oh, no, Alexei Sergeovich," said Svyatoslav softly, "I think this time *you* are the one to be damned." And as the young man froze, staring, stunned at the realization that he had just admitted his own guilt, the prince continued, voice trembling with rage, "I cannot punish you as I would. What you've done is not, strictly speaking, treason against the crown. But I will not have such—such foulness as you in my lands, either! Alexei Sergeovich, hear my decree:

"Within three days, you must be clear of those lands, alone and friendless. May every man's hand be turned against you! And should you be found within the boundaries of Stargorod once the three days are past, your life shall be the price!"

And so, thought Finist, refusing to feel the slightest pity, *farewell, Alexei.*

Now came the pardon for Maria's father, that the *boyar* Danilo Yaroslavovich "be restored, without penalty or fault, to all his former rights, rank and privileges."

Well and good, thought Finist, *that's settled.* But he couldn't return to Kirtesk, not yet. There was still one matter to be finished.

And so, when Svyatoslav at last returned, alone, to his royal bedchamber, he found Finist standing there, waiting. But before the younger prince could say anything reassuring, he saw, to his disgust, that Svyatoslav was tensing, going on his guard once more.

"Prince Svyatoslav, please. I'm not here to attack you, or carry you off or steal away your soul! I *am* here to tell you where to find *boyar* Danilo. Or were you planning to simply search blindly for the man?"

Svyatoslav, embarrassed, shot him an angry glance. "All right, then, where is he?"

"In the forest, where— *Now* what is it?"

The other's eyes had gone wild with alarm. "Is that it? Are you in league with the forest?"

"What?" Finist suddenly remembered the *leshy,* and

the armored men, the mysterious hunters. "They *were* your men, then," he murmured; then, seeing Svyatoslav stare, hastily added, "No, I am not in league with the forest, or those who dwell within it. But I do know something about them. And I promise you this, if your men enter the forest in peace, the forest shall not harm them. Now, let me give you proper directions . . ."

WHEN the messengers of Prince Svyatoslav rode, uneasy, into the forest, they were met by a stranger in an ugly deerskin robe, an amber-eyed stranger who bowed, polite as any wary peasant, and pointed the way to Danilo's farm. Watching those royal messengers ride away, Finist smiled.

Now they can't possibly miss the way. And his smile broadened a bit at the thought of the joy to come to Maria and her family. Soon they would be safe and honored and free.

If only he could be part of that joy . . .

Oh, nonsense. He had his own life and duties. This was nothing, the settling of a debt, that was all. Love—no, it was just gratitude.

Then why couldn't he believe himself? Confused, Finist searched till he found a small, still forest pool. Quickly the prince focused his will, fighting aside emotion; quickly he made the proper gestures, said the proper words, and watched his reflection mist and fade. The mist began to clear, obedient to his wish, and . . .

Maria was there before his eyes, Maria and Vasilissa. And he heard, faintly but clearly, Maria's patient, weary voice.

"Lissa, dear, listen to me. I was only gathering forest herbs, not communing with demons!"

"Don't jest!"

"Lissa, it's *not* evil out there! The forest is really very beautiful and—"

"And filled with pagan rites and sorcerers—ha, yes! Sorcerers like your Finn, appearing out of nowhere, disappearing into nowhere!"

"He wasn't a sorcerer, and you know it. Lissa, he saved our father's life, remember?"

"And what did he take in exchange, eh? Your virtue?"

"Is quite intact," the young woman snapped impatiently. "Finn took nothing from me but gratitude."

"But where did he go? Answer me that, Maria! If he was so very innocent, why did he disappear as though— yes, as though by magic!"

Maria winced. But she said, calmly enough, "I'm sure there's some perfectly reasonable explanation for—"

"Stop it! I don't want to hear about him anymore! He's gone now, Heaven be praised! He's gone, and you're safe, and—and— Pray, Maria! Pray you never see him again! Maria, I love you! I—I don't want to see you doomed!"

"Lissa, really—"

"No! Remember this: magic is evil, *evil*, Maria! And all who practice it are damned!"

Argue with her, Finist silently urged. *Akh, Maria, say something to defend me!*

But she said not a word. Finist sighed, and lost his hold on the image. He found himself staring bleakly down at his own reflection once more.

"You fool," he told himself softly, "oh, you fool, to give your heart at last, but to someone who can't ever return your love, someone for whom you and your magic must always be of the Darkness." Slowly he got to his feet, stretching stiff muscles. "You'll never know this, Maria, but I wish you joy and ever joy."

With that, the prince resolutely turned his back on his own hope for joy, and began the long flight home.

XX

THE FOREST

"THIS CAN'T BE HAPPENING! It can't be happening!"

The dazed Alexei had been repeating that over and over through that nightmarish midnight ride back to the estate—Danilo's estate once more.

Damn him. It was *always* Danilo.

Alexei glanced at the soldiers who'd been sent to escort him. They were all studiously bland of face, trying their best to ignore his ravings. *Damn you all, too!* thought Alexei savagely. This wasn't the end, not yet! He'd be back, he always landed on his feet, and then—oh, then, Danilo beware!

They'd reached the main house. "You, Sasha!" Alexei commanded imperiously. "See that my horse is made ready! And— Did you hear me, man? *Move!*"

"Oh, I think not." Sasha had plainly already heard the news of his banishment. Look at the man, fairly smirking at him, not moving a muscle. The insolence was more than Alexei's overwrought nerves could endure.

"How dare you!" he shrieked. "Obey me! I am your master!"

"Never that," replied Sasha coolly. "Certainly not now. Traitor."

Shaking with fury, Alexei raised a hand to strike him, but Sasha calmly stepped back, just out of reach, leaving the young man staggering to regain his balance. "Tsk," said Sasha. "You never should have betrayed Master Danilo, now, should you?"

"Curse you, I—"

"Aren't you wasting time? Don't you think you'd better be out of here and away as soon as possible? That is, of course, assuming you really want to reach the border and safety before those three little days are up."

That sent a chill through Alexei. He glanced in sudden unease at the impassive soldiers who were waiting to make sure he left, and turned away from the coolly smiling Sasha, wishing the man dead, desperately trying to plan what he'd need take with him. Clothes, of course, and gold. He would take as much of Danilo's gold as he could find.

It wasn't much. The servants, curse their treacherous souls, had simply hidden almost everything of value. And there was no time to worry about it. The dawn was almost here, and he'd have to be on the road and riding as soon as possible to clear the border before it was too late. Alexei shot another quick glance at the guards, and what he saw in their hard eyes made him shudder. *If it's not already too late! Oh God, if they* let *me clear it! I'm going to have to escape them, and survive as well.* The young man thought in sudden fierce determination, *I will survive. Come what may, I* will *survive!*

SVYATOSLAV hadn't been able to return to sleep, not with his mind racing as it was. Alone in his bedchamber, he sat and mulled over the bizarre events of the night.

Finist. The magician-prince had actually been here. But had he been telling the truth? Was that sorcerer really interested only in justice? Or had he been plotting something? Trying to find a way to use Svyatoslav? Looking for a chance to invade—no, that was impossible, there was too much wild land between Kirtesk and Stargorod. An army couldn't get through, and even a sorcerer couldn't hope to take an entire city all by himself!

But why was he so interested in Danilo? Was the *boyar* a spy? No, no, that didn't make any sense, either!

The prince sighed, confused and frustrated. Could he trust Danilo? Of course; it was madness to think otherwise. But just the same, he'd test the man. He'd set a watch on him, and at the first sign of betrayal—

Alexei had betrayed him; at least there was no doubt

about that. Alexei had made him look like some ridiculous weak-minded old man!

Svyatoslav winced. The only other who'd betrayed him so blatantly had been Rostislav, treacherous Rostislav who had nearly had his throne and his life. Overwhelmed by memory, the prince snatched up the goblet from his bedside table and hurled it across the room in anguish and rage. That time, the traitor had escaped him. And now he'd been forced by law to let Alexei go, too!

But if Alexei didn't leave his lands in time . . . Svyatoslav smiled thinly.

I've lost Rostislav. But Alexei, I will at least have your life!

HE'D tried outracing them. He'd tried simply telling them, "It's quite all right, you can tell your royal master I'm well on my way." But the cursed guards had stuck with him faithfully. Alexei glanced at the weapons hanging at their saddle bows, so well-worn, so close to hand, and winced. Would they never give up? Ahead of him now, the road twisted, skirting the wall of forest—

The forest? Alexei looked at his unwelcome escort again, more closely. The men were uneasy—and more than uneasy. The superstitious fools were actually afraid of the forest!

And aren't you? wondered a malicious little inner voice. *After all, didn't you lose men to it?*

"Nonsense!" he muttered. "These damned guards probably killed them, that's what."

All right, no time for hesitation. The road wasn't going to get much closer to the trees, and there was the hint of a path trailing into the forest.

With a wild cry, Alexei spurred his horse into the sea of trees. Behind him, he could hear startled shouts, but then, almost as though he'd plunged into a sea indeed, all noise was shut off behind him. Alexei forced his frightened mount on along the dangerous, narrow path, frantically ducking and dodging branches that seemed determined to sweep him from the saddle. There, now, there was some kind of wide-trunked tree whose branches drooped to form a perfect screen. Alexei hastily reined in his horse, pulling the reluctant animal under the shield of branches with him, hand ready to close over the horse's nose to keep it from whinnying. Heart racing, Alexei stood listening frantically to the crashes of mounted soldiers following him.

"I don't see him, sir," said one. "The forest being what it is, I think we've lost him."

The desperate Alexei prayed, *Yes, yes, you've lost me, go away!*

And to his heartfelt relief, he heard, "Bah, our orders weren't to follow him in here. Let the forest take care of him!"

They were leaving, they were actually leaving, and he was safe.

Too safe: safe from a way out of the forest.

Somewhere amid all this heavy greenness there were roads, Alexei knew, roads that would lead him to some nice, civilized city where he'd never have to see another tree. But he'd been riding for what seemed like days, and for all he knew, he'd been going in one great circle. Give the horse its head? No chance! If he did that, the fool beast would almost certainly take him right back to Danilo's estate.

The trees grew thick together on either side of the overgrown path he was following, forcing him to keep twisting in the saddle to avoid having a hip or thigh bruised against rough bark. Leaves hung heavily on the wide-spread branches, motionless in the still air, screening out the sky. Somewhere up there, Alexei knew, the sun must still be shining. Down here, it was perpetual dim green twilight. Where were the birds? Birdsong to break the stillness would have been a joy. But he guessed that whatever birds there were had been frightened away by his presence. Silence shrouded him, without even the familiar clop of hoof to relieve it; the horse was picking its delicate way over muffling layers of damp, rotting leaves. The overripe stench of them made him gag and raise a screening hand to his face. God, for a breeze!

What was that? A quick, sharp rattle of a sound—he

could have sworn he heard a laugh—*Dammit, I'm getting as bad as those dolts of soldiers!*

Was he? Something was watching him; that was no superstitious fancy. Something inhuman, something hostile, was watching him. He knew it. Something was virtually breathing down his neck, playing with him, preparing to strike—

Alexei whirled in the saddle, staring back over his shoulder, half expecting to see the trees quietly closing in behind him.

Nothing.

Of course, nothing, he told himself angrily. *Don't be a fool.*

But the blood was surging in his ears, his heart pounding so sharply he thought it must burst . . . It was the forest pursuing him, the forest itself that didn't want him here . . .

With a startled snort, Alexei's horse almost fell out of underbrush onto a road, an undeniable road, and he could have kissed the beast. He didn't know where he was, he didn't know where the road led, but surely it had to get him out of the forest!

But which was the right way? The branches even overhung the road, and in this cursed sunless gloom, he couldn't even begin to judge direction. Gnawing on his lip, Alexei picked a direction at random, forcing his horse forward. The animal didn't seem very happy about his choice, its ears flicking nervously until he could have shouted at it to be still. Save for the clop of its hoofs on dirt and the continued surging of blood in his ears, there still wasn't a sound, not even the faintest stirring of wind in leaves. The sense of being watched, of riding ever deeper into nameless peril, grew till he could have screamed.

Suddenly Alexei's nerve broke. He whirled his horse about so sharply the animal reared in protest, then kicked it into a frenzied run—

Just as something heavy came hurtling down on him out of the trees. Alexei was sent flying from the saddle, landing on his back with an impact that knocked the breath from him. Dazed, he saw men peering down at him—

dirty, ragged, perfectly human robbers—but his attention was on his horse, galloping off with an eagerness that said it wasn't going to stop till it was safe in Stargorod. Galloping off with all his possessions and his hopes of getting out of the forest!

"No!" he gasped, and again, in rising panic, *"No!"* Oh, God, the thought of being trapped here forever— "Damn you!" It was a shriek. "You've stranded me. *Damn you!"*

Blazing with mindless rage and sheer terror, in that mad instant blaming these fools for everything that had gone wrong, Alexei sprang to his feet, sword in hand, and descended on the amazed robbers like a demon out of the old tales. He was dimly aware of knives flashing out, improvised clubs being raised, but just then he didn't care what weapons these peasants bore.

"Damn you!" he repeated, and when one of them, better-armed than the rest, dared to lunge at him with long knife raised, Alexei swung his blade, two-handed, and felt a savage surge of joy at the impact of steel on flesh. His victim fell, spouting blood, nearly decapitated, and the other robbers cried out angrily. The sound penetrated Alexei's killing rage, and he looked down at his ghastly handiwork in sudden horror. He'd never had to kill anyone before; not like this, not with his own hands. God, the mess of it, the ugly, reeking mess . . . But he didn't dare be sick, as his churning stomach was insisting, because these creatures would almost certainly murder him if he showed any weakness.

Yes, but why did they all seem more shocked now than angry? Surely they'd seen violent death before. *Oh, fine,* thought Alexei in sudden realization, *that was their leader I just killed. And now they're going to kill me.*

The fading of his killing frenzy had left him fairly shaking with reaction. Alexei thought of those dirty peasant hands tearing him limb from limb, and all at once wanted nothing so much as to beg their mercy. Not that he would ever dishonor himself like that! But right now, he had to think of something clever, and fast.

And to his amazement, Alexei heard himself saying, in a cold, casual voice, "The fool is dead."

There was a muttering of anger from the robbers.

"Fool, I say!" repeated Alexei sharply. "Look at you—half-starved, ragged, filthy. Is *that* the sort of leader you admire, a man who couldn't even keep you fed, let alone show you riches?"

"What makes ye think ye're better?" came a grumble. "Ye, with yer fine city clothes and yer fine city words."

Oh, God, now what? Alexei located the one who'd spoken, and started towards the man as boldly as he could, praying his weak-limbed gait would be taken for brash swagger, letting his sword droop in his hand in what he hoped was a convincingly casual manner. Face to face with the man, trying not to breathe in the stench of him, Alexei simply stared, the unblinking stare of a *boyar* trained to cow servants. And to his great relief, he saw the robber blink and look angrily away. Alexei smiled. "That should be obvious," he said coolly.

"Ye a thief, then?" came someone's not-quite-hostile query.

"Some have called me that," Alexei answered carefully, wondering if he'd made the right answer. What if these scum felt some sort of professional jealousy? "What of it?" he added, fear sharpening his voice.

"Eh, no need to get hot about it!" They evidently thought he was about to go back into the bizarre fighting frenzy that had killed their leader. "No shame in bein' a thief."

"A good one?" someone asked, and Alexei sneered.

"Do I look a failure, now? Do I?"

"If yer so fine a thief, what ye doin' runnin' for yer life?"

Alexei managed a reasonably casual shrug. "Misfortune." He glanced at them slyly, feeling how hostility, bit by bit, was being replaced by curiosity. *They're harboring no loyalty towards their late leader,* realized Alexei. *But why should they? The man was a failure—I proved that by killing him.* The young man smiled in suddenly restored self-confidence. Did these peasant scum actually think they could get the better of him?

Alexei straightened as a sudden, fantastic idea struck him. After all, he'd need help to get out of this forest, particularly now that these fools had left him afoot and nearly penniless. Not one of these slow-witted creatures seemed eager to replace their late leader, so . . . "You see," said the young man carefully, "I did make one small mistake. I needed a band of good, skilled men behind me. I didn't have one at the time. But something tells me I just might have one now." With a coolness that wasn't quite feigned any longer, Alexei pulled a golden ring from his finger and tossed it to the robbers, a *boyar* tossing a scrap to his dogs. And the dogs scrambled for it.

"Yes," repeated Alexei softly, watching them, "I do think I have a band behind me now."

He waited a moment, but there were no arguments.

And so it goes, thought Alexei wryly. *From* boyar *to leader of a scruffy bandit troop in one short day. God, what a ridiculous change. Oh, Danilo, what I owe you for this! But I'm still alive. And,* he added savagely, *I will have my revenge! Hear me, Danilo, wherever you are: I will have my revenge!*

XXI

RESOLUTIONS

It was a mild spring day, and she'd taken her mending outside, meaning to do her sewing by sunlight. But for some time now, Maria had been sitting, simply sitting, staring moodily off into space.

Finn, akh, Finn . . . She couldn't believe the ridiculous things Lissa had been saying about him. But why had he left them so suddenly, without so much as a good-by? *Even to me?*

Maria hurried over that last, over the silly hurt; of course she'd been nothing to him, no more than his nurse, no more than he'd been anything to her! A nameless wanderer; she should be ashamed of herself for even considering—

Enough of this! There was work to be done.

And yet, why *had* he left so abruptly? And for that matter, *how* had he managed to leave so abruptly? Maria sighed, bending over her mending, determined not to think about it any longer.

Until now, the forest birds had been chirping, there'd been the normal little rustlings of creatures in the underbrush. But suddenly the forest fell into so abrupt a silence that Maria looked up again, heart pounding, listening intently.

And then she heard the invading sound of hoofbeats. Maria sprang to her feet, letting the mending fall, unheeded, to the ground.

"Father," she called, then more fiercely, "Father! Come here! Hurry!"

It was a troop of soldiers come riding up. Prince Svyatoslav had finally found them.

". . . AND I must admit you gave me quite a fright," Danilo said, smiling, to the captain of Svyatoslav's guard. The man grinned in return.

"You gave me a bit of a fright, too, *boyar* Danilo, standing there with that axe. Thought you were going to take off my head before I could give you the good news!"

"Is it true?" breathed Vasilissa. "The pardon—is it really . . . ?"

"Quite true, *boyarevna.*" The captain glanced about, plainly trying not to show his embarrassment at the poverty all around him. "The *boyar* Danilo Yaroslavovich is to return to take his rightful place as counselor to our Prince as soon as he is able."

Danilo snorted. "Which is, as I'm sure my daughters will agree, today!"

But Maria hesitated. "Please, tell me this: how did you find us?"

"Well, our Prince gave us directions. But we were pointed onto the shortest way by some peasant or other."

"A peasant?"

"A man in a crudely made deerskin caftan."

Maria exchanged a startled glance with her father. "Finn?" she asked. "But how could he have known . . . ?"

Her father waved her to silence, and got down to business with the messengers, checking the condition of his estate, of his status, pleased to hear that Alexei hadn't quite managed to deplete his finances. "It sounds as though it won't take much to make everything quite liveable again."

"No, *boyar*, I would think not. And Prince Svyatoslav does expect you back in Stargorod as soon as possible."

"Yes," said Danilo.

"No," said Vasilissa, and when everyone turned to look at her in surprise, she repeated, quite calmly, "No. Don't you see? We have already lived in enough shame. To go back now, dressed as peasants, sitting on horses behind common guards—we cannot accept that. Good Captain, we shall wait here till all is ready for us. And then we shall return to Stargorod not as beggars trying to steal into the city, but as noble folk properly clad, in a proper carriage, in proper style.''

And, while her father and sister stared at her, amazed at this longest coherent speech she'd made in some time, Vasilissa smiled at them and gave a little sigh of delicious anticipation.

LJUBA awoke with a start, looking up to find her maid, Anya, standing over her, a worried expression on her face. Ljuba frowned, puzzled, looking around. She was in her bed, with no memory of having come here!

"What is this? What's going on?"

"Ah . . . you've been asleep, Mistress."

"I gathered that! How long?"

"Well . . . you did wake, or almost wake, a few times, enough to take some water and then some soup. You don't remember?"

Ljuba shook her head impatiently. "How long? Altogether."

"Nearly five days, Mistress."

Ljuba stared up at her in sheer disbelief. But the look of stupid honesty on that bovine face just couldn't have been feigned. And Ljuba had to admit she did feel amazingly drained. But why . . . ?

And then memory returned with a rush:

How long had she been staring like this into her mirror? Ljuba had long since lost track of time. But it didn't matter, because at last she'd located Finist—in Stargorod, of all places.

And though the image was dim and uncertain, she watched while the prince paid his visits to Alexei and Prince Svyatoslav, while one *boyar* was condemned and another reprieved, she watched in complete bewilderment.

Why should Finist care what happens to a man who isn't even of his court? She couldn't, for a moment, accept that someone would go so far out of his way just to satisfy an urge for justice. *Some sense of obligation? Or is it more?*

Her head was beginning to ache fiercely now, her muscles to cramp. Ljuba knew there was a danger in spending too much time mirror-gazing, the danger that she might lose herself in visions, separate mind from body; it could happen to someone like her, someone without the strength of sufficient innate magic. But what was Finist about? It must be very important; he was too conscientious to leave his people so long for anything else.

And Ljuba persevered. She saw, through a haze of forest-magic, the faintest image cast in a small, still pool: the image of an ordinary, plainly clad, brown-haired young woman. And, just for an instant, she saw, or thought she saw, a look of despair cross Finist's face.

I don't believe it. He's become infatuated with some dirty little peasant girl!

It struck her as funny, so ridiculously funny that laughter burst out before she could stop herself. With her loss of control, the mirror-image that she'd labored so hard to achieve wavered, then slipped out of existence. Choking on her laughs, Ljuba let out a strangled oath instead, and set wearily about trying to establish the image once more. But this time there was nothing, nothing . . .

LJUBA sighed, staring up at the canopy of her bed. Five days. Five lost days of semiconsciousness. God! But magic did have its price, and that collapse was the price she'd had to pay for exhausting herself at her mirror.

But then, remembering, Ljuba tensed. "Has there been any word from the prince?"

"There has, indeed," said a sudden voice.

"Finist! Cousin, I—"

He gestured to Anya. "Leave us." As the servant hurried to obey, he turned to Ljuba, face impassive. "You shouldn't try to spy on me, cousin. It's too exhausting for you."

Ljuba didn't like that note of disinterested coolness in his voice. In almost unthinking response, she moved subtly in her bed so that the blankets molded themselves interestingly about her body, and let them slip, ever so slightly, back from one smooth, bare shoulder. "I worry about you, cousin."

"Thoughtful." He reached down and calmly pulled the blankets back into place. "But totally unnecessary. I'm quite myself again, cousin. And I do intend to stay that way. Good day to you."

With that, he was gone, and Ljuba was left staring. "My God," she said fervently, "it isn't infatuation at all! Finist is actually in love with that little peasant slut!"

But such an outrageous situation wouldn't—couldn't— last for long. And Ljuba would be ready to . . . console him.

XXII

APPEARANCES

DID YOU REALLY THINK everything would go back to normal, just like that? Maria asked herself. Already, after little more than a month, the ordeal of exile and that long, painful winter seemed more like a dream than reality, but it was going to take a long time for memories of that dream to fade. Of course everyone was wildly pretending, of course she and her sister had been invited to more social gatherings than ever before. *Gatherings at which we're the prize exhibits, like heifers on market day. Everyone's so eager to see the daughters of the reinstated boyar.*

And Lissa? Lissa was fever-bright and fever-gay. Maria doubted her sister realized the reason for their sudden popularity, which was almost certainly due to the novelty of seeing someone actually returned to royal favor, a novelty spiced with an intriguing touch of danger—after all, one never knew when they might be banished again, or worse— but the young woman did seem to be holding up fairly well. At least she was keeping up a convincing facade. And if she wasn't quite as rational as Maria had hoped, if her spirits did seem too relentlessly high, presaging a fall into depression once more, at least she was far better than she'd been in the forest. For Lissa, for the moment, the nightmares were fading. And she'd surprised Maria by summoning enough inner strength to face down Afron when that shallow young man, prodded by his father, had begged for her forgiveness and asked that their betrothal be renewed.

Of course: suddenly it was a politely advantageous match once more. Maria gave a thin, humorless smile. Bless Lissa! The Lord knew *she* had wanted to spit in Afron's face, but all Vasilissa had done was refuse him, quite politely and calmly. That she'd then gone home to a storm of weeping was very understandable.

As for Danilo . . . Maria sighed. Things weren't quite so simple for her father. Try as he would, he couldn't quite hide the shadow of mistrust and tension still within him. And she couldn't fault him for that, because she felt much the same unease herself. A prince so easily swayed just might change his mind again, and then—

No, she wouldn't even consider that! But faced with the falseness, the artificiality, of everyone at court, there were times when she could almost wish they'd never returned to Stargorod.

Maria glanced down at hands still red and work-roughened, and gave a dry little laugh. Not that she wanted to spend the rest of her life farming, and growing old before her time from overwork, either! It was just . . .

Finn?

Oh, what nonsense! Who knew but that the man, given the chance, might not have proven just as false as Afron?

But right now . . . Maria sighed, leaning moodily on her bedroom window's sill, blindly looking out over her father's estate. And for once she was quite unable to mock herself, for once unable to stop herself from wishing for what she knew she could never have, dreaming of what could never be.

NOBLE self-sacrifice might, Finist mused, be all well and good in its proper place, but it certainly wasn't helping him function as head of state. For all that he was back in his own land, back in his royal palace, the prince found his mind still wandering to the forest, found himself brooding and pining for Maria, and snapping at courtiers till he was disgusted with himself. And in the middle of reading some document, it dawned on Finist that he hadn't the vaguest memory of what he'd just read, and he threw down the parchment with a cry of:

"This is ridiculous!"

Semyon's startled eyes met his, so full of sheer astonishment that the prince had to laugh in spite of himself. "No, Semyon, I didn't mean this report. It's only—I just realized what a fool I'm being!"

They were alone in the small chamber. Semyon moved to Finist's side and asked softly, "Who is she, my Prince?"

"What do you mean?"

"Oh, come now! I may be older than you, my Prince, but I'm hardly old enough to have forgotten what love is like!"

Finist glanced sharply at him, ready to explode at the first sign of condescension, but saw on Semyon's face only a warm and genuine concern that made the young man redden. "No," he muttered, "of course not. It's only . . . she can never be mine."

"Is she . . . married, my Prince?"

"No."

"A woman of some holy order?"

"No!"

"Ah." Semyon considered for a moment. "My Prince, if the problem is that she's not of sufficient rank, remember that you do have the power to ennoble anyone who—"

"No, no, it's nothing like that. Semyon, I— Never mind."

"My Prince," said the old *boyar* bluntly, "any other young man might be permitted the luxury of feeling sorry for himself. You don't have that option. You're not doing yourself or your land any good like this." He paused under the weight of Finist's insulted glare, but continued firmly, "If you won't talk about her, won't you at least grant me a glimpse of your forbidden lady?"

Finist hesitated a moment, wondering uneasily if the older man was, somehow, subtly mocking him. But the thought of seeing Maria again, even if only by magic . . . "Very well. Watch."

They stood before a mirror, and Finist began the proper spells. And soon enough the mist had cleared, and . . .

. . . Maria was there before their eyes, Maria and Vasilissa together, no longer in that shabby farmhouse, but in some elegant, well-appointed room. *Ah,* thought Finist in satisfaction, *they* did *return safely to Stargorod!* Vasilissa looked a bit . . . saner, though there was still a touch of wildness to her lovely eyes. And Maria . . . Maria . . .

But he wasn't going to spy on them. Quickly Finist let the image fade, and turned rather defiantly to Semyon. He caught the old *boyar* staring at him in some alarm, and after a startled moment, puzzled out the cause, and gave a wry little laugh.

"No, Semyon! I haven't been pining over that—ah—rather wild-eyed young woman. That's Vasilissa Danilovna, and . . . Maria."

"She's the one," murmured Semyon. "Maria."

Reddening, Finist nodded. "She is Maria Danilovna, Vasilissa's younger sister, and the two of them are daughters to a *boyar* of the Inner Circle of Svyatoslav of Stargorod."

"So!" Semyon was plainly relieved to learn that she wasn't a peasant. "But, my Prince, I'm afraid I still don't see your problem."

"Akh, Semyon . . . They hate magic, the whole family, hate it and fear it as they fear the very Devil himself. How can I possibly—"

"Excuse me, but does this young woman know you for what you are? When you were taking shelter with her family—those are the folk you mentioned, yes?—when you were with them, weren't you disguised?"

"As Finn," agreed Finist with some distaste.

"So she doesn't know who or what you truly are?"

"No. Why?"

"And you really plan to leave things like that?"

"What else can I do?"

"You're afraid, aren't you?"

Finist straightened. "You forget yourself."

"Perhaps. But you *are* afraid. Afraid that if she sees you as Finist, and rejects you, it will be over for you. But . . . my Prince, is this sort of mooning about really better?"

"I— No— But—" Finist stopped short. *Dammit all, the man's right! I went running off like some idiot of a boy afraid even to speak to his sweetheart in case she might say she didn't love him! How do I know Maria shares her family's views on magic, when I never once had the nerve to ask her?* The prince hesitated, eyeing his counselor warily. "I don't suppose I really have to order you not to let this conversation go beyond this room?"

"Oh, my Prince, of course not!"

"I . . . Semyon, you're right. I *have* been a fool!"

"No," the old man said gently. "Just young."

"Ah. Well. At any rate, I must go back there, Semyon."

The *boyar* nodded complacently.

"Maria must learn the truth. One way or another, things will be settled between us!"

XXIII

THE FEATHER

"BUT DO YOU REALLY HAVE TO LEAVE?" wailed Vasilissa.

Danilo smiled reassuringly. "My dear, Kotina's just a short ride away. If I leave tomorrow, I should be back in less than two days."

"But why do *you* have to go, you yourself?"

"Don't you see?" said Maria. "By sending Father off to discuss business with the *boyars* of a vassal town, the prince is showing Father how much he trusts him. Lissa, it's as good as an out-and-out royal apology!"

Maria added wryly to herself, *For whatever that's worth!* But Vasilissa was still nervous, so Maria smiled reassuringly at her sister, and hid her own skepticism as best she could.

THANKS to a favorable wind, Finist reached Stargorod in less than two days, circling Danilo's estate by nightfall. When he was sure the household was lost in sleep, the prince, who'd been nervously preening his feathers, trying to plan, stretched his wings and searched for Maria's bedchamber. Here it was, a small, lovely thing, all soft carpets and floral wall paintings. Maria was alone in it, and sound asleep. Finist huddled on the sill like some timid sparrow, the sight of that sweet face relaxed in slumber almost more than he could bear. He dared go no closer lest he forget all sense, alter shape, and recklessly sweep her into his arms.

166

Damn! I'm acting like a little boy mooning over his first sweetheart!

He'd brought a regal caftan with him, elegant brocade, almost more weight than his falcon-shape could comfortably bear. And Finist hesitated, toying with the idea of appearing before Maria in sudden, princely splendor—

And she, not remarkably, screams at the sight of a stranger in her bedroom, and you have to scramble out the window like some idiot of a thief. Very clever.

Now what? He briefly considered waiting till day and boldly appearing before the family as himself, and only gradually introducing the tricky subject of magic. But that would take weeks, and he didn't dare be away from Kírtesk and his throne *that* long.

Reckless, romantic, Finist decided to introduce himself and his magic together directly to Maria. And so he sent a dream to her. Admittedly, it wasn't the most coherent of dreams; just then, it wasn't easy for him to coolly focus his will. But he sent an image of himself, and a message . . .

Maria smiled in her sleep and reached out an arm as though to Finist, and that almost finished his resolve. The prince felt his shape beginning to shift of its own accord, and firmly fixed it back into falcon-form, though he wasn't so sure he could hold it. The prince hastily flew out that window as desperately as though he was being pursued. Which in a way he was.

But did she get my message? And will she heed it?

He'd have to wait till morning to find out.

DANILO sat his horse well, looking brave and noble in his splendid riding clothes, he and his escort all bright colors and rich fabrics in the clear morning sunlight.

"A fine day for a ride to Kotina," said Maria cheerfully. "Enjoy it!"

"Thank you, child. Eh, don't fret, Lissa. I'll be back in a day, I promise." He leaned forward in the saddle. "Come now, the two of you, tell me what presents you'd like from Kotina."

Vasilissa smiled faintly. "Slippers," she said in a

dreamy voice. "Golden dancing slippers, just like the ones I used to have. Before Alexei destroyed them."

Hastily, Danilo cut in, "Of course, dear, and maybe a ruby brooch, too, to wear at your pretty neck. You'd like that, yes? Now, what about you, Maria?"

"Oh, Father! Just bring yourself back safely!"

"I plan to do just that!" he said with a laugh. "Come, pick something pretty for yourself, girl!"

But Maria hesitated, remembering . . . Feeling a little smile forming almost of its own accord, she murmured sheepishly, "This is silly, I know it, but I had a dream . . . Father, bring me one thing only: the feather of Finist the falcon."

"A feather?" echoed Vasilissa. "Maria, that's the most ridiculous thing I've ever heard!"

"I *said* it was silly! And I can't explain it, Father, but that really is what I want—that, and the three of us back together here."

"And both you shall have, child." But Danilo muttered, so softly that Maria almost didn't hear him, "A falcon feather. Heaven help us, what next?"

DANILO never suspected he was shadowed by a falcon. He never suspected that the falcon was waiting patiently while he completed the brief, friendly, routine meetings with the *boyars* of Kotina. Business completed by midday, the man set off for the town's small rich market square. Kotina was noted for the mineral wealth in the nearby hills, and in only a short time, Danilo had purchased the promised ruby brooch and dancing slippers.

"But . . . a feather of Finist the falcon?" he muttered.

The bird-seller, a weatherbeaten man whose leathery skin was crossed and crisscrossed with faint white scars— mementos from countless beaks and talons—stared at him blankly. "M'lord, I got all sorts a' birds here. Got pretty little singin' birds for the ladies, hawks for the gentles, even got an eagle. None of 'em got names, though." His eyes were wary. "And ye said ye didn't want a whole bird, that it?"

Danilo sighed. "I want," he said, very carefully, "the

feather of Finist the falcon. No more, no less. Can you help me?''

"Sorry, m'lord. Yer pardon, but I don't know what yer talkin' about.''

"Never mind, man. Good day.''

Danilo walked on, trying to ignore the curious stare following him, thinking dryly, *He doesn't know what I'm talking about, eh? I don't know what I'm talking about!*

By now he'd spoken to every dealer of birds in all of Kotina, and managed only to convince them all that the *boyar* must be quite out of his mind.

"Maria,'' Danilo murmured aloud, "I hate to disappoint you, but I think this 'Finist' of yours is nothing more than a fantasy!''

"Is it?'' asked a harsh, crackling voice. "Is it indeed?''

The *boyar* whirled. Before him stood a bent, mysterious figure hidden completely in a hooded cloak that looked as though it had been hastily cobbled from every scrap of cloth in Kotina. "You know of Finist the falcon?'' Danilo asked warily, trying in vain to catch a glimpse of the face hidden beneath that bizarre hood.

"Oh, I do, I do indeed! And here is his feather!''

Danilo gasped. The strange figure held out what had looked like a common bird's feather—until it caught the sunlight. Then—how it gleamed, shining bright silver, splendid as something from the forge of a master metalsmith. Stunned, the *boyar* let the gorgeous thing be put into his hand, hearing the figure give an odd, anxious little laugh.

"It is to be a present for your daughter—yes, I overheard you—a present for your daughter, Maria. Come, take it to her, the feather of Finist the falcon.''

"But the price—''

"No price! Take it home to your daughter as a gift from me!''

Danilo, bewildered, glanced down at the shining feather in his hand. But the sun had gone behind a cloud, and all the magical glow was gone. The *boyar* glanced quickly up again, with a cry of "Wait! Who are you?''

The stranger was already gone, vanished into the market crowd as though into thin air.

* * *

HE had agonized long and hard over giving his daughter something that seemed so blatantly magical. But, Danilo decided reluctantly, he *had* promised her the feather of Finist the falcon. And the look on Maria's face, that compound of open amazement and sheer, delighted wonder, was almost worth all his doubts.

Vasilissa, cradling her father's presents in her arms, stared dubiously at Maria's prize. Now in shadow, it really did look like the drabbest of feathers. "Is that . . . thing what you really wanted, Maria?"

"Yes." Maria didn't know why she'd said that; yet it was true. "Yes," the bemused young woman repeated, looking down at the feather. "Somehow I really think it is."

MARIA sent her well-meaning but fussy servants away, and sat, alone, on the edge of her bed, still completely dressed for all that the hour was late, turning the silvery feather over and over in her hand, watching it glitter in the candlelight, shivering a little at this overlapping of dream and reality.

That dream . . . Maria couldn't remember all of it, only that there had been a mysterious young man in it, vaguely seen, yet strikingly handsome. In that odd, unquestioning way of the dreamer, she hadn't wondered about the fact that something her sleeping self had known to be magic had been shimmering about him most alarmingly. And yet she hadn't been alarmed.

Maria frowned, trying to remember details. His hair had been of a strange hue, so fair as to be nearly true silver, just the shade of this remarkable feather. And he'd said something to her . . . about seeking the feather of Finist the falcon.

Whomever or whatever *that* might be.

But his voice . . . There'd been something so oddly familiar about it, so teasingly familiar . . .

"Finn!" said Maria.

The dream-figure's voice had been Finn's. Maria reddened to think how handsome she'd dreamed him. And magical, too. But was it really only her imagination? It had all seemed so real, and— Oh, nonsense, dreams were nothing more than fantasies!

Were they? Then how explain the reality of this shining feather? And how explain her certainty that she was suddenly on the edge of wonder?

POISED just outside Maria's window in the warm spring night, Finist waited with ever-mounting tension. *Call it!* he urged her silently. *Oh, Maria, call my name!*

THERE had been more to the dream, Maria remembered. Once she actually held the feather, she was supposed to call the name of the falcon. Bemused, the young woman turned the glinting feather over in her hand. "Finist?" she said tentatively. "Finist the falcon, I, uh, summon you."

The unlatched shutters slammed open. A wild wind swirled through the room, pulling at her clothes and hair, tearing the feather from her hand. Maria bit back a scream as a falcon, a silvery falcon clutching a golden cloth in its talons, dove smoothly into the chamber. Once it circled the room, twice, three times, then came to a landing before the window. As Maria stared in disbelief and wonder, the gleaming form seemed to grow, to alter, though a sudden swirling of silver mist kept her from seeing what . . .

Then the mist was gone, and the falcon with it. The shining-haired stranger of her dream stood before her, dressed in a most splendid caftan of gold-worked silk.

For a moment, they regarded each other in silence. Then Maria recovered her senses enough to gasp, "Who are you?"

The stranger swept down in a deep, courtly bow. "Why, Finist the falcon, of course," he told her, and smiled.

XXIV

SURPRISES

YOU FOOL!

Alone in her chambers, the servants having fled her rage, Ljuba paced restlessly, berating herself for want of any other victim. She had let Finist go his own way, she had been so sure that if she simply left him alone, he'd quickly tire of peasant squalor and stupidity— But he *hadn't* tired. For all that she had surprised many a look of honest lust for her in his eyes, for all her attempts to build up an image of a chastised, dutiful, loving young woman, he'd spurned her. He'd gone his own way, all right, right out of the palace, without so much as a word to her!

Finist had returned to his little peasant slut, and as though that wasn't enough, he'd left Semyon to hold the throne for him: Dull Semyon. Honest Semyon. Semyon, who, with his smiles and politeness and sheer, deliberate, calculated stubbornness, was going to drive her mad.

And did Finist really think he would get away with his amorous intrigues? Did he really think she would let him insult her like this?

Ljuba glanced quickly about to be sure no servants lingered, then cast off the protective drape from a precious mirror. For a moment she hesitated, struck by the memory of how her last magical spying had exhausted her. But then she caught herself staring fearfully at her reflection like some simpering little idiot terrified of consequences. Well, damn those consequences!

* * *

IT had been a long, wearisome search. Ljuba had to struggle just to focus at all on forest that resented her intrusion. And she couldn't help but remember that wild-eyed, mocking forest demon. She'd been lucky to locate Finist the last time without rousing demonic wrath. But what if he—it—sensed what she was trying to do, and attacked her? She knew how to deal with psychic assaults from other humans, yes, but if the attack came from the forest itself, the Old Magic that was so terrifyingly uncontrollable . . .

Enough of this nonsense. She was losing her hold on the mirror's image. And all the stupid agonizing had been for nothing, because now she realized that Finist wasn't in the forest at all.

Wonderful. Just wonderful. Then where in the name of God was he?

Delicately, Ljuba widened the scope of her search. She saw the hint of a city . . . Stargorod! Bewildered, Ljuba hunted for the essence that was Finist—carefully, lest he detect her prying. Yes, there he was, and with someone . . .

With a little hiss of fury, Ljuba recognized the peasant wench. That plain, nameless little slut—

But Ljuba stopped, noticing the woman's clothing for the first time. Rich, silken brocade . . . And her surroundings were never that of a peasant's hut, not with those elegant furnishings . . .

"No!" moaned Ljuba. "Damn her!"

This was no peasant, no common little light-of-love to be used and discarded. This was a noblewoman, a *boyar's* child, no doubt of it! That made her a genuine rival. And Finist—

"Oh, no, Finist! You won't get away with this!" Ljuba said viciously.

"I think that he will, lady."

The quiet, unexpected voice made Ljuba whirl in surprise.

"Semyon! How dare you enter without—"

"My apologies, lady. Royal orders. And the door *was* unbarred." The old *boyar* gave her the most courtly of bows. "My Prince left me this command, lady. If you were found to be using your mirrors to—ah—observe him about his business, all reflective surfaces were to be removed from your presence. My Prince and his father both trained me to be sensitive to the *feel* of anyone attempting such scryings, and so . . ."

Enraged to speechlessness, Ljuba could only gasp, *"You dare!"*

"Those *are* the prince's orders."

"I—I'll—" Ljuba floundered helplessly for words as embarrassed servants searched her quarters, removing mirrors, silver perfume flasks, anything which might hold a reflection. "Stop! Don't— You can't— Oh, curse you, leave me alone!" But she didn't dare offer any real resistance, because resistance to a royal command was as good as treason, and she didn't dare cast any sort of suspicion on herself, not now.

"One thing more, lady," Semyon said softly. "This too is the prince's command: you are to be confined here within your palace, within these private quarters, until Prince Finist returns."

The look of grim satisfaction on the *boyar*'s face was just too much for Ljuba. Suddenly unable to hide her hatred, she stared into Semyon's eyes and hissed, "If I ruled Kirtesk, *old man*, you'd be wise to flee for your life!"

He didn't so much as flinch. "Then it's fortunate for us both that you do not, lady. I make a very poor runner. Good day to you."

XXV

REVELATIONS

FOR A MOMENT, Maria could only stare at her elegant visitor and try frantically to muster her bewildered thoughts. It wasn't helping that he was fair, so very fair, with those fine, high cheekbones and shining hair . . . She supposed that the proper thing to do would be to scream for help. But this was hardly some common intruder. He had been a falcon just a moment ago . . .

Well now, Maria admitted to herself, *I'm certainly not going to call for help until I find out who he really is, and why he's come.*

"Finist the falcon," she echoed, rather amazed at how calm she sounded. "That doesn't tell me very much. Who is Finist the falcon?"

"No one to harm you." His amber eyes—hawk eyes, thought Maria—were very bright. "Ever." He hesitated a moment, then said simply, "Lady, I am Finist, Prince of Kirtesk."

Kirtesk . . . "Oh. Oh! The magician-prince!" To her astonishment, she felt herself grinning. "Oh, my. You'd better not let my father know you're here. He—ah—doesn't care for magicians."

He grinned in return. "I know. That's precisely why I didn't appear to him."

There was something about his voice, something so teasingly familiar . . . But that was impossible! "And why *have* you appeared?" Maria asked, adding belatedly, "Your Highness—"

"No, please, that's not necessary!"

But now she'd placed that voice. "Finn. . . ?" she whispered.

"You know me?" That came out as such a yelp of astonishment that Maria had to bite back a laugh.

"Then you *are* Finn! But why this disguise?"

"Ah, no, what you see now is my true self."

"Then why . . . ?"

"Was I hiding all that time as lowly Finn?" He sighed. "Because, thanks to my own foolishness, I got caught aloft, in falcon-form, by a storm that finally dumped me close to where your father found me."

Maria nodded. "And it wouldn't have been wise for a prince alone in a foreign realm to advertise his presence."

"I bow to your wisdom."

"But what I don't understand . . ." Maria stopped, horrified to feel tears welling up in her eyes, then determinedly started again, "What I don't understand is why you slipped away from us like—like some criminal, without so much as a farewell."

"Oh, Maria!" Finist breathed. "I never meant to hurt you, believe me! It's only that I had to be elsewhere, swiftly. And knowing your father's views on magic, I didn't want to frighten you by taking falcon-form in front of you." He took a wary step forward. "Am I forgiven?"

"It's not for me to forgive a prince."

"Please, don't . . ." He stopped, studying her with a birdlike tilt of the head. And Maria, bewildered, saw a hint of joy lighten the fine-boned face. "Ahh," the prince said, very softly, "but this is something more than mere insulted pride, isn't it?"

Maria felt a little shiver run through her at the brightness of that amber gaze. Despite herself, she found herself remembering becoming so sharply aware of Finn as male, as desirable . . . He was still desirable, more so in this new, exotic guise . . .

And this was a dangerous train of thought! Alarmed at herself, Maria said, a bit too sharply, "I don't know what you mean."

"Don't you?" There was the faintest, most alluring hint of wildness hidden in that urbane voice. "Maria . . ."

Hastily she took a step back. "That dream was your doing, wasn't it? The one about seeking out the feather—your feather! Yes? But, why?"

To her amazement, he reddened. "I was afraid."

"Afraid!"

"Oh, yes. I couldn't think of any more direct way to introduce myself, as myself, as a magician. I thought you might share your father's views."

"About magic." Maria thought of the forest, and the *leshy,* and smiled faintly in spite of herself. "No. He'd probably have me in a convent for saying this, but no, I don't fear it. But that doesn't explain what you're doing here! Unless . . . There were rumors at court about you, and— It *was* you, wasn't it? Speaking to Prince Svyatoslav, I mean, clearing Father's name—it was you."

"Yes. Oh no, Maria, don't."

She'd swept down to the floor in a deep curtsey. "Prince Finist, I offer the deepest gratitude of my father and myself."

"Please, Maria." He knelt beside her. "I couldn't *not* have done it, for the sake of justice. And . . . for your sake. But I didn't come here to hear words of thanks."

Before she could rise, he captured her hands in his. Confused, overwhelmed by his nearness, Maria looked up into the bright amber eyes, wondering, seeing something of the same wonder she felt mirrored in their depths.

"Then . . . you can care for me . . ." Finist breathed after a time. "You can, you *do!*"

Maria panicked. Struggling to free her hands, she gasped, "No, I . . . Finist, please, this—this is improper. If my father should—"

"Come, admit it!"

"Please! Finn—akh, I mean Finist— You've got me so confused I don't know *what* I mean! Let me up."

"Not till you confess it. Maria, you *do* care for me! Admit it!"

She stared into the falcon-fierce eyes, so unlike those of Finn in their alien color, so familiar in their warmth. And all at once that warmth was racing through and through her, till all she could do was cry out, "Yes, I do! Finn, Finist, I always did!"

She felt his arms close about her, marvelling at their strength and gentleness; she felt his lips brush her cheek, her neck, tender, demanding, felt the warmth within her blazing up into a new, wonderful, terrifying fire, in that moment caring nothing for silly rank, propriety . . .

Then Finist was drawing away, so sharply it made her gasp in surprise. With one fluid leap, he was on his feet again, the falcon-wildness fading from his eyes as he used what was plainly a magician's trained will to get himself back under control. Maria, struggling to catch her breath, told herself she should appreciate that self-control, showing concern for her honor as it did. But deep within her, a wicked little voice was ruing it just a bit . . .

Embarrassed, Maria blurted out, "I'm sorry," exactly at the same time as Finist. As one, they continued, "I didn't mean to—" and broke off in astonished laughter.

"Oh, enough of this!" gasped Finist. "Come, my dear." He chivalrously offered Maria his hand, pulling her lightly to her feet. Dazed, bewildered, rejoicing, she felt a surge of sheer joy bubbling up inside her until she had to giggle like a little girl and say:

"It's going to take some adjustment of thinking to get used to you like this."

He drew back, staring at her in genuine dismay. "You preferred me as *Finn?*"

"Now, did I say that?" teased Maria. Dizzy with her new joy, she pretended to study the prince as he'd studied her, trying to match the personality of Finn with the exotic handsomeness of Finist. "It really *is* going to take some adjustment." There now, she could feel the giggles stealing out again. "But I do think I'll manage it!"

Handsome, oh yes. The sudden harsh thought cut into her giddiness, chilling as a wave of icy water. *He's handsome as something out of the old tales. But you . . . Oh, fool!*

"Maria, what is it? What's wrong?"

"How can you, *you,* care about me? I mean, I have a mirror, I know I'm no raving beauty, I'm not even—I—"

"Akh, Maria, dear one, don't be foolish!"

"But—"

"Hush."

And the warmth of his lips against hers quite silenced her.

XXVI

GAMES

"AIN'T RIGHT. Ain't right at all."

Alexei, late of Stargorod's nobility, now as torn and filthy as any other bandit, glared at the man who'd spoken. *"Now* what's wrong?"

"Ain't right, cuttin' down a good, healthy tree like this. *They* won't like it."

"What superstitious rubbish are you—" Alexei glanced around at the others, and swore under his breath to see them, all these ruthless, murderous men, afraid of—fairy tales. *"They* let you live here, don't *They?"* he said with heavy sarcasm.

"Sure, because They don't care what we do to people, They don't care about people, only the forest! But They—"

"All right, spare me the lecture! Just cut down the damned tree, and on my head be the guilt!"

More than impatience lay behind Alexei's outburst. In the days he had been trying to lead this ridiculous excuse for an outlaw band, their fear or mistrust or sheer, stupid stubbornness had effectively checked every move he'd attempted to make. He had tried and tried to convince them that this skulking about in the underbrush wasn't the way to fortune, that if they only showed him the way out of here, the road to some city—other than Stargorod, of course—he would have them wealthy in no time. But the damned fools were afraid! They had skulked out here for so long, preying on the occasional farmer, that the thought

of possibly coming up against a city's trained guards made
them whimper like puppies.

If only I could forget the whole thing, Alexei fumed.
These oafs were stupid and boring and at the same time
so unpredictably quick to take offence, dangerous as so
many mindless bulls. And they stank. Akh, so did he by
now, for that matter! The thought of a hot bath, clean
clothes . . . *If only I could get away from them. I'd be
better off trying to find my own way out of here!*

He could simply up and abandon them—and wouldn't
they take kindly to that? These would-be bandits might be
idiots, but they would have no scruples at all about slaugh-
tering anyone they thought a traitor. And there was never
a time when he was alone, never a time when he could
simply slip away and forget they existed—

That wasn't the whole of it. Granted, he'd only been
their leader for a short time, but already they were getting
restless, waiting for him to prove himself, to lead them to
the treasure he'd promised, and even his most logical arguments about treasure being found only in cities didn't
move them. If he didn't produce, and soon . . . Alexei
glanced about at the rough, hard-eyed lot of them, and
fought back a shudder.

"All right," he said once more. "We all know there's
a merchant's party that's going to be riding through this
part of the forest, yes? Merchants carry gold. Agreed?"

"Yeah, but he's got soldiers with him, lots of 'em!"

Alexei bit back an impatient oath. "We've been through
this before! Cut down that tree, block their path, attack
them from the shelter of the underbrush—they'll be down
before they can figure out who's attacking them!"

Yes, added Alexei to himself, *and if it doesn't work, if
those soldiers manage instead to massacre my gallant
band, why then, I become not the bandit chieftain, but a
bandits' captive, as noble and refined as can be, and oh-
so-grateful for the rescue— If only I can get these idiots
to cut down the damned tree!*

Desperate, raging, he snatched an axe from one gape-
mouthed fool and started hacking away at it himself, with
more vigor than skill. The others stood, staring, presumably waiting for some forest ogre to rend him limb from

limb. But when nothing happened other than Alexei showering them all with flying chips of wood, someone took the axe from him and began silently, and more efficiently, to finish the job.

THE falcon, its wings bright in the sunlight, flew, radiant with delight, now and again making sweeping loops in the sky for sheer joy.

She loves me, she loves me, she loves me!

But after a time, reality intruded into his euphoria, and Finist sighed, and circled over forest till he'd found a clearing that held a small, clear pool within it, then swooped down for a landing. "Forest, forgive the intrusion once more," he remembered to say, both aloud and with psychic emphasis. "I shan't be here very long."

It was probably just as well. Head up, listening to elusive sounds that were just beyond anything physical, Finist frowned, warily letting feathers begin to re-form. The forest was angry at someone, no mistaking that restless stirring, dangerously angry . . .

But after a moment he nodded, relieved. Although the forest had become instantly aware of his magical presence, that strange, inhuman anger wasn't directed at him, so for now, at least, he could ignore it. The little lake was so clear he could see its pebbly bottom, so still it was as fine as any man-crafted mirror, and Finist set about his work.

"Semyon. Can you hear me?"

The old *boyar*, his image clear on the surface of the pool, started. "My Prince! How—ah—how goes it?"

"Oh, well, Semyon! Well indeed!"

"Really!" Semyon beamed. "Is it all settled, then? And so quickly! Will you and she be returning together, or—"

"Hey now, not so fast!" Finist had to laugh. "She's just barely admitted that she—that there's some hope for the two of us!"

"I see." The *boyar*'s eyes twinkled. "Ah, to be young again!" he murmured. "But, my Prince, how are you surviving in Stargorod?"

Finist grinned. "Well enough. Most of the time I'm falcon. Otherwise . . . I—ah—liberated clothing and funding from Svyatoslav. Leaving a properly apologetic note behind, of course. I must remember to send him a regal letter of thanks, prince to prince, when I return to Kirtesk. Which reminds me: Are things peaceful at home?"

The *boyar* understood instantly. "Quite peaceful. No one suspects you're undertaking anything but a—political mission." His smile widened. "Have no qualms about continuing your courtship."

Finist hesitated. "What about my cousin?" he asked warily.

Semyon's smile faded. "She . . . did try—I mean, your royal cousin did attempt to—to—"

"To spy on me," Finist said coldly. "Did you obey my commands?"

"To the letter, my Prince. I fear the Lady Ljuba hates us all most heartily, but there she is, mirrorless, in her quarters, and there, till you countermand your orders, she will stay."

Will she? "Semyon, I will check back with you at the next turning of the day. Keep me informed—about everything. Till then, farewell."

He let the image fade and sat back, staring blankly, suddenly uneasy. "Cousin, *now* what game are you playing?" This incredible persistence wasn't like her. Could she be jealous? It stretched his imagination almost to the breaking point to picture cool, controlled Ljuba in thrall to any such mundane emotion. And yet, a plaintive cry echoed faintly through his memory, Ljuba's desperate: *"I love you!"*

Finist shook his head. "Aie, cousin, what am I to do about you?"

"What is that to me?" asked a harsh voice, and the prince let out a startled yelp.

"Ah, my lord *leshy.*"

"Magician-man. Why have you returned? For your men?"

The mutable being was, for the moment, nearly as tall as Finist, lean as any predator, face sharp and narrow and green as grass, eyes flickering with an eerie light that in human eyes might have indicated the onset of madness. In a *leshy*—who knew?

Finist had no intention of staying to debate the subject.

"Your pardon. I did not mean to intrude. In fact, I'm just about to leave, and—'' He stopped short. "My men? *Leshy*, I assure you, I have no men here.''

The alien eyes burned into his, dizzying Finist with tantalizing hints of ancient magics. But then the *leshy* turned away. "Mm. You tell the truth. So be it. Farewell, magician-man.''

And with that, the being was gone, leaving a very bewildered Finist behind. *Go*, said the forest softly, wordlessly, and *By all means!* agreed the prince, and gladly took wing. Whatever had angered the *leshy*, it was surely none of his affair.

"FINE,'' said Alexei, wiping his brow. "That's done it. Eh, careful. Don't let it fall, not yet. Balance it . . . That's right.'' He pointed to one of the—he hoped—more intelligent of his men. "You, stand watch! As soon as you hear the merchant's party approaching, give the signal—Yes, fool! The usual bird-call!''

"Uh—then what?''

Alexei sighed. "What do you think, dolt? Then we let the tree fall to block the road, take that screen of thorns we spent so much time weaving and pull it across the road behind the soldiers to block their retreat, and . . .'' He gave an expressive shrug.

CLEVER, thought the watching *leshy*. *But not so clever as I!*

Silly humans—stupid humans. To kill here, in his domain, to kill one of his trees! He stood still as stone, invisible to merely human eyes, while all about, the birds fell silent, responding to the *leshy*'s softly swirling anger.

Shall I play with them? the being wondered, eyes glowing with alien malice. *Shall I lose them in the forest?* For a moment, he hugged himself in glee, picturing the wild-eyed, frantic things. But then the *leshy* sighed.

Fun must wait. The wasted tree-life must be avenged. Yes, and he must find something to do with this new human, this city man who called himself the leader of those ugly creatures.

At least they have always feared me, respected me. But

he—oh, he fears, yes, but not me. *And he respects no one, nothing.*

The *leshy* laughed, very softly, the sound of winter wind in frozen branches.

I shall play a new game with him. And he shall learn respect. Oh yes, I think he shall!

XXVII

BY MOONLIGHT

VASILISSA AWOKE with a start, staring blindly up at the canopy of her bed, her heart pounding. She'd had the dream again! As before, it had begun innocently enough, with Maria, smiling and happy, in the company of a fine, handsome young man. But slowly the mood of the dream had changed, slowly Vasilissa had come to realize that Maria was helpless, fallen completely under the young man's spell. No wonder, no wonder at all, because Vasilissa knew the horrible truth: this was no man, but a devil, a demon! He was out to steal Maria's soul, but no one seemed to care. Only Vasilissa knew the truth, but no one would believe her, no one would believe—

"This is silly, it was only a dream of course, only a dream."

But then Vasilissa sat bolt upright, listening intently. Voices . . . Akh, it must simply be her father talking to one of the servants.

So late at night? It must be past the mid-hour. And wasn't that the sound of a muffled laugh? Two of the help having a romance? Here? In their master's private quarters?

No, she recognized Maria's laugh. And that other voice . . .

It was the voice in her dream!

Shivering, Vasilissa pulled aside the bed curtain and padded silently to the wall that divided their two bed-

186

chambers, ignoring her slumbering maidservant, pressing her ear to the cold, painted surface, listening . . .

"OH, Finist! It's lovely!" Maria exclaimed as the prince held the thin, shining chain up to the candle's flickering light. "It looks almost like woven moonlight!"

"Why, it *is* woven moonlight, love! Don't expose it to sunlight, or—poof!—it'll dissolve into mist."

"Really?"

Finist couldn't keep his face sorcerously somber. "No," he admitted, grinning. "It's silver. Truly. I wanted to give you something more substantial than those silly toys and flowers."

Maria laughed. "I *like* those silly toys! Even if they're only illusions that fade the minute you turn away."

He sighed. "I only wish it were more. You understand, the limitations of falcon-form, I can't carry anything very heavy and still get off the ground."

"But how wonderful to fly at all! I envy you, love."

"You should," he said, staring at her.

"Eh?"

"Having your love—what more could any reasonable man want?" There was a moment of awkward silence, then Finist forced a hasty laugh. "Now, let us see how this necklace fits."

Maria reached out to take it from him, even as Finist started to slip it over her head. In the brief confusion, their hands locked. The silver chain wrapped itself about both their wrists in a shining bond that abruptly seemed to distort time and space so that for an alarming, wondrous moment Maria found herself looking at herself out of Finist's eyes, feeling his love, desire, longing—

Then he quickly disentangled the chain, and the moment was over.

"What was that?" Maria asked breathlessly.

Finist looked just as shaken. Maria reddened, realizing that he'd been sharing her emotions as well. But he answered steadily enough, "That, love, was a phenomenon known as linking. Mind-to-mind linking."

"But what does that mean?"

"It means," Finist told her carefully, not quite meeting

her gaze, "we are so right together that our very ways of thinking were joined for a moment. No," he added hastily, seeing her start, "you don't have to worry about that sort of thing happening all the time, I promise you. It usually only occurs in moments of great emotional strain." The prince paused thoughtfully. "In fact, I've never heard of it happening at all, save between two magical folk— Ah. I know what caused it."

Confused, Maria protested, "But I'm no magician!"

"That doesn't matter." Suddenly the professional, he continued, "The silver was the thing. The chain is of silver pure enough to have acted as a focal point, particularly since I was foolish enough to try to have something to do with its forging and ended up accidentally cutting myself and spilling a drop or two of blood into the mixture. The magic of blood could only have strengthened the focus, so that—"

"Finist," Maria said gently, "I repeat, I am not a magician."

"Ah. Sorry." His grin was quick and rueful. "This isn't frightening you, is it?"

"You know what's going on, and it doesn't frighten you, so why should I be alarmed?" she retorted, almost truthfully, and Finist gave a delighted little laugh.

"Maria, my clever darling, I *do* love you! Come, I'll try to explain. You did know that silver is the most magical of the pure metals?"

"I thought that was only a fable."

"Hardly. You see, it gets its Power from its ties with three of the most Powerful natural forces: Earth, its parent; Moon, its mystic twin; and Night, time of the Old Magics." He grinned. "Just as gold has ties with two forces."

"Earth, of course," hazarded Maria, "and . . . Sun?"

"Exactly. Earth doesn't dim gold's brightness, Sun doesn't fade it. And copper, while we're on the subject, is the Fire metal, since Fire only heightens its color."

"That leaves out iron. What about iron?"

Finist winced. "The magician's foe," he said shortly.

"But why? It's of the Earth; surely—"

"Maria, iron is the only metal without ties to other forces to temper its strength. It is bound only to Earth."

"I don't see what . . ."

"Air and Water rust it, Fire alters its basic form." Finist sighed. "Love, to put it simply, most of my magic comes from within me, from the focusing of my will, my energies, my life-force if you will. I can, however, use certain rituals to tap into outside Forces."

"Such as Earth, you mean?"

"You say that so lightly! Think of the strength of Earth. Think of mountains upthrust and land torn apart with the ease of a child smashing a toy. Do you think *that* is something any merely human soul can command? Iron bears within it all that Force. Magic *can* be worked on it, but that's a perilous thing to try. Worse, the contact of iron against a magician's skin overwhelms the will with Earth-force, confusing any spell— In short, its touch bans magic."

Finist stopped, frowning slightly. "Now I *have* frightened you. Love, please don't worry. I'm not a demon, to disintegrate at iron's touch! I don't become fatally poisoned if I cut myself with the stuff, either!" He added with wry honesty, "Though I must admit that iron-wounds are uncomfortable things for magicians, causing spectacular fevers, and healing much more slowly than other injuries. It's a small enough price to pay for magic!"

The prince struck a dramatic pose, laughing. "There. You've lasted out my lecture. Now, my lady, your reward."

He slipped the silver necklace smoothly over her head, this time being careful not to touch her. As she settled the chin in place, touching the shining links with a wary hand, Finist breathed, "Ah, lovely!" adding with a jokingly melodramatic flourish, "I am indeed fortunate to bear the love of the *boyarevna* Maria Danilovna."

With extravagant gallantry, he bent to kiss the hem of her gown. But a suddenly chilled Maria pulled away, the mention of her full name reminding her, as it must, of her father.

It's none of his affair! she thought defiantly. After all, aside from the scandalous fact that she and Finist had spent several nights together, alone, they'd done nothing for which either of them could truly be censured, even though she knew he—and to be honest, she, too—burned for more than those few reasonably chaste kisses they'd exchanged in their brief meetings.

"Finist . . ."

"What is it, love? What's wrong?"

She bit her lip. "Nothing."

But she was thinking of how it was with more ordinary couples. While, properly, it should be the fathers, not their offspring, who first suggested alliances and betrothals, it still wasn't unheard of for two young people to fall in love quite on their own. But in such a case, the young man *must* go to his beloved's father to sue for her hand, the father *must* give his permission; he had all legal rights over his daughter, after all, and without his consent, there could be no marriage.

Marriage. She wasn't sure Finist even had such an idea in his mind. She wasn't even sure *she* wanted it.

For an instant, a wicked image raced through her mind, she and Finist running off to live in delicious sin . . . But then it was as quickly replaced by her father's face, sad-eyed and anguished for his daughter's sake. Dear Heaven, how could she ever think of hurting him like that?

Maria sighed. Why try to pretend? Oh, she was grateful to Finist for respecting her honor, or at least she told herself she was. And these past nights had been the most wonderful in her life. But they'd have to end unhappily. How else? As soon as Danilo learned the truth, he'd try to exorcise Finist, or—royalty or no—have him burned!

How much longer can I remain chivalrous? wondered Finist.

And yet the prince was forced to admit that something besides honor controlled him. He couldn't quite forget the memory of a sleek golden form, lit by candlelight, half-hidden by candlesmoke, of a room close with the scent of burning wax and perfume, of joyless lust where there should have been delight . . . Oh, no. There would be nothing like that for Maria. When they came to share a bed, let it be with wonder, with honest pleasure, not with shame.

I want her, all at once he knew it, *I want her as my wife.*

The impact of that so sudden, so final realization quite stunned him.

My wife . . . Finist repeated weakly. But at the same time, something deep within him was singing, *Yes, oh, yes!* And now that the first shock was wearing off, he wondered why he had been surprised at all. He had known virtually from his first sight of Maria that she was the one for him, that he must love her then and now and forever. And she—oh, the wonder of it was enough to leave him weak and shaken, but—she loved him! She did love him! And after all this midnight courting, after the magic of their linking, it should be clear to both of them that they belonged together, so let him gather up his courage and be bold, just like any ordinary man with his love, and say what he meant to say.

Come now, Finist chided himself, *it shouldn't be so difficult.*

Shouldn't it? Amazed, bewildered, the prince suddenly found himself shaking, as dry of mouth as though he'd tried some spell far beyond his powers.

Ridiculous. He swallowed nervously, and began, "Maria . . ."

"Yes?"

"Maria, I . . ." The prince stopped again, struggling for words. This really *was* the most ridiculous— He'd faced down angry *boyars,* sly ambassadors, all without a trace of nerves to him, but now—

"Maria," he began once more, doggedly. "We've been together now for a time, before, when I was—ah—Finn, now, here in Stargorod, where I can be myself, and I think I must ask—I mean—" Finist stopped with a little exclamation of self-disgust. "Do you love me?"

"My dear, you know I do!"

"You know—at least, I pray you know—that—that I love you, as well."

"Finist, love, what *are* you trying to say?"

"I— Few princes ever have to worry about this sort of

thing. It's taken care of by their ministers in cold-blooded political deals, the sort of thing into which emotion never enters. But I—I—'' *Dammit!* ''Maria, will you marry me?''

The young woman stared at him blankly, plainly as stunned as he'd just been. ''Are you allowed to ask that? I mean, aren't you supposed to clear things with your *bo-yars* first, and—''

''I am their prince,'' Finist said flatly. ''They will support my wish.'' He stirred uneasily. ''Akh, but I don't mean to sound so pompous! Maria, love, they won't protest. That is, if you—Maria, please! *Will you marry me!*''

He saw the realization of what he'd said at last sink in. And to his horror, he watched her eyes well up with tears. Blinking fiercely, biting her lip, Maria turned sharply away.

''Oh, Finist, I can't!''

''I . . . see.''

''No, it's not like that!'' She whirled to face him again, pleading, ''Believe me, I want to say yes—more than anything, I want to say yes! But I can't, not without my father's approval!''

Finist stiffened as though she'd struck him. ''Maria, he'll never give his approval, you know that, not to a magician, someone he sees as damned.''

''We—we don't know that,'' she lied painfully.

''Oh, believe me, we do.'' The prince gave an angry, weary little sigh. ''You see, in a manner of speaking, I've already asked him. Oh, no, not in so many words. I . . . spoke with him in a dream. And what I learned . . .''

At first, there'd been nothing but hatred, blunt, unreasoning hatred, and fear so strong Finist had been sure the man would wake, and wake shouting. But behind the fear had been grief, such painful grief that Finist, pitying, had nearly broken contact then and there. Then all at once Danilo's sleeping self had cried out in anguish:

''Sorcery slew my wife!''

And, in response to Finist's shocked query, he'd continued, *''She—Maria's birth was a difficult one. After that . . . there could be no more children after that. But—but she would never believe me when I said that it didn't mat-*

*ter to me, that all I wanted was my dear one alive and
well . . . She wanted so to give me a son . . . And when
prayer seemed useless, she . . . In secret, she went to a
sorcerer. She did whatever foulness he demanded. She
drank his foul potions.* And they killed her!"

Shaken, Finist had tried to insist that it hadn't been a
sorcerer, but some fool of a charlatan who'd poisoned her
through his sheer ignorance, that magic, true magic, had
had nothing to do with it. But he couldn't pierce the wall
of hate.

*"My wife was avenged at the stake! But magic didn't
die in that fire! Oh, no, its seductive evil is still very much
alive, waiting for other poor innocent souls— If any sorcerer ever dares touch either of my daughters, I swear that
I shall see him writhe in flames—and my hand will hurl
the first torch!"*

Finist repressed a shudder at the memory.

Maria was staring at him. "Finist? Are you all right?"

"I . . . Do you know how your mother died?"

She blinked, surprised. "Why, not really. Lissa and I
were both very young—Father told us she died of fever.
Why do you ask?"

Finist sighed. He couldn't tell her the truth, he couldn't
hurt her like that. "Akh, never mind. Let's just say I know
without a shadow of doubt that your father will never, ever
give his approval to our marriage."

"Ah . . ."

The resignation in her eyes angered him. "All right,
then! Forget him!"

"Finist!"

"You say you love me—"

"I do!"

"Then come with me, now!"

"What are you saying?"

"Nothing dishonorable, I swear it." He rushed on before she could interrupt, "My powers will see us both
safely to Kirtesk. And then . . . oh, Maria, can't you
imagine it?" Fighting to keep his voice level and cajoling,
Finist continued, "Picture the two of us together, on the
throne, in our bed, picture us as husband and wife, happy
people all about us, our people, shouting benedictions.

Picture it, Maria, and come with me. In Kirtesk we can wed as we will, and—"

"We couldn't. Finist, our marriage wouldn't be legal."

"But it would! In Kirtesk, the law allows a woman to marry as she will, assuming, of course, she isn't trying to wed close kin, or—"

"I can't. Finist, I'm sorry, I just can't."

"You can! Maria, listen to me. There's no shame about this. We'll wed, and be happy, and—" But she wasn't listening. She was still her family's slave, and Finist added in a savage burst, "And Danilo can go to—"

"He's my father!" Maria gasped, anguished. "I can't just leave him!" She turned away, biting her lower lip so hard that Finist ached to cry out to her, Oh, my love, I don't mean to hurt you like this! Back to him, Maria continued, very carefully, "Maybe you're wrong. We haven't tried him, after all. Yes, I admit it, he hates magic, but he does want me to be happy. If he only has a chance to see the love between us— Maybe if we both go to him and—and explain how things stand, he'll give his consent after all."

"And maybe Stargorod will go floating off into the clouds!"

"Stop that! I—I don't know what else to do!" The weary curve of her shoulders made him take a step towards her, but before he could put his arms about her, she added softly, "Finist, love, what about magic? Can't you . . . bespell him?"

He stared at her back. "Do you know what you're saying?"

"Oh, I don't mean anything dangerous, just some harmless little spell, just enough to soften his heart so he'll give his consent and not worry about—"

"Any spell powerful enough to alter his thinking," Finist said flatly, "would not be harmless."

"I—I'm sorry. I didn't know."

"Akh, Maria, enough. Don't let him do this to you!" It was a cry of sheer frustration. "Don't let him spoil your life! Leave him here with his fears. Come with me."

She whirled to face him, eyes enormous in a wild, flushed face. "Oh, it's so easy for you, isn't it?"

"Now, what does that mean?"

"You, who can just fly away from anything that bothers you!"

He winced. "It isn't like that."

"Isn't it?" She continued in a soft, fierce, anguished voice, "You're a prince! Who would dare say no to you? No one! No one save me!"

There comes a limit even to magical self-control. "And is that what you want?" Finist shouted. The force of it snapped Maria back to herself, gesturing to him frantically, and the prince belatedly lowered his voice. "Do you want it to be over between us?" *Oh God, if she says yes . . .*

"Akh, Finist, what do you think? Of course I don't! But Lissa and I are all Father has left to him. I can't hurt him like this."

"And what about me?" Finist knew how selfish that sounded, but he was past the point of caring. "What about us?"

"Don't do this to me! Father—Lissa—they depend on me, they always depend on me—"

"And you prefer it that way, don't you? Of course, I should have realized. It's safer that way." He saw her flinch in pain, but kept on relentlessly, "You don't have to think about the outside world, no, your father and sister need you, you don't have to worry about leading your own life or—"

"No! How dare you mock my life, you who've never suffered any hardship and—"

"Maria! I only wanted you to see how your father is using you!"

"Stop it!" Hands over her ears, she burst out, "I don't want to hear this! I don't want to talk about it! Please, leave me alone!"

"Maria—"

"Leave me alone! I—I need some time to myself."

"Time, is it? Then time you shall have!"

His shout became the shriek of a falcon. Raging, aching, Finist hurled himself out into the night sky, shutting his ears to the sound of Maria's hopeless sobs behind him.

* * *

AND in her bed-chamber, Vasilissa moved away from the wall, smiling. All was well: Maria had cast out the demon. Oh, the girl might weep and wail for a time, instead of being sensible enough to fall to her knees and thank Heaven for her deliverance. But at least it was over, and Maria was safe.

XXVIII

REVENGE

SOBBING FOR BREATH, shaking with exhaustion and the residue of terror, Alexei tripped over a branch and fell, for perhaps the hundredth time that night. But this time he'd passed the point of recovery. He could do nothing more than to roll painfully onto his back, staring wildly up at the black mass of leaves overhead, thinking that at least he'd be able to see his attackers before they killed him.

How could it have gone so wrong? They'd been all ready for the attack, his men—

My men. Ha! Fools! Superstitious fools!

Was it only superstition? Surely it hadn't been chance that had twisted the tree out of their hands, surely it hadn't been chance that had sent the heavy trunk crashing down, not on the road but on two of his men, the two who'd done the most to chop the tree down— No, he was becoming as insane as they!

But Alexei couldn't rid himself of the sight of that fallen tree, and the two men crushed beneath it, and the slow flow of blood . . . The merchant and his party had fled, unchallenged, while Alexei and the robbers had stood motionless, staring in silent horror. And then . . .

"It was yer doin'." The sound was a low, feral growl.

"Nonsense! It was an accident—sheer clumsiness on the part of whoever was holding the—"

"Ye did it."

"Did *what,* for God's sake?"

197

"Ye kept after us. Made us kill the tree."

Good Lord, they meant it! And they were moving slowly forward, menace in their eyes . . . Alexei took a step backwards despite himself. "Don't be ridiculous!"

"Ye brought the forest devils down on us."

"There aren't any—"

"Killed two of our own, the ones who dared cut it— Ye took an axe to it too. Why didn't it kill ye?"

"Maybe 'cause we're supposed to do it," came the ugly snarl. "Forest devils want *us* to do it, show we ain't forgot the proper ways."

"Have you gone mad?"

But then they'd attacked, beating at him with their clubs, and there wasn't room for swordplay in those close quarters, there wasn't even room to simply draw the blade. He could only try to ward off the blows as best he could, and pray they wouldn't think to use their daggers as well. A club connected with his arm with agonizing force, a second smashed against his side, a third grazed his head, and in the dodging, he lost his balance and fell, thinking, *Oh, God, now they've got me, they'll beat me to death!* But somehow he managed to scrabble free, panic overwhelming pain, tearing his way through the underbrush on hands and knees, not even feeling the thorns ripping his flesh, till at last he could struggle to his feet and run quite literally for his life.

He'd been running ever since, clutching his wounded arm to his wounded side, running through the ever-darkening forest, falling, scrambling up, falling again, sure he could hear the robbers right behind him. Or was it only robbers? Was it the guards, the royal guards from Stargorod? No; it was all impossible! Could any mortal have kept up with him all this way?

—And Alexei found himself staring into two wild, cruel, inhuman eyes. He screamed aloud in a terror sharper than any he had ever felt.

"No!"

Somehow he managed to find his feet again and stagger on, blindly, lungs aching with the strain—

And a hand, an inhuman hand, brushed his cheek. With

a gasp, Alexei swerved aside, hearing laughter behind him—

"Ahh!"

Strong fingers pinched his arm, and now the laughter was all around him, cold, mocking laughter that filled him with renewed panic. He found one last burst of speed with in him, but then something—someone—was tripping him, and he was falling down a steep, rocky slope, coming to rest at the bottom in a crumpled, sobbing heap.

"No, oh God, no! Leave me alone!"

Weakling. You are no son of mine.

"Father . . . ?" Alexei shook his head in frantic denial. "This can't be! You're dead!"

But the cold voice continued, *Little whining boy blaming your mother for her peasant blood, blaming me for taking her, blaming everyone and everything but yourself.*

Yet the voice no longer belonged to his father. Alexei gave a little moan of horror as he recognized the rough sound of the men with whom he'd gambled away his inheritance. *Big-talker. Full a' no-good promises. Never your fault when it all goes wrong. No, course not, always someone else's fault.*

Alexei heard himself whimper as he tried to find a way to hide from those sneering voices, but they were all around him. And now Danilo's voice had joined them, saying:

Traitor. Foolish, empty, pitiful traitor.

"Leave me alone! Just—just leave m-me alone!"

The voices drowned him out. The voices dragged out his secret dreams of glory, mocking them, showing him what a small, sorry, *ridiculous* creature he was. And the laughter, the cold, pitiless laughter was all around him, there in the darkness, and there was no place to run, no place to hide, nothing but torment—

All at once it had gone quite beyond endurance; all at once there was nothing for Alexei to do but simply surrender. Lying submissively where he'd fallen, letting the voices beat at him till they'd faded into the darkness, he quite calmly gave himself over to whatever fate awaited him. After all the terror, it was almost a relief not to even try to fight back, to just let go, to feel fear and pain and sanity slip away from him. Now that the voices and the laughter were gone, he could see that the darkness was quite beautiful, the beautiful darkness all around him . . .

And when the forest spoke to him, he wasn't at all amazed. When it asked him, "Do you fear me?" he nodded, smiling cajolingly.

"Yes, oh, yes."

"And have you learned? Do you respect me now?"

"Yes, oh, yes!" repeated Alexei.

All at once it struck him as funny, everything struck him as funny, the fact that he'd gone from *boyar* to bandit chief to nothing, no one at all, it struck him as wildly, wildly funny. And there in the darkness, the beautiful darkness, with who knew what unseen devils looking on, Alexei put his head back and laughed and laughed and laughed.

XXIX

DEMONS

THE CROW, bearing a small vial in its claws, squirmed and struggled its way through the missing slat in the locked shutters barring the window, let the vial fall, and smoothly transformed back into golden Ljuba, a bit breathless, but smiling a small, contented smile.

Did the old fool really think he could keep her captive?

Ljuba's smile thinned. All this time, she'd been acting the docile, resigned, helpless lady, and so far, the act had worked well enough. Let Semyon believe he had her imprisoned in the inner chambers of her own palace. Granted, she had no way to unlock the iron chains with which he'd had the shutters of her windows fastened. But quiet, patient pryings had worked loose that slat, letting her pull it out or fit it back into place as she would. As long as she could continue to change to crow-shape and squeeze through the narrow opening, she was hardly a captive.

Of course, Ljuba reminded herself, replacing the slat, she still had to be wary of the chains. Iron was a perilous metal even for someone with only weak magic in her blood. Her avian true-shape wouldn't be affected by accidental contact, but catch a wing or claw in a chain and her Power would be bound, too; if she couldn't free herself by simple struggling, she'd be left hanging ignominiously till someone thought to rescue her. Worse, if she tore feathers or skin on the iron, she would almost certainly damage her will or her Powers.

For the moment, that wasn't a problem. Right now, she wasn't interested in escaping.

Ljuba had been cautious enough to bar the door before removing the slat and taking flight; this time there would be no unwelcome intrusions. Kneeling, she pulled back one of the rich carpets covering the floor, then spilled the contents of the vial she'd brought from her experiment-room—a room from which Semyon thought he had barred her—onto the smooth marble. Eyes shut, the young woman concentrated, calming her mind, cooling her thoughts . . . She spoke a few cold, careful words, and felt the Power stir . . .

Ljuba looked down at her handiwork: the potion had frozen to a smooth sheet of ice. It would melt of its own accord soon enough, leaving nothing but a trace of damp-ness for prying Semyon to find, but for now, it formed as fine a mirror as anyone could want. Carefully, she began to concentrate, and saw the icy surface grey, then clear. Gently, now, gently . . .

There he was, there was Finist, and with him, that young woman—Maria Danilovna. Ljuba stared at them both in-tently, and what she saw was . . .

Love—clear, strong, shining love.

"No . . ." It was an involuntary moan. "Akh, no . . ."

But there it was, no denying it. Finist did love this Ma-ria, she loved him, there was no room at all for Ljuba . . .

And why should that hurt? Why should she care? For a bewildered moment, Ljuba didn't know herself at all. She trembled on the verge of something new, something won-drous . . .

Something weak. Something stupid and useless and weak. Recoiling in self-disgust, frightened at how near she'd come to losing precious control, Ljuba forced out as ugly an oath as she could find, taking fierce joy in the vileness of it.

Fool, fool! Just because he was the first man in God knows when to be gentle in your bed, there's no reason to wail like some stupid girl bemoaning the loss of her vir-ginity! He's your road to power, no more, no less.

It was a long time before she could force herself to be-lieve that. But at last, staring into the icy mirror, Ljuba managed to calm her mind till she could watch almost dispassionately. Soon she saw Finist fly angrily away. But what was this? She sensed someone else's triumph at that. Not the sobbing Maria, but someone akin, closely akin . . . Delicately, Ljuba widened her scan and found Vasilissa.

"Why, you little fool!" Ljuba told her contemptuously. "Don't you realize this is only a lovers' spat? Don't you realize he'll be back?"

Wait, now . . . Idiot indeed, this young woman, weak and fragile of mind. Ljuba could sense the uneasy workings of that mind even from here, feeling how it teemed with old fears, old superstitions . . .

"So very fearful," Ljuba said slowly. "So ready to believe almost anything, anything at all . . . So willing to be led."

The young woman licked her lips thoughtfully, a cat considering potential prey.

VASILISSA awoke with a start. Someone was calling her name. The demon? Had the demon returned for revenge?

No, this was surely a woman's voice, sweet and warm and loving. Bewildered, Lissa pulled aside the bed curtain, and gasped.

There, shimmering and faint as heat-haze, a woman stood. Woman? This radiant being was surely more than that, this being with the waterfall of golden hair and the beautiful face and the rich, glittering, golden robes . . .

"An angel," breathed Vasilissa. Hastily she stumbled from bed and fell reverently to her knees. "Are you an angel?"

"I am . . . Call me a messenger," said the shining being. "Come to tell you how to save your sister."

Vasilissa drew in her breath sharply. "But she's already safe! The demon is gone!"

"Gone, Vasilissa, but not banished. He will return."

"No!"

"Do you doubt me, child? Do you dare?"

"Oh, no, I didn't mean any discourtesy! I only meant—"

"Come, child, enough. Would you save Maria's soul?"

"Her soul!" gasped Vasilissa. "Of course I would!
Please, tell me what I must do!"

The golden being smiled faintly. "Listen, then . . ."

LJUBA broke contact with a gasp of exhaustion, falling
full-length on the floor. Ugh, but the melting potion was
cold and slimy! With a little cry of disgust, the young
woman wearily dragged herself to her feet, and collapsed
onto her bed. Lying there, staring up at the embroidered
canopy, she began to laugh.

The little idiot had thought her an angel, and believed
her every word! But would she be able to carry out her
instructions properly? Ljuba's laughter faded. All at once
she found herself shaking with a chill that had nothing to
do with the physical. What if the stupid girl went too far?
What if, in her zeal, Vasilissa decided to act on her own,
or tried something too dangerous, or—

Stop this! Ljuba snapped at herself. It would work, of
course it would! She didn't dare start doubting now. It
would work, and Finist would be hers.

But . . . if it failed . . .

Ljuba groaned in dawning horror. If her plan failed, she
might just have given what amounted to Finist's death sentence.

I've got to stop her!

Struggling to her feet, Ljuba tried again and again to
restore the mental link with Vasilissa, tried till her head
ached and her body shook with exhaustion. But it was
useless; she hadn't the strength. Whether she willed it or
not, her plan had been set into motion.

SHE wouldn't weep anymore, Maria told herself fiercely.
Yesterday had been . . . yesterday, and though she ached
to recall the words she'd said in anger, the past wasn't to
be changed. Tonight she'd sit here in her bed-chamber,
and hope—no, she would *believe* that Finist would forgive
and return. Together, they'd find a way out, a way that
would see Danilo yielding to them, and letting them wed.

"Wed," Maria said softly. "Wed to Finist . . ."

That he was a prince did give her pause, just a bit, and
the fact that she'd be a princess in a city foreign to her.

But she could endure anything, adapt to anything, with Finist at her side. And at any rate, as a *boyar*'s daughter, she'd been trained to accept that someday she would marry a noble who would almost certainly be a stranger to her, who might take her away to foreign lands. Who just might turn out to hate and abuse her . . . Maria shivered at the thought. Wonderful, to think of Finist as her husband instead—warm, kind, loving Finist . . .

Why was I such a fool? When he asked me to wed him, why didn't I just fling myself into his arms? Why, oh why did I send him away? She bit down on her lip, hard. *He must return to me. Dear Heaven, he must!*

HE'D been flying for what seemed an eternity, right through the night and the next day, pausing only to snatch a dove on the wing—as falcon, he wasn't squeamish about raw food—flying on till sheer wing-weariness drained the anger from him.

Akh, Maria, why was I such a fool? Why did I pressure you like that? Why didn't I give you more time to think things through? The prince stabbed his talons fiercely into the branch on which he perched. *I can't leave it like this! God, no, I've got to go back!*

Wings spread, Finist leaped into the air once more.

MARIA started violently as someone knocked on the door to her bed-chamber, thinking for one wild moment, *Finist!* But that was ridiculous, he'd have no need for a door.

"Maria? Are you still awake?"

"Lissa!" Maria cast one last, longing glance at the window and the empty night sky beyond, then sighed and went to open the door to her sister. "Lissa, love, what is it? What's wrong?"

The young woman was virtually shaking with tension, but she blurted out, almost defiantly, "Nothing! Why should anything be wrong?"

"Akh, Lissa. What is it? The foul dreams again?"

"No, I—I just couldn't sleep, and I thought I'd see if you were awake, too. See, I—I had the servants prepare us some warm milk. I thought we could drink it together, the way we used to do when we were children."

Gigglings and gossipings and childish secrets . . . fragments of warm memory raced through Maria's mind, and she smiled faintly. Although warm milk was the last thing she wanted right now, the young woman said gently, "Of course, love. Come, sit here beside me."

Lissa had poured the milk into two goblets. "To happiness," she toasted diffidently.

"To happiness," Maria echoed willingly, and drank. She stopped, puzzled. Lissa, who'd been watching her intently, straightened.

"What's wrong, Maria? Is it too sweet?"

"Not sweet enough! Are you sure this milk is fresh?"

"Oh, it is, it is! Look, I've brought honey to sweeten it . . . There. Is that better?"

She looked so concerned that Maria could only sigh and drain the goblet. "There, now. Finish yours, and we'll . . . I'll . . ."

"Maria?"

"Odd . . . Suddenly I'm so sleepy! I . . . can't seem to . . ."

"Hush, dear." Vasilissa was moving around her, helping her out of her clothing and into bed. "Sleep, Maria, sleep well."

"This—this is . . . silly . . . I . . ."

But she couldn't fight the heavy tide a moment longer. Her eyes closed, and Maria let the dark ocean sweep over her . . .

For a long while, Vasilissa stood frozen, staring, heart pounding. Dear Heaven, was Maria all right? Was she breathing regularly?

"Yes . . ."

It was a sigh of relief. She'd never prepared a sleeping potion before; that sort of thing was usually Maria's task. She hadn't been quite sure the dosage had been correct. Yes, and then, when Maria had questioned the taste of the drugged milk . . . Vasilissa had been all but ready to confess, to beg her sister's pardon. But somehow she'd managed to hold out.

Of course she had: Maria's soul was at stake. And for Maria's sake, she would be brave. Suddenly obsessed with a need for haste, Vasilissa let her goblet fall and snatched up the bundle she'd brought. Oh, but the angel would be so proud of her! The angel had wanted her to use simple nails set in wood, barely enough to tear at the demon's skin. She'd sworn the bite of cold iron would be enough to confuse his mind and magic, and make him flee back to his demonic home.

Vasilissa smiled. How much more effective would the demon-trap be since she'd used, instead of petty little furniture nails, good, strong spikes, horseshoe nails, stolen from the estate's stables? With one last glance at her deeply sleeping sister, the young woman hurried to the window and began to prepare. Maria's window was the exact same size as the one in her own bedroom; she had been able to work out the precise measurements she needed, and had even had a chance to try this out once there already.

There. It was done. The window was barred by a criss-cross of wood, laths studded with horseshoe nails and jammed crosswise into the frame, the iron spikes pointing out into the night, invisible in the darkness. Vasilissa gathered up all traces of her visit, took one last, lingering glance at Maria, then stole quietly out of the room. Soon she would know if she'd succeeded. Soon she'd know if Maria was safe and the demon banished—forever.

IT was a strange time to come visiting, Finist admitted to himself, past the midnight hour, nearer to morning than tonight. But Maria just might still be awake . . . At any rate, he didn't think he could bear to wait a whole day through till the next nightfall to straighten out things between them.

Danilo's estate crouched like some vaguely seen sleeping beast in the moonless darkness, and even with his falcon-keen vision, Finist had to strain to pick out the shape of Maria's window. But there it was, and he wasn't going to waste a moment more! Finist soared silently towards the window on outspread wings, planning a smooth swoop that would—

No, something was wrong! He sensed a wave of hatred, the cruel, cold blaze of iron. Frantically, Finist tried to pull out of his dive, but it was already too late. He cried out his pain as iron tore into him. For a terrible moment, he thought he'd been fatally impaled; then, desperate, he managed to wrench himself free. Wild with agony, bright feathers stained and torn, Finist fought to stay airborne. The iron, the cold, burning iron, beat at his mind, driving away clear thought, driving away humanity. No longer rational, the falcon gave one last, despairing mental cry:

Maria! Maria, save me! Kirtesk— Seek Me— My love! Save me!

And then he lost all hold on his human self. The wounded falcon flew wildly away, lashed by pain, knowing only that it must reach safety, it must reach home, *home!*

XXX

THE FALCON

LJUBA SPRANG to her feet, frantic and confused. She hadn't meant to fall asleep, but her magic-weary body had betrayed her. God, how long had she been unconscious, while who knew what had been happening in Stargorod? The potion— No, only a gummy residue was left, nothing that could be frozen into a mirror. Ljuba began a frantic search, hurling aside clothing, jewelry, everything, hunting for anything with a reflective surface, anything that would let her know about Finist. What if something had gone wrong? What if he was—

Ah! She straightened, holding an elegant brooch set with a clear crystal, a small thing but perhaps large enough . . . Someone was beating at her barred door, Ljuba was dimly aware of that—evidently she'd been asleep long enough to worry people—but right now the mirror-spell was more important than setting some fool's mind at ease.

Finist was no longer in Stargorod; that much she knew right away. Then, where . . . ? For a desperate time, Ljuba couldn't find a trace of him, not the slightest hint of his aura, for a desperate time she had to fight down her growing fear lest she lose the scanning image altogether.

"Finist, where are you? *Where are you?*"

Wait . . . There was something . . . not so much seen as felt: a wild, confused tangle of pain and bewilderment and sheer, mindless terror, a bird's emotions—

No. Not quite a bird. Not quite human, either. Ljuba moaned in horror, but just then—

209

"Lady." Semyon was in the chamber with her. They must have forced open the door; lost in the concentration-trance, she hadn't heard a thing. Ljuba supposed she should feel something of gratitude that they'd thought to worry about her, but right now she didn't have time for this nonsense, and—oh, curse them! Curse them all! She'd lost her hold on the image of the frantic, pain-wracked falcon!

Just at that moment, an enraged Semyon, seeing only that she'd dared disobey a royal command, snatched the brooch from her hand. Without thinking, Ljuba whirled and slapped him hard across the face.

"You old fool! I had him—get out of my way!"

He stood rigidly, blocking her. "I've told you, lady. The prince ordered—"

"The prince, yes, that's what this is all about! Finist needs me! No, curse you, I'm not being hysterical! He's been hurt, hurt by iron, he's lost in falcon-form, and I doubt he'll have the strength to make it all the way back to the royal palace! Semyon, if I don't reach him quickly and bring him back to himself, Prince Finist may be lost forever! Now, *get out of my way!*"

THERE was pain with every wing-beat, pain with every breath . . . The falcon no longer had a memory of a time without pain, but to fail now would be to die; dimly it knew that, and struggled on. A great object was beginning to loom on the horizon. A mountain? The bird-mind could understand it only as some sort of strangely hued mountain. But something seemed to whisper, *city,* though the concept had no meaning to the falcon; *Kirtesk;* and then, *Home.*

Home. The falcon quickened its wing beats, hunting for whatever air currents might carry it more swiftly, no longer soaring over forest, but over open space, the fields that surrounded Home. But now the fickle currents were failing it, now the falcon's strength was failing, too. Struggling against the suddenly heavy air, it made one last valiant attempt to remain in flight. Then, with a sharp, despairing cry, it began to fall, spiralling helplessly down and down, at the last possible moment managing to use its aching wings to brake its fall as it landed amid tall grass in a crumpled heap of feathers, and lay still.

"Finist. Finist, hear me."

The falcon stirred as something touched it. Frightened, it weakly tried to bite, to claw, but the something was holding it fast, the something was making odd sounds, over and over . . .

"Finist. Yes, look at me, look at me. You are Finist. Remember, you are Finist."

Finist. Something stirred in the avian mind. *Finist.* Once, it seemed, it might have borne a different form . . . *Finist.* Once, it might have had a different self . . . Once, it had been more than bird, much more, once it had been—

"Finist."

The falcon-shape blurred and was gone. Human once more, the prince lay where he'd fallen, naked and torn, too sick with shock and pain and weariness to move, wondering feverishly where he was, how he'd gotten here, remembering almost nothing of that nightmarish flight. Someone was gently slipping a caftan about him, but the touch of even that soft silk against the ugly gashes across his chest and upper arms made him gasp in pain and look up. Through the reddish haze of rising fever, he saw Ljuba, and some ingrained sense of wariness wanted him to pull away. But he was past the point of escape.

"Cousin." His voice was a dry, anguished gasp. "Help . . ."

"Oh, I shall, Finist. Believe me, I shall."

She smiled at him. And the sight of that smile, sly, cruel, and possessive, was the last thing Finist saw before darkness took him.

XXXI

DECISIONS

MARIA! Maria, save me! Kirtesk— Seek me— My love! Save me!

Those scraps of anguished thoughts echoing in her mind, Maria dragged herself up through layers of sleep to a dazed awakening, head aching, throat dry, vaguely aware that something was terribly wrong.

With a great effort, she managed to swing heavy, barely responsive legs over the side of the bed and sat up, so dizzy she thought she'd be sick, feeling as though she had been drugged . . .

That goblet of milk . . . that odd-tasting milk Vasilissa had insisted she drink! It must have held a sleeping potion. And, judging from the way she felt, she was probably meant to sleep right through until midday, but . . . Maria blinked at the predawn sky. Vasilissa plainly hadn't known how to calculate the proper dosage.

Akh, I'm lucky she didn't poison me. Though why she would want to drug me . . .

Somehow her sister's motives just didn't seem so urgent, not compared to the dream . . . If only she could remember—there was something about that dream . . .

Confused, Maria struggled to her feet. The cold night air would help revive her. The window—

She stopped short, staring at the bizarre wooden cross that blocked the opening. Moving warily closer, Maria realized she was looking at two crossed laths, their ends jammed firmly into the windowframe. They could only have been put there by Vasilissa once she'd known Maria was safe in drugged sleep. As a bewildered Maria stared more closely, horror swept the residue of slumber from her mind, because the laths were studded with spikes, cruel iron spikes that were dark with blood.

"Finist . . ."

It was his blood, she knew that as surely as she knew anything at all! Finist had come back to her and not seen the trap in the darkness, and she'd not been awake to warn him—oh, dear God, did he think *she'd* set the trap? Did he think she'd tried to kill— To kill! No, no, he wasn't dead, he couldn't be dead!

And then, cutting through the rising panic, came the memory of her dream. All at once Maria knew it hadn't been a dream at all, but Finist's desperate cry to her, and she could have sobbed aloud because at least it meant he must still be alive. But that cry:

Kirtesk— Seek me— My love! Save me!

Maria straightened. Whether he'd meant it or not, behind those broken, pain-wracked words, there had been a second, even more alarming message. About . . . Ljuba?

Ljuba, yes. In their time together, Finist had, of course, told Maria something about his lands, light, amusing tales of Kirtesk, of his people, his *boyars*—and of Ljuba, his cousin, his sorcerous, ambitious cousin. At the time his voice had seemed a little too light to be convincing, a little too casual.

And in that faint, second layer of dream-message, Finist had plainly feared that in his weakened state he would fall under his cousin's control. If she could control Finist, she could control Kirtesk as well. That had been his greatest fear, for his people. It seemed that since they had been exposed to magic all their lives, the folk of Kirtesk had become attuned to it, enough for them to have lost the resistance to sorceries usually present in the human mind. They'd be easy targets for Ljuba. The desperate message had been clear enough about that: Only an outsider, with that natural resistance still intact, could hope to stay free of sorcerous seduction long enough to stop Ljuba.

Me? Maria shuddered in sudden, cold terror. *Against*

sorcery . . . A chasm seemed to open up before her, a chasm filled with all the horrors of the dark, frightening unknown . . .

But her glance fell to the cruel iron spikes and their grim stains, and Maria drew herself slowly erect. No time now to indulge her fears. And she was no longer the girl she had been, not after the ordeal of exile, not after the joy of Finist.

If only I'd been brave enough to go with him when he asked, to wed him, none of this would have happened.

The thought of Finist—poor Finist, alone and wounded, and in God knew what peril . . . She had always thought those tales of folk willing to actually die for love only so much melodrama, but now she realized that life without Finist truly wouldn't be worth the living.

All right. If she didn't gather the shreds of her courage together and do something, Finist was lost. It was as simple as that.

The door creaked softly open, and Vasilissa began to tiptoe in, candle in hand, only to stop short at the sight of Maria grimly facing her.

"Checking up on your handiwork, Lissa?"

"I don't know what you mean."

"No? Do you usually wander about the house at this hour?"

"No! I just . . . didn't think you'd be awake yet. I mean, I was only looking to see—"

"If your trap had worked?" Maria cut in quietly.

"Trap? What—"

"Enough, Lissa! Why did you do it? Were you so envious? So jealous? In God's name, Lissa, *why?*"

"For you!" Vasilissa cried. "For the sake of your soul!"

That surprised Maria. "Now what nonsense are you—"

"It's true!" her sister screamed. "It's true—Maria, you never would have seen the truth in time! That was no man, that was a demon, a devil! He would have ravaged you, body and mind! But I saved you! An—an angel told me what to do, and I saved you!"

An angel told her. "Akh, Lissa . . ." Sick at heart,

Maria bit back tears. How could she hate Vasilissa for being what she was? "Lissa, I know you meant well. But now, go back to bed. Please. Just . . . go back to bed."

"You'll be all right?"

"I'll be fine. Lissa—"

"No, wait! First, let's both kneel and say a prayer of thanksgiving for—"

"What in the name of Heaven is going on?" asked a sudden, stern voice, and Maria sighed.

Wonderful, just wonderful. Vasilissa's hysterics had awakened Danilo. "It's nothing, Father. Lissa was only . . . dreaming."

She gave her sister a warning glance, but of course, Vasilissa ignored it. "No," she insisted angrily, "it wasn't a dream! Father, Maria was consorting with a—a devil, but I saved her!"

"A devil!" Danilo repeated, amazed. But his face darkened with dawning anger. "A lover, you mean!"

"No," protested Maria. "It wasn't—"

"Oh, so you admit it!"

"*No!* I—"

"Wait. Vasilissa, child, leave us."

"But don't you want to hear about—"

"Not now, Lissa! Leave us!"

As soon as the young woman was gone, Danilo whirled to his younger daughter. "How dare you—"

"Father, please. No one could have gotten past you and Lissa to get to my room, you know that."

"The window."

Maria fought to keep her voice level. "But this room is on the second floor, and the outside wall is quite smooth." She forced a laugh. "You don't really believe Lissa and her—her devil?"

"No. Of course not." But he did just what she had feared: he started towards the window. "Eh, stand aside, Maria. Stand aside!"

God, let him not see the spikes! Let him not see the bloodstains!

But he saw, and touched a wary finger to the stains. "Blood. You lied to me, girl."

"I . . ." There was no way out of this, no way short

of the truth, fantastic though that might be. "First, I swear to you by our family's honor that nothing shameful happened between us."

"Who is he?"

"A—a man of—yes, of honor! Of high rank, indeed! Fin—"

"Finn! That—that nameless—" He stopped short, staring out at the unclimbable wall. "No place to attach a rope . . . Lissa was right all along! The man *is* a sorcerer!"

"The man is Finist, Prince of Kirtesk!" cried Maria fiercely, but her father spun about and caught her a stinging slap across the face.

"You dare!" he shouted. "That accursed sorcerer— You *dare!*"

Shaking, Maria shouted back, "That accursed sorcerer saved your honor! Who do you think went to Prince Svyatoslav, eh? Who do you think proved your innocence?"

"Silence!"

"No! Not this once! Finist is a good, kind, honorable man! He loves me! And I—*I love him!*"

"Why, you little fool! And have you slept with him yet? Have you let this good, kind, honorable *sorcerer* into your bed?"

"I have not! And he *is* honorable! He wants to marry me!"

"Liar!"

As lord of the house, he'd always been within his rights to discipline his children as he saw fit, though up to this time, Danilo had never abused that privilege. But before Maria could defend herself, he struck her again and again, raging and terrified all at once.

"Enough," he said at last, panting. "Enough. But you shall spend some time alone, girl, thinking on your sins!"

He dragged the dazed, struggling Maria to a windowless storeroom and threw her inside. "Stay there till you repent!" Danilo shouted, and slammed the door shut. Maria, aching, heard the bolt slide into place, and sank slowly to the floor.

I should have known. He's so afraid of magic—if Svy-

*atoslav himself should praise Finist's worth, Father
wouldn't believe him.*

Maria sighed, rubbing sore arms. Danilo hadn't hurt her
badly, and she knew he had acted more out of fear for her
than genuine anger. The young woman shook her head,
ashamed. What truly hurt had nothing to do with bruises
or injured pride, but the fact that she had been too foolish—too childish—to accept the strength of her father's
fear. She should never have tried to challenge him. And
no matter what she did, no matter how contritely she be-
haved, Danilo was never going to help her—or Finist.
There was no one to help Finist. No one save Maria.

Oh, fine! Right now she couldn't even help herself!

After a time her physical aches and mental shock began
to wear off a bit. And in their absence, Maria, much to
her amazement, felt her spirits begin to rise. She wasn't
going to abandon Finist, no matter what. And if she must
rescue him all by herself, so be it! But first, she'd see
about getting herself out of this fix.

The storeroom was piled with various musty-smelling
boxes and barrels. Getting stiffly to her feet, Maria began
to rummage through them, holding her breath against the
dust. They contained bits and scraps of household gear,
the sort of things to be found stored in most homes, things
too worn or rusted for use yet too good to be simply thrown
away. Maria grinned.

Oh, Father, I do think you've underestimated me!

IT took her most of the day. Twice she had to stop and
quickly hide her work when a silent, embarrassed servant
brought her food and drink and, blushing fiercely, a cham-
berpot. But by late afternoon—Maria guessed the time
from the light that filtered into the storeroom—she glanced
down at her handiwork and grinned all over again. It had
taken some trial and error, but she'd managed to use scraps
of wire to bind together the skinny haft of what might once
have been a dainty dagger—though the blade was long
gone—to a sturdy kitchen hook, ending up with a tool that
should see her out of this makeshift prison.

It did. She could slide the thin haft sideways through
the crack between door and frame, and use the hook to

catch the bolt. With a little care and effort, she would be able to slide the bolt free. And as soon as it was fully dark, and everyone in the estate was safely asleep, she would be up and away from here.

HER father came to see her at nightfall.

"Maria. I hope you've had a chance to repent your foolishness."

He waited, but she, afraid of what she might say or do, kept resolutely still, fiercely pretending to be asleep. After a moment Danilo said sharply: "Come, girl, I know you can hear me! Answer me!"

She kept her eyes shut, willing him to go away. But Danilo persisted, more softly:

"My dear, I don't want to hurt you, surely you know that! I only want you to be happy, and safe. But you can be neither with a—a godless sorcerer as your lover!"

Maria bit her lip but said nothing. At last she heard Danilo sigh in frustration, and dared open her eyes a crack, just in time to see him leave, looking so dejected that she ached to call after him. But he wasn't so dejected that he didn't remember to bolt the door after him, and Maria held to her determined silence.

For a long time she could do nothing but stare after him, thinking, *I may never see him again. After today, I may never see him, or Lissa, or home, again.*

No: if she let herself start thinking like that, she'd never have the courage to act.

She would have to wait until it was fully dark before slipping away; she might as well use the time in planning. She would need clothes, peasant clothes—it wouldn't be wise to travel as a *boyar*'s daughter. Sturdy peasant clothes, and good, stout shoes . . .

NIGHT: Through the darkened house, one small shadow moved quietly to the servants' quarters, where it tucked plain, serviceable clothing into a pack, then to the kitchen, for food that could be easily carried, and for flint and steel. Maria hesitated, then stole back to the family's private quarters. There, barely daring to breathe, she tiptoed past her father's room and into her own chambers. Watching the door nervously, half expecting to be interrupted at any moment by Danilo or her sister, Maria gathered up several small pieces of jewelry—but nothing so large or so blatantly valuable as to attract attention. She paused, looking desperately around the room. Now that the moment had come, she didn't want to leave.

But . . . the stars were dimming. If dawn was coming, there was no time to delay. Maria turned to go, then sighed and turned back again. With a small grimace at her sentimentality, she gathered up the fine silver chain, Finist's gift—

—and at the touch, she saw him; just for a moment he was there with her, warm and loving. At least some of the link the silver had created between them must still exist, and her heart ached for want of him—

Then that fantastic moment had passed. Maria stared down at the chain in her hand, now merely a pretty silver necklace, and shook her head. She really must be overwrought if she had started seeing visions! Smiling wryly, the young woman quickly slipped the chain about her neck, hiding it under her blouse.

"So," Maria Danilovna whispered. "Let me be off."

XXXII

THE GIFT

HE'D TAKEN to wandering at random through the summer-heavy forest, eating whatever came his way, never bothering with a fire, sleeping wherever the night took him. It was simpler that way, simpler than facing fear and the shame of what he'd become, what he once was . . . Though with each day, the memories of Past seemed to become more and more nebulous . . . vague images of bright colors and noise and himself as *boyar* Alexei . . . No, it hurt to think of that. It was so much simpler not to even try to think, just to wander, never realizing that something was driving him east and east and east . . .

THE *leshy* stood in shadow, watching with distaste as the ragged figure stumbled its way along. *Phaugh,* how the human reeked. No wild thing bore such a stench—every forest animal knew at least enough to keep itself clean. But this city man, whose mind had fallen so easily apart, had lost all pride, all sense of what was right and proper to the forest.

I could slay him. Let a tree drop a branch on him, that would do the trick. Slay him—bah, and then be left for days with the reek of his filthy corpse! No, no, and there's the fact that he did do me homage, mad though he is, he did. The *leshy* gave a wind-in-leaves breath of a sigh. *And so I am reduced to doing an . . . honorable thing, and merely put within his mind the urge to travel east, away from me, away from my realm.* The being shivered in sudden, delicious humor, and the bushes all around shivered as though sharing the jest. *Let my brother leshy of the eastern forests have him! Oh, how witty, how fine a joke! I did owe Brother Leshy a gift from our last meeting, when we two gambled and he won, and I never could prove he cheated. Let this creature be my gift to him!*

The *leshy* hugged himself in mischievous joy, while all around him the trees stirred, branches shaking where there was no wind.

THE sunlight hit him like a sudden blow. One moment Alexei had been making his aimless way through the forest; the next, he'd fallen quite literally out of the forest and into this unexpected meadow, and for a time he just lay where he was, arm flung over his face for protection. How long had it been since he'd seen the sun? Really seen it, without the shifting curtains of leaves in the way? Its rays soaked through him, warming him to the bones, to the corners of his mind that always seemed dark and cold these days . . .

He was free, at least for the moment. Free of the forest, its magics and its madness . . . He'd been quite insane for—God only knew how many days, but now he could begin to think clearly once more, and know that he was Alexei Sergeovich, late of Stargorod. Akh, but look at this, he was in rags, and he stank, actually stank!

Alexei rolled over, leaning on his elbows. This was a good-sized meadow, surrounded on all sides by forest. He suspected very strongly that if he tried to go back the way he'd come, that bizarre madness would overtake him once more; he could feel the darkness hovering just out of reach of consciousness, just waiting to strike.

"Very well," he said aloud, and winced at the rusty sound of his voice. "I have no intention of going back! I'll go east, instead. But . . . not just yet." Alexei shuddered. "I—I'll find shelter here, or just sleep out under the stars; the weather's mild enough for that. I . . . don't want to reenter forest, no, not yet."

Wait. Was that sound . . . water? Rushing water? Alexei got to his feet to investigate, and found that a stream bi-

sected the meadow, widening at one point into a pool.
With delighted thoughts of a bath, he hurried forward.

But he froze at the brink of the little pool, staring in
horror at his reflection. Was that thin, rough-bearded, wild-
eyed face truly his?

And as he knelt and stared down at his savage self,
Alexei felt a familiar wave of hatred come stealing through
him, and he welcomed its return as he would welcome
some old, old friend.

This is Danilo's fault, all my suffering, his fault. Alexei
delighted in the force of his hatred as he'd delighted in the
warmth of the sun. *And he will pay, oh, yes!* The young
man grinned in savage humor. *I will see him beg for mercy.
He and his dear, sweet daughters shall beg for mercy, but
I shall give them* none!

THE *leshy* stood just at the edge of the magic meadow
created by himself and his brother *leshy* to mark the verge
of their two domains, stood shrouded by trees, and stared
contemptuously at the raging, laughing man. *City-man,*
the being mused, *with his fragile, foolish hates . . . I think
no more city-folk shall pass unscathed through my forest,
no, not for a long time!*

Trees whispering all around him, the *leshy* shook his
head and began his call:

"*Brother* Leshy! *Hear me!*"

He waited, head to one side.

Silence.

With a little hiss of annoyance, the *leshy* began again,
"*Hey, now, Brother* Leshy, *hear my call!*"

Silence once more. But the being felt a consciousness
brush his own, a wary "*I hear. What would you?*"

"*Why, Brother* Leshy, *do you not recall our game of
gambling? Do you not recall the debt I owed you?*" The
being hugged himself in glee. "*My payment waits there
in the meadow between our two domains.*"

There was a pause. The other *leshy* said dubiously,
"That? *What do I want with . . .* that? *I will not take
him.*"

"*You must, you must! By the rules of our game, you
must accept my gift! And there he is, Brother* Leshy! *There*

is my gift to you! With time and patience, you should be able to drag him into your domain. And then, my Brother Leshy, enjoy your gift as you will!"

"I'll repay you for this!" hissed the other *leshy* in not-quite-feigned anger. *"I shall steal your squirrels from you, or your foxes!"*

"Storm away, storm away!" laughed the being. *"The man is yours, and yours he will remain! Farewell, Brother Leshy!"*

Oh, a wonderful jest! And how glad he was to be rid of that ugly human!

And with that, trees swaying to his laughter, the *leshy* vanished into his forest domain once more.

XXXIII

REGRETS

"MARIA?" Vasilissa tapped nervously on the storeroom's bolted door. "Maria, please!"

She had firmly approved of her father punishing the girl for her scandalous behavior. But poor Maria, having to spend the night on the cold floor of a dusty storeroom— The very thought of it had kept Vasilissa awake half the night. And now it was nearly morning, and Lissa couldn't stand it any longer. Whether or not Danilo approved, she meant to see that her sister was all right.

"Maria!" Vasilissa rapped with a bit more force. "Maria, answer me. Maria!"

The girl *couldn't* be sleeping that soundly; something must have gone wrong. Maria must be ill, or hurt, or— had the demon come for her?

"Maria!"

Hands trembling, Vasilissa fumbled with the bolt until she finally managed to pull it aside. She flung open the storeroom door—

And screamed.

Suddenly Danilo was catching her by the shoulders. "Lissa! Lissa, what is it?"

"The demon! Oh, Father, the demon came for Maria and carried her off. She's gone!"

Danilo nearly shoved her aside in his haste to get into the storeroom. But after a moment he returned, holding a thin little metal blade to which a hook had been carefully wired.

224

"No," Danilo said in quiet despair. "No one carried her off. Don't you see? Maria has run away to join her sorcerer."

MARIA huddled in the wagon, hidden under the pile of sacking, heart racing. It had been almost ridiculously easy to steal out of the estate in the early morning light, when their watchmen had plainly gone off their guards. *I must warn Father,* Maria thought, then gave a silent, wry laugh at her foolishness. Who knew when she'd see her father again?

The wagon lurched, and Maria frantically snatched at her concealing mound of sacking. It might smell of onions, but it was shelter. The peasant driver, on his way home to wherever, had no idea he was carrying a passenger out of Stargorod, and this was hardly the time to enlighten him.

Just keep going, Maria urged him silently. *Please, just keep going!*

There, they'd gotten safely over the rut or hole and were on their way again. Maria, holding her breath, heard the driver exchanging bored greetings with the guards at the city gate. And then the wagon was rumbling out of Stargorod. Maria peeked through a hole in one of the sacks, saw the city walls receding slowly behind her, and shivered in a mixture of fear and excitement.

There was no turning back now. Like it or not, she was on her way.

AFTER his first shock, Danilo, ablaze with frantic energy, called for his overseer. "Sasha, come here! Hurry!" And to the trembling Vasilissa, "Don't worry, child. She can't have gotten very far. We'll find her before— Sasha where are you, man?"

The servant came hurrying up, panting. "Ah— You're up early, master. Just as well, you see."

"What *are* you talking about? Sasha, I'm in no mood for riddles!"

"No—no riddles, master. It's orders—orders from our Prince just arrived a few moments ago. He—uh—wishes to see you and the rest of the council as soon as possible."

"Damn!" That escaped Danilo before he could stop it, but it was quite heartfelt. Just because Svyatoslav seemed to need less and less sleep as he aged, he expected his counselors to be the same! Danilo bit his lip to keep from saying something in front of Sasha that he'd regret. Dammit all! Surely Svyatoslav must realize that these early morning meetings never accomplished anything, not with all the *boyars* sitting around blinking sleepily at each other! And to be summoned now, with Maria missing—

"I can't go, not now! Tell the messenger— No, wait." Danilo gave an angry sigh as he realized: *I don't have a choice. If I don't go, Svyatoslav will certainly wonder about my loyalty again.*

"Sasha," Danilo said bluntly, "my daughter has . . . disappeared."

The servant glanced hastily at Vasilissa, then exclaimed incredulously, "What, young mistress *Maria?*"

"She has. I suspect she may be trying to reach Kirtesk."

"Kirtesk? But—that's a long way to go! And for a young lady, alone—"

"I know, man, I know!" Danilo hesitated a moment. "I'd hoped to be supervising this myself, but . . ." He shrugged helplessly. "You'll have to be in charge, Sasha. Send out as many men as you trust to search."

"Of course." Sasha bowed, then paused just long enough to give Danilo a quick, sympathetic smile. "We'll find her, master," he said gently. "All will be well, don't fear."

"Thank you. Go now. While I," the *boyar* added wryly, "go to attend my Prince."

Danilo sat with the other *boyars* in Svyatoslav's small audience chamber, and nodded when it seemed he should, and agreed with whatever the others said, and couldn't keep his thoughts from his daughter, his poor Maria, alone in the middle of—of— God, if only he hadn't been so harsh with her. He had driven her away! And yet, what else could he have done but—

"Boyar! Boyar Danilo!"

He came back to himself with a shock. "Ah, my Prince, I—"

"You." The regal sweep of arm took in the other counselors. "Leave us. You." He pointed directly at Danilo. "Stay." As soon as they were alone, Svyatoslav frowned. "What is all this about?"

"My . . . Prince?"

"This mooning and dreaming. Were I a gambling man, I'd wager you haven't heard one word in twenty that we've been saying!"

"I . . . Forgive me, my Prince."

"Not till you confess! What troubles you?"

Danilo had meant to give some vague, pacifying reply: an aching head, a poor night's sleep. But instead, he heard himself blurting, "My daughter is gone. My Maria has—has run—"

"Has run away, eh?" Svyatoslav shook his head. "There it is: children are always betraying one."

How would you know? Danilo thought savagely. *You never sired any.*

But he wisely kept silent, and the prince, with surprising gentleness, said, "Come, tell me. It shall go no further than this room. What is it? Has the girl a lover?"

"Yes— No— I mean, her virtue is—is intact; I trust Maria's sense that much. But she . . . swears she's in love."

"With someone at court? If he's unwed, surely there's no problem to arranging—"

"No problem," Danilo said bitterly. "She's chosen to love a sorcerer! Prince Finist of Kirtesk—"

He stopped short, realizing to his horror that he'd been about to condemn royalty to royalty. But Svyatoslav, unheeding, murmured, "So that's it! 'Justice,' bah! I knew he was after more than that! Why, he *used* me!" The prince stared at Danilo with such sudden intensity that the *boyar* had to fight the impulse to squirm. "So, Danilo. It seems we have a common bond between us."

"My Prince?"

"We've both been betrayed by those we love."

It was on the tip of Danilo's tongue to gasp out a ridiculous *You love Finist?* But he bit that hastily back, realizing just in time that Svyatoslav could only be referring to his treacherous cousin, the exiled Prince Rostislav.

"So!" the prince continued. "I will never see my cousin again, not while we both live. But your daughter, at least, shall be found."

"My Prince?" Danilo repeated, abandoning any hope of following the man's train of thought. "I don't understand—"

"Why, it's simple!" Svyatoslav's smile was almost beatific. "I will send my own guards to search for her. No, no, get up, man! Don't thank me till it's all over. And don't fear, *boyar,* Maria Danilovna will be found. Her betrayal shall be ended!"

XXXIV

FEVER DREAMS

ABOVE HIM, so cruelly far above him, the sky beckoned, the wide, open, free sky. The falcon ached to be up there, ached with every fiber of his being to be soaring up and out on the wind. But he couldn't move. He was snared, his wings were bound, he was trapped here, helpless amid all this cold, close stone, while within him, he burned with thirst, and the fire—the dry, cruel fire . . .

IT was a hushed and nervous gathering of *boyars*, there in the royal palace, all of them worrying about the state of their prince's health. Since his sad return to Kirtesk, carried limp and unconscious into his private chambers, the Lady Ljuba had taken charge of him, as was her place as Finist's kinswoman and a healer in her own right, and allowed no one to disturb the prince's rest. Predictably, in the absence of hard fact, the rumors had already begun to fly, among these *boyars* no less than among the commons.

"He might not recover."

"I heard his strength has been permanently damaged."

"I heard he's been crippled."

"*I* heard that . . . it's his mind that's been hurt."

Old Semyon had been stirring impatiently during all this wild speculation, but that last was just too much for him. He sprang to his feet with an angry cry of: "Enough! Are you *boyars*, or a pack of old gossips? If you're all so afraid of the Lady Ljuba that none of you dare intrude and learn the truth—I am not!"

With that, he marched boldly towards the prince's private chambers, hearing the others whispering nervously behind him. *Fools!* the old man thought sharply.

But Semyon was brought up short, staring in disbelief at the guards who moved to block his path.

"What's this?" he said indignantly. "Stand aside!"

"I'm sorry, my lord. But we are to let no one pass."

"Nonsense! I have a perfect right to enter the princely chambers, unless Prince Finist himself denies me! Has he? Well? Has he?"

"Uh—no, my lord."

"Then who dares to stop me?"

The closed door to the prince's bed-chamber opened slightly. "I do," said Ljuba. "Kindly keep your voice down, *boyar.* Your prince is asleep."

For all Semyon's angry words to the others, he had to admit that this new Ljuba, all soft submission gone for the moment, fierce-eyed and positively sorcerous of aspect, was enough to give anyone pause. And for a moment, Semyon found himself wondering if it had been wise to leave Finist in her hands. Then Ljuba was looking directly at him, her eyes so wide and deep . . . so deep . . . Semyon shook his head at his foolishness. Who better to tend the prince than someone skilled in the preparation of healing potions?

But why were her eyes so cold? Now that she wasn't staring at him, Semyon found himself fighting down a shudder, and asked hastily, embarrassed at himself, "How is he?"

Ljuba winced, slightly. "Still feverish."

For a moment, the cold perfection of her control seemed to slip, just enough to let Semyon remember with a shock that this was still, for all her poise, only a very young woman. In sudden compassion, he murmured, "Akh, don't be afraid. I know you're doing your best."

"Don't pity me!" The words were sharp as a slap, and Semyon flinched. "Go away, old man," Ljuba continued savagely. "Go and tell the others that the prince lives and will recover. Do you hear me? He will recover!"

With that, she slammed the door in his face.

* * *

ALONE in the royal bed-chamber save for the restlessly sleeping Finist, Ljuba fell against a wall and desperately fought back shaken sobs. The strength needed to control Semyon's will, even for that little time, had nearly finished her. But she couldn't let go, not now!

And yet it had all seemed to be going so well. True, she'd been horrified at her first sight of Finist's injuries, prepared to find nothing worse than iron-scratches, just enough to throw off his magical and mental balance, and finding instead those deep, ugly wounds. Had Vasilissa been there by her side, the meddling little idiot would have died. But after that first fright, she'd realized that Finist was not fatally wounded; the iron-gashes, for all their ugliness, weren't so severe. And he wasn't some forest devil, to be poisoned by the mere touch of the metal!

Finist stirred in his sleep, moaning, and Ljuba winced. Everyone of the royal blood had gone through iron-fever at one time or another; it was impossible to live in an iron-oriented society without eventually getting cut by a knife or jabbed by a pin. But no matter how high the initial fever soared, it never lasted long, not unless there was a death-wound to go along with it. And Finist just wasn't that badly injured! What was wrong with him?

You know, her inner self whispered. *It was the potion. It was the will-destroying potion.*

"That's impossible!" Ljuba said aloud. Oh, granted, she hadn't wasted any time, she'd given some of it to him, mixed with wine to sweeten the taste, as soon as they'd first been alone; feverish and raging with thirst, Finist had drunk it without question.

But it should only have lowered his resistance to my will. It couldn't have hurt him, not really!

Couldn't it? Ljuba realized with a sudden shock of horror that she'd never thought to test her potion on other than healthy subjects. She'd never even considered it!

And what effect might it have on someone weak from wounds, from fever . . . *Oh, Lord above, what if I've poisoned Finist?*

Cold with fear, Ljuba turned sharply way. He *must* live! Finist *must* live, or all her hopes and dreams died with him.

XXXV

OLD MAGIC

MARIA STIRRED gingerly under the protective mound of sacking, trying to stretch stiff muscles without letting the driver know his wagon was carrying a secret passenger. Not, she thought dryly, that he could have heard her over the monotonous creak, creak, *crack* of the uneven wooden wheels. But gradually she became aware of a new noise, counterpoint to the wheels' groaning, a rhythmic sort of rumbling . . . Thunder? If so, the storm was speeding towards them, because the sound was rapidly growing louder—

No, not thunder, but the sound of cantering horses.

Maria groaned. Things had been going so well—the driver had even taken the forest road towards Kirtesk. But now . . .

Maybe, she told herself hopefully, the riders had nothing to do with her. Warily, she peeked out, and quickly stifled a gasp. Those were her father's men, and with them, riders in livery—royal soldiers!

Father must have gotten the prince to help him.

And he must have figured out that she was trying to get to Kirtesk. This was the only road, so surely the soldiers would just keep patrolling it until they found her. And that meant they'd be searching the wagon again.

What if she abandoned the road altogether? Maria hesitated, thinking of all those *versts* of forest. It was one thing for Finist to fly lightly over them. But for all the time her family had spent on that farm, she was the first to admit how little she knew about actual wilderness survival.

Here came the soldiers, back again. *There's no hope for it,* Maria thought desperately, and dove into the forest.

At first all she sensed was silence, immense and alive. But slowly her ears adjusted to the faint stirrings of leaves, the rustlings of small creatures in the thick underbrush. Maria took a wary step forward, trying to judge direction through the heavy canopy of leaves.

A strange, intense warmth at her throat startled her: *Something's burned me!* But it wasn't really painful, not really hot—

And it was coming from the silver chain. Finist's gift.

Quickly she pulled it free of the neckline of her blouse, staring at it. Surely it should be glowing! But it looked the same as it had always looked, the finely wrought links glinting faintly in the dim forest light. Puzzled, she took a second, tentative step, back the way she had come.

Nothing happened.

Let's try this again.

Maria turned back to where she'd begun—and that was it! As long as she faced this way, the silver chain radiated warmth.

Magic? she wondered, then laughed at herself. Naturally, magic! She'd already had one experience of mind-to-mind linking, thanks to this chain. And, though she'd been too dazed to take much notice of it at the time, Finist had mentioned he'd accidentally spilled a drop or two of his blood into the molten metal. And blood, according to the old tales, was strong with the Power of Life. Now, even though the prince wasn't here, Maria guessed that the forest's magic, Old Magic, had stimulated the Power of silver and blood a new. The necklace did still seem to be attuned to Finist.

Maria grinned in sudden delighted relief. If she was correct, all she need do was follow the chain. No matter how dense the forest might become, this wonderful, magical chain would guide her right to Kirtesk—and to Finist.

THE *leshy* frowned. He had felt the presence of the human riders, of course he had. But they had stayed on the road, that uneasy compromise between Human and Forest. They hadn't trespassed, and therefore didn't concern him. Yet there *was* someone, some fool of a city-bred intruder! The being moved silently forward, tracking, then stopped, hidden by dappled shadow, to watch.

He remembered this one, this young female human . . . the girl from the farm. The girl who'd saved his son! But now there was a difference to her . . . The *leshy* hissed in displeasure. Now she bore the unmistakable taint of City about her.

Yet I am still in her debt, the *leshy* admitted reluctantly. *Just as much as I was with Brother* Leshy. *Debts must be paid. Aie, but I have sworn not to let city-folk pass!*

It was a dilemma. He stood for a time, more still than anything of mere human flesh and blood, and pondered.

Aie, but these humans are such boring things!

With a whoop and a laugh, the *leshy* swarmed up a tree, startling a squirrel, tickling its nose, then froze again, thinking of that itch of a debt. He leaped lightly down to the forest floor with a sigh, and all the leaves about him stirred.

Vows are magic, not safely broken. So the forest shall not welcome her; no, it shall not.

He would let it do what it would do. And if, in the doing, the human was harmed or slain—that was the way of things.

Yet . . . the debt . . . I will not aid her until and unless she thinks to call upon me. The being paused, considering, then gave a foxlike bark of a laugh. *Yes. It is the way it must be.*

The human promptly forgotten, the *leshy* turned away and vanished into the forest's depths.

WELL, *what did you expect?* Maria chided herself. *A gentle stroll in the country?*

For what had seemed like days, she'd been struggling through summer woodland that seemed grimly determined to stop her, thrusting out roots to trip her, branches to snag clothing and flesh. The ground beneath the deceptively smooth carpet of old leaves had proven so treacherous that she'd had to pick her way, thankful for her sturdy shoes, lest she do something as disastrous as twist or break an ankle.

"I don't remember the forest about the farm ever being as tangled as this, or as rugged!"

Still, the pull of the silver chain was leading her on. Maria stopped to wipe stray strands of hair back from her overheated face, then grimly continued. Akh, the fallen log she'd thought secure had rolled under her feet and sent her sprawling! Scratched and aching, Maria lay still for a moment, catching her breath, feeling the life-force of the forest all around her, powerful, indifferent . . .

No, not indifferent. It knew she was here, and it didn't care for the knowledge—

Oh, nonsense! She was beginning to think like Vasilissa.

Maria scrambled to her feet, trying in vain to wipe bits of twigs and leaves from her skirt, then started forward once more—only to stop short as she realized she'd been about to walk right into a gnarled giant of a tree. Shaking her head, she started around it, only to find her way blocked by a thorny thicket. After a vain attempt to find a safe way through the dangerous thing, she backed away— only to find herself backing right into the gnarled tree once more. She moved hastily aside, then froze, listening with all her might. Was it illusion—or the faintest, most inhuman sound of mocking laughter?

The wind, Maria decided after an anxious moment. *It must have been the wind in branches.* The *boyarevna* drew a deep breath, telling herself to go on. She had to find some safe, dry place to camp before nightfall, and night wouldn't be long in arriving. Though she guessed it must be late afternoon, the forest was already growing dark.

Maria shivered, anticipating the chill that would soon rise from the cooling earth. A fire, now—a nice, warm, cheerful campfire . . .

The forest seemed to flinch about her, almost as though it had caught her thought. Branches lashed at her as though the wind had caught them—but there *was* no wind. Gasping, Maria fought her way forward again, away from the old tree and the barricade of thorns—only to find her

way blocked this time by two larches grown close together.

*They weren't here like this a moment ago, I could
almost swear it!*

And the air had grown so still, so heavy, almost men-
acing. No, impossible. This was a forest, only a forest,
not some demonic being!

Maria heard the softest slither behind her, and turned
to see the impossible.

The branches of the thicket were stirring and spreading
themselves, moving with slow, dreadful purpose, blocking
the path she had just taken.

Heart racing wildly, Maria spun about again, suddenly
terrified that the two larches might be working some darkness behind her back. But there they stood, innocent of
any trace of that obscene, impossible motion, two solid,
stolid young trees. And now she realized that there was
space between them, just enough space to let her squeeze
through, were she careful. This was hardly the time to
worry about it! Hastily, Maria began to worm her way
through . . .

And the two larches began, creaking, to move together,
closing the gap between them, very plainly sentient, very
plainly intent on crushing the life from her.

In a burst of sudden, desperate inspiration, Maria struggled against the ever-increasing pressure till she could
reach the neckline of her blouse and whip out the magic-
drenched silver chain. The larches froze, then seemed to
flinch away, just enough to let her force her frantic way
through to safety. But as soon as she'd passed, the motion
resumed, and the two trees crashed together with such
terrifying force that Maria nearly screamed.

Something grabbed at her skirt. She looked wildly over
her shoulder, to find that the hem had been caught between
the trees. Fighting down hysterical sobs, Maria tugged
fiercely until it tore and she was free. But not safe: the
forest was all around her, hostile . . .

Pure, primitive rage burned away her fear.

"Dammit, I've done you no harm. Enough!"

It wasn't working. The forest wasn't interested in anything she might say. But Maria remembered one other—

"Leshy!" she shouted. *"Leshy* of the forest, I call upon you! Honor your debt!"

The forest grew very still, a mighty sentient beast holding its breath. And a voice, strange and cold and never human, said out of nowhere:

"I am here. What would you?"

Maria let out a shaken gasp. "Safe passage," she said, trying to keep her voice level. "Safe passage through your realm."

"Indeed? You ask for no small thing, human-girl."

"I saved your son's life, *leshy!* Surely that was no small thing, either!"

The trees about her stirred restlessly, and Maria tensed, wondering if she'd gone too far. Then she heard the faintest of rustling sounds, and realized to her amazement that the *leshy* was laughing.

"Ah, the nerve of these human-folk! The sheer, foolish, ignorant nerve!"

"That's as it may be," Maria replied sharply. "But will you honor your debt?"

"Why, I must. Stand as you are, human-girl, stand still."

Something stirred in the darkness, something reached out a branch or a hand to her brow. She gasped and bit her lip as a burning like ice seared her forehead. But as soon as it had come, the pain was gone, and Maria reached up a tentative hand to touch her forehead. No harm seemed to have been done . . .

"Now you are marked," came the *leshy*'s cool wind-whisper of a voice. "Though it is nothing mortal eyes can see. Now the trees shall not crush you, the paths not disappear before your feet."

Why did she feel he was mocking her? What was the *leshy* deliberately not telling her? She pondered a moment before speaking.

"That's well and good, *leshy,* and I do thank you. But what about those beings that might be living in the forest? Does the protection extend as far as—"

A hiss, sharp and angry and alien, made her flinch. Then the *leshy* spat out, "No more, human-girl! I have granted you enough! Go through the forest as you dare, but tarry no longer within than you must. Our debt is paid!''

With a wild laugh and rustling of leaves, he was gone. But Maria was almost sure someone else was watching her.

''Who's there?''

''Don't be afraid, mortal-child,'' came a soft voice.

Maria blinked. ''You're the *leshy*'s wife, the *lisunka!*''

The being chuckled. ''Indeed. Don't let my husband frighten you, human-girl. He brags and blusters, but forgets that I am as much the forest as he. Child, you did us the greatest of good when you saved my son. Now I, in turn, shall aid you.''

Maria felt a small, smooth object being forced into her hand. She peered down at it in the darkness. ''A wooden egg?''

''Guard it well. Draw it out only when you are in despair and darkest peril.''

''But what is it? What does it do?''

''Guard it well!'' the *lisunka* repeated. And then she too was gone, and Maria was alone in the night.

XXXVI

VOWS

THERE WERE TIMES when he could feel himself trying to swim back through the layers of darkness. At times Finist was vaguely aware of a chamber, his bedchamber . . . But it was difficult to hold to consciousness; he felt so weak, so ill . . . Blinking, trying in vain to clear his swimming vision, he managed to force heavy eyelids open long enough to dimly make out someone's face through the haze . . .

"Ljuba?" he whispered.

"Hush, cousin. Drink this."

"No, I . . ." There had been something about the last drink she'd given him, something that seemed to be bewildering his wits. In a wild surge of defiance, he flung out an arm and sent the goblet flying. "No, cousin, I don't yield so very easily! I . . ."

But he hadn't the strength. The fever burned in him, and he was weary, too weary for defiance.

"No . . ." Finist said weakly, and sank back into the world of dreams. "Maria, where are you? Maria . . ."

LJUBA, drenched, let out a hiss of frustration. Weak as he was, dangerously ill as he was, where had Finist found the strength to resist her?

He could only have found it, she realized abruptly, in the discipline necessary for true magic. And for a moment, Ljuba caught herself staring down at him with all her old jealousy. But jealousy was ridiculous right now.

And of course, a magician's mind was schooled to control arcane forces by will alone, so it wouldn't yield so easily to something as natural as disease. Even iron-enhanced disease.

Akh, but that very stubbornness was endangering Finist's life. Once his mind finally surrendered to her control, once he stopped weakening himself by defiance, his body would begin to heal—she was sure of it. She'd carefully diluted her potion to the point where it should only be helping him by relaxing that fierce will. But he wouldn't surrender, and all her attempts to feed it to him were meeting with failure.

And would he never stop moaning for his dear Maria? Ljuba frowned, astonished to feel a twinge of pain mingling with her rage. Still . . . what if he called to *her* with such longing in his voice . . . ?

Akh, foolishness. She was getting soft-minded for want of rest. Ljuba rubbed tired eyes, trying to remember when she'd last had a chance to sleep, really sleep. Slowly she got to her feet, shedding the potion-soaked caftan and slipping into a fresh one. She dared do no more than nap, not till Finist was safely under control and out of danger.

Aie, there he went again, calling for Maria!

"Maria, Maria, Maria!" Ljuba mocked under her breath. "Let me see what your little slut is doing. Ha, she must have forgotten you by now!"

SASHA bowed low before his master, stalling for time, trying desperately to think of some gentle way to deliver his news.

"Sasha?" Danilo had risen from his table so quickly he still clutched a precious glass goblet. "Come, man, out with it! Is there any word of my daughter?"

No, Sasha decided, there wasn't any gentle way. "No, master," he confessed, and then added formally, "I regret to tell you that neither our men nor those of our good Prince Svyatoslav have been able to find the slightest trace of the *boyarevna* Maria."

"That's impossible!" Danilo snapped. "Sasha, don't lie to me!"

"Oh, I only wish I were!" Sasha said miserably.

"But . . . My lord, your daughter seems to have . . . vanished. She might have run off into the forest, see, to elude us." He stopped, wincing, hating what he was going to have to say next. "The—the forest is large. A young woman lost in there might . . . never be found."

"No!" It was a shout more of pain than of rage. "I won't accept that. I can't!"

"I'm sorry—"

"Sorry! Is that all, that you're *sorry?*" Danilo knew if he didn't shout, he just might weep. "Get out of my sight!" he stormed. "Go back out there and search, and don't dare to return unless you—"

"Father." Vasilissa laid a gentle hand on his shoulder. "Don't be afraid. I'd know it were Maria . . . dead. She's alive and unharmed, I swear it."

"Akh, Lissa, you can't be sure of that."

"I can." Vasilissa's mouth tightened in a grim line. "And I can guess what's become of her."

"What do you mean?"

"Send men out to search the forest, yes. But also send an envoy to Kirtesk, to the court of that—that sorcerer!"

Danilo gave his daughter a sharp, searching glance. She might be delicate of mind, he couldn't deny it, but there were also times when she spoke with surprising wisdom. Who knew? Maybe Maria's sorcerous lover had been waiting to meet her and carry her off.

"Yes," Danilo said slowly. "Thank you, child. I shall send men to Kirtesk, whether our Prince approves it or not! And should it turn out that this—this sorcerer-prince has connived to take advantage of Maria's innocence, if he harms her in any way . . ."

The *boyar* clenched his hand so fiercely about the goblet he'd been holding that the delicate glass shattered.

LJUBA drew back in disgust at the sight of Danilo, his hand bleeding, staring blankly ahead with hatred in his eyes. "*That's* the father of Finist's beloved?" she murmured dryly, letting the image fade. "Oh, my dear fool of a cousin, you might as well have fallen in love with an out-and-out burner of witches!"

So Maria was gone, was she? Run off to find Finist?

Ljuba gave a little cry of mingled rage and contempt at the thought of her out there somewhere, trying with all the earnestness of her pious little soul to follow her lost love. It was as irritating as a thorn Ljuba couldn't reach to remove.

Of course, Maria would almost certainly get lost in the forest, or murdered by bandits, or eaten by something.

But what if she didn't?

Worse, what if she and Finist were magically attuned, by a spell, perhaps, or his gift to her? What if Finist, in his near-delirium, was using that link as a healthy magician might use a crystal, making that outside magic a focus for his resistance to his cousin? The link would last as long as Maria lived. And continued resistance might weaken Finist to the point of death—and kill all Ljuba's hopes at the same time.

Ljuba turned sharply to her little crystal mirror again. "I'm sorry, my dear Maria. I'm afraid you really are going to have to be removed."

XXXVII

THE PACT

MARIA PAUSED to impatiently braid her wild hair, wishing for perhaps the hundredth time that during her frantic, hurried preparations she had remembered to pack a comb.

By the time I reach Kirtesk—she glanced down at her ragged, scratched, unkempt self—*it'll be a marvel if the guards let me enter the city.*

No wonder that she didn't look the elegant *boyarevna:* All too soon she had discovered that not even farm work had prepared her for a wilderness trek. And there was more than physical strain: Even with the *leshy's* grudging cooperation, Maria was only protected from the forest. But she could sense other beings watching her from the shadows, softly following her. So far, they had seemed harmless enough, merely curious—attracted, perhaps, by the silver chain's aura of magic. But Maria could remember all too well Finist telling her that each *leshy* ruled only a portion of the great forest. Who knew whether one *leshy's* protection held true beyond his domain. And Finist had told her that the force which was forest magic, Old Magic, grew stronger the further east one went. . . .

It all seemed far too much. Footsore, aching, more alone than she'd ever been in her life, Maria cried out:

"I can't do anymore!"

If only she could find the road! Even though she'd been travelling for nearly half a month, if her reckonings were still accurate, the soldiers must surely still be patrolling it; her father and Svyatoslav were not men to give up eas-

ily. The soldiers would take her home, and all this would
be over. Maria glanced wildly about and saw nothing but
forest—unbroken, untouched forest, gloomy beneath the
canopy of leaves. All around her a hundred little chirping,
rustling lives went on their way, not caring whether she
lived or died, and the young woman bit back a despairing
sob.

Finist, oh, Finist . . .

Falling to her knees amid the litter of ancient fallen
leaves, she clutched the silver chain to her, feeling its
warmth stealing into her chilly hands, wonderfully com-
forting, reminding her that human love still lived, even in
this nonhuman place. Hugging the chain to her, Maria
determinedly remembered Finist as she'd first seen him as
Finn, remembered how she had warily begun to love him
even then. And when he had first, nervously, come to her
as Finist . . . Maria smiled wanly at the thought of those
magical nights.

For an instant she could have sworn Finist was there
with her, soothing her fears. When she looked up, wondering, Maria found herself alone; yet somehow she did
feel comforted.

*Akh, Finist, I can't abandon you. Come what may, I
love you.*

She let out a long, shaken sigh, then scrambled to her
feet, brushing off leafy skeletons as best she could. Now
that she was determined to go on, there was no need for
hysteria. The forest wouldn't hurt her; she would just go
on believing that. As for food . . . Well, as long as she
kept her head, that wouldn't be too much of a problem,
either.

The scanty provisions she had been able to carry with
her—the cheese and bread and dried meat she'd stolen from
the kitchen back home—had soon begun to run dangerously low. But during her farm days, Maria had talked to
peasants and hunters, and had learned a good deal about
foraging. There were berries aplenty now, in the heart of
summer, and edible roots; frogs were easy to catch bare-
handed, and quite tasty if one didn't think about it too
much. There were fish to be seined from streams with her
shawl. She had already swiped a rabbit from some hunter's

snare, and might be able to do it again. And since she and
the forest seemed to have come to a sort of truce about
the lighting of fires—small, well-tended fires—she could
cook whatever she found. Maybe it wasn't a luxurious life,
but . . . Maria gave a chuckle, rather surprised to feel her
spirits rising once more.

"I refuse to worry about What Might Be," she said
aloud. "I've managed to survive so far, and I firmly intend
to go right on surviving!"

With that, she shifted her pack to a more secure position, took a deep breath, and started forward.

ALEXEI had built himself a shelter there in the meadow, a
rickety hut contrived from fallen branches and bits of bark.
He'd kept himself fed on whatever he could find, and refused to consider that someday the summer would end,
and the winter come on. But—he was a prisoner, as surely
as though walls penned him in, for the moment he entered
too deeply into the forest, Alexei knew with dreadful certainty, the forest would take him.

There must be a way out of this, a way back to civilized
lands . . . But so far he had not found it. No matter how
hard he tried to hold to dreams of power, wealth, revenge,
his will kept slipping away. And right now, Alexei simply
lay in the warm meadow sunlight, as empty of thought as
any of the small animal lives about him.

But—there was a flicker of movement, there at the far
end of the meadow. Alexei came bolt upright, staring,
thinking, *God, oh God!* That was a human form—a girl
form!

Overwhelmed by shock, his muscles wouldn't move; he
could only sit and stare. But if he didn't do something,
she'd get away, and he'd be alone again. Struggling frantically to his feet, Alexei shouted in a voice grown harsh
with disuse:

"Wait! Stop!"

Aie, he'd been too slow to react. All unaware of his
presence, the girl had already scampered from one end of
the meadow to the other—almost as though she was afraid
to be caught out in the open—and vanished into the forest
at its far side. Alexei let out a little moan. She hadn't heard

him, and now it was too late. Desperate, he began to lunge after her—

No, he dared not. Enter that forest, and he was lost, he knew it.

And the girl? She was lost, too. The forest would never let her go. The forest would keep her, forever and ever.

"A pity. What a pity. She was so young. Young, and warm, and soft . . ."

Head all at once full of dim memories, of private rooms and woman-scent and secret, midnight games, Alexei sank back to the grass and vagueness once more.

LJUBA bit back a frustrated curse. What good old Semyon deigning to allow her a mirror once more if she couldn't keep her emotions under control long enough to bend its image to her will? But—Maria! The forest's hostility had allowed Ljuba only tantalizing bits of vision, but she had seen that—that—Maria—had somehow managed to charm it into letting her pass. Bah, more than merely let her pass. The girl had already gotten surprisingly far, quite unscathed.

"I don't believe it!"

That sheer, quiet persistence was maddening. And it certainly wasn't helping to have to listen to Finist's incessant calling for his love. Particularly since she suspected he wasn't so far from lucidity that he couldn't taunt his cousin.

"Oh—*dammit!*" Ljuba exploded.

She must be rid of that girl. She hadn't a chance of controlling Finist completely till that—that gadfly was crushed!

Raging, Ljuba turned her full attention to her mirror. There must be someone human in that forest, a hunter, a bandit, someone she could contact, someone quite without scruples . . .

Yes . . . There was a meadow, clear enough without the forest's magic-haze to fog it, though it did seem to have its own magical aura, and a figure within that meadow— a man, or what passed for one. Ljuba curled a fastidious lip in disgust at his raggedness.

Yes, but she didn't care if the man wasn't a vision of

masculine beauty! He need only have two things: greed, and a certain ruthlessness. And a man in such sorry condition was almost certain to be greedy, and eager enough for any reward she might offer to be ruthless.

Ljuba's smile was thin and cold.

AT first, he thought the woman only a part of his fantasies, this radiant golden creature whose image seemed to waver ever so slightly, a vision, a lovely, sensual dream of pleasure . . .

"Have you finished staring?" the vision asked him. "Come, fool! Answer me!"

The startled Alexei sat sharply up. Pleasure-dreams didn't scold! Was she a . . . hallucination? Alexei looked at the beautiful creature, and shook his head. He doubted his madness could ever be *that* artistic!

"All right, you're real. Who are you?" That strangely wavering image made him add warily, "And, for that matter, *where* are you?"

"Who and where I am doesn't concern you."

"Why, you're a magician!" Delighted to realize he wasn't *that* far gone into madness, Alexei managed to summon up an echo of his former charm, his former cunning, enough to make him ask urbanely, "But, dear lady, why bother sending your image to me? What could you possibly want from such as myself?"

"An errand." If the woman was surprised by his sudden courtliness, she didn't show it. "The removal of . . . a nuisance."

"Ah." Alexei's voice was bland. "A living nuisance, I take it?"

"Why, the man has some wit about him after all!" Her smile was humorless. "I shall be blunt. There is a girl somewhere in the forest near you."

Alexei tensed. "The—forest . . ."

"Yes, of course! You may even have seen her pass." The lovely eyes had gone quite cold. "I wish her to disappear."

"But . . . to go into the forest . . . I don't dare—"

"What nonsense is this? I didn't think you were a complete fool—ahh, I see what it is! You're trying to bargain with me, aren't you? Very well, man, what do you wish? Come, name your price!''

"You—don't understand. I can't enter the forest. The— the demon will seize me again."

He saw a flicker of unease cross her face. *She knows,* Alexei thought wildly. *She knows about the demon! She knows I'm telling the truth!* And he wondered nervously if she was simply going to abandon him.

But the woman said sharply, "No demon will touch you, not if you obey me. My magic will shield you. And the girl, Maria Danilovna—''

"Danilovna!" Alexei shot to his feet, grabbing for the woman's shoulders. But of course, his hands merely passed through the wavering image, and fighting fiercely for self-control, Alexei stepped back. "Maria Danilovna," he repeated savagely. "Are you sure?"

"So-o! You have no love for the slut, either!"

"I have no love for the whole damned family!" Too tense to remain still, Alexei began pacing nervously in a tight circle. "To have her in my hands, to start my revenge . . . And with magic to shield me . . ." He stopped, looked up. "Your magic *will* shield me?"

"Why, of course," the woman said smoothly. "You'll do it, then? I have your word on it?"

"Not—not so fast. I—want more. I—I was a *boyar* once."

"And you wish a return to power, do you? Why, man! In a few short days, I shall rule a realm! Serve me well now, and you shall have a place of honor at my court."

To be a *boyar* again! Oh, no doubt this woman, whomever, whatever she was, would try to trick him, to be rid of him, but he'd outwit her, magic or no, he'd outwit her and survive. And he would triumph!

"Done!" shouted Alexei in savage joy. "Oh, done, done!"

XXXVIII

RUSALKI

DANILO'S MEN HAD BEEN RIDING along the forest road in silence for some time, now walking their horses, now trotting, now cantering, covering *verst* after *verst* that way. But all around them loomed the trees, dark with shadow, mysterious, dangerous, and at last the men took to singing to keep back the darkness. After a time, though, they had finished all the songs (polite and otherwise) that they knew, and before the ominous silence could fall again, one of them, young Ivan, said hastily:

"It's been a week. Must be halfway to Kirtesk by now."

The others weren't in the mood for small talk. "Mm," said one, noncommittally.

"Think the sorcerer has her?" Ivan persisted. "Young mistress Maria, I mean."

That earned him a scornful glance. "Now, what do you think? Of course he has her!"

Stung, Ivan continued, "And we're going to ride right up to him, yes? And tell him we're from her father? And—and demand the *boyarevna* back again?"

The others glanced at him impatiently. "Of course!"

"We're really going to ride up to a sorcerer, and insist he give back the woman he probably went through a lot of trouble to get. Fine. But what," asked Ivan simply, "are we going to do if the sorcerer says no?"

They were trying not to think about that. A nervous silence fell, broken only by Ivan's worried murmur, "I only pray the young mistress is safe. I truly do."

* * *

"You are not my brother *leshy's* gift."

Maria whirled at the voice, stifling a yelp. "I, uh, no," she said warily, realizing that somewhere along the way she must have crossed over into this second *leshy's* domain. "I don't think I am."

"Yet you bear his mark of safe passage."

"Yes." Maria peered into forest shadow, trying in vain to locate the being. "He was paying a debt."

"Ah." It was a sound of perfect comprehension. "But you carry another's sign as well."

Maria raised a tentative hand to the silver chain about her neck. "Do you mean this? This was a—a gift."

"From the human-magician."

"You know him? Oh, please tell me, is he well? Is he—"

"How should I know that? His realm is city, mine forest." The being sighed—a soft stirring of leaves. "But he has always been in harmony with the forest way. There is peace between us. You love him?"

The suddenness of the question caught Maria off balance. "Yes!" she gasped. "Please, may I go to him?"

"You may go where you will." The *leshy* sounded surprised that she had even thought to ask. "A warning: You have passed safely through my brother *leshy's* domain. But that domain has been softened by the new, human ways from the west." Was there a hint of superiority in the wind-in-leaves voice? "The forest-magic here is older, stronger. Walk warily."

"What do you—"

But the leshy was already gone.

"I wish *I* could move that efficiently," said Maria. She gave a sudden shiver, remembering branches that stirred without wind, trees that moved to slay . . . "Softened," echoed the young woman. "If that was his idea of 'softened,' then what must *his* realm be like?"

She would find it out, sooner or later, whether she liked the idea or not.

"But the road, as the saying goes, doesn't get shorter for the waiting."

And, with a quick touch of the silver chain for luck, Maria started eastward once more.

IT had taken time for Alexei to gather enough courage to enter the forest, even with the magician-woman's assurance of protection, even under the goad of his own shame. Maria's trail had nearly grown cold when Alexei had finally mastered himself and plunged in, but now he found that he could still follow it. Somehow, magically, no one, no *thing* was moving to stop him.

Magically! The woman had been right, she had been telling the truth, her powers *were* protecting him! Alexei squirmed in delight. Let the forest demons rage as they would; they couldn't touch him, not with that beautiful and most powerful magician as his ally! And as for the girl he was pursuing—she couldn't be travelling too quickly, and soon enough he'd overtake her, and then . . . Alexei hissed with savage laughter as he tore his hungry way through the underbrush.

So *that* was his brother *leshy's* gift! The being stared at the ragged creature in distaste, thinking that Brother *Leshy* had a dubious sense of humor at best. No wonder the foxes were always sneaking out of his domain! The *leshy* gave a dry wind-whisper of a laugh, remembering the last time Brother *Leshy* had gamed with him, and lost, and been forced to give up almost all his squirrels from leaf-birth to leaf-death.

He moved smoothly after the human, chuckling soundlessly in the joke of seeing but unseen. Well now, maybe he was, indeed, bound by the rules of the *leshiye* games to accept this . . . gift. But no rule said he had to actually *do* anything with it! The being hugged himself with delight. There is was! He'd let the creature pass as it would, and maybe it would be eaten by something, or simply make its way right out of his domain. Either way, Brother *Leshy's* jibe at him would be spoiled!

THEY'D been following her for some time, the whatever-they-were, drawn, Maria guessed, by the magical aura of her necklace. And while they hadn't actually done anything—yet—she was beginning to feel unnerved by the glimpses at the very corners of her vision of shadowy forms and pale, glowing, inhuman eyes. Something cried out— a bird? an animal?—with a sound very much like shrill, tittering laughter, and Maria started violently.

"Enough of this." She held the silver chain out from her neck so it was clearly visible. "See? It's a necklace, that's all, a chain of silver. It was given to me by a magician. You may even know him: Finist, Prince of Kirtesk. Now, are you satisfied?"

They were, to judge from the whisperings in the bushes. But as she turned to go on, Maria found that she'd picked up a new, equally fascinated audience, the members of which—as far as she could tell in the deepening shadows— seemed to look something like hedgehogs. Hedgehogs with green fur, bright green eyes, and a tendency to giggle.

"Wonderful."

At least the things—some type of forest sprites, she assumed—all seemed harmless. They were even, in their own strange way, a sort of company. But if so many magical creatures were able to gather by daylight (when, according to all the old tales she'd heard, nothing enchanted was supposed to be out and about), just what might be waiting for her by night?

No, Maria told herself firmly. *I refuse to start worrying.*

And yet, it was already twilight, and rapidly turning towards the night . . .

Akh, this was ridiculous! She had come all this way, she wasn't going to let herself be afraid of nothing.

But the swift forest darkness was overtaking her. She was beginning to have to peer to see her way. Better to stop for the night now, while she could still—

A sharp squeal of alarm made her jump. All her little green-eyed, giggling friends vanished in a frightened rustling of bushes. Then the forest was still, unnaturally still. Remembering the deadliness of two innocent-seeming larch trees, Maria, hand going to the silver necklace, turned, ever so warily . . .

What was that shadowy Something? Strain as she might, she couldn't see it clearly in the darkness, save to note that it was large and filled with a strange, boneless, supple power. And it was stalking her. Silent as death, it was stalking her, radiating a dreadful cold amusement at her fear.

"All right!" she shouted at it defiantly. "Maybe I *am* afraid! But I'm not going to run! And I'm not going to stand here like a little fool and let you scare me right into your jaws, either!"

But how could she fight something she couldn't even see clearly? How could she fight something that was sending wave after wave of terror at her?

The *leshy?* No, she had no hold on him; he would have no reason to answer her.

The necklace? It was silver, and magical—

Quickly she pulled the chain over her head and held it up, silver glinting bravely even in the darkness, and the Something, darker still than the night, flinched. But it stood its ground. And that cold mockery radiated from it, beating at her mind till Maria ached to simply turn and flee. But blind flight would surely be the death of her.

Maria straightened, listening intently. Now that the forest had fallen so still, she could hear other sounds, and one of them . . . Water? Free, rushing water? All the old tales said that creatures of evil couldn't cross rushing water! Maybe the tales were right, maybe they were wrong, but right now, they were the only hope she could find. Gathering up her skirts, Maria ran towards the sound of water with all her might. The moon was rising, the cold silver rays beginning to pierce through the forest, casting a ghostly light, just enough to let her see where she was going.

Then the earth was crumbling beneath her feet, and Maria threw herself backwards, just in time to keep from tumbling down the slight embankment into the water:

No mere stream, this, but a lake, fed at one end by a narrow ribbon of a waterfall, a lake silent and beautiful and eerie in the chill night, a flat mirror of silver shadowed here and there by grey or indigo or black shadows, its boundaries hidden by mist.

Beauty wasn't going to stop her pursuer. Maria glanced wildly back—and a cold, slim, inhumanly strong hand closed about her wrist, pulling her backwards, towards the lake. Desperate, Maria lashed out with the silver chain as best she could, feeling the magical metal whip across cool flesh. There was a wild hiss of pain, then she was free, scrambling about on the damp, slippery earth to face her attacker.

A woman!

She was naked in the moonlight, standing half out of the lake waters, one hand languorously brushing back long curtains of hair as fair as her pale, pale skin. She was too slim, too long of arm and leg for true humanity, from the sharp, triangular face, broad at forehead, narrow at chin, to the sleek, supple muscling beneath that smooth skin. Her eyes were green and wild and empty as emerald flame as she stared at Maria and gave a soft, throaty laugh.

Maria asked in shaken wonder, *"Rusalka?"*

"Rusalki," corrected the woman-thing. "See, here are my sisters."

They were all around her, the strange creatures, slim and lovely and deadly as any predator. And predators they were, these women who had drowned by chance or design and been reborn to this parody of life, hating humanity, feeding off it when someone fell into their grasp.

As I have done! thought Maria in horror. *That great, dark thing was illusion,* their *illusion, to drive me here to them.*

"Pretty maid," one of the *rusalki* was crooning. "Brave, pretty thing. We shall not make you suffer, no, not like the others. We shall drown you swiftly, and feed. And who knows? Perhaps your spirit will join us, and play in these waters forever."

"Thank you, no," said Maria wryly. "This is a lovely lake, and I—I'm sure you're very happy in it. But I'd really rather not join you."

"No? You have no choice, pretty maid!"

They were closing their circle about her. In another moment, she would be forced into the water—

"Wait!" cried Maria in desperation. "You—you see, I *do* have a choice!"

They stared at her with those fierce, disconcertingly empty eyes, waiting with inhuman patience, and Maria racked her brain frantically. What did the old tales have to say about *rusalki?* That they were deadly, yes, that they were cruel and alien as cats . . . What else? *Someone* must have found a way to escape them!

"Riddles!" Maria cried, and the green eyes blinked. "I challenge you to a riddling contest!"

"So-o!" one of the *rusalki* crowed. "And do you dare, little human?"

"I dare!" Relieved to see the deadly ring draw back, Maria continued hastily, "It's to be a contest in the old style, three riddles for one of you, three for me!"

The *rusalka* who had first spoken gave her soft laugh. "I shall be your opponent, pretty maid. And if you cannot answer one of my riddles, mine shall be the hand to draw you underwater."

"Fair enough. But if you can't answer one of *my* riddles, then I go free, and you have no further hold on me! Agreed?"

The *rusalka* smiled thinly. "Oh, agreed."

"Do you swear it?" Maria persisted, not liking what she saw on that thin, fair face. "Swear by . . . by whatever you hold sacred."

The lake-woman chuckled at that. "Oh, brave little human! Few are the things such as we hold sacred! But I will swear, by the moon and the lake and the living forest. Will that do for you, pretty maid?"

"It, uh, yes. It will."

Maria hesitated, licking suddenly dry lips. "You—you're the challenged party, so you have the right to choose the first riddle."

"Do I, indeed? Silver living, silver dead, upon me are others fed."

She'd said it so smoothly, it took Maria a second to realize that the *rusalka* had just spoken a riddle. "Silver living, silver dead . . ." The first thing that came to mind was her necklace. But: ". . . upon me are others fed."

Oh, good Heavens. It was simple enough, almost too simple. "A fish!" cried Maria. "The answer's a caught fish!"

There was the faintest of whisperings among the clustered *rusalki*. One of them moved smoothly forward, and Maria hastily said, "My riddle! My first riddle:

> "I speed through city, forest, field,
>   Before my touch, the strongest yield.
>   I stir the wheat and bend the tree.
>   I am the one no man can see."

For a long moment, there was silence. Then her opponent laughed softly. "The wind, little human. The answer is the wind."

"Uh . . . yes. That's right." It had been an easy riddle; it had also been the only one Maria could think up in her haste. "Your turn."

The *rusalka* smiled sweetly. "So, now:

> "An emperor of wide renown,
>   Pale of face and horned of crown,
>   Rules in darkness all alone,
>   Cold as winter, cruel as stone.
>   But a usurper comes in golden crown,
>   To cast the silver emperor down.
>   The golden tyrant's loved by men,
>   Until the darkness comes again."

She drew back in the water, watching Maria with such an unblinking stare that the young woman had to turn away—only to find herself facing the other *rusalki*, all of them with eager, hungry faces. Fighting down a shudder, she turned back to her opponent, trying desperately to think. An emperor with a horned crown . . . ruling darkness . . . a usurper king . . . Oh, it all sounded like a history out of some sorcerous land! What hope could she possibly have of solving a riddle based on such a—

"Have you no answer, little human?" crooned the *rusalka*.

"Of course I do!" snapped Maria. "Just give me a chance to think!"

An emperor of darkness . . . a golden-crowned usurper . . .

Wait a moment! Here she'd been thinking in terms of

actual rulers, flesh-and-blood kings, but what if . . . ? Yes, that must be it! Trust a *rusalka,* a creature of night, to see things in reverse to the human way! A "golden tyrant"— ha!

"The moon," said Maria. "The pale emperor is the horned moon ruling the night. And the golden tyrant's the sun, ruling the day till the night falls again!"

The sound the *rusalka* made could have been a soft laugh or a hiss of disappointment. "Clever, pretty maid. You will do well among us."

"I have no intention of joining you, thank you! Besides, I still have two riddles left."

"Come, speak. We are waiting."

All right, she'd have to come up with something beyond a *rusalka's* experience if she was going to get out of this fix . . . But her mind seemed to have gone blank, quite blank . . .

"Come, little human! Speak!"

"I will, I will! What, are you in such a rush?" Maria asked in sharp humor. "You, to whom mortal time means nothing?"

"Perhaps it's that we ache to have you share our time-lessness."

"Cute. Very cute." Dear God, she had to think of *something,* and quickly— Aha! "Here's my second riddle:

> "I stand all day in empty space.
> I move, but never leave my place.
> One head, one crest, one body, one wing,
> One leg in all on which to swing."

The *rusalka* blinked, plainly taken aback, plainly going down a hasty mental listing of fantastic, magical creatures. *Search all you like!* thought Maria triumphantly. *You'll never find* this *beast!*

Time passed. "Come, come," prodded Maria. "You didn't give *me* this much time to think!"

The *rusalka* smiled at her, an unnerving flash of sharp white teeth. "No need for more time, little human. I, too, was human once. And I have not forgotten all the trappings of humanity. Your little one-legged creature is noth-

ing more than a weathervane in the shape of a cockerel."
She tossed the wild, wet hair back from her face. "Am I
not correct?"

"Yes," Maria admitted reluctantly.

"So now! One more riddle to go for each of us, then
you shall die, and your spirit live again as *rusalka.*"

"Don't be so sure of that. I guessed the answers to your
first two riddles."

"Ahh, but you haven't guessed the third one yet! And
even if you should, by chance, by luck, by wit, guess the
answer, you are still bound to us unless I cannot guess the
answer to *your* third riddle, remember that!"

"How," murmured Maria, "could I forget?"

"Come, now, enough delay! Here is my third riddle,
little human. Listen well:

> "I am the silent, stalking one.
> If once I want you, no use to run.
> No prey eludes me, none win free.
> I am the doom of those I see.
> I end all longings, end all fear,
> Bring final peace when I draw near.
> King or peasant, fear my cry.
> Rank is nothing to such as I.
> I stalk you, be you *boyar,* slave.
> No one escapes me, no one save
> The one who dares to play my game,
> Who dares risk all to call my name."

With that, the *rusalka* fell silent, dipping smoothly beneath the water, surfacing again without a ripple, smiling
at the human through a veil of hair. "Well, maid? Can
you answer?"

"Give me a chance to think!" Maria snapped, but she
was thinking, *What an ill-omened riddle. What a* deliberately *ill-omened riddle!* She hesitated, considering.
Could the answer be Death? The seemed too obvious. And
the answer could just as easily be Plague! She fought down
a shudder. *I'll only have one chance at this, and if I pick
the wrong answer . . .*

"Why, what's wrong, little human? Why so silent? Do you yield?"

"No, damn you, I do *not* yield!"

"Oh, pretty maid, we are already damned! Your little curses cannot harm us! Come, choose! Answer—or die!"

At least it would be quick. The *rusalka* had promised her that it would be quick, the lake waters closing over her head, a few moments of fear and pain, swiftly over.

And then an eternity spent as a soulless lake spirit? Learning to hate the mortal folk? Learning to stalk them, deadly and inevitable as—

"Good God!" Maria cried out, and the *rusalki* stirred uneasily. "That's it!" She broke off, staring defiantly into her challenger's empty green eyes, and began again, deliberately, "The answer to your riddle, *rusalka*, is *you*, you yourself, you, *rusalka*!"

The lake-woman's eyes were full of malice. She said nothing.

Oh, no! You're not getting away with that! thought Maria, and insisted, "Well? Isn't that right? Don't just look at me! I know enough about riddling games to know that you *must* answer me, or forfeit the game! And I did guess the proper answer, didn't I?"

"Yes." It was almost a hiss. "Oh, wise little human, let me hear your third riddle now. Be sure that I shall guess its answer before you can take a dozen mortal breaths!"

You want me to fear you, don't you? Maria asked silently. *Well, you've succeeded. I do fear you—but not so much that I'm going to let myself be rattled!* "No . . ." said Maria aloud. "No, I really don't think you shall. Here it is:

> "I sit in judgment in the court,
>   Or fly with shining wings for sport.
>   The sunlight is no foe to me.
>   Day or night, I'm equally free.
>   I walk, or fly, or, sporting, swim.
>   I play with storm winds for a whim.
>   Sometimes one form, sometimes another,
>   I call the *leshy*-man my brother.

On foot, on wing, I am the same.
Come, tell me, if you can, my name!''

She finished with a grand flourish, although she was
thinking wryly, *Akh, what dreadful poetry!* Still, considering that she had made it up on the spur of the moment,
maybe the thing wasn't so bad—particularly since it had
made the *rusalka* sink down into the water till only her
green eyes showed through the tangle of pale hair, eyes
blinking quickly in confusion.

"There's no such creature, human!"

"No?" Maria forced a smile. "Believe me, *rusalka*,
there is! Why, I, myself have seen . . . ah . . . it."

"But nothing walks *and* flies *and* swims!"

Maria, still smiling, said nothing. The *rusalka* eyed her
suspiciously for a moment, then continued, almost to herself:

"It must be magic. No mere human could befriend a
leshy!" The *rusalka* gave a hiss of impatience. "Yes, but
no magical being rules three of the four elements! And no
magical being can walk by day *and* night and take no
harm! Aie, impossible, impossible!"

"Are you giving up, then?"

"No! No!" There was tense silence for a time, then
Maria heard her opponent muttering, over and over, "A
being that walks and flies and swims!" The *rusalka* broke
off abruptly, glaring at Maria. "There is no such creature!"

"Ah, but there is!"

"No!" The *rusalka's* eyes were ablaze with savage
frustration. *"There is no such creature!* This is a lie you
tell, only a lie!"

"It's no lie."

"It is! It is! A creature that walks and flies and swims—
Bah! Your riddle has no answer! You cheated, you cheated!
You've doomed yourself and forfeited the game and—"

"Are you finished?" asked Maria mildly. "There *is* an
answer, *rusalka*. Would you care to hear it?"

"If you would live, speak!"

"The answer is a—a 'mere human,' as you put it—"

"No!"

"Yes. *Rusalka,* the answer to my riddle is: Finist, Prince of Kirtesk." She saw the lake-woman draw back with a hiss, heard the others stir uneasily, murmuring among themselves, "The magician, of course, the magician . . ." and added wryly, "I see you know him."

"We know," said her opponent shortly. "We should have remembered. You have won. Go."

With that, they dove into the lake with smooth, silent grace, one after the other, and the water closed behind them, still as glass. Stunned by the suddenness of it, hardly daring to believe the ordeal was over, Maria backed away from the lake, wary at first, then gave up any pretense of caution and simply turned to run—

Right into arms that caught her roughly and held her fast.

XXXIX

THE HEIR APPARENT

"MARIA!"

She was in peril, he knew it! But his body wouldn't obey him! He couldn't move, couldn't go to her, couldn't even remember any magic that might help her, he couldn't do anything at all but suffer this dreadful certainty . . .

"My Prince . . ."

The words seemed to be coming from a hundred *versts* away.

"My Prince, can you hear me?"

He knew that voice . . . Dimly, he seemed to realize that he knew that voice . . . And Finist began to fight his way up through layer after layer of fever-haze.

SEMYON sat anxiously by the royal bedside, watching his prince struggle against who knew what invisible terrors.

"My Prince," he repeated. "Can you hear me? Do you recognize me?"

The amber eyes opened the barest of cracks, looking up at him vaguely. But then their vacant gaze sharpened. "Semyon."

It had been the barest whisper of sound, but the old *boyar* felt a rush of relief sweep through him. *Akh, my poor Prince! At least the fever hasn't damaged your mind!* "What is it?" he asked gently. "Something's been disturbing you. What is it?"

Finist seemed to be struggling against invisible bonds,

straining to speak, his fever-brightened eyes frantic. "I
. . . can't . . ."

"Boyar!"

Semyon started, and turned guiltily to face the angry
Ljuba. "Lady, I—"

"I allowed you in here only under the agreement that
you'd do nothing to disturb my cousin's rest! And yet here
you are, causing him such distress— Hush, now, cousin,"
she added in a sudden croon. "Rest, my dear. No, no,
don't try to talk! Just rest. Drink this . . . that's right . . .
and rest."

To Semyon's bewildered eyes, it seemed almost as
though Finist had been fighting Ljuba. But that had been
the fever, surely, for now he was sinking into sleep. Sleep,
the boyar told himself firmly, was what the poor youngster
needed the most. He hesitated despite Ljuba's patent impatience, looking down at the drawn, flushed face, heart
aching with mingled pity and fear, then reached out an
impulsive hand to gently smooth strands of shining hair
back from Finist's face.

"Boyar." It was a warning, and Semyon sighed.

"Yes, lady. I'm leaving now." But he stopped, and
turned to her. "Lady, this may seem to be in dubious
taste. But . . . that terrible fever . . . He . . . seems to be
weakening with every day, and . . ." Semyon bit his lip,
hating what he must say. "For the sake of the land, the
council must know this: Is our Prince going to recover?"

"Am I God, that I should know that?" she snapped.
"Go away, old man! I'm doing all I can!"

"Lady, please. We must know. Will Finist recover?"

To his shock, he saw genuine fear flicker in Ljuba's
eyes. "I . . . don't know," she whispered. "I've never
seen a fever burn like this. I truly don't know."

THE other boyars had been waiting for him. Now, as
Semyon wearily entered the Ruby Chamber, they all
sprang to their feet, assaulting him with questions:

"Did you see him?"

"Did he know you?"

"What about the fever? Is his fever any lower?"

"Akh, *boyars*, please." Semyon sank to a chair, feeling very old. "Give me a chance."

There was silence in the chamber for a time. And then one voice asked quietly, "Is our Prince going to die?"

"I pray to God he is not."

"But you don't know."

"I— No." Semyon took a deep breath. *"Boyars,* I never thought to have to say this. I am old, our Prince is young, I never thought I . . . might outlive him, but . . . The time has come to discuss the problem of the succession."

Stunned silence fell once more, at least for a moment. Then Semyon sat back and listened for a time to the storm of debate raging all about him. Prim-faced *boyar* Andrei, elegant in dull red velvet—*matching the decor,* thought Semyon—seemed to be winning.

"But we can't go against the proper order of things!" he was saying. "If Prince Finist dies without an heir— which God forbid, of course—then his uncle inherits the throne."

"Prince Vasili," muttered someone from the rear of the room, and Andrei blinked and continued, "Why, naturally, Prince Vasili!"

"Monk Vasili, you mean."

"Well, yes, he may have taken monastic orders, that's true enough, but he's a good, kind, gentle man, and I'm sure—"

"That his reign would be a disaster," finished Semyon, waving to silence Andrei's reply. *"Boyars,* let us face facts. Good, kind, gentle men tend to make terrible rulers. There are enough historical examples to prove that point! Granted, Vasili was trained in the proper princely studies, but said training was a long time ago. He's been in that monastery, shielded from secular life, for almost as many years as our Prince has been alive." Semyon paused, letting his words sink in. "Do we really want to put an unworldly monk on the throne of Kirtesk?"

"But it's the proper order!" sputtered Andrei.

"My dear *boyar,* we're talking about the survival of our city, not the etiquette of some royal dance!"

There were scattered ripples of laughter at that, quickly stifled. "All right," said the blunt *boyar* Mikhail, grizzled of hair and beard, humorless of mind. "If not Prince Vasili, who?"

"Prince Finist's first cousin, then," exclaimed the indignant Andrei. "Prince Demyan is, legally, next in the succession."

"Prince Demyan," someone drawled, "is also regrettably weak of wits, and growing ever weaker. And his son can't be anywhere near of age yet."

"He's not." Mikhail's voice was sharp. "I'm sure none of us want to place a minor on the throne."

"Then—then . . ." stammered Andrei, "what about Princess Marya of Astyan? She is next in line."

"I'm afraid not," Semyon paused. "While the young woman seems to be proving a most able ruler of her own lands, I'm afraid she also seems to be quite deficient in one royal requirement: she has no magic." He glanced about at the dismayed faces. "Come, *boyars,* we're wasting time. There's only one possible alternative. Marriage."

"To his cousin Ljuba, you mean," said Mikhail. "I thought you disliked the lady, Semyon."

"My personal likes or dislikes have nothing to do with this," Semyon said flatly, annoyed at Mikhail's unexpected touch of malice. "I have always served the crown faithfully, and will continue to serve the crown."

"No matter who's wearing it, eh?"

"Akh, Mikhail, what would you have me say? Ljuba is capable enough, and intelligent. And unlike Princess Marya, she *does* have something of the Power." He looked sharply about the room. "Come, come, this won't be the first time we've thought her the most suitable mate for our Prince!" *Forgive me,* he said silently to the girl he'd never met, to Maria Danilovna, *forgive me, but we haven't time to consider love, not now.* "Well, *boyars?* What do you say?"

Andrei shrugged. "God knows *someone's* going to have to take over the reins of power."

Mikhail grunted. "And better her than that—what did you call him, Semyon?—that unworldly monk. So. I'm sure the lady in question will raise no objections. Let us only pray our Prince lives long enough to wed her!"

"Let us only pray our Prince lives!" corrected Semyon, and everybody obediently bowed their heads and murmured "Amen" to that. He stood apart as the other *boyars* left, stood staring blindly out the window at the midnight sky, all at once remembering his wife, dead these many years, thinking of the son he'd never had, thinking of Finist . . . "Live!" he whispered urgently. "Oh, Finist, *live!*"

XL

PREDATORS

STRUGGLING FIERCELY against her captor, Maria twisted about in his arms and caught a glimpse of a wild-eyed face, rough-bearded but undeniably human. Undeniably filthy, too—his stench was enough to gag her. Frantically kicking, trying to claw and bite, Maria fought him with all her strength. But he had such a good grip on her, she couldn't get so much as an arm free.

"Let—me—go!" Maria gasped, even though she was shouting at herself, *Oh, you fool! That isn't going to sway him!* But she couldn't help it: "Let—go!"

Even as she gasped those useless words, Maria loosed a savage kick that struck bone. The man gave a yelp of pain, but only tightened his grip, lips bared in a fierce, predatory smile.

"Oh no," he hissed, "no, my dear Maria."

She froze. "How did you . . ." Maria's voice trailed off into silence as she stared at him there in the cold moonlight. "My God . . ." she said slowly. "Alexei! It *is* Alexei, isn't it?"

He gave her a mocking little grin. "I always did say you were a clever thing!"

"But how did you get here?"

"How do you think, my dear? I was exiled, remember? Thanks to your dear father, I was exiled—"

"Justly!" Maria snapped without thinking; but to her relief, he only laughed. Still, there was a glint in his eyes, something not quite right, not quite normal . . . Chilled,

Maria stammered, "Never—never mind, Alexei. I'm not going to—to argue with you. Just let me go, and maybe I can help you—"

His laugh, charming, sophisticated, totally inappropriate, chilled her even more. "You, help me? Oh, no, I don't want your charity. I don't need it! No, I have someone else helping me, someone with Power, true Power."

Oh, dear God, he's insane. "I—I see. And—ah—who is this—someone?"

"A magician, dear Maria, a woman who knows my true worth, who'll gives me riches, honor, power! Her Art saved me from the forest demons, her Art brought me right to you! And in return, she asks one thing of me, only one little thing. And that is—your life, Maria."

"No!"

"Yes! You will be the first of your line to die, you, the daughter of damned Danilo— You, who mocked me, scorned me—God, you'll die, you and all the rest of your kin!" His eyes stared savagely into hers, hot with hate and lust. "Aie, but death's too swift! First, oh, first . . . Remember that day in Stargorod? I wanted you then, honorably, I would have wed you—"

"Damn you, you would have raped me!"

"Oh, yes, oh yes!" His eyes were ablaze. "You scorned me then, you tricked me! But this time, there shall be no tricks! This time I'm taking what I want! Yes, you'll die— but not at all so quickly!"

His hand shot up, closing so cruelly about a breast that Maria gasped in pain. As his lips came down bruisingly on hers, pure, mindless fury blazed through her. She bared her teeth and bit down as hard as she could, tasting blood. With a strangled yell, he jerked his head away, instinctively pushing her from him. But before she could run, he was at her again, trying to hook a leg around one of hers, trying to bring her down, and—curse him! He was laughing at her! Ha, but her sturdily shod foot caught him sharply on the knee with an audible crack. She heard him yell again, felt him begin to lose his grip, and savagely wrenched herself free.

No—a wildly outflung hand had closed about her wrist, pulling her back so sharply she lost her balance and fell, landing with bruising force on roots and bits of rock, desperately gasping for breath, the reek of decaying vegetation and Alexei's stench in her nostrils. Alexei tried to throw himself down on her, but Maria, grimly determined, brought her hand stabbing up at his face, narrowly missing his eyes, opening long furrows on his cheek. He sat back with a curse, hand going to his bleeding face.

"Why, you—*bitch!*"

He threw himself at her again, but Maria, savage as any wild thing, brought her knees up to her chest and kicked with all her strength. Alexei staggered back, losing his balance, falling, rolling helplessly down the sloping earth towards the lake.

And Maria sat up, hearing the sudden cruel, delighted laughter coming from the lake, and screamed:

"Alexei, get away from there! Hurry!"

"Oh, no, bitch! I'm not listening to anything you say!"

"*Alexei!*"

But it was already too late. A pale hand had come snaking up out of the lake, a pale arm encircled his neck. Heart pounding, Maria heard Alexei's shout of fear as he was pulled over backwards into the lake with a mighty splash. Fighting frantically, he was dragged beneath the surface so quickly that Maria didn't even have a chance to move. Horrified, she scrambled to her feet, in time to see him struggle helplessly against the inhuman force of *rusalki* strength. For one desperate moment, he managed to pull his head free of the water, eyes wild and pleading and most terribly sane. For one desperate moment, Maria tried frantically to find a way to save him, even him—

Alexei's face contorted in a scream of agony. In the next instant he was gone, and the lake was settling into innocent stillness once more. But on its surface was a dark, slowly spreading stain . . .

It was too much. Overwhelmed by shock, by horror, Maria turned and ran, stumbling blindly, ran till at last she could run no more and fell, sobbing for breath. Oh, God, the horror of this night! And which had been the worst of it? The inhuman cruelty—or the human? Too shaken for rational thought, Maria murmured over and over again:

"Please, please, just let this night be past!"

Huddling under a low-branched old tree, pressed up against the shelter of its broad trunk, she clutched the silver necklace as though it were some mystic thing to guard her from all harm. And gradually, too drained of strength and will to hold to fear or shock or even thought, Maria lost her hold on everything, and almost gratefully slid away from consciousness.

XLI

THE BINDING

SHUDDERING, Ljuba watched the *rusalki* take Alexei. The mirror's image was wavering and faint, forest-magic, as ever, interfering with her own. But she saw . . . enough.

Not that she would waste sympathy on the madman. He'd been a tool, merely a tool; if he had reached Kirtesk, she would have had to eliminate him herself.

Still, to die like that, at the hands of forest demons . . .

Ljuba roused herself, angry at her own weakness, and turned her attention grimly back to the hazy, flickering image in the mirror. Green, everywhere she scanned, nothing but a canopy of green . . .

"Come on," she urged under her breath. "Come *on!* Show me Maria! Did the creatures slay her, too? Show me . . ."

Ah, there, the image was clearing—

Clearing to show a hint of green fur, cold, alien eyes— the *leshy!* With a gasp, Ljuba hastily broke contact, and merely sat where she was for a time, fighting to regain control.

All right. She wouldn't be able to learn any more. But if the lake-demons slew a grown man, mad or sane, a mere girl couldn't have escaped them. No, Maria was dead, she must be dead. And now Ljuba could turn her full attention to Finist.

She gave him a quick, almost guilty glance and froze, hocked to realize how alarmingly prominent those high cheekbones were becoming in that increasingly gaunt face.

Was he truly going to die . . . ?

No, no maudlin weaknesses now! Worry only about whether he's going to live long enough to make you his wife!

Surely the *boyars* would be taking up the delicate mental suggestions she'd been planting on just that subject, and coming to see their prince any moment now?

Finist moaned and stirred. His eyes opened, and for a moment they were aware, and staring directly at her, the angry fire in them enough to make her flinch. Almost enough. Right now, his anger was as futile as a child's little rages because, hate her though he might, Ljuba was well aware he just didn't have the strength to threaten her or her plans.

"Give in, cousin," she whispered. "You are under my will now. The potion holds you. You are under my will."

But: *Am I?* those raging eyes seemed to say. *Oh, my treacherous cousin, am I indeed?*

WAVERING between sanity and delirium, Finist was dimly aware of Ljuba's plottings.

Ljuba . . . traitor . . . I was a fool, a fool! Never should have trusted you, never allowed you so much freedom . . .

But what good to rage now? Whenever he tried to speak, whenever he tried to resist her, psychic bonds held him fast, body and mind.

She hasn't the magical strength for this, not alone. The potion! Her damnable potion!

It must have been in every sip of water or wine she'd given him. Finist groaned, feeling the fever burning at him, searing every bone. No matter how he tried to resist, the fever-thirst would win in the end, and he'd have to drink . . . Eventually, it would kill him. But by that point, it would be too late for Kirtesk, because he knew, grimly, that if she ordered him to announce to the *boyars* that he would wed her, even from his sickbed, for the sake of the succession, the potion's strength would force him to obey.

The soothing, maddening escape of delirium was pulling at him, urging him to simply give in, but Finist fought it with whatever scraps of will he could find. He'd not leave Kirtesk in the hands of a tyrant! And if he couldn't overcome the potion's power over him, perhaps he could, at least, find a way to confuse the issue . . .

His memories were painfully cloudy, but he recalled something about when he had landed, when Ljuba had called him back into being human . . . something about a caftan . . . She had clothed him in one, he was almost sure of it. And it would have been stained by his blood.

Would Ljuba have kept the thing? Probably. After all, she knew as well as he that blood, the very stuff of life, held Power, and the spilled blood of a magician more Power than most.

Of course she's kept it! Ljuba, I do believe you've made a mistake. One that's truly going to amaze you!

With that, the exhausted Finist let himself slide back into unconsciousness once more, his last waking image the so satisfyingly alarmed look on his cousin's face as she stared at his faint but decidedly sardonic smile.

"BOYARS." Ljuba dipped her head to them, politely acknowledging their bows.

"Lady." Semyon was evidently acting as their spokesman. "You know why we've come?"

"I do."

"And . . . the prince? Is he—lucid?"

"He knows what's happening, yes."

They bowed again, and solemnly filed into the bedchamber. *Like so many crows at a funeral!* thought Finist in dark humor, struggling desperately against fever and the potion's grip. *No, boyars, there isn't going to be a funeral! Not yet!*

But he couldn't manage to say any of that aloud, and now Semyon was bending over him, eyes sorrowful, to ask:

"My Prince, do you know why we've come?"

Finist vainly fought the psychic bonds holding him, gasping out involuntarily, "For . . . a wedding."

"Ah. You do understand the—the need?"

"Succession . . . Matter of succession . . ." Damn, he hadn't wanted to say that! But the potion was binding his mind, Ljuba's will was pulling and pulling at him . . . *No,* Finist thought savagely. *I will not—be your puppet!*

"Lady!" Semyon was stepping aside in dismay. "What is it? What's wrong?"

Ljuba dove to Finist's side. He tried to pull away, but she quickly caught his hand, holding it in apparent solicitude. "It's nothing, *boyar*, nothing—nothing worse than I've already seen, a surge of the fever, that's all. See, he's quieting now."

But at the same time, she was telling Finist, quickly, coldly, mind-to-mind, *Don't fight me, cousin. It won't do you any good. You can't escape, so just relax, relax and yield to me.*

Like Hell I will! Finist managed to retort with such force that he felt Ljuba wince. But his defiance was useless against the fever and the potion and his cousin's will. Horrified, despairing, Finist heard himself calling to Semyon, heard himself saying in a strained, distant voice that didn't sound at all like his own:

"Boyars, I—name my cousin, the—the Lady Ljuba—as my betrothed. We—shall be wed—as soon as it may be arranged. And till the day that I recover, my—wife-to-be shall rule—as Regent. You shall—obey her as—you would me. So be it done!"

There was a collective sigh of relief from the *boyars*. As one, they bowed deeply, murmuring, "It shall be as you wish, my Prince," and backed away. Exhausted, Finist fell back against the bed cushions, head swimming, longing to let himself simply collapse. But he couldn't give up, not yet! There was a vague memory teasing at the edge of his mind, of his father, his tutor in magic, telling him . . .

"The Power is in our blood, in our very essence. As long as there is still breath within you, your magic lives."

And when, a boy drained and weary from his lessons, he'd tried to protest, he had been silenced with a fierce:

"There is no room for weariness in true magic! Your will must always be stronger than your body's weaknesses—or you are no magician!"

But I am, Finist told that stern ghost. He turned his being inward, seeking the heart of his Power, fighting the dizziness that was trying to overwhelm him, desperately summoning up the last shreds of his strength. Heart pounding painfully with the strain, blood roaring in his ears, the prince shouted:

"*Boyars*, wait!"

Astonished, they stopped, staring at him. Feeling Ljuba frantically trying to silence him, Finist cried, "By all the Powers of Magic, by all the strength of Day and Night and Warm Mother Earth, I swear this vow!" Dead silence fell; even the magicless *boyars* knew better than to try to interrupt a spell, and Ljuba, for all her fury, wasn't about to risk having unspent Power recoiling on her. Caught in the trance of his own inner Power, Finist continued, blind and deaf and insensible to all but his magic, "By all the force of Life: No woman shall wed me till the spilling of my blood shall be avenged, till she has washed my blood-stained caftan clean of treachery!"

As he felt the hastily fashioned spell come properly to life, locking itself firmly about him, Finist's trance shattered. He fell back into his aching, illness-wracked self, drained, panting, blazing with renewed fever, only now hearing the ghost of his father's final warning:

"*But no matter how wondrous your magic may seem, remember this: scorn the physical self too much, weaken your body beyond hope, and Power or no—you die!*"

But even now, he still managed to gasp out the shadow of a triumphant laugh. Turning his head to the dazed Ljuba, he added in a savage whisper:

"The caftan must be washed clean. And that, my treacherous cousin, spiller of my blood, you shall never do! Do you hear me, Ljuba? That, you shall never, never do!"

"A temporary setback," the young woman muttered grimly. "Only a temporary setback. The throne will still— Finist!"

But he had already escaped her into exhausted sleep.

XLII

LESIELO

GIGGLING, Marfa scurried down the narrow forest path, hearing Stefan laughing and panting somewhere behind her. Of course, she didn't plan to run *too* fast! She had no intention of outpacing him, not with those lovely thoughts of capture and delicious surrender dancing in her mind. As an old married couple of nearly a year, they were supposed to be somberly working in forest and garden, not cavorting about like a couple of spring-mad deer—didn't she, after all, have her hair coiled up on her head in a married woman's braids? But you couldn't be expected to be serious all the time, not when you were young and alive and—

Marfa stumbled to a stop. "Stefan! Stefan, come here. Hurry!"

By the time he caught up to her, she was kneeling beside the crumpled form. "Marfa, what— A woman! But she isn't from the village . . . Is she dead?"

"N-no. But she's all bruised and scratched, and I think she's got a touch of fever." Marfa glanced earnestly up at her young husband. "Oh, Stefan, we've got to get the poor thing to shelter right away!"

SHE ached. Mind and body, she ached, and her throat was so painfully dry that when she tried to groan, no sound came out. But this wasn't the hard forest floor, surely.

Maria opened her eyes in bewilderment, to find a bright-eyed young woman staring down at her. "Where . . . ?"

"Don't worry. You're safe, now. You're in our house, in the village." The young woman was cradling her head, letting her drink something that was cool and herbal and very soothing. "There, now. That's better."

Maria attempted a smile, and drifted right back into sleep.

IT was early morning when she awoke, and Maria blinked in confusion, trying to straighten time out in her mind. Had she actually slept through the day? It seemed very possible. At least she felt better now, less weary, less filled with despair.

Warily, she sat up. Sore muscles complained, but the ache wasn't anything she couldn't bear, and after a moment, Maria gingerly swung her legs over the side of the bed—

"Akh, be careful!"

It was the bright-eyed young woman, small and pretty, who'd given her something to drink. Maria frowned, trying to remember. . . . "You were the one who found me, weren't you? I mean, in the forest."

The young woman nodded. "I almost stepped on you. Nearly scared the life out of me! Thought you were dead—no, don't try to stand up yet!"

"I'm all right now, really." Maria stretched carefully, wincing at bruises, trying with fierce determination not to think about who had caused them, or of his fate. Instead, she glanced about, finding herself in a small, clean one-room house that reminded her of the farm of her family's exile. Nothing they'd had there, though, had been as lovingly carved and painted as these chairs and table and—"I've pushed you out of your own bed, haven't I?" Maria asked contritely, and the other woman gave her a quick grin.

"It's all right. You needed it more than we did. Besides, it was . . . kind of fun, Stefan and I snuggling on the floor by the fire!" She blushed. "We . . . haven't been married all *that* long, you see. Akh, but here I am, keeping you standing with nothing more than a shift on you! Wait, now . . ." She rummaged about in a chest for a bit, then came up with Maria's pack. "The clothes you had on—Well, I did my best to wash 'em and mend 'em, but . . ."

Maria shuddered. "That's quite all right. I . . . don't want them back."

The other was looking at her in sudden sympathy. "It was a man tore 'em like that, yes? And gave you those bruises, too? He didn't, ah—I mean . . . You know what I mean. He didn't—"

"Rape me?" Maria finished bluntly. "No." Seeing the unease on the young woman's face, she added, "He wasn't one of your village men, either; you don't have to worry about that. And, at any rate, he's . . . dead."

"Well, good! Yes, I mean it! Anyone tried that with me, I'd have the pitchfork in him, or—or the butcher knife!" The small, fierce thing nodded in satisfaction. "That's it! He'd be singing all the high notes in the choir when I was finished with him!" She stopped in sudden dismay. "Oh, now, I'm sorry! I didn't mean to start you crying!"

"I'm not!" Maria gasped between bursts of giggles. "Singing—singing all the high notes, indeed! Thank you! I—I haven't had too much to laugh at lately." Sobering, she added, "But I'm forgetting my manners. I am . . ." She stopped at the last moment, remembering caution, and finished lamely, "Maria."

The other woman merely nodded. Peasant she might be, as her accent and surroundings proclaimed, but that didn't make her either stupid or tactless. "And I'm Marfa. My husband, as you've heard me say, is Stefan. And our village is called Lesielo, and it's under the"—she stumbled over the unfamiliar word—"sovereignty of Finist, Prince of Kirtesk."

Suddenly Maria's legs wouldn't support her. "Finist. Oh, God, Finist . . . Am I finally near Kirtesk?"

Marfa was watching her with bright-eyed curiosity. "I knew you were more than you seemed!" she said triumphantly. "What with that pretty silver necklace, and your fine way of speaking—I knew it!"

"Marfa . . ."

"Don't worry, I won't betray your secret. Whatever it is." The last was said with a good deal of hope. But when

Maria said nothing, Marfa continued, "Oh, but I shouldn't speak too lightly of our Prince. Not with him being so ill and—"

"Ill! What do you mean? Marfa, please, tell me!"

The peasant woman stared at her in astonishment. "Hey, now, gently! We don't get much news from Kirtesk, here in the forest. But a peddler told us poor Prince Finist flew back from who knows where—you did know he can change his shape? Into a beautiful, shining falcon?"

"Yes, of course. Please, Marfa, go on!"

"Well, he came flying back maybe a month, a month and a half ago, with gashes all over him. His cousin is tending him, the Lady Ljuba—"

"Ljuba!" That was the name of Finist's dangerous kins-woman. *Dear God, when Alexei was raving about the woman "with Power, true Power," that could only have been Ljuba, too! That means she knows about me! That means—she wants me dead!*

Maria froze in stunned horror at the realization. Sor-cery, aimed directly at her . . . But if Ljuba had been able to strike her down, surely the woman wouldn't have needed the dubious aid of a madman. Surely that meant Maria was safe, as long as she stayed in the protection of the forest.

But I can't stay here forever! Her journey cross-country had plainly used up at least a month already. *I've got to get to Finist! What am I going to do?*

"Maria?" Marfa asked warily. "Are you all right?"

"I—Oh, yes, of course. Please, go on."

"Well, uh, the Lady Ljuba is something of a sorceress herself, but whatever she's doing isn't working too well, because Prince Finist is supposed to be . . . I'm sorry, but he's supposed to be burning up with fever, and no one knows for sure if he's going to live."

"No, that can't be—"

"Uh . . . there's more. The Lady Ljuba is his Regent, since he's too sick to rule. And she . . ." Marfa hesitated, looking about warily. "She's not like our Prince; she's a real tyrant. And she's gotten herself betrothed to Prince Finist—but he said some sort of spell, and now she can't

marry him until—until she manages to wash the bloodstains out of his caftan—easy, now! Don't faint!''

"I'm not about to faint," Maria said grimly. "Marfa,
you and your people love the prince, don't you?"

"Saints above, yes! Stefan and I in particular! He—he
saved us, you see, saved us from something that—well,
never mind. We'd do anything for him, anything." She
hesitated, then added defiantly, "Not like for that . . .
treacherous Lady! She's got to be treacherous! If she were
so good, why'd our Prince put such a spell on her, eh?"
Her eyes were suddenly very serious. "You love him, don't
you? Not as subjects love their ruler, no, as—as woman
loves man. Please, don't try to deny it. It's clear as sunlight on your face. So. I'm not asking who you really are,
name or rank or anything. But if I were you, I wouldn't
risk going straight to Kirtesk, not with that jealous sorceress waiting."

"What other choice do I have? Marfa, it's true, I
do love him. And the thought of Finist in such terrible
peril—"

"Whoa, now. I'm not saying you should just give up."

"What *are* you suggesting?"

"Did you ever hear of Prince Vasili? No? He's Prince
Finist's uncle. And though he went into a monastery years
ago—I guess so he wouldn't confuse the line of succession
or something like that—it's said the royal magic runs in
his veins, too. Go to him; he's a kind, saintly man. Who
knows? Maybe he'll have some sort of counterspell that'll
make the lady just"—she made a shooing gesture—"slink
away."

Maria hesitated. How wonderful it would be to be able
to turn to someone magical for help . . . "But if he's a
monk—"

"Well, as a monk, he'd be sworn to combat evil,
wouldn't he? Surely he can help you—and our Prince!"

"Akh, but it's been so long already. And Kirtesk is so
close."

"Not as close as all that. Look you, it takes a good
fortnight to get to Kirtesk from here, and that's riding, not
walking. It takes only a week maybe, not much more, to
get to the monastery. We'll lend you a horse, I promise.

And if the magician-monk can help you, you haven't wasted any time at all, have you?''

"Marfa, I— Thank you!"

"Don't be thanking me just yet, not till all is well. But when it is—do be reminding our Prince of Marfa and Stefan . . . Stefan, the—the wolf. Oh, but you can't be meaning to leave right away!"

"I can." Maria's hand went to the silver necklace. "If Finist is as ill as you say, I can't afford to wait another moment.''

XLIII

THE REGENT

LJUBA LAY STARING up at the canopy of her bed, too worn, too weary for sleep even though her body ached for rest.

Finist, why didn't I realize what you were going to do? How could I have so sorely underestimated your strength?

That spell! That impossible, ridiculous, unbreakable spell! She'd tried, tried with every counterspell she knew, with every soap and powder and potion at her command, but the magic held fast, the bloodstains remained set in the silken fabric, she remained Regent but not ruler.

And Finist was weakening with every hour. If he died . . . God, if he died, with the spell in force and he unwed, Ljuba would be finished. The *boyars*—damn them all—would never support her claim, nor would the guards—not a mere lady, not when they were all talking only of pious Prince Vasili!

Ljuba slammed her hand down on the bed cushions in helpless frustration. Akh, Finist! Since that dramatic demonstration of his magical strength, she'd been afraid not to keep feeding him at least the weakened form of her potion.

Yet his fever was so high. That Powerful outburst of his had nearly slain him. But . . . if she released her hold on him, let the potion's effect gradually drain from him, might that not give him a better chance for survival?

Still, there was no proof that the potion was harming him. And even if she stopped it, he would only have a very slight chance for recovery. At any rate, Ljuba didn't dare try it. She'd already gone too far: if she let him go, and he did recover, his first act would be to see she paid the traitor's price.

To be trapped in avian shape till the human mind was lost forever . . . No, no, *no!*

Ljuba let out a strangled sob. This had to be what those stupid peasants meant by "catching a wolf by the ears": having to make such an impossible choice. Keep Finist in thrall, and she might risk slaying him. Let Finist go, and she'd almost certainly be slaying herself—

Oh God, what am I going to do?

She clenched her jaws till they ached, refusing to give way to tears, huddling amid the disordered cushions in silent misery. But her body's demands for rest at last outweighed her anguish, and Ljuba slipped, reluctantly, into a restless sleep . . .

"And did you think I'd let you rest?"

"Who . . . Finist! This is a dream!"

"Is it, my treacherous cousin?"

"Get out of my mind! Leave me alone!"

"Get out of my mind! You would enslave me! You would dare! Traitor, you'll never know peace, not from me!"

She could feel the wildness of his thoughts burning at her, close to madness in their fever-frenzy. Ljuba cried out in her sleep as it came to her that, reduced to the most primitive levels as he was, gentle Finist meant to destroy her mind:

"Saints in Heaven, help me! Help me!"

"What, call on Light? You?"

"Finist, no! Please!"

And: *"No!"* screamed Ljuba aloud, and woke herself, sitting bolt upright, shivering in fear.

THE falcon stirred restlessly in his prison. Why was he here, trapped behind these cold stone walls, when he could be out in the free night sky? Yet his wings were bound. He fought . . . fought . . .

And suddenly he was up and soaring out over open country, out over forest, free . . .

* * *

DEEP in the forest, the *leshy* paused, frowning, staring into the night. Now, what had he sensed . . . ? It had the feeling of the human-magician's aura, yet with a chaotic strangeness to it . . . Humans were usually unable to bear such chaos. And even stranger, there was nothing of tangible form behind the aura . . .

Suddenly he had it puzzled out, and said, quite reasonably, "Is this wise? Human-magician, is it wise to leave your body behind when it has been so weakened? Go home, forest-friend, before it's too late."

"Too late!" came the echoing mind-cry. *"It's already too late! My cousin has poisoned me. She holds me ensnared! She will slay me, slay me!"*

The *leshy* shivered, leaves stirring about him, confused by the force of human illness, by the unfamiliar tangle of human emotions. Yes, but the man, human or no, had always been a forest-friend. While the woman . . . Oh, the *leshy* knew of whom the magician spoke! He knew that woman well! How many times had he felt her hatred of the forest? How many times had he heard her gloat at the very thought of its destruction?

"I think I will help you, forest-friend," the *leshy* said thoughtfully. "Go, now, back to your body," he added, almost gently. "I do believe the forest shall help you!"

LJUBA sat on the throne of Kirtesk, her form regal in gold brocade, her face a beautiful, impassive mask. This was the moment of which she'd dreamed, yet right now she could feel no triumph, no pride, nothing but fear.

I can't go through another night like that!

The worst of it hadn't come from Finist—not directly. After that first, terrifying attack on her sanity, Finist had fallen into so deep a slumber that she'd had to check to be sure he still breathed. No, the messages had come from the forest, there'd been no doubt of it, messages of hate, warning her, *Walk warily*, mocking her with *Fool! Your doom is very near!* Ljuba surreptitiously clenched her fists beneath her caftan's long sleeves. Those forest devils knew she feared them!

They knew, too—curse the things!—that she had no way to defend herself against them.

Don't I? thought Ljuba savagely. *It's Finist who's to blame, Finist who sent for them, Finist's who's always thought nothing of consorting with those demons. He sent his spirit-self roaming free to summon them—but I will bind it back in his body, bind it fast. He shall not elude me, body or soul. And if any of his demon-friends try to stop me, I will crush them!*

"Your pardon, lady," said a voice, and Ljuba started, glancing sharply down from the high dais.

It was old Semyon, dipping his head to her in a brief, formal salute. Ljuba stared at him, unblinking, eyes cold as midwinter ice, till the old fool got the point and went down on one knee before her. She let him stay there long enough to think things over, then calmly bade him rise, smiling thinly at his aura of frustrated anger.

Too bad, old man! Ljuba mocked him silently. *You yourself vowed to serve the crown. And, like it or not, right now I am the crown.* Aloud, she asked curtly, "What is it?"

"Emissaries from Stargorod have just arrived, lady."

Ljuba tensed. "What, from Prince Svyatoslav?"

"Ah, no, lady. Not officially. They seem to have no royal backing at all, but—"

"Common messengers?" From the late Maria's family, perhaps? She couldn't afford that! She didn't dare have anyone raise potentially awkward questions, not when her authority was still to be firmly established. "Let them wait," said Ljuba regally.

"But, lady, they—"

"Did you hear me?"

"Yes, of course, lady, but—"

"Then obey me! If these so-called messengers have no official status, let them wait for an audience, just like any other common folk!"

Semyon started to argue, then sighed, bowing in reluctant submission. "So be it, lady."

Ljuba glanced about the chamber at the other *boyars*, seeing them wary, skeptical, hostile, and her thin smile sharpened a touch. Thanks to the edict she'd forced from Finist, they must obey her, or be named traitors to the crown. And in these short days since she'd come to sit as

Regent of Kirtesk, she was already beginning to bend these fools to her will, showing them just how spoiled and soft they'd become under Finist's gentle hand—showing them what a true ruler was like!

"Think of me as you will," murmured Ljuba under her breath. "Mistrust me, fear me, even hate me. But—obey me, you shall!"

XLIV

THE EAGLE

MARIA GLANCED ABOUT bemused. After all that weary time afoot in the wilderness, she had forgotten just how fast a good horse on a—well, a relatively good road could travel.

Of course, her being here at all was thanks to Marfa and Stefan, and the village of Lesielo. Those folk had done more than merely lend her one of their precious horses. It said a great deal for their loyalty to their prince that so many of them had chosen to take valuable time from their farm work to escort Maria safely to the very gates of the monastery. *Of course,* thought the young woman with a touch of pride, *it also says a good deal about Finist's loyalty to his people!*

So even with the necessary stops for food, for rest, she and her escort had managed to reach the foothills of the Khomensk Mountains in under a week. Another day had been spent in climbing up to the isolated monastery. Now here she was, staring at the high, grey walls, and wondering if anyone was ever going to answer the visitor's bell.

Wait, here was someone opening the small window set high in the heavy door and peering through. All Maria could make out were two blinking, reddened eyes, *Like the eyes of a turtle!* she thought in sudden wild humor, and started when the turtle snapped, "Yes? What is it?"

He didn't seem to be pleased to find himself faced by a stranger—a woman, no less, and a young one at that—and Maria, having an image of him simply slamming shut the window again, said hastily, "I've come to see one of your brothers."

"Have you?" The cracked voice was suspicious. "Which one?"

Maria took a great breath. "I don't know his holy name. But in the secular world he was called Prince Vasili."

There was the hiss of sharply indrawn breath from the other side of the door. "He sees no one from the outside world! No one save his royal nephew."

Finist! "Oh, please! I've come on behalf of that nephew!" Feeling those turtle-eyes staring skeptically, Maria continued, "I beg you, take word to Prince Vasili. Tell him—tell him Prince Finist's in peril! Tell him it's quite literally a matter of life and death! Please—"

Suddenly she realized she was speaking to empty air.

How long had they kept her here outside the gate, waiting in suspense? Maria shifted her weight restlessly from foot to foot, thinking that it had been long enough for her to have remembered every worry she'd been trying to forget!

What if Vasili wouldn't see her?

What if he were ill? Too ill for visitors?

What if he wasn't even here, or alive, or—

The anguished groaning of ancient wood startled her. The monastery's heavy door was being pulled slowly open, just wide enough to reveal the figure of a carefully bland-faced young monk—a novice, she supposed.

"Please," he said, "follow me."

Maria bid a hasty, grateful farewell to her village escort, and squeezed through the narrow opening, only to find herself in a narrow courtyard, facing a second wall. Beyond it were hints of the red-tiled roofs of various buildings, *kelii*, the monks' individual cells, she guessed, plus the main chapel and whatever else was deemed necessary to an isolated mountain retreat.

Of course, the monks weren't going to let a young woman onto the actual monastery grounds. Instead, her guide led her down the length of the inner wall, the only sound that of his sandals slapping against paving stone, till they reached a little herb garden.

Neutral ground, Maria thought dryly.

Then she saw the man who stood tranquilly awaiting her, and forgot her sarcasm. He was tall, dignified—somehow, even after all the long years away from the world, he still looked regal. Even in the plain, dark, monkish robes, this could only be Prince Vasili. And oh, he did look so much like Finist! A Finist grown old, hair gone white, skin more tightly drawn over the high, elegant cheekbones . . . Overwhelmed, Maria began to sink into a respectful curtsey, but in two smooth steps he was at her side, and strong, gentle hands were reaching out to pull her up again.

"No, child. I am Brother Feodosi, no more than that."

Seen up this close, the resemblance to his nephew wasn't quite so stunning. Brother Feodosi's face was softer than Finist's, his eyes not the falcon's fierce amber, but a subtler gold—the eyes, Maria thought, of an aging, gentled eagle.

But as the man studied her, those golden eyes brightened, surprised and warm.

"Why, my dear, you are Finist's love! How wonderful!"

"You—you know—" Maria stopped, blushing. "Oh. Of course you'd know. The magic . . ."

The man gave her a wry little quirk of a smile. "The magic, yes. It does still flow in my blood. Though now I use it only for healing. But you are . . . ?"

"Maria Danilovna of Stargorod." Maria shook her head impatiently, abruptly remembering, now that the first shock was past, why she'd come. "But that's—"

"Stargorod! You've come a long way!"

"Yes, but I—"

"And to see me." All at once his voice was very serious. "At the gate, you spoke of my nephew. And of peril."

"Yes." Maria paused, trying to organize her thoughts, then dove headlong into her story, of herself, of Finist, of that strange, sudden illness and—Ljuba.

Odd. When she first mentioned Ljuba, the man's face had grown very still. And when she finished her story, the first thing he asked was:

"Are you sure? That . . . the Lady Ljuba is to blame—are you sure?"

Maria gave a sharp, incredulous little laugh. "Oh, very! I assure you, Alexei *was* trying to kill me. And it *was* at Ljuba's command."

"Yes, but you admitted that the man was insane. He might have been lying, or indulging some mad fancy. You might have misunderstood him. That's only understandable, what with the shock and fear you must have been feeling. You might very well have been mistaken."

Maria stared at him, bewildered. "No, I most certainly was not mistaken! Neither were the villagers of Lesielo, for that matter. Ljuba was and is to blame—of that I am very, very sure."

"Ah." It was a sound almost of pain. "I . . . see."

Maria waited anxiously, expecting him to continue. But when the man said nothing more, she prodded, "But aren't you going to do something? Can't you help? I'm not worried about myself, not—not really. But Finist—poor Finist! Can't you—"

"No."

"W-what?"

"I'm sorry, child. There's nothing that I can do."

"That doesn't make sense! You're a magician, you can't be afraid of a sorceress!"

"It isn't fear," he murmured. "Not of that."

"And you're Finist's uncle! Surely that matters to you!"

"It does." The golden eyes were dark with pain. "I love my nephew dearly. Please, child, believe me. But . . . there really is nothing I can do. I'm sorry."

"Sorry!" exploded Maria. "He—he's desperately ill, he may even be d-dying, he and his people are at the mercy of that ambitious, murderous sorceress, and all you can say is that you're *sorry!*"

"Maria, child, please. You don't understand. I . . . can't return to Kirtesk. You see, my dear, many years ago I swore a sacred vow. In short, I swore never again to enter that city's walls."

Maria blinked, confused. Why on Earth would he swear something like that? Because Finist's father held the throne? Because Vasili didn't want to get in the rightful ruler's way? She shook her head, impatient. "That's as it may be. But you say you swore that oath years ago! Surely such a vow isn't still binding, not when the life of your nephew and—and the safety of all of Kirtesk is at stake!"

He wouldn't meet her gaze. "A vow, child, is a vow. I may not break my word."

" 'May not,' " Maria echoed, "or *will* not! Surely you can't believe that the—the good Lord would strike you down for—"

The golden eyes flashed in sudden anger. "You speak lightly of something you know nothing about!"

"I know that if it were *my* prince and *my* people in peril, nothing in all the world would stop me from rushing to help them!"

"No!" he insisted. "I will not break my vow!"

"Why not?" snapped Maria, forcing down a frantic little voice within her that was screaming, *Don't get him angry! He's a monk, but he's still a magician! Don't get him angry!* "It's not the vow, is it? No, there's more to this than that! What is it, envy? Are you so envious of Finist for having the throne that—"

"No!" The man turned sharply away from her in a swirling of dark robes. "I never wanted the throne!"

"All right, then!" With Finist's life at stake, she wasn't going to waste time in meek courtesy. "If not envy, what? For God's sake, why won't you help Finist and put a stop to this—this Ljuba?"

"Because I . . ."

"Why?"

"Because I can't." It was a cry of anguish. "Because in Ljuba, my sin has come home to me!"

As Maria looked at him in utter bewilderment, the man who'd been Prince Vasili sank to a stone bench, staring blankly into space.

"Efrozinia . . . She was so beautiful, the Lady Efrozinia." The words really weren't for Maria's ears. "And how I loved her! My brother was already the sire of a fine, healthy son; surely I was free to love where I would. But she . . . she turned from me to another, a mere petty nobleman. She could have had a princely mate, but she wed that—nobody!"

He stopped to catch his breath, glancing at Maria, but continued as though, after all the years of silence, a dam within him had finally burst.

"Of course, it was not a happy marriage. How could it be? He was but one or two grades above the commons, while she . . . My Efrozinia was used to court life, to light and song and laughter. It happened that she and her . . . husband came to the palace—at my brother's invitation, not mine, for the festivities surrounding his son's first birthday. I . . . She . . . Akh, there's no excuse for what happened next. We'd both been drinking, she and I, we forgot all caution, all shame. We stole away together, and I cast a spell of secrecy about us. And then . . . The sin wasn't Envy. It was Adultery."

He glanced up at her again—a brief, anguished flash of gold. When she said nothing, he continued in a soft, frenzied rush of words:

"After that, Efrozinia avoided me, but I still burned for her. With my Powers, I forced her to my bed. And after that . . . Oh, God, how could I stay at court after that? *That* was when I swore my vow and left the world behind, hoping to atone in quietness and gentle deeds. Everyone thought I was being so wise and noble and self-sacrificing, when actually—" He broke off sharply, fists clenched. "It still hurts. After all these years, it does still hurt."

Maria hesitated, knowing she should say something, anything, wondering how she could possibly dare condemn or pity this man who was so many years her elder, this man who was both monk and prince.

"You . . . got her with child, didn't you?" she asked, very, very carefully, wondering if he was going to strike out at her.

But: "Yes," bitterly. "Though I swear before Heaven I didn't know it when I left! And her husband—" Monk though he was, the man couldn't keep the scorn from his voice. "Oh, he must have guessed the truth of it, he wasn't that great a fool! But what could he do? I was a prince, brother to his liege lord! He daren't attack me or his wife. And after all, he had no proof, no real proof, that the babe wasn't his."

"She bore you a daughter."

"She did: Ljuba." The man shuddered. "Poor child. The man whom she called Father hated her, her mother turned from her in shame. And I . . . Here in my monastery I could do nothing to help, nothing but watch from afar . . . And what I saw . . ." He gave a little groan. "My sin has twisted her!"

"Twisted—"

"Oh, I'm not speaking of her outer shell! I meant her heart, her magic. My daughter's Power is dark. I thought with time she would learn to control her inner shadows, I prayed she would learn to love, to pity, but she hasn't, and I am to blame!"

Maria let her gaze fall, too uneasy and embarrassed to stare at him. And yet, she couldn't help wondering why, for all his anguished words, the man had never tried to help his child. Why had he, knowing her to be alone and unloved and bearing the seeds of Shadow within her, never once tried to leave this safe place to which he'd fled? Even now, he spoke not about Ljuba, but about himself, *his* guilt, *his* shame.

His self-pity.

Sickened, Maria looked at the worn, gentle face, and saw the weakness behind the gentleness.

Dear Lord, how could I ever think you looked like Finist?

"All right!" she said, as brusquely as she could. "I'm sorry for what's happened, but you can't change the past! Don't you want to atone for your sin?"

The barest hint of royal pride and anger flickered in the golden eyes. "You dare to ask me that?"

"That's right, get angry at me! Shout at me! But whatever you do to me won't change the facts: Finist is deathly ill—by Ljuba's hand. And if he died—it'll be Ljuba, *your daughter*, who slays him!"

"No!"

"Yes! You *know* I'm telling the truth! Can you live with the knowledge that your daughter damned her soul with murder while you did nothing?"

"Stop it! I *will not break my vow!*"

There was a moment's tense silence, the two of them glaring at each other. But then the golden gaze fell.

"You're right." It was barely audible. "To my shame, you are right. So, child, I won't break my vow—"

"But . . . ?"

"But I will do what I can." He looked her up and down, an impersonal, professional stare. "Now. If Ljuba isn't to know you at once, we must disguise you."

Maria blinked, glancing ruefully down at her worn self. "By now, I don't think my own family would recognize me."

"Your own family doesn't have Power. First, child, give up that pretty silver chain." As Maria raised a hand to it, reluctant to part with the gift that had brought her so far, he added a touch of impatience, "Come, be sensible! The thing fairly glows with Finist's aura! For safety's sake, you must carry nothing of magic about you."

"Ah . . . what about this?" Maria fished about in her pack till she'd found the odd little wooden egg the *lisunka* had given her, so long ago, in the forest. The man raised a surprise eyebrow.

"You've made some peculiar friends, I see!" He reached out a hand to the egg, then drew it sharply back again. "No, child, keep it with you. The forest-magics are the Old Magics, alien to our little human charms. If I couldn't detect the egg, there's small danger that Ljuba shall. And I suspect you may have need of forest-magic in the times that lie ahead. Now, stand still, Maria. Hold your breath and shut your eyes . . . I haven't worked this charm in many a year, but I haven't forgotten the way of it . . ."

She heard him murmur something soft and bizarre, the words curling and curving dizzyingly about themselves like the threads of some incredibly intricate weaving. There was no sensation of change, nothing strange at all. But all at once the monk was giving a sigh that mingled weariness with satisfaction.

"Yes, that does it. Come, child. Open your eyes and look at yourself."

He held up a mirror of shining bronze. Maria stared in

wonder at the reflection of a stranger's face, a broad, coarse-featured peasant face framed by mousey brown hair. The man smiled at her awe.

"Nicely done, eh?" He stopped to catch his breath; the magic plainly hadn't been as easy as he pretended. "Oh, granted, it's not the most secure spell in the world. Any other magics performed nearby will almost certainly break it—as will the calling of your rightful name, remember that—and return you to your own likeness. But till then, you should be safe enough, Heaven willing. Since the spell is one that radiates little true Power, it's difficult for most magicians to detect. Ljuba . . . shouldn't have the skill to sense it."

At least I hope she doesn't, thought Maria. "I—thank you."

She turned to leave, glad she'd managed to get this much help out of the man. But he called, "Wait!" and when Maria turned back to him, puzzled, he added nervously, "How are you going to get to Kirtesk?"

"Why, walk, I suppose."

"Your friends can't help you?"

"The villagers? Oh, no, they've already started back for Lesielo. Farm work doesn't go away for the waiting! It's all right," she added with a touch of humor. "I've been doing a great deal of hiking lately. I only wish I could be already there, at Finist's side . . ."

"Yes, of course . . . There's one more way in which I may aid you. Climb up on this bench and look out the window slit, there, to the horizon. Do you see it?"

"That city?" Maria's heart gave a great leap. "Is that Kirtesk?"

"It is. And I will shorten your journey a bit, my dear."

Maria turned to him, puzzled, then drew in her breath with a sharp gasp. Apparently avian forms ran in the royal family, because Finist's uncle had just shed his monk's robes to become a great golden eagle.

A golden eagle large as a man.

It isn't possible! thought Maria wildly, then, *Don't be a fool!*

Of course, a magician could alter size as well as shape. After all, she had suspected Finist's shape-shifting magic included a casual changing of mass as well as form. How else could a tall young man shrink to falcon-size? Apparently such changes could go the other way as well . . .

Gentle golden eyes turned to her, bidding her to approach.

"Uh . . . you want me to ride you?" Maria hesitated, recalling how tired he'd been after casting that disguise-spell over her. Surely carrying what would now be a super-avian weight, plus her own, would be much more of a strain. Not wanting to insult royal pride, the young woman added delicately, "I won't be too heavy for you?"

The eagle shook his head.

"And it's all right? Leaving the monastery like this, I mean?"

That merited only a rather condescending glance. *Of course*, Maria realized. *He's still royal. Ha, for all I know, he may even be the abbot!*

Gingerly, she seated herself on the smooth-feathered back, feeling the unexpected strength of the muscles beneath the skin, smelling, bemused, a faint, strange scent midway between the sharpness of human and the warm dustiness of bird. After a few awkward moments spent figuring out a way to hold on, she managed to lock her legs around the base of the eagle's wings, hoping she wasn't going to interfere with his flying, and threw her arms about his neck, hoping she wasn't going to strangle him. Those powerful muscles bunched beneath her—

And the great golden bird was aloft, spiralling up. Maria clung with all her might, giddy with fear and exhilaration. At first the eagle seemed to struggle in the air, plainly rusty in the mechanics of flight. Then the wide wings steadied, catching the wind beneath them.

With a wild cry of joy, the golden eagle soared out over the mountains towards Kirtesk.

At first, Maria didn't dare look anywhere but straight ahead. But after the first shock was gone, she found herself staring boldly down at the wild tapestry of a thousand different greens that was forest and field below. Oh, it was wonderful! Someday she must find a way to fly on her own, somehow there must be a magic to let her ride the winds by herself, or with Finist at her side—

Akh, Finist! Maria looked ahead to the walls and towers of Kirtesk with new hope. Surely things would all be well. Surely—

Abruptly the eagle lurched in the air. He'd plainly lost the current he had been riding. Now, judging by the frantic beating of his wings, he couldn't find another. Maria froze on the feathered back, terrified that if she moved, she would upset the eagle's precarious balance.

In a moment he was in control again, wings beating rhythmically. Maria felt each stroke of the wide golden wings surging through her.

But how this must be wearying him! And carrying my weight, too. How can he possibly—

He couldn't. The sound and feel of his wingbeats were growing ragged, uncertain. The eagle staggered in the air, caught himself, staggered again, trying in vain to find a current steady enough to let him rest his wings by soaring. Maria's heart lurched each time he slipped. She should have known it, after seeing how that transformation wearied him. For all his pride, she never should have let him try this. The man was aging, gentle, used to quiet monastery ways; he didn't have Finist's young strength. And he was tiring with every wingbeat.

"Land!" she shouted to him over the wind's roar. "Please, don't try to go on! Just land!"

But stubborn, determined, he fought on. Maria glanced down at the fields still so far below, and heard herself moan.

"Please, please, land!"

The beat of the great wings was growing slower as current after capricious current slid away from him . . . Maria could hear the eagle gasping for breath. He lurched sideways—

And lost his hold on the sky. Maria screamed, clinging to the eagle with all her might, wondering in panic if it could possibly matter to her if they fell together or separately. Earth and heaven whirled together in a sickening blur of colors as they went plummeting down, but the only thing that came to Maria's mind was a despairing:

Akh, Finist! If only I could see you one last time!

XLV

EARTH MAGIC

THE FOREST WAS ALL ABOUT HER, dark, terrible, in the moonless night. The air hung heavy and still, stifling with the smell of rotting vegetation—

The forest was all about her, waiting . . .

Her magic had fled, she couldn't recall even the simplest spell. And what was that strange stirring, that creaking . . . ? The trees were moving. Slowly, terribly, they were closing in about her—

Crushing her.

LJUBA came starkly awake, trembling, heart racing. Again, these dreams, these terrible dreams— Night after night, always about the forest, always ending with forest-demons slaying her, painfully, horribly.

Forcing herself under control, Ljuba got to her feet. She'd had her bed moved into Finist's quarters so that she might always keep an eye on him in his illness, and now she stood grimly over him.

Look at him, sleeping so peacefully, as though nothing is wrong. Ljuba clenched her fists in frustration. *Damn you, cousin! I don't know how you're doing this, but these dreams can only be your sendings!*

Enough. She was foolishly letting him drive her to the brink of hysteria, instead of concentrating on her plan to stop him. Oh, it was a dangerous sorcery she meant to try, no denying it. But if it worked—no, *when* it worked— the sendings would stop. Tonight she would—

Tonight? Blinking, Ljuba saw that light was shining through cracks in the closed shutters. Morning already, and in a moment her servants would be entering to dress her. Right now, she was in no condition for any of them! Reluctantly, Ljuba murmured the twisting phrase of a restorative spell, sighing with relief to feel new strength flooding through her. It was a false strength, she knew, and she would pay for it later, but for now . . .

For now she would cope.

IT was the day when all folk could bring their petitions before their prince—or, in this case, before his Regent. Ljuba eyed them all with distaste, wondering why Semyon hadn't just cancelled the whole thing. Trying to make her look bad? After all, the old fool hated her, he knew it and she knew it, for all the mask of courtesy. And she'd had trouble with him already, arguments about her policies, about her ways of doing things. When she had challenged him, he'd turned a meek face on her and murmured something about her being Regent, only Regent . . .

One of these days, Semyon, you're going to go too far. And then . . .

Ljuba sat sharply erect, recognizing those in the front of the crowd. Damn! It *must* be Semyon's doing—these were the messengers from Stargorod. And this time he knew she had no excuse not to hear them out.

Haven't I? Angrily, she got to her feet. "It is time for me to return to tend our Prince. I declare this audience at an end!"

"But lady . . ."

How had the fool guards let them approach this closely? "I said the audience is at an end. Now stand aside!"

"Lady, please. We're sorry to hear of Prince Finist's illness. But we only wish to know whether our master's daughter is here. Her name is Maria Danilovna, and—"

Out of the corner of her eye, Ljuba saw Semyon start. "No!" she snapped, fighting down a wave of panic. "I know nothing of her."

"Are you sure? She was headed this way, her father's been so worried— Please, lady, are you sure?"

Without warning, the false strength drained from her.

Dizzy, shaking, furious, Ljuba forgot all caution and snapped, "She's dead! What more do you want? The girl died in the forest. Now get out of here!"

She hurried off toward the prince's quarters—but Semyon moved to block her path. His eyes were quite unreadable.

"How did you know?"

"What do you mean, old man? Get out of my way!"

"You said, 'She died in the forest.' How would you know that?"

"Don't try to question me! Stand aside, or I—"

"You couldn't have known she was dead. You couldn't even have recognized the name Maria Danilovna—a girl you'd never met—unless . . . you killed her."

She should have challenged him, she should have laughed him away as mad, but Ljuba, shaken by the quiet horror on his face, could say nothing at first, nothing at all. Then she said, very softly, "A dangerous accusation, old man," and felt a surge of Power within her. It would be so simple, a psychic clenching of his heart . . . He was old, after all, no one would suspect . . .

Semyon must have known his peril. But he said, almost calmly, "There is a scroll stored in the royal chapel, its location known only to one priest. If I should die mysteriously, that scroll shall be read . . ."

He let his words trail off suggestively. Fuming, Ljuba stared, seeing nothing but bland self-control on his face, unable to get past that smooth, practiced facade. Despite herself, she was shaken, wondering . . . Was this only some desperate bluff? He *couldn't* know about Finist, and the potion—but what other hold could Semyon possibly have over her? What evidence might he have been able to collect?

After a moment or two of tense silence, Ljuba bit her lip in frustrated rage. Damn him, he'd overmatched her; she dared not call his bluff. Her authority was shaky enough. The slightest bit of scandal, and farewell Regency, farewell hopes of power.

"I think," said Ljuba carefully, fighting to keep her voice steady, "that it might be best for you if you were to retire. Are we in agreement?"

He looked as though he was aching to argue. But Semyon evidently realized he'd best not push an angry magician too far, and yielded.

"You understand, lady, that my estate lies within the city walls."

"I don't care where you go, old man! I just want you gone from here!"

"So be it. Lady, you shall have my written resignation by midafternoon."

"I shall be expecting it," said Ljuba flatly. "Now get out of my sight!"

SEMYON bowed in reluctant obedience as Ljuba swept by, then straightened slowly, painfully, a storm of rage behind the practiced blandness of his face. Curse her! After all the long years of service, to be casually thrown aside by that fickle, malicious child!

That sorcerous child.

Damn it, why did I try to challenge her?

If only he'd kept his mouth shut! Maybe Ljuba *did* have something to do with the death of poor Maria, but such things could have been settled when Finist recovered. Now it was too late. Words spoken couldn't be unspoken, and now he must leave the palace—and Finist.

Akh, Finist! As long as I was still within the palace, you had at least one loyal protector, old and worn though I may be. Now . . .

But surely Ljuba wouldn't hurt her own cousin.

"Or, rather," murmured Semyon with more than a touch of cynicism, "she wouldn't hurt her one real hope for genuine power!"

Would she . . . ?

But the guards were eyeing him with wary, sympathetic glances—sympathetic glances that certainly wouldn't stop them from following their Regent's orders. Rather than suffer the shame of being formally thrown out of the palace, Semyon gave them the curtest of bows, and left.

MIDNIGHT: The chamber was small and dark and window-less, there beneath Ljuba's palace, almost featureless, the door bolted fast by iron and magic both. And in the center of the room, within a circle marked—for those who could see it—by glowing lines of force, Ljuba stood, naked, trembling more from exertion than cold, her golden hair a long, wild mass clinging to skin glistening with perspiration there in the candlelight.

As always, it had been a struggle to form the circle properly, to hold the mystic forces properly in place. But now it was complete, the correct scrolls were open before her, the correct items stood on the small table beside the scroll-stand, all of them properly aligned to the four directions. There was no reason to delay.

No reason save fear. There on the table was the object of her magic, no great or terrible thing, just a small pin such as a woman might use to hold back her hair, nothing frightening at all. But that pin was made of iron. Pure, cold, magic-hating iron.

And Ljuba didn't know whether she had the strength to work with iron. If she failed, even for a moment, and the force of it broke free . . .

She would be dead so quickly she'd feel nothing. And no magic at all could be worked through a fog of self-doubt! Ljuba set about casting her mind inward and inward . . . calming . . . calming . . .

Cool-eyed, she began. Stretching out her hand to the eastward item, a candle red as flame, Ljuba murmured, "Svarozits, hear my call," dimly aware that the force she invoked had once been a god of the old, pagan days. "Svarozits, Lord of Fire, hear my call."

The candle burst into flame at her touch.

"Svarozits, once I call you, twice I call you, thrice I call you: as this candle burns, so shall this iron pin burn Finist's will. In your name, be it!"

Too soon to tell if her charm was working. Quickly Ljuba reached out a hand to the southern item, a clod of dark, fertile earth.

"Syra, hear my call. Syra, Lady of Earth, hear my call."

She crumbled the earthen clod, let it sift to the chamber's floor.

"Syra, once I call you, twice I call you, thrice I call

you: as this earth covers the floor, so shall this iron pin bury Finist's will. In your name, be it!''

Odd; the air within the circle seemed to be growing so close, so heavy, making her eyes burn. Ljuba wiped a hasty hand across them to try to clear them, then reached out for the third item, the westward item, a small bowl of water.

''Vodyankoi, hear my call. Vodyankoi, Lord of Water, hear my call.''

Slowly she poured out the water.

''Vodyankoi, once I call you, twice I call you, thrice I call you: as this water falls, so shall this iron pin drown Finist's will. In your name, be it!''

Akh, the air *was* heavy, making her head ache, making her lungs labor, making it difficult to remember the next step . . . How she longed for sleep. She wanted nothing so much in all the world as to sleep . . . but she dared not. If the charm were left unfinished, if the Power was roused but not controlled, she might as well slit her throat here and now and be done with it. Grimly determined, Ljuba reached out to the last item, the northern item, one shining feather lost by Finist in falcon-form.

''Perun, hear my call. Perun, Lord of Sky and Wind and Storm, hear my call.''

With a sharp Word, she hurled the feather from her. It whirled about and about as though caught in the heart of the wind.

''Perun, once I call you, twice I call you, thrice I call you: as this feather is conquered by the wind, so shall this iron pin conquer Finist's will! In your name, be it!''

Hot, it was so hot, stifling, dry heat—the iron! The power of the iron was aroused. She must bind it—now.

''By Fire, Earth, Water, Air I bind you! By the Power of Day and Night I bind you! By—by the—'' She couldn't think. There was wild, terrible pressure on her mind, on her body, crushing her.

Savage with determination, with pain, Ljuba shouted, ''By the Power of Light and Dark I bind you! By the power of my will you must yield to me! By the Power of my will—*you are mine!*''

The force of magic, the force of iron, whirled up in one

great, silent explosion. Ljuba had time for a sharp, anguished scream—

Then she knew nothing more.

ACHING, groaning, Ljuba forced her heavy eyelids open, forced an unresponsive body to its knees. The circle had burst wide open in the explosion of raw Power: Shreds of her scrolls and splinters of the table littered the floor, and the walls were darkened with scorching. Shaking, she glanced down at herself, half expecting some hideous, dying ruin. But she seemed whole; the magic she'd conjured had flung itself out and away from her. And the iron pin? Ljuba reached out for it with a trembling hand, seeing it glowing red with heat. But as she gingerly touched it, the heat drained away.

She had done it. The magic was complete—and now Finist would be hers.

Shaking with exhaustion, Ljuba struggled to her feet, wearily pulling her caftan about herself. Soon the pin would be in place. Soon she'd be able to sleep.

FINIST stirred as she approached him. Amber eyes opened, too bright, too mocking. "You . . . don't give up . . . do you?" It was a painful whisper of sound. "Poor cousin . . . never have real power, never . . . Never break my binding . . ."

"I shall," she hissed.

"Shall you?" he taunted with feverish glee. "Have you washed the bloodstains from my caftan? No? Then you shall never wed me, cousin! Never have the throne of Kirtesk!"

Enough of this! Ljuba stabbed the iron pin into the shining locks of his hair, feeling him tense with the shock, then collapse into deep, mindless slumber.

"So, cousin." Ljuba smoothed his hair back to hide the pin. "No more defiance. No more taunts. No more disturbing my dreams!"

She managed to reach her own bed before collapsing, sinking immediately into a well of sleep.

But . . .

Eyes were watching her in her slumber—mocking, inhuman eyes. A voice, the whisper of wind on leaves, laughed softly.

"Did you think to escape so easily? You have roused the forest's wrath, oh woman! You have harmed a forest-friend and threatened the forest—you shall never know peace again! Sleep well, oh woman! Sleep while yet you can!"

And Ljuba awoke with a start, head pounding, aching for sleep, alone and afraid and at last despairing.

XLVI

KIRTESK

MARIA CLUNG FRANTICALLY to the smooth-feathered back
as the golden eagle plummeted helplessly, wild wind pulling the air from her lungs. Seeing the fields once so far
below them seeming to rush up at them, she tried to pray,
but the only thing that came to mind was an anguished
memory of Finist's face, eyes warm with love . . .

Just when she was sure she was dead, the eagle, with a
very human groan of effort, managed to drag open his
wings and began backwatering fiercely, braking with all
his might. Those wide wings swept out sharply, throwing
her forward onto his neck, struggling to keep her seat.
Then their fall was levelling out into a long, sweeping
glide.

*But we're already so close to the ground—is there room
for him to land safely?*

Not quite. They hit the ground with stunning force. Maria was thrown from the eagle's back and went rolling
helplessly away, ending up at last on her back, staring
blankly up at the night-darkening sky, too dazed and
winded to move.

Yes, but she was beginning to realize she'd landed right
on top of her pack, and it was uncomfortable, to say the
least. And the eagle—she didn't hear a sound from him.
Was he all right?

When Maria painfully managed to sit up and turn
around, she saw him, no longer eagle but man, half-hidden
by the bushes into which he'd fallen, lying quite still.

307

She hurried to him, and let out her breath in a sigh of relief: He wasn't dead. Drained of strength, he had collapsed into heavy sleep. Maria hesitated, glancing toward the walls of Kirtesk, now so temptingly near. Akh, Finist! If she left now, she might be at his side this very night.

Maria sighed and turned back towards the unconscious man, spreading her shawl and scarf over him for warmth and modesty.

It was going to be a long night.

VASILI awoke with a cry, blinking in confusion at the sleepy Maria there in the cold grey light of early morning.

"What— Oh. Yes." He clutched the shawl frantically to him. "Was I asleep all this time?"

"You were."

"Ah." The fair skin reddened a bit. "Child, forgive me, I thought I'd outgrown the sin of Pride, but . . . it was so glorious to fly again." He shook his head in self-reproach. "I should have heeded you and landed before I'd exhausted myself."

You should, indeed, thought Maria, but all she said was a carefully bland "No harm done. But are you all right?"

For answer, he shifted smoothly back to eagle—a normal-sized eagle this time—offering her shawl and scarf with a careful talon. Golden eyes looked from her to Kirtesk and back again.

Maria sighed. "I know, I know. You still will not break your vow by entering the city."

The eagle gave her an apologetic glance. He reached forward to rub his head against her cheek in a gentle caress, then took to the air in a rush, flying back to his monastery. Maria got to her feet, watching till she couldn't see him any longer, then turned to face Kirtesk, feeling a surge of something near to panic.

Finist, Maria reminded herself, and started determinedly forward.

THE guards hadn't even looked twice at the plain-faced peasant girl entering their city. Maria scuttled through the vast main gate before they could change their minds, but then had to stop, overwhelmed by the realization that she was in Kirtesk. After all these days and hardships, she was actually in Kirtesk!

For a moment, Maria seemed to hear Vasilissa's voice in her ear, warning her, *A boyar's daughter doesn't stare; a boyar's daughter doesn't gawk at things like a peasant.*

Right now, I am a peasant! Maria retorted, and stood and gawked as she would.

Even consumed by worry as she was, Maria had to confess that this was a lovely city. It wasn't as large as Stargorod, but unlike that hectic, complicated place, it was *clean*. The streets—all of them, by Heaven, not just those leading to the market square—were paved with smooth planking. The houses were mostly of fine stone, though some were of wood beautifully carved and painted. And the people—Maria raised a surprised eyebrow. In Stargorod, only the *boyars* wore anything more exotic than linen. Here, it seemed that linen was reserved for the poor. Everyone else wore a wild riot of color, tunics and trousers for the men, gaily embroidered blouses and *sarafans*, overdresses, for the women, brocaded caftans for the wealthy. The fabrics of choice seemed to be either the finest, thinnest of wools or even silk!

Well, Finist did *mention to me once that Kirtesk is on one of the silk routes.*

It wasn't just the material prosperity, though. Kirtesk had a feel of joy to it, of contentment—something Stargorod had always lacked. Although Maria knew she had never been here before, she felt very much as though she had come home.

But what sort of home could it be without Finist?

The sheer anguish of that thought brought her sharply back to reality, and all at once Maria found herself staring at the people she passed—staring with a new and ever-increasing fear.

Why do they all have such sad, worried faces? Why is the city so quiet? It's almost as though everyone's in mourning. Oh, dear God, am I too late?

Surely she would know if Finist were dead. She would *know* it.

Panic wasn't going to solve anything. Mimicking Marfa's accent as best she could, Maria asked a cloth merchant, "Something wrong here?"

He looked at her in disbelief. "Just come in from the countryside, have you? Haven't you heard about our poor Prince?"

"He—he isn't—"

"Dead? No, praise Heaven! But he's so ill, we don't know if he will recover. Eh, wait! Where are you going?"

Maria had hurried blindly off, mind tumbling with wild thoughts. She had to get into the royal palace. She had to get to Finist's side before it was too late. But how could she manage it? They would never let a mere peasant in there. And if she dropped all disguise, Ljuba would kill her.

As she wove her way through the crowds, a familiar name caught her ear.

"Pity about it. *Boyar* Semyon's a good man."

Finist had spoken of a Semyon. He'd told her how the old man was ever loyal, a good friend and a true support. Could this be the same *boyar*? Maria edged warily forward.

Not warily enough. The merchant who'd been speaking to his fellow stopped to glare at her, and she hurried meekly away.

Yes, but now that she was attuned to Semyon's name, she seemed to be hearing it everywhere, in various snatches of nervous gossip:

"Pity the *boyar* went and resigned from court."

"Especially now."

And: "It was the lady made *boyar* Semyon resign."

"Hush! Never know if Her Sorcerousness might be listening!"

And: "*She* made *boyar* Semyon leave, you know. It's only truth. The Lady Ljuba never did like him."

"Well, at least she let him stay here in Kirtesk."

"Shh! He's here, right behind you! See him?"

Slowly, casually, Maria turned. Akh, but Semyon looked so weary, so worn. So old. *Not surprising, under the circumstances*, she thought wryly.

But this might be her only chance. Without stopping to think, Maria hurried to the *boyar*'s side. Startled servants quickly moved to block her path and protect their master, and Maria hastily called, "Please, *boyar!* I must speak with you!"

He can't think me a threat, an innocuous peasant girl!

Sure enough, Semyon was waving his servants aside. "What is it, child?" he asked courteously. "How may I help you?"

Maria hesitated. She hardly wanted to discuss this where everyone could overhear. "It's about—about the prince's health," she said warily, and saw Semyon tense. "Please, *boyar,* I must speak with you alone, just for a few moments!"

"My lord?" The servants weren't too happy about it. But their master gave a short, humorless laugh.

"What, after all I've survived so far, do you really think one little peasant lass could possibly hurt me?" He paused, glancing about with well-trained caution. "Come, girl, this innkeeper knows me. We shall have at least the illusion of privacy."

"I can't tell you my true name," Maria began. "No, it's not a trick, I swear. It's only— You see, there's—" She stopped, took a deep steadying breath, and started anew. "It has something to do with a fragile spell of disguise. You know about such things? Akh, of course you would! You remember when Finist was hidden as Finn!"

Semyon's eyes widened. "How would you know—"

"Because I was there! *Boyar,* I'm the one of whom he's spoken, the—ah—the daughter of that exiled *boyar* from Stargorod. Please, before you interrupt, let me tell you why I'm here."

"I wouldn't dream of interrupting!" Semyon said.

". . . AND SO," Maria concluded, voice quavering, "Finist was gone."

"And you came all the way from Stargorod to find him," Semyon said carefully, "all by yourself."

"I didn't have a choice. There wasn't anyone to go with me."

She stopped to catch her breath, fighting back sudden tears. "Oh, don't you see? How could I not come? He—

In a dream-message, he cried out to me to seek him, to—
to save him. How could I not come to Kirtesk?'' Maria
hesitated, studying Semyon's face. ''You—you do believe
me?''

''I do.'' His voice was grim. ''But—my dear, do you
know what you're doing? The, ah, lady will not be gentle
with someone who tries to stand in her way.''

Maria stared at him. ''And would *you* willingly abandon Finist?'' she asked.

Semyon winced. ''No, I would not.''

He fell silent for so long that Maria felt her spirits sink.

''But. . . . for all and all, you're not going to help me,
are you?''

The *boyar* gave her a startled look. ''Of course I am!''
he said. ''Now,'' he added thoughtfully, ''I have only to
figure out a way to get you safely into the palace.''

LJUBA glanced at herself in the mirror, then looked quickly
away. Face wan, drawn, eyes haunted and dark-circled—
God, she looked like an old woman!

But how could she look any other way? Every time she
dared relax her guard and sleep, the forest and all its demons taunted her. Sick for want of rest, she was finding
it more and more difficult to keep the *boyars* in check—
why, this very morning she'd overheard them murmuring
something about her and madness in the same breath! And
Finist—

She glanced down at him, lying motionless, only the
faint movement of his chest proving he still lived. The iron
pin had worked too well, subduing his will so firmly that
he was nearly in coma. But at least the thing was doing
some good! While it kept him in that deep, dreamless
sleep, his fever-exhausted body had a chance to heal. In
fact, the fever seemed to have broken, much to Ljuba's
relief.

But what about the effects of the potion? Had he sweated
that out, too? Ljuba sighed wearily. She didn't dare give
him another dose, not as weak as he was. If she left the
iron pin in place, he'd never be able to truly wake. But if
she removed it, and the potion no longer bound him, she
was doomed.

It was all too much for her to bear. Ljuba rushed from the room, leaving orders to the servants to summon her if there was any change in the prince's condition, hurrying she knew not where. She narrowly avoided a collision with some homely young woman servant.

"Fool! Get out of my way!"

"Ah—Lady Ljuba?"

"Of course, you idiot!"

"Wait, lady, please. I've heard of your troubles, with that stained caftan, I mean, and— Well, I think I just may be able to help you!"

MARIA had been hard put to keep her voice light and casual. It hadn't proven too difficult for Semyon to smuggle her into the palace with some of the real servants, it hadn't been too difficult to wander her way towards the royal quarters, she hadn't even had too long a wait before Ljuba had come tearing out of there as though possessed. But now that she was actually face to face with the woman—

Akh, Ljuba was beautiful! Even now, looking haggard, she was so beautiful that Maria's heart ached.

How can Finist love plain, unbeautiful me, when every day he's faced with this golden wonder?

And yet . . . he had wanted to wed Maria, not treacherous Ljuba.

But this was no time for self-doubt, while Ljuba was shouting angrily for her to stand aside. Maria saw the sorcerous rage in those lovely eyes, hot as the heart of hate, and was very much able to believe that this exquisite creature had tried to kill her. Fighting down her terror, her urge to run, Maria stood her ground and told Ljuba, with feigned cheerfulness, how she knew of that stained caftan. She concluded with:

"Well, I think I just may be able to help you!"

Ljuba tensed. "What do you mean?"

"It isn't nice perfumey stuff such as you ladies use, but . . ."

"Out with it, girl! What are you trying to say?"

"Only that I've got a concoction of sorts, a soap we use back in my village. It gets most any stain out of anything.

And I don't doubt it'll take the bloodstains right out of that caftan you've got, and let you w-wed your prince!''

Would Ljuba accept Maria's story? It was a bluff, of course. Still, to judge from those marks of strain on Ljuba's face, she must have reached the point of being willing to try anything.

And so it was. ''What is your price?'' she asked.

''No more than you can pay, lady,'' answered Maria, rather surprised at her own blitheness.

''So.'' Ljuba hesitated, absently tapping a long, elegant finger against a perfectly curved lip. ''Come with me,'' she said. ''You'll have your chance. Of course,'' she added over her shoulder, in so casually cruel a voice that Maria shuddered, ''you do understand that if you fail, if you damage the caftan in any way at all—you'll die.''

XLVII

COUNTERSPELLS

LJUBA WALKED AHEAD, not once checking to see if Maria—who, not being as tall as the elegant sorceress, had a shorter stride—was keeping up with her. It was only to be expected, Maria thought. Why should the Regent of Kirtesk care about the comfort or discomfort of a mere servant? At least this frantic scuttling didn't give her time to be afraid.

A respectful servant cast open a door so finely crafted and ornate that it could only lead to the royal suite.

"There," said Ljuba.

For one brief moment, Maria thought they were facing some manner of bizarre altar, complete with silken altar cloth. Then she saw dark, brownish stains marring the shimmering fabric.

The caftan—and Finist's blood.

Ljuba gave her a sharp glance. "Have you suddenly turned squeamish?"

"Uh . . . No, lady, of course not. I was . . . only pitying the poor, wounded prince, that's all." Boldly, Maria moved forward to the caftan. But when she tried to pick it up, her hand was stopped by empty air that felt quite solid. "There seems to be a magical barrier around it, lady."

"Of course there is, fool! Did you think I'd let any idiot touch it?"

Ljuba gestured with a flicker of supple fingers, and the

barrier was gone. *Convenient,* Maria thought, and gently picked up the caftan.

Ljuba was watching. "There is purified water in that basin. Do you need anything more?"

"No, lady." Maria hesitated, waiting for Ljuba to leave. But Ljuba showed no sign of stirring. "Uh, lady, it's all right, you don't have to stay, really."

A corner of that perfect mouth turned up in a wry, cold little smile. "Did you think I'd trust you alone, girl?"

"But—"

"No. Come, you made your boasts! Clean the caftan, or learn to regret your lies."

Maria turned away, clutching the caftan to her, heart pounding. She rummaged frantically about in her pouch— there *was* a sliver of soap in there. At least she could go through the motions of washing. But even a sorceress couldn't remove those sad stains. How could Maria ever hope to succeed?

At least she would go down fighting. Filled with a sort of desperate courage, Maria lowered the caftan into the water.

LOST in a fathomless sea of sleep, Finist stirred restlessly. Someone was touching him, touching his heart . . .

DEEP within the forest, small green-eyed beings nudged each other and giggled softly, and the *leshy* stood staring at the scene his magic showed him, and began to laugh . . .

MARIA froze, staring in disbelief at the caftan. She had only touched it to the water, and the dried bloodstains had simply melted away, leaving the silk shining and unharmed.

Dazed, terrified and joyful in one, Maria turned to Ljuba. The sorceress was stunned, face blank with shock.

It lasted only a moment. Then the beautiful eyes went cold and flat as blue marble. "Why, well done, girl." It was an urbane croon. "You shall be truly rewarded."

Maria's heart gave a frightened leap. Rewarded—by death? Everyone in the realm knew the terms of Finist's spell: Only the woman who washed the caftan clean with her own hands would be able to wed him.

Only she and Ljuba knew the truth about what had just happened. If the sorceress let her live, no matter how far away she sent her, Ljuba would never be free of the fear of blackmail. And, as far as the sorceress was concerned, Maria was a nobody, a nameless peasant, quite expendable . . .

She doesn't dare let me live, Maria realized in horror. *All she has to do is get rid of me, tell everyone she cleaned the caftan, and she can wed Finist and live happily ever after!*

Ljuba raised an elegant brow. "I promised you a reward for cleaning the caftan. Come, name your price!"

Maria shivered, only too well aware of how easy it would be for Ljuba to see that she disappeared: an accidental fall down a palace stairway, a stumble off the edge of a parapet . . . Who'd notice the death of a peasant? Ljuba wouldn't even need to risk using magic.

"Come, girl, speak!" There was the faintest edge of menace to Ljuba's voice. "Name your reward!"

Akh, she couldn't seem to think straight. The only thing that came to mind was a thought of Finist—that if she could just reach Finist's side, all would be well—

"I only want this," said Maria boldly. "I've heard so much about our magical prince, how kind he is, how much he's done for everybody—well, now that he's sick, I want to do something for him. I want to spend the night at his bedside, try to heal him." Seeing Ljuba's disbelieving gaze, she hurried on, "I've got some simple songs we use to soothe the sick children back home. Who knows? They might soothe him, too."

Ljuba gave a short, contemptuous little laugh. "Is that really all you want? Are you sure you don't want to try to help yourself to some royal jewels as well?"

"Oh, no, lady!" Maria's indignation was genuine. "I said I wanted only to help the prince, and I meant it—"

She broke off abruptly, staring at Ljuba, who had become as alert and fierce as some deadly hunting cat. Now what—? Maria glanced down at her hands, and gasped. Those broad, coarse, convincingly peasant fingers were blurring, becoming more refined, returning to their true shape. Terrified, she remembered Vasili's warnings about the fragility of the disguise spell. Dear Lord! When the magic binding the caftan had unravelled at her touch, the disguise spell had begun to unravel as well! Maria stood, stunned, as the last of it dissolved, leaving her defenseless.

Ljuba's glance sharpened in recognition.

"You!" It was almost a scream of rage. "You didn't die in the forest!"

"Ah, no, I—"

"Don't try to talk your way out of this one, fool! Not now!"

Ljuba's eyes blazed with blue fire. "You've been the thorn in my side all along, but that's over. Now there aren't any forest demons to protect you. Now, Maria, you *will* die!"

XLVIII

THE LISUNKA'S EGG

IT WAS SO SOOTHING here in darkness, no fever-fire scorching mind and body. Here one could float in peaceful, mindless sleep . . .

But something was wrong. Finist heard the faintest echo of sound, felt it stirring and prickling at his psychic senses . . . Someone was in peril, someone he loved . . .

Maria!

Finist fought a battle that was no less fierce for being of the mind alone, fought to master his will, fought to wake—

But the iron bound him, cruel as any chains. Despairing, he felt himself sliding, bit by bit, over the edge of consciousness once more . . . felt himself drowning in the sea of sleep, the endless, peaceful, mindless sea of sleep . . .

MARIA could feel the Power gathering about Ljuba, the death-magic that was going to strike her down, and there wasn't anything she could do about it. Ljuba had her in a corner of the room, there was nowhere to run, to hide, to even try to dodge! Frantic, Maria thrust her hand into her pouch, trying to find something, anything, that could be used as a weapon. And she came up with—

The little wooden egg the *lisunka* had given her.

What good could such a toy be against sorcery? But Maria refused to doubt forest-magic, especially now, and fiercely held the little thing up.

* * *

LJUBA froze, staring, as the wooden egg cracked open on the girl's outstretched palm.

No, she cried in silent terror, *it can't be!*

For the forest was flowing out of that little egg, the forest was all about her—the terrible darkness, the Power that was so much greater than anything she could hope to wield! The forest was crushing her—the demons were mocking her, reaching for her to tear away her soul and leave her trapped in avian form, forever a mindless crow—

BEWILDERED, Maria stood watching as Ljuba, her eyes wild, turned and ran, screaming.

What could she have seen? Maria didn't see anything at all. It must have been illusion—and it must have been a masterpiece!

But Ljuba's panic wouldn't last forever, and as soon as she regained composure, she would return twice as deadly.

Maria hurried anxiously through the maze of rooms that was the princely suite, expecting at every moment to be stopped by palace guards. But there didn't seem to be any guards. Ljuba must be *very* confident in her ability to guard Finist.

Finist, Finist, where are *you?* Maria worried. Desperate, she flung open a door, and found herself at last in the royal bed-chamber. There lay her love in the great canopied bed. At his side sat a plainly clad young woman, who turned at Maria's entrance to stare at her with dull, bovine eyes.

"Come here!" Maria ordered. "Hurry!"

"You—you aren't the mistress. How did you—"

"Of course I'm not! She sent me to get you!"

"Where is she?"

"Come here and I'll show you! She's waiting for you, right through this door!"

"I dunno. I'm not supposed to leave my post."

Maria bit back a scream of impatience. "Do you want the mistress angry at you? Well?"

That did it! With a fearful look around, the servant got to her feet and hurried forward. *A little closer,* thought Maria, *come just a little closer to me . . . Yes!*

"I don't see—" began the servant, peeking warily around the half-opened door.

But she got no further. With a mighty shove, Maria pushed her out of the bed-chamber and bolted the door.

She was bound to yell for help, but at least Maria had bought a few moments alone with Finist.

But for all the need for haste, Maria could only stand by the bedside, looking at the sleeping Finist, quite overwhelmed by the force of her love, and her shock, too. Even knowing how desperately ill he'd been, she hadn't really been prepared for this:

Oh, my dear, my poor dear! So wan, so painfully thin!

But all would be well now. As soon as he woke, and saw her, all would be well. She didn't dare let herself think otherwise.

"Finist? Finist, love, it's me."

There wasn't the slightest response. Maria continued, a bit more intensely:

"Finist! Come now, wake up!"

He didn't so much as stir, and Maria, staring at the wan, peaceful face, felt the first stirrings of alarm.

"You really *are* asleep, aren't you? I'm sorry to have to disturb you, but—come, wake up! Finist! Wake up!"

But he slept on, composed and still as death.

"Finist!" Maria shook him, gently at first, then with increasing frenzy. "Oh, please, please, wake up! *Finist!*"

Dear God, it was useless! He wasn't going to awaken, no matter what she did. Ljuba wasn't going to let her prize escape, not so easily—she must have bespelled Finist while he was weak and defenseless from illness. And that meant . . .

A little sob of despair escaped Maria. She certainly didn't know how to fight sorcery.

Akh, but Finist . . . Aching with love, Maria reached out a gentle hand to caress his face, tenderly brushing back the wild locks of bright hair from his forehead.

But what was this? Something sharp was tangled in his hair.

Carefully she worked it free.

A pin? Maria held the ugly little thing gingerly between

thumb and forefinger. It looked like iron—a very odd metal for a magician to be wearing.

Unless this was part of Ljuba's charm? With a sharp cry of disgust, Maria hurled the pin from her, then, shaking, turned to Finist—

But Finist slept on. And nothing she could do, not pleading with him, not shaking him, not even—wincing as she did this—slapping him, could make him wake.

"Finist . . ." It was a weary moan. "I've come all this long way for you! I've borne all my trials for you! Won't you waken for me? W-won't you . . ."

He stirred not the slightest of stirrings. And it was more, suddenly much more, than she could bear. Maria, who prided herself on never weeping, Maria, who hadn't wept during all her journey, at last felt her strength give way. Arms flung about Finist's still body, she sobbed in complete despair.

"How touching," said the coldest, most mocking of voices. "How very touching."

Dear God, in her haste to get to Finist's side, she hadn't stopped to think there might be other doors into the royal chambers! Maria whirled, choking on her tears—and saw her death before her.

It was Ljuba.

XLIX

POWER PLAY

TRAPPED, *chained, wings pinned closely to his sides, the anguished falcon strained against his bindings, aching for the sky, staring painfully up at that endless, dizzying sweep of blue, at that open freedom he could never reach—*

And then, all at once, it happened! Miraculously, the iron chains were falling away from him, and he was free, free! Breathless, bewildered, trembling with joy, the falcon leaped into the air on fiercely outstretched wings, soaring up and up and up.

But something was wrong. The fierce blue sky was turning overcast, grey as grief. And something was striking his upturned face—rain? Warm, salty rain? Confused, he felt his wings begin to falter . . . And now the sky was fading . . . and he was—

HE was awake, and Finist, man, not falcon, and the warm, salty rain wasn't rain at all, but tears—

Who would be weeping for him? Surely not Ljuba! Finist blinked, trying to clear his hazy vision. As his senses returned, he froze, staring up in sheer, stunned wonder.

Oh kind, merciful, wonderful Heaven, could it be? These were Maria's tears! She was here, his dearest, somehow she was here!

"Maria . . ." Finist gasped.

But before he could say anything more, before he could see more than the very first, faint dawnings of joy on her

323

face, she was turning wildly from him, staring with horror.

Ljuba stood in the doorway—a fierce-eyed Ljuba gathering Power to her to strike Maria down.

How could she know about— Aie, no time for questions! "Ljuba, stop!" Finist shouted, or tried to shout, struggling to get to his feet and— Oh, damn, damn, he didn't have the strength. He wasn't going to be able to stop Ljuba in time, and Maria was going to be slain right before his helpless eyes.

"No!"

There wasn't time for finesse. Finist abandoned the fragile physical, and desperately threw all the essence of his will at his cousin even as she struck. Power flared dazzlingly—there was a soundless, agonizing rending of reality about them—

And the world of flesh-and-blood was gone. Around them was . . . nothing.

Nearly nothing. There was no sense of *hot* or *cold* here, no clearly defined *up* or *down*, there was only a featureless, boundless blue-grey haze—a haze that fairly glowed with Power. And after a second of confusion, the prince realized with a surge of triumph what had happened. This place had nothing to do with any of the Realms of Flesh or Spirit:

We've thrown ourselves onto a plane of pure energy, of pure magic!

Granted, he could still kill himself here; though he had left his physical self somewhere back in reality, he was still linked to it, and there was always the chance he would exhaust that weakened body beyond the point of recovery.

It's worth the risk, thought Finist, drawing Power to him.

This time, he knew with a little shock of horror, it couldn't be a case of merely stopping his cousin. This time there could be no reprieves. After all the years of forgive and forgive, this time only one of them could survive.

Oh, my cousin! It was a cry of silent pain.

LJUBA struggled to get herself back under control. God, that had been a shock! First to find Finist conscious—and

frighteningly coherent, too—then to be hurled roughly out
of herself and dumped in this . . . wherever it was, at the
mercy of her almost certainly vengeful cousin—

Akh, wait. This place had a strangeness to it, a tingling,
electric strangeness that meant they could only have fallen
onto a plane of pure magic.

*Oh, Finist, you fool! I may be a weaker magician than
you in the real world. But here, with Power all around
me, I am truly your equal!*

With that, she seized magic from the richness all about
her, glorying in the ease of it, and hurled it at her cousin
in a wild, raw, deadly wave of Power.

OFF balance, Finist barely managed to defend himself
against the savage attack that had plainly been meant to
slay his mind and leave his body helpless. *Of course,* he
thought, *she still needs my body as her puppet.* Staggering
beneath the dizzying impact of that arcane wave, he sighed
with relief to feel it striking, recoiling, breaking apart
against the psychic wall he'd hastily hurled together.

Ljuba, too, was staggering, dazed by the backlash of
unspent force.

Now's your chance! Finist shouted to himself.

But he couldn't strike to kill—curse him for a fool, he
couldn't! Even knowing what she was, even knowing what
she'd meant to do—he couldn't block the memory of the
past. There she lingered in his mind, not the ruthless,
lovely woman-who-was, but the girl-who'd-been, the girl
he had been too young to know how to help, child-Ljuba,
unloved and so alone . . .

*You idiot, forget your misplaced pity! She's a traitor to
the crown; she tried to break your mind. She tried to kill
Maria! Will you let her escape?*

Shaking, Finist pulled Power to him, all the wild, terrible Power his being could control, and hurled it at Ljuba
in one blazing, deadly spear—

But the memory of a smooth golden form, warm and
radiant in candlelight . . . the thought of that perfect form
lying torn and broken in death . . .

And even as he hurled that blazing Power, Finist cried
out in despair and cast it wide.

* * *

As the terrifying force engulfed her, burning, a horrified Ljuba had only time enough to think, *I'm dead!* But then that force had hurtled by and burst apart, to leave her untouched, and she nearly laughed in her shaken relief. *You can't kill me, can you, cousin? You're not quite free of my potion's control yet! While I . . .*

She stared fiercely at him where he sagged, drained, exhausted, and knew that now he was hers.

Yes, and yet . . . did she really have to destroy him? Ljuba blinked, astonished to once again feel that sudden, unwanted twinge of . . . love?

Oh, no, not here, not now! It was a silent scream of rage. *There's no time for this!*

She'd strike him now, mind to mind, conquer him without the need for potions or foolish iron pins. She would use this Power to burn out his will and make Finist and Kirtesk her own.

Then, without warning, the blue-grey haze of this plane was swirling up about her, as though it were Earthly fog seized by a terrible wind—but there couldn't be any wind, not in this place of Not-Quite-Real—sweeping over her in glowing waves. Surrounded by the wild, silent whirlings of Power, she couldn't see or hear or feel—she was alone in nothingness.

Finist! What have you done to me?

WHAT was happening? One moment Maria had been in Finist's bed-chamber, seeing Ljuba about to strike, sure that she was going to die, the next moment Finist had been struggling to his feet, magic swirling wildly about him. Though his body hadn't moved from the bedside, she had still *felt* him leaving the physical, leaving her, as surely as she'd *felt* his emotions when the silver chain had been binding them together. She remembered screaming out:

"No, I can't lose you, not so soon!"

Then, too anguished to think clearly, she had thrown the entire force of her love and longing and despair after him, sensing her mind brushing his just for an instant before a terrible pressure seemed to rend body and spirit apart—

And was this death, this strange blue-grey, swirling fog? Surely not. Because, even though she didn't seem to have a proper body, even though she didn't seem to be breathing, she could still feel, she could still hear, she was still *she*, Maria Danilovna!

Caught in a fresh surge of panic, she glanced wildly around, trying to orient herself. But there weren't any landmarks here. There didn't seem to be *anything* here, save this eerie fog—

All right. Maria forced herself sternly away from hysteria. *If I'm not dead, this must be one of those bizarre magical Realms Finist once mentioned when he—*

Finist! Even as she thought that name, the haze about her seemed to clear, and Maria stared in disbelief.

"Finist!"

Without air to breathe, there couldn't be any sound, but he heard her. Without solid ground beneath her feet, she shouldn't have been able to run to him, but she did—right into his arms. And how wonderful was that embrace, strangely weightless though it was!

"Oh, Finist, my love!" This must be some sort of magical nonvocal speech, she decided, then stopped worrying about it altogether as their lips met in a quick, frantic kiss.

Then Finist was drawing back, eyes anguished.

"Maria, forgive me, I didn't stop to think—I didn't mean to pull you here after me!"

"No," Maria protested, *"it wasn't you. I did it. Truly. I knew you were leaving your body behind, for my sake. And—and I couldn't bear to think I might be losing you a second time, and—"*

"Maria, do you know what you're saying?"

"That . . . we are attuned?" She stared up at him in dawning comprehension. *"That's it, isn't it? Even without the magic of the necklace, we're still attuned."* Maria heard the nervous delight quivering in her words. *"I mean, for such a thing as this to happen—"*

"Yes, of course, love—but I've got to get you out of here before Ljuba senses you!"

Shaking, Maria *felt* the prince making a heroic effort to control his magic, heedless of the damage he might be doing to his weakened body. She knew with him that it was going to work after all, she felt with him the proper psychic tingle that was magic stirring through him . . .

But as quickly as it had come, the Power had drained away again, and Finist was left sagging in Maria's arms. For a moment, Maria found herself sharing his storm of emotions, feeling his fear for her, his despair, his aching weariness—*Akh, Finist, my poor dear!*—and with it, a tangle of something else, a darkness composed of grief and shame and . . . lust?

Not for myself, I hope—not like this, anyhow, so very mixed up with guilt and hatred.

And then she tensed, staring.

"No." Maria wasn't sure whether she'd groaned that aloud or not. But there before her was the object of Finist's hatred:

Ljuba. Ljuba, whose only lust was for power. Ljuba who, untouched by fever-weakness, meant to destroy her cousin. Maria knew it, saw it, *felt* it.

But what could she do? Ljuba was drawing the raw stuff of magic about her and it was flaring brighter, a deadly aura encircling the sorceress. Her long, golden hair stirred and crackled eerily in that place where there was no wind, no sound; her eyes blazed till they were no longer merely human.

Beside her, Maria could feel Finist trying to gather Power to him, but she knew with a dreadful sort of calm that he could never control it in time, not drained as he was. Ljuba would win, and Finist would die—no, worse, his *mind* would die, and the empty shell of his body live on—

"I won't let it happen!" The cry burst from her, tearing through the wild tangle of her emotions, Finist's emotions. *"Ljuba, I won't let you do this!"*

Her fierce, despairing gaze locked with the sorcerous stare. There was a sharp, dizzying sense of impact, almost as though she'd struck Ljuba a physical blow. Then—a rational corner of Maria's mind insisted that what happened next could only have been caused by that continued link with Finist and the Power around him. And yet surely the force of the love and hope and fear she felt for him was more powerful than any magic. For in that next, stunned instant, Maria found herself looking past the mere chance of luck that was Ljuba's outer beauty, past the confusion that was Finist's love and hatred, looking more deeply and more truly than ever she'd seen anyone before. And what Maria saw:

Oh, the poor thing!

Far worse than simple physical abuse was the total lack of love. There was a girl who knew she bore the seeds of darkness in her, yet had no way to fight them, who cried and cried for help, but silently, always silently, because she knew there was no one to aid her, no one to care, no one to trust—

But at last young Ljuba had learned to build a wall about herself and call it strength. She had come to accept the dark within, to welcome it, come to lust for power and for Power, the only things sure never to betray her, the only things without the weaknesses that were love or trust or pity—

Maria couldn't stand any more. Blinking back stunned tears, she cried out, *"Oh, my dear, no! It isn't like that!"*

And accidentally, in all innocence, she showed Ljuba to Ljuba.

WHAT was happening? There'd been that sudden locking of their glances, startling but not alarming, though Maria had astonished Ljuba by the force of that magicless will. But now, before Ljuba could even begin to resist, the images were here, flooding over her, overwhelming her, drowning her, the images of herself—

No, not me! I was never like that!

—images of the inner Ljuba, the secret self she'd thought safely locked away since childhood, the piteous, shrivelled being with all her weaknesses, all her fears, so helpless, so lost, so afraid . . .

There was no eluding that merciless flood of truth . . . *Finist:* She had tried to believe she loved him, but it wasn't love, she didn't really understand love. It had been a hunger for dominance, no more, a hunger for power . . .

And what's wrong with that? she thought defiantly. *Kings have ruled with less.*

But the images were still flooding her mind, sharper,

clearer images from deeper within herself . . . And all at once Ljuba was seeing not that crippled, love-starved child, but the thing she'd deliberately become, the cold-hearted, empty creature—

The *pathetic* creature! The *laughable* creature, unable to love, unable to trust, unable to feel anything save lust and hate and fear.

Stop it! Please, please, stop it!

Ljuba fought to flee the torment of her own mind, but there was no escaping that prison, and so she found instead the very heart of her fear, found the forest there within her, there with all its ancient, terrible Power, the forest that hated her, had always hated her! It was mocking her with a bitter, deadly wit, calling:

Traitor! You would have slain your kin! You would have murdered your prince!

Aie, this was Maria's fault. If only she could find the girl, kill her, this torture would stop, and she'd be in control again and all would be well—

But the forest's cry was continuing savagely, *Traitor, you've lost! It's over and you've lost*—

—and she couldn't think, she couldn't act, she could only scream out:

"No, no, you don't understand! I—"

But still it continued, shouting at her, taunting her in her own voice:

Traitor—hopeless, loveless, soulless traitor!

"No! Please!"

Traitor! her own voice screamed. *Traitor!*

Semyon was before her, echoing, *Traitor!* the entire court was watching her, echoing, *Traitor!* and most terribly Erema, who'd died for her, was with them, the nameless man in the forest who'd died for her was with them, all of them crying, *Traitor!* and there was no escape from them, no escape—

WHAT inner horror could Ljuba be seeing? Maria had sparked it—in all innocence, Finist was sure. Overwhelmed by the Power she didn't know how to control, she had turned Ljuba's vision inward, though Finist knew from Maria's very plain bewilderment that she hadn't the faintest idea what she had done.

As Ljuba shrank back into herself, wild-eyed, Finist felt a sudden, wonderful surge of returning strength. His cousin had just lost her last, tenuous psychic hold over him.

Finist knew what he must do.

Grimly shutting his mind to pity, Finist steeled himself to strip away Ljuba's Power and return her to the real world, and a traitor's fate. Arm protectively about Maria, the prince focused all his restored will and called himself, his love, and his cousin back to the room they'd left. The blue-grey fog agreeably parted and faded . . .

It wasn't as easy as it should have been. For an instant that seemed to drag into forever, there was nothing about them, and he couldn't seem to find the right path, or any path at all.

Then the familiar lines of his bed-chamber were re-forming about them, and Finist gave an unashamed sigh of relief. Abruptly returned to mortal solidity and a body that was still weak from illness, the prince staggered, only the residue of the other plane's magic keeping him upright. He felt Maria, who, poor love, must be nearly as dizzy as he, make a valiant attempt to steady him. For a moment, linked in that afterglow of the magical plane's Power, their minds touched, warm, loving . . .

Yes, but Ljuba—

Desperate with terror, Ljuba huddled against a wall, staring at him as though he were her death. Drawing the magical residue about himself, enhancing his own depleted strength as best he could, Finist gently pulled free from Maria, physically, psychically, and reached out for his cousin. What must be, must be.

But before Finist could even touch Ljuba, she screamed: the sound of it rang with the anguish of a lost, lost soul.

THEY were back, they were back, and Finist was coming towards her, shouting without words, *Traitor! Traitor!* Didn't Maria hear him? Didn't anyone hear him? *Traitor! Traitor!* Oh, God, and it was true—all her plans, all her hopes and schemes, had come down to this. When Finist reached her, when he touched her, her fate would be sealed, she would be lost, forever lost—

Ljuba screamed and, screaming, tried to flee. But Finist blocked her path, shouting in his silent rage, *Traitor, traitor!* She couldn't let him touch her, she had to escape, but there was no escape! No escape save one—

"LJUBA!"

Just as he touched her, just as his hand closed about her arm, she changed. There was a dizzying blurring of shape, a wild stirring of feathers and a rush of wings, and all at once there was no Ljuba, nothing but a crow flapping frantically away, nothing but an empty caftan falling to the floor.

SOMEWHERE deep in the forest, strange beings stirred. Somewhere deep in the forest, the *leshy* laughed softly to himself and whispered, "Meet your fate, oh forest-foe!"

"FINIST . . . ?"

The prince came back to himself with a start, realizing belatedly that he had tried to follow the crow. He stood at the window, staring after her. Swallowing convulsively, he glanced down at his hands, trembling with shock there on the sill, and clenched them about the smooth stone to try to stop their shaking.

"Finist? Please, Finist, what is it? What happened?"

Slowly and painfully as an old man, the prince turned from the window. "Ljuba's gone."

"Well, yes, I saw her fly. But—"

"You don't understand, love. She's gone forever." For a moment he couldn't continue. "Ljuba . . . broke. She took her guilt upon her before she could be formally accused. And she—she not only took her avian shape, *she sealed herself into it.* Maria, I felt it happen!"

"I don't—"

He couldn't hide his shuddering. "It—it's the fate of the royal traitor, to be bird forever, body and—and mind." Finist saw the dawning of comprehending horror on Maria's face, and gasped, "You understand! Oh, Maria, she will never, never return!"

She said nothing, only watched him, her face pale as death. And Finist broke, and flung his arms about her, and clung to her as though he'd never let her go again.

At last the shock wore off. Finist pulled free enough to look down at Maria and smile, a touch uneasily.

"Forgive me. I didn't mean to . . ."

"You—you don't hate me?"

"Hate you!" He drew back even more, staring. "Dear God, Maria, no! Why should I—"

"Ljuba . . . It was my doing. Her—collapse, I mean."

"Nonsense."

"It was! I—I don't know what happened, I don't even know what I did!"

"You showed her the truth, that's all," said Finist, very gently. "You simply showed her the truth. You . . . did what I would have had to do."

"But—"

"Maria, love, believe me, you did nothing wrong! What happened to my cousin was inevitable." For all his attempts at calm, Finist couldn't keep a faint tremor out of his voice. "You see, love, if she hadn't d-doomed herself, it would have fallen to me as prince and magician to—to destroy her."

"Oh, Finist, no!" Maria looked up at him with anguished eyes. "And you loved her, didn't you?"

"No. I . . . No," said Finist after a moment, truthfully. "No, I never really did." He shook his head impatiently. "It's *you* I love, Maria, never doubt that. It's you I love."

What if she didn't believe that? What if he had frightened her away? Suddenly terrified, Finist stared into her eyes. But what he saw there was warmth—wonderful, reassuring warmth. And the prince let out his breath in a long, happy sigh.

"So. There are a good many things that must be done, to undo what—" He stopped short, reluctant to mention Ljuba's name. Ah, it was going to take a long time for healing. "What was done," Finist finished firmly.

"Akh, yes." Maria understood. "The first thing to do, I would think, is to restore poor *boyar* Semyon to his proper place."

"Indeed! And then get word to Stargorod and your father that you're alive and quite safe."

"Yes, thank you!"

"Mm, and perhaps I can find a way to coax the man to Kirtesk. I can always use someone of his integrity at my court. Even if he does insist that I'm a child of the Devil!"

"And Vasilissa . . . ?"

"I'd like to see her again, too. Love, I just might be able to help her. Strengthen her mind, I mean, with healing magic."

Maria's eyes shone with startled joy. "I never thought—Finist, could you?"

"I can at least try. Akh, but we're leaving out the most important task of all!"

She blinked. "What's that?"

"My dear Maria, my poor people have been living in desperate anticipation of a royal wedding for a good long time!" His breath caught in his throat. "We can hardly disappoint them, can we?"

To his relief and delight, she didn't pull away, but moved comfortably into the crook of his arm, fitting there as neatly as though she'd always belonged there. "Indeed we cannot," Maria said, and smiled.

EPILOGUE

Two months, thought Finist. *Has it really been only two months?*

The time till he and Maria could be wed had seemed like an eternity:

Two months of slow boredom, as his worn body gradually regained its strength.

Two months of frenzied preparations, with all the city in such a whirl of busy confusion that the psychic overflow of excitement had left his mind spinning.

Two months of sheer torment, longing for Maria, yet not, thanks to the stern rules of royal propriety, being allowed to so much as touch her.

But now, at last, the time of waiting was over!

The day of his wedding passed for Finist in one shining, dizzying blur of light and music and joy, with only one constant: Maria. Maria, there by his side in the royal chapel, Maria aglow in robes and veiled headdress so splendid with gold, so stiff with pearls and priceless gems she'd needed the handmaids to help her kneel beside him. Lost in the radiance in her eyes, he hardly knew whether or not he was making the proper responses, his voice that of some hoarse stranger. When the time came for the exchange of rings, Finist, mortified, found his hands shaking so wildly he had a horrible image of the ring flying right out of his grip and rolling all the way down the length of the chapel. But somehow he managed to slip the ring on

Maria's finger, feeling her hand warm and dry and trembling only slightly in his own. When he must kiss her, there before all the assembled *boyars* and the crush of commons behind them—God, he didn't want to ever let her go.

The day sped on. Before Finist could credit his stunned senses, he and Maria were royal newlyweds sitting at their wedding feast. The great banquet hall was ablaze with torches, their light reflecting dazzlingly from the bright, ornately painted walls, striking many-colored sparks from the rubies and emeralds worn by the *boyars*, transmuting the strings of harps and *gusli* to gold as minstrels vied with each other to sing finer and ever more intricate songs of royal glory, struggling to be heard over the chatterings and laughter of the crowd. The air was heavy with the scents of savory meats and pastries, with perfume and slightly overwarm humanity.

Finist looked down at the food before him, and realized he couldn't eat a bite to save him. Maria, he saw with a shy sideways glance, wasn't eating either, her cheeks flushed from the warmth of the room, her lashes lowered. But she must have felt his gaze on her, because a small hand slipped unobtrusively into his own.

Akh, he mustn't forget his honored guest! Finist turned to the man at his left, to Danilo Yaroslavovich. Danilo looked very much like a man in a complete state of shock. After all, thought Finist in a flash of sharp humor, he'd just seen the fearsome, damned sorcerer not only enter a holy chapel, but complete a holy service without once vanishing in a cloud of smoke.

"Enjoying yourself?" Finist asked the man softly.

"As it pleases you, Prince Finist."

"Oh, come now, man, unbend a bit! You *are* my father-in-law."

Danilo's glance was cool. "Again, as it pleases you."

"What, still so hostile? Yet you and Vasilissa came."

The cold facade shattered. "How could I not come? When you sent me that message . . ."

"You didn't object to its being a magical one, eh?"

"I . . . Anything that could get to me so swiftly, that

could let me know my dear one was alive, and safe, and happy—How could I object? I love my daughter!''

''As do I,'' said Finist.

His heart was in the simple words. And, just for a moment, the two men were in complete accord, just for a moment the prince felt the wall between them start to crack.

A beginning, he thought, and smiled.

OUTSIDE, night darkened Kirtesk. Within the banquet hall, merriment still reigned. Though now, since all but Finist, who, as ever, dared not risk too much drink, and Maria, who was too wary to drink, had been liberally helping themselves to the sweet, dangerous mead and the rare wines from the East, the conviviality was taking a bawdy turn. Vasilissa, much to her father's shock and Finist's amusement, actually seemed to be enjoying herself, eyes bright with delight. She really did love her sister, the prince realized, really did wish her joy. But Maria, though she continued to smile valiantly, was beginning to droop.

Poor thing, Finist thought, *weighed down by her robes and probably ready to faint from exhaustion.*

He bent to her, whispering, ''Want to get out of here?''

She shot him a grateful look, whispering back, ''But how? They'll all want to see us to—to our bed and . . .''

Finist heard the quaver in her voice, and said firmly, ''They'll just have to be disappointed. Watch.''

Delicately, feeling the force of Power bubbling up within him as though he'd drunk too much of that heady wine, the prince built up a haze of illusion about them. It wasn't the neatest spell he'd ever worked; Finist was tired from the long day, too. In fact, it probably wouldn't have fooled a sober soul for a moment. But by this point, none of the guests—including Danilo, who was trying with ever fading coherency to explain his views on magic to an owl-eyed, beaming Semyon—were even remotely sober. Finist grinned. The haze should be just enough to confuse drink-befuddled sight even more! He caught Maria's hand and peeled her carefully away from the delicate illusion, leaving behind two smoky, almost solid images of themselves.

"Beautiful!" giggled Maria in his ear.

"Shh! Mustn't let them realize where we're going."

Fighting down laughter, Finist and Maria tiptoed off, hand in hand, for all the world like two errant children, stealing up stairways and down corridors till at last they were safely behind the doors of Finist's private chambers.

"There, now! Home at last," the prince managed to get out, and then he and Maria were bursting into gusts of helpless laughter.

"They—they'll never forgive us!" gasped Maria.

"I suppose not!"

But as he looked at her, at his wife, Finist felt his laughter fade. Maria turned to him, eyes wide, and for a moment, dazed and wondering, they stared, quite speechless, at each other.

Overwhelmed by a sudden hot rush of love and desire, Finist murmured, "Akh, Maria, come. No one will disturb us now."

Hand in hand, they entered the bridal chamber. Servants had been here before them, had strewn the floor with flowers and sweet-scented herbs. *Herbs for good fortune,* realized Finist, *for fertility.* He heard Maria give a little gasp as the implication of those herbs dawned on her. She pulled her hand from his and turned away, trembling, and he thought in pity, *She's frightened.*

He would be gentle. He would use every bit of his love and his magic to ease the way for her, and—

A sharp, half-stifled little oath startled him. "Ah, Maria?"

She turned a flushed face to him. "I wanted to be bold and—and daring for you, and let these robes just—fall where they would. But I can't get these d-damned laces open!"

He burst into laughter again, and after a moment, she joined him. Finist struggled with the stubborn knots, the warmth of her flesh beneath his hands feeding his impatience till at last he cried:

"Akh, enough of this!"

A surge of Power sent bridal finery flying from them both. Maria gasped again, reddening, but stood facing him for a moment before shyness sent her scuttling for the shelter of the bedclothes. Finist stared after her in sheer, joyous wonder. Deep within him, he realized now, there'd been the lingering fear that the memory of Ljuba might come cruelly between them. Now that fear seemed so foolish. Ljuba's golden loveliness had been too perfect, sterile. Maria was full-breasted, full-hipped, all that was womanly, all that was warm, living, happy beauty.

"Oh, my love," he breathed, "my heart, my life!"

For all that she continued to blush fiercely—with a surge of new delight Finist watched the spread of that blush down between those charming breasts—Maria's eyes never left him, caressing the length of him. And all at once she gave a delightful little chuckle.

"Finist, love, you're going to catch a chill standing there like that. Do come to bed."

Grinning like a fool, he obeyed. The touch of her skin, satin-smooth against his, sent desire raging like wildfire through him, racing from his mind to hers and back again in a sudden wonder of shared love and need: the psychic link they'd shared before would now, it seemed, grant them an added, unexpected delight.

Unless this last bit of strangeness was just *too* strange for Maria? For a moment the linking quivered and threatened to fall.

But then:

"Oh, I *do* pity women with mundane mates," said Maria smugly.

Finist gave a joyous laugh, and pulled her to him.

AFTERWORD

THE WORLD OF FINIST and Maria was, as the reader has certainly realized, inspired by Slavic history and folklore. An equivalent time period in our own world would be the early Middle Ages, about the end of the eleventh century, an era just after Viking expansions added blond hair and blue eyes to the indigenous Slavic stock, and a century before the first of the invasions of Genghis Khan's Golden Horde. That was a time of small city-states in much of the region, principalities kept fairly insular and independent primarily because of the problems of travelling over poor roads through what must have seemed like endless expanses of forest and steppe. A good deal of the Eastern European forest still survives in the form of the Siberian taiga, some of which is virgin wilderness even today. Anyone who's ever spent any time alone in dense forest can certainly understand why the Slavic folk peopled their forest with such creatures as the *leshiye*—who, with their unpredictable whims and fancies, are the very personification of the forest's complete indifference to humanity—and the *rusalki*, those cruel creatures who are all the more deadly for having once been human. The *rusalki*, like their Slavic cousins, the *vily*—who turn up in the ballet *Giselle*—are always female, and sometimes out-and-out sadistic, hating all humanity in general and men in particular, since it was suicide from unhappy love or murder at a false lover's hands that brought about their watery transformations.

Inspiration for this story came from several sources.

Chief among them was the music of Nikolai Rimsky-Korsakov, in particular his fairytale operas, not so much for subject matter as for mood, brimming as they are with folk melodies and magical events. Other inspirations include books of history and archaeology of the period, including the highly readable *Kievan Russia* by George Vernadkey, and several of the collections of Slavic folklore made in the field towards the end of the last century and the beginning of this one. Last, but hardly least, inspiration came from the stories of actual Slavic life told to me by my grandmother.

Josepha Sherman is that rarity: a resident of New York City who was actually born there. Her short stories have appeared in the *Sword and Sorceress* anthologies, *Dragon Magazine, Fantasy Book,* and elsewhere, and she has written a novel for children, *Vassilisa the Wise,* set in the same culture as *The Shining Falcon,* her first novel for adults.

Ms. Sherman earned her M.A. in Ancient Near Eastern Archaeology at Hunter College. She writes, "I have participated in such salvage excavations as the ones taking place in York, England—where we discovered that ancient Roman cesspools retain an amazing amount of aroma. Ah, the romance of archaeology!"

UNICORN & DRAGON
BY LYNN ABBEY

illustrated by
Robert Gould

A BYRON PREISS BOOK

An epic tale of two very different sisters caught in a fantastic web of intrigue and magic—equally beautiful, equally talented—charged with quests to challenge their power!

UNICORN & DRAGON *(volume I)*

75567-X/$3.50US/$4.50Can

"Lynn Abbey's finest novel to date"—*Janet Morris*
author of *Earth Dream*

AND IN TRADE PAPERBACK—

CONQUEST
Unicorn & Dragon, (volume II)

75354-5/$6.95US/$8.85Can

Their peaceful world shattered forever, the two sisters become pawns in the dangerous game of who shall rule next.

Buy these books at your local bookstore or use this coupon for ordering:
....
Avon Books, Dept BP, Box 767, Rte 2, Dresden, TN 38225
Please send me the book(s) I have checked above. I am enclosing $_____
(please add $1.00 to cover postage and handling for each book ordered to a maximum of three dollars). *Send check or money order*—no cash or C.O.D.'s please. Prices and numbers are subject to change without notice. Please allow six to eight weeks for delivery.

Name _____

Address _____

City _____ State/Zip _____

U&D 9/88

NEW BESTSELLERS
IN THE *MAGIC OF XANTH* SERIES!

PIERS ANTHONY

VALE OF THE VOLE

75287-5/ $4.50 US/ $5.50 Can

HEAVEN CENT

75288-3/ $4.50 US/ $5.50 Can

*and coming in
October 1989—*

MAN FROM MUNDANIA
75289-1

Buy these books at your local bookstore or use this coupon for ordering:

Avon Books, Dept BP, Box 767, Rte 2, Dresden, TN 38225
Please send me the book(s) I have checked above. I am enclosing $_____
(please add $1.00 to cover postage and handling for each book ordered to a maximum of
three dollars). *Send check or money order—no cash or C.O.D.'s please.* Prices and num-
bers are subject to change without notice. Please allow six to eight weeks for delivery.

Name _____

Address _____

City _____ State/Zip _____

Xanth 3/89